"Son of . . . !" he trailed off. "No one was supposed to have live ammunition. Who in the hell is that?"

From slightly behind him, the calm quiet voice of Frank Monday replied. "Don't rightly know, sir."

Rockham lay still while closely studying the opposite slope in an effort to find the assassin hidden on a Colorado mountain side. Slowly, a moving figure emerged in his field of view. He watched the man work his way sideways along the slope.

"Look straight ahead," Rockham said to Monday. "Four hundred meters to your left."

Monday studied the slope through his compact Nikon 7=15x35 Action Zoom binos.

"I got him," he said. "No, wait, there's another one . . . Make that three. One has a sniper's rifle."

Monday replaced his field glasses in their case and positioned his weapon, an SDV Russian sniper's rifle, exactly like the one that had shot at Rockham.

"It just happens that I brought along some live ammo, too," he said, aiming the weapon, taking up the "military slack" in the trigger.

In seconds, all three targets were down.

Now, the question was: who the hell were they?

Books by S.M. Gunn

SEALS

SUB STRIKE
OPERATION EMERALD RED

S.M. GUNN

AVON BOOKS
An Imprint of HarperCollinsPublishers

This is a work of fiction. Names, characters, places, and incidents are products of the author's imagination or are used fictitiously and are not to be construed as real. Any resemblance to actual events, locales, organizations, or persons, living or dead, is entirely coincidental.

AVON BOOKS
An Imprint of HarperCollins*Publishers*
10 East 53rd Street
New York, New York 10022-5299

Copyright © 2005 by Bill Fawcett & Associates
ISBN-13: 978-0-06-050289-8
ISBN-10: 0-06-050289-4
www.avonbooks.com

First Avon Books paperback printing: November 2005

Avon Trademark Reg. U.S. Pat. Off. and in Other Countries, Marca Registrada, Hecho en U.S.A.
HarperCollins® is a registered trademark of HarperCollins Publishers Inc.

Printed in the U.S.A.

10 9 8 7 6 5 4 3 2 1

SEALS

SUB STRIKE

OPERATION EMERALD RED

PROLOGUE

★ ★ ★ ★

1996
1635 ZULU
Room 3D526
The Pentagon
Arlington, Virginia

Lieutenant Greg Rockham, CO of the Special
Materials Detachment—a SEAL organization under the direct control of the United States Special
Operations Command—received an order to attend a meeting at the Pentagon. It came during
an intensely difficult training period. Needless to
say, the top SEAL commander found it annoying.
When he reached Room 3D526, Rockham met
with a rank-heavy group. Present were five admi-
rals, two captains, a man in a gray business suit—
the uniform, Rockham knew, of the upper echelon
of the CIA—and a honey-blonde civilian woman.

Admiral Cromarty, the vice commander of USSO-COM, was also there.

Cromarty was responsible for all of the SEAL Teams, SDV Teams, and the Special Boat Units. That made him the highest ranking SEAL in the Navy. He took the lead after a round of introductions, then gave Greg Rockham a thorough rundown on what the Navy had in mind. It didn't fail to impress the young lieutenant.

"The United States will soon meet a very different class of enemy, Lieutenant," Cromarty said. "Some of us think that meeting will take place much sooner than others expect." He went on to describe the threat posed by the existence of highly sophisticated biological and chemical weapons—specifically those in the recently collapsed Soviet Union—and the possibility that some of those weapons might well fall into the hands of rogue states and terrorist groups. Worse still was the chance of a nuclear device reaching Al Qaeda, or some other terrorist organization, and being used against the United States or Israel.

Admiral Cromarty summed up with a distinctly disquieting observation: "Run-of-the-mill terrorists are something the SEALs have dealt with. But there's a new class of terrorist coming up in the world who's a different kind of animal. This killer is educated, smart, and fanatical—his fanaticism based in religious extremism—and he could soon be armed with weapons of mass destruction."

Rockham produced a lopsided smile. "That seems to be right up our alley, sir."

"It is," Cromarty agreed. "The biggest and most urgent matter we face is that the immediate threat of a proliferation of WMDs rests with an old enemy of yours—Senior Captain Grigoriy Rostov."

CHAPTER 1

Spring 1996
Safe House Apartment of Grigoriy Rostov
83 Pushkin Alley
Novosibirsk, Lower Siberia
Russian Republic

Senior Captain Grigoriy Mikhailavich Rostov sat in the darkened apartment he used as a safe house and squinted at the thirteen-inch black-and-white TV screen that flickered with images broadcast by State Television. The program was *Brimyah*—"Time," in English—the major news program produced by *Svet Rebvoste*—the World News Network. What he saw hardly pleased him. His country had fallen apart around his ears.

Rostov could no longer deny the obvious. His beloved USSR had collapsed; the highly vaunted Soviet Union had disintegrated into a collection of mutually antagonistic states. Each one claimed to represent the "True *Rodina*." Rostov could not believe that the Motherland had ever spawned such disobedient children. He drank heavily of his glass of tea—the strong brew liberally laced with a generous portion of Kremlin one-hundred-proof-vodka—and leaned forward to turn up the sound. As he listened vaguely to a report that Russia now sought membership in NATO—traditional enemy of his beloved country—his memory ran back over the past to when the dissolution of his icon began.

It was June 12, in the summer of 1987. The American president, Ronald Reagan, had come to West Germany for a conference with Chancellor Kohl. On this particular day, Reagan went to the Berlin Wall, to make a speech to the German people and the people of the Western nations. Many were not aware that the speech could be easily received in Eastern Europe as well. Reagan opened his remarks with the usual polite acknowledgments of those to whom he spoke. Then, as Rostov saw it, he suddenly changed gears and spoke with an iron determination, laced with smug and condescending superiority.

"You see, like so many presidents before me, I come here today because wherever I go, whatever I do: *Ich hab noch einer Koffer in Berlin.*" It meant: "I have a suitcase in Berlin." The applause, as Rostov remembered, had been a roar of approval. Reagan continued: "Behind me stands a wall that encircles the free sectors of Europe. From the Baltic south those barriers cut across Germany in a gash of barbed wire, concrete dog runs, and guard towers . . . Yet, it is here in Berlin where the wall emerges most clearly. Here, cutting across your city, where the television screens have imprinted this brutal division of a continent upon the mind of the world."

As Grigoriy Rostov saw it, when Reagan reached the heart of his message, he made a chilling demand. "General Secretary Gorbachev, if you seek peace, if you seek prosperity for the Soviet Union and Eastern Europe, if you seek liberalization: Come here to this gate! Mr. Gorbachev, open this gate! Mr. Gorbachev, tear down this wall!"

There had been much more, but Rostov marked that moment in time as the start of the destruction of the political and military power of his homeland.

Tragedy also fed the fall of the USSR, Rostov had to admit. In April 1986, when the nuclear reactor at Chernobyl exploded and sent radiation three times above normal levels into the atmosphere, the Soviet government denied that any accident had occurred. They claimed it to be an invention of the Western media intended to discredit and harm the *Rodina*. Seventeen days later Gorbachev appeared on *Mir* state television with the utterly surprising admission of what had happened. Things got worse, by Rostov's estimation, in 1987 when "Gorby" declared in a speech that for their own internal progress, the USSR must be open to normalizing international relations.

That opened the floodgates, as Gorbachev gave the world two new slogans *peristroika* (restructuring) and *glasnost* (openness). Under increasing pressure, the Soviet premier was compelled to promote a market economy, including the right to possess private property. Religious freedom came next, and the avalanche grew.

Rostov's depression deepened as he recalled the terrible chain of events. In May 1989 the communist system was abolished in Hungary, and in East Germany the disturbances proved even more remarkable. Within a month after celebrating the fortieth anniversary as a socialist workers state, even with Gorbachev as honored guest, the Communist party in that country collapsed. On June 11, 1989, the walls began to tremble. Three days later Reagan's prediction came to pass and the first hole was made in the Berlin Wall. On that day, Rostov cursed as he did now, recalling the sorry spectacle of East Germans flocking into West Berlin. Nervous East German police stood by, helpless. Czechoslovakia, Romania, and the rest of Eastern Europe quickly followed, bringing an end to the Warsaw Pact nations.

When all was said and done, Rostov lamented bitterly, the revolution of 1989 meant a victory for the Western governments and its way of life.

* * *

Former Senior Sergeant Vladimir Frolik, the senior NCO of Rostov's Spetznaz unit, applied the stout, case-hardened jaws of a bolt cutter to the chain securing the former Red Army arsenal doors. With a sharp *pop!* the link parted. Frolik looked nervously over his shoulder and spoke in an agitated whisper. "Are you certain we're safe doing this, Captain?"

Despite this being their first adventure into a bold raid on a military warehouse, Rostov answered, "Of course. Major Koznikov accepted the bribe I offered—one large enough to keep the major and his entire maintenance unit silent. There were five thousand cases of Kalashnikov rifles in there, and our friend Saddam requires fifty cases to issue to new recruits to his army."

Frolik grunted and worked quickly to open the tall double doors. Once open, ex-Sergeant Pyotr Adamenko backed the truck into the gaping warehouse. Adamenko cut the ignition, and the engine of the Zil-135, ten-ton truck died. Rostov gave instructions to Frolik, along with Adamenko and fellow ex-sergeants Josef Dreshko and Konstantine Gorenko. Working as a well-coordinated team, they swiftly began to load cases of AK-47s. Cognizant of the value of incentive bonuses, Rostov then indicated a corner of the arsenal where individual units of AGS-17 *Plamya*, or flame, grenade launchers had been assembled and arranged on the concrete floor.

"Take four," he commanded Frolik. "The Iraqi

army will make good use of them." He then went to a stack of wooden crates behind the launchers and selected two cases of each type of ammunition—HEAT (high explosive antitank) and AP (antipersonnel) rounds, with warheads that sprayed lethal steel spheres over a kill radius of seven meters. Frolik next secured a number of the easy-to-load drum magazines holding belts of twenty-nine rounds each. Their linked belt carrier system jingled musically as the arms dealers brought them aboard the truck.

"We are done here, comrades. Secure the doors with the same links and lock," Rostov said, smiling.

"While you were busy," he then told them, "I had time to pick the lock. Except for being a link short, they will not likely suspect anything. At least until the next time they routinely open the doors, and by then, dust will have covered the floor space where we took our goods. I will contact our customer at 0900 Baghdad time tomorrow. *Mytniy!* Uday Hussein never awakens before one in the afternoon. We will have to wait for details of the delivery—not to mention our final payment for the goods. For good socialists, these Husseins certainly understand the indolent lifestyle of the filthy capitalists."

"Do we need to deal with them, Grigoriy Mikhailavich?" Senior Lieutenant Ivan Tsinev asked seriously.

Rostov produced a rueful grimace and spoke sardonically. "We do if we wish to sell any of the arms left so conveniently unguarded. We deal with Saddam Hussein and any of the terrorist organizations, or we do not do enough business to make a living. Outside of ourselves, the Chinese, Cubans, North Koreans, and in the Middle East, the only place we find genuine anti-Americanism these days is among the Muslim terrorists. Let us be grateful they exist. Perhaps," Rostov went on to speculate hopefully, "we can enlist the assistance of former General Koriev of the KGB to create some ingenious euphemisms, such as 'Arab militants' or 'freedom fighters'?"

Frolik hid the grimace his former captain's words forced him into. For his part, this was strictly for the money. Whatever political importance could be attached to stealing arms from their brother soldiers paled in the light of millions in American dollars that would be theirs for successfully completing a contract. Let Captain Rostov find some proper Marxist rationale behind what they did, *he* did not care. In the rearview mirror Frolik saw the face of former Sergeant Adamenko, a worried expression on his face.

"What is it, Pyotr Simonovich?" Frolik asked testily.

Adamenko peered into the rearview mirror as well, a frown forming on his clear, high forehead. "There is a car following us. The lights are out and I suspect it is the police."

Frolik stiffened but kept his voice calm. "Pray it

is not the new State Security Service and keep on watching."

"*Da,* Vladimir Konstantinich, I will watch closely." Less than five minutes later, Adamenko reached through the opening and tapped Frolik on the shoulder. "They are closing in, comrade. I see weapons in the hands of several occupants."

Is it truly the Security Service? Frolik wondered. He relayed this information to Rostov.

Without a moment's hesitation, Rostov snapped an order. "Stop them."

Konstantine Gorenko and Josef Dreshko paused only long enough to charge their weapons, then sent streams of full auto 7.62mm steel-jacketed rounds into the windshield of the car they believed to be from State Security. Safety glass fragmented and fell inward, and the experienced soldiers raised their point of aim only slightly to chop down the passengers in the rear seat. The fight was over almost before it began.

With a dead man at the wheel, the sturdy black BMW wavered and crashed almost a hundred kilometers an hour through the tubular steel barriers of a bridge, plunging down with racing engine to splash into the Volga River. Rostov's truck sped away into the distance unseen by any save an old drunk, slouched in the entranceway of a narrow alley, his hands held possessively around a half-liter bottle of cheap vodka wrapped in a strip of newspaper. It was this close call that convinced

Grigoriy Rostov to move his operation south to the relative safety of Novosibirsk.

"Perhaps this will work to my advantage," Rostov mused as he digested the import of what he had mentally reviewed. With the Soviet Union dissolved, it would make it easier for him to obtain the stock of his new trade. His military experience greatly aided him in this enterprise. It was a lucrative business, albeit one fraught with enormous risks and dangers. In light of the rapid collapse of the Soviet Union, his present clients' request and the half pay in advance he demanded took absolute precedence over all other considerations. Frolik would be the one who conducted the demonstration firing of their client's requested product; an *Igla*—or needle—shoulder-fired launcher for the 9M-39 homing missile. Rostov considered his planned presentation for the day. First, he would pick up Frolik at the ex-sergeant's hidden digs in Krasnayrsk and meet the client in the prearranged location for the demonstration.

Vladimir Frolik eased his lanky, lean frame into the driver's seat beside Rostov. He drove away immediately in the Zil-135 army truck that had recently been converted to a garish yellow-green-blue color scheme that declared it a civilian vehicle. Rostov directed him. They drove in silence, conscious of the cargo that rested in the covered rear of the truck. The missile was a thing of deadly beauty, sleek and painted a dull, nonreflective gray. Its nose cone had a hole in the tip, and the proximity detonator lay in a padded box that sat between the two former Spetznaz troopers. Smiling, Rostov finally broke the silence as he patted the small box.

"*Eto khorasho,*" he said, indicating that everything was good for the test.

"*Spashibo ha Bog.*"

"God! Vladimir Konstantinich, since when do you give thanks to God? We are Spetznaz. The only godlike being we should acknowledge is Karl Marx," Rostov snapped in genuine displeasure.

Frolik produced a weak smile. "Communism is dead, Captain. Maybe it is time to go back to the old ways?"

Rostov growled in an effort at rejecting the idea. "Nonsense, I say! If communism is dead, then I have no god."

"You are a brave man, Captain," Frolik replied, thinking of the inevitable fate of his admired leader's soul. "Ah . . . where do I turn to reach the test area?" Frolik asked to change the subject.

"Turn left on the Great Circle and go around to *Stalyin Oolnsa*. From that point we go east, into the Baykal Mountains. There is an old quarry some twenty kilometers into the mountains. That is where we will meet our clients."

Frolik frowned. "I do not like dealing with Orientals, Captain. They make me feel unclean, and—truth to tell—they frighten me."

Rostov chuckled and patted his sergeant on the shoulder. "That is because of our previous operations against the Chinese. They, my friend, are a different breed of cat. Given five thousand years of culture, they can be quite formidable. But believe me, these members of the Taiwanese cabal have no more love or resemblance to the Mainland Chinese than we do. They have no political motivation and are doing what they are doing only for money. Beijing has paid them well, and they will pay us excellently."

Their broad smiles, as wide and menacing as those of a shark, made the first impression on Grigoriy Rostov and Vladimir Frolik. The Taiwanese gentlemen bowed graciously. After dismounting from the truck, Rostov got directly to the point.

"Dobre posleobedeonfoe bremyah, tovarichi." Then he repeated in universal English, "Good afternoon, comrades."

They returned the greetings somewhat stiffly.

Rostov gestured to the truck bed. "In a few moments we will be displaying for you the Igla launcher and two 9M-39 homing missiles set up for ground or air attack." Like a ringmaster at the circus, Rostov went on describing the particulars of the test. "Only one of the missiles will be fired— they are quite expensive and somewhat hard to come by at present."

One stout Taiwanese peered through beer-bottle

glasses. "I quite understand, comrade," he allowed gracefully.

"Thank you, Mr. Youang," Rostov assured him. "I have cornered a large quantity of these modified missiles, all with hollow warheads like these two examples. You can place within them any material of your desire."

Quai Wang Xi smiled frostily. "And of course your firm will be more than happy to provide us the nuclear weapon we seek?"

Grigoriy Rostov hesitated and frowned. "Not at once. That will require considerable time to obtain at the source—not to mention the expense. Nuclear materials are still closely guarded, and will cost a great deal. Even so, it will be only a small delay—an, ah, inconvenience for you. We can provide any other weapons you wish within three days of you making a fifty percent deposit on the missile system and the payload substances you order."

Frowning at this mention of fifty percent, the Taiwanese hesitated only a second. "Very well, Captain Rostov," Quai responded. "Proceed with the demonstration, if you will."

Frolik set up the launch platform and inserted a missile. Then he turned and invited the Taiwanese to examine the powerful weapon. As they took a close look, he kept up a steady commentary in broken English. "You saw how the missile is loaded from the front of the launcher. The tail fins slide down this rail until clicking into their retention joints, which hold until sufficient thrust is established for launch."

When they had gawked to their fill, Frolik hefted the weapon and placed the padded yoke over his shoulders. Years of experience permitted him to hold the launch unit steady. He removed the safety wire from the missile propulsion system and released the launcher firing mechanism. "I have now enabled the missile and opened the firing circuit of the launcher," he said. "When I fire, the projectile will break free on its own and fly to the target."

Youang Fu Genn leaned forward for another look. "And what is the target this day, Sergeant Frolik?"

Rostov answered for his lead NCO. Pointing, he said mildly, "See that flock of sheep over there?"

Squinting, the Taiwanese barely made out the gray-white balls of sheep on a far-off hillside.

"What is the range?" asked Quai.

"Twelve hundred meters," Frolik informed him. "Now, watch."

Immediately, he settled into his firing stance and took aim. His finger tightened on the trigger and the clients heard a muted click. A fraction of a second later a hiss grew into a roar. With a lurch, in a tail-heavy attitude, the 9M-39 missile left the launcher and wobbled into the air. Its speed increased with each half second while farther down-range, some of Rostov's associates aimed the homing device. With it, they would direct the missile into the center of the flock of unwitting sheep. At the precise moment, one man pressed a button.

The missile suddenly arched upward, turned nose down, and descended in a rush to strike among the wooly animals. With a large portion of its fuel still aboard, it ruptured and sprayed the volatile fluid around. Sparks and hot metal instantly ignited it. A dull boom reached the ears of the onlookers.

Quai stood in awed silence for a while. "What is the actual range of this device?"

"It has a maximum range of five kilometers, with a payload weighing 1.25 kilos."

"Most impressive, Captain Rostov," Mr. Youang purred with satisfaction. "We should not need more than four launchers and ten missiles each to cover the area we intend to devastate. What is the asking price of one of these systems and how many missiles come with it?"

Rostov responded coolly, without turning a hair. "The launcher units each run $25,000— U.S. dollars. They come with two 9M-39 missiles at a price of $4,000 each. That gives us a total of $260,000 per shipment." He paused. "Additional missiles can be purchased at a lower rate in groups of fifty."

"What will the chemical filler cost?" Quai pressed his question with an anticipatory frown of disapproval.

Rostov told him without hesitation or discomfort. "We are asking one-half million U.S. for the entire purchase." Quai Wang Xi gasped in genuine astonishment, then realized that Rostov continued to talk through a tight smile. "Actually, it is quite cheap for items on the underground illegal arms circuit. We are not Rosoboron Export"—the Federal State Unitary Enterprise—"but then, we offer advantages they do not for the price you pay. For instance, we are considerably more flexible in consideration of the buyer supplying an end-user certificate. We do not ask for one."

Quai considered this lack of documents to make the shipment legal most attractive. "That is decidedly to our benefit."

"Then we have a deal, yes?" Rostov prompted.

All of the Taiwanese exchanged glances, then bowed in acknowledgment and acceptance of the transaction. "Thank you, Captain. We will no doubt return for additional business that will prove mutually advantageous."

Rostov smiled with satisfaction at this. The huge sum he would reap from this one transaction would allow him to retire and live in opulence for the rest of his life. Naturally, provided he wanted to quit the game before it had run its course. "As a sign of good faith, we shall deliver this first installment to your place of departure."

"That would be Pier Six at the Posnin Terminal in what used to be called Leningrad," Quai told him.

"It is now returned to being Saint Petersburg," Rostov responded glumly, reluctant to use the name in open conversation. "It is a long way, but we shall be there in a week's time."

Quai spoke for them all. "That will be sufficient. Thank you for your aid in our cause."

"Fools!" Rostov exploded as Frolik drove their truck back from the demonstration site. "If they believe their activities will escape the attention of the *Goanbu*, they are in for a rude shock." He referred to the *Guojia Anquan Bu*—the Ministry of State Security for the People's Republic of China.

"True enough, Captain," responded Vasili Rutil, former lieutenant of Intelligence in Spetznaz. "The only thing we do not know is against exactly whom they propose to use these chemical agents. Were we not aware they are being operated by agents of the famous Black House?"

Rostov dismissed that with a frown. "Actually, that is of no concern to us, Vasili. No matter which side they seek to kill off, we win, eh?"

Rutil nodded. "You are right as usual, Grigoriy. *We* make lots and lots of money; they take lots and lots of chances."

"What makes it even nicer is that the only ones who will be upset by it are Kim Jong Il, the Vietnamese, and Cuba's Fidelistas."

Rostov laughed—a harsh bark—and then sobered. "But none of that impinges on us. Our goal is to enrich ourselves, and keep off the radar screen of the police while we're at it," he added, reflecting on their first excursion into criminality.

Rostov and his scratched together crew sweated out the next three days, waiting for the inevitable knock on the door. When none came, they began to breathe easier. Few if any of them believed that the hard-faced, silent men of the *Komitet* had actually faded away along with the politicos. To a great extent, they were right. KGB operatives had joined the new federal police and Security Service of the new Russian Republic with an enthusiasm that would have done any bureaucrat proud. Yet, for all the diligence they practiced, the loss of the iron-fisted totalitarian methods they had been so fond of employing made them nearly helpless. The police especially felt helpless in the face of a burgeoning criminal element, the so-called Russian mafia. Frequent and plentiful breakdowns of communications aided in the failure to curtail these outlaw bands.

To their relief, there was no reaction to the killing of the suspected Security Service agents who had died at the bridge. In retrospect, Rostov saw it as a good omen. Since then, he had only prospered. He did not doubt that his success would continue, whatever the consequences to some of his clients.

CHAPTER 2

Three hundred fifty men gathered in the rows of benchlike seats at the Topside Gym at Little Creek at 0830 local time. Newly promoted Lieutenant Commander Greg Rockham had already selected the core members of his new unit. He'd asked Shaun Daugherty, now promoted to full Lieutenant, to be his assistant platoon leader. Senior Chief Boatswain's Mate Frank Monday would once more serve as his platoon chief. Mike Ferber had rushed to volunteer as leading petty officer for the newly enlarged SMD Team. Hospitalman First Henry Limbaugh was the next tapped for the SMD following his promotion to First Class. His addition came as a tie with Larry Stadt, who had also been upped to First Class. Now Rockham stood at a slender rostrum and addressed the men of SEAL Teams Two, Four, Six, and Eight.

"Gentlemen, I'll not bandy words. I am in need of a few good men." Laughter rippled across the assemblage at Rockham's theft of the Marine Corps slogan. "Specifically, we are enlarging the Special Materials Detachment. I want a number of volunteers from among the best special operators in the world . . . you SEALs. I'll not lie to you— this is not going to be any walk in the park. Special Materials Detachment has been created to kick ass and take names in some of the dirtiest, most dangerous and decidedly unfriendly places in the world. Our job is to break things and kill people. If you can't accept that policy, you are free to leave the gym now. I'll wait three minutes for you to respond."

At once the SEALs proved that Rockham was not the only one to steal a phrase now and then. "Hell no! We won't go!"

Rockham grinned like a kid in a candy store with unlimited credit. "Good, I thank you all. I appreciate your sentiment. But I'll level with you. Hot operations are few and far between, but you will be training hard. When we do go on an op, I expect only perfect performances from all of you who qualify for SMD."

It took very little time to fill the ranks of the reorganized SMD Strike Force and to thank those

SEALs who had not been included. "Gentlemen, being left out is not a reflection on your abilities or level of training. You simply happened to be too far back in line. Please leave your names, with copies of your 201 jackets and SEAL operational records," Rockham instructed them. "Following in-depth interviews and physical tests, if there are still any openings you will be promptly notified by rank and rating. Thank you all for coming. Your interest and enthusiasm are duly noted."

Examining the list of those who had volunteered, Rockham's concern over the likelihood of having to face Rostov again dissipated somewhat. Every member of squads one and two, Fourth Platoon, had signed on, and some from squads three and four filled out many of the other vacancies. Rockham considered it a tribute to his leadership and evidence of his personal influence on the enlisted men. After the last of those who had missed out departed, the interviews began immediately.

Not surprisingly, Lieutenant Matt Fisher, the mustang officer who commanded the SDV Detachment and served as captain of one of the boats, was first to be screened. He had been with the SDVs since the mid-seventies, taught operating SEAL Delivery Vehicles for a number of years, and also participated in the development team for the Dry Deck Shelter Detachment. Fisher saw SMD as likely his last chance to engage in an operational use of the boats he commanded. It didn't hurt morale that he had a sense of humor that infected everyone he encountered. He could find something funny about the tightest situation. It was a bonus for anyone involved in the tension-loaded world of Special Operations.

Rockham saw only one drawback to Matt Fisher; what he called the boat commander's "hostages to fortune." Matt had been married ten years to Irene Miller, and they had two sons, seven and nine, living in Virginia Beach. Greg broke off thoughts of his own home and family. He roughly dismissed intruding reflections on his wife Sharon and his son Matthew when Fisher cleared his throat.

"You can start the grilling, Sergeant Friday," Matt quipped.

"We don't do third degree here, Matt. We've been through enough operations together. I'm quite familiar with your qualifications, and we both deserve to be considered old salts. So I have only one question. If you happened to be captured by one of the terrorists we're going to be operating against, do you believe that organization could get to you through your family?"

Fisher sat in contemplative silence for long seconds, then drew a deep breath before responding. "I have to answer that in two parts. First, yes, they could get to me that way. But secondly, if they went after my family, they would be a lot of sorry sons of bitches. Irene is an expert marksman with her Kahr Arms MP-40. And she is deadly with her Mossberg twelve-gauge, ATP-8S police riot shotgun. And Jimmy, my oldest, is already qualified as expert with his .22 and the CAR-15. He qualified Sharpshooter with his M-08 Colt pistol." Matt quickly raised a hand to forestall an obvious objection. "I know it's an antique and a subcaliber, but the 380 is the best of the breed and it fits his hand perfectly."

"Jeez, Matt, Jimmy is only nine."

Matt grinned with a father's pride. "Sure, but he's one hell of a shot. I taught him until this year, along with the VFW Post rifle instructor. He's learning pistol from his uncle Willie."

Greg summed up his friend's comments. "So you're saying that your wife and son would blow away the bad guys and all would be well?"

Matt produced a rueful grin. "Well, not entirely them alone. But they could hold off any terrorists until the cops arrived. After all, most of them aren't good shots, and they're ignorant of basic infantry tactics. Irene would call 911 on her cell and tell them to expect automatic weapons in the hands of the attackers. The Virginia Beach cops would bring out the big stuff, and that would be the end for the terrorists. So, with no leverage, the terrorists get no results. They'd either kill me or I'd be held until someone came to get me out."

"And we'd come for you, buddy, you can count on that," Rockham assured him. Then he continued apologetically, "Now, that statement brings up another question. Suppose—just suppose, for a moment—that the terrorists' U.S. cell members overpowered your wife and son and killed everyone in the house, but told you that they were still alive and captive? You know, in order to suck you in. What would you do then?" Rockham watched his subject intently.

Fisher furrowed his brow but spoke after only a momentary pause. "I would probably go batshit and try to kill as many of them as I could with my hands."

"Wrong answer. You would be wise to concoct some BS story to feed them to keep them happy and you alive until we could get there. Then, together, *we* would kill them all."

Fisher's face sagged. "Does that disqualify me, Commander?" he asked formally.

"No, not at all. As a father myself, I can see why you answered as you did. But we've always got to suck it up and keep on going for the good of the mission." He paused a second. "Truth to tell, if I found out my family had been killed, I'd probably go rogue and slaughter every bad guy I could find."

Fisher grinned for the first time since the questioning began. "Attaboy, Greg—uh, Commander."

"Greg's good," he said, to make light of his promotion. "We'll be working even closer than on earlier ops. And I haven't a long time to be here, as the song says."

Curious, Matt asked, "Really? What's next?"

"I'm not entirely sure, but I've heard scuttlebutt that our old enemy, Rostov from Spetznaz, is back and involved in illegal arms deals. Worse than that, I'm getting kicked upstairs to staff at NavSpecWar before any op against Rostov."

Fisher was impressed. "That's far out! You become a head honcho and we peons need only obey. Don't let it go to your head," he quipped in conclusion.

Rockham cocked an eyebrow. "Are you kidding? Sailing a desk will piss me off big-time. Anyway, welcome aboard. Who is next for an interview?"

"If I'm not mistaken, it's Edgar Lopez. He's a hell of a good boat jockey and a top-notch warrior as well," Fisher said of the coxswain.

"Thanks for the recommendation. See Chief Monday on the way out for instructions. We begin exercise drills tomorrow morning."

"Aye aye, sir." Fisher rose and exited from the gym.

With Daugherty, Monday, and Ferber conducting interviews, the session went quickly. They found only three interviewees who failed to qualify for the positions they sought. When they and Rockham discussed it afterward, Rockham personally made phone calls to contact six more of those aspiring to join.

They came eagerly and quickly. Out of the six, one was selected. Another call went out, this time for ten candidates. They proved no less enthusiastic than their predecessors. The last two positions were filled and the rest dismissed.

Leaving nothing to chance, all members of the newly expanded unit were notified to meet at SMD headquarters the next morning at 0600 hours to begin intensive training in counterterrorist tactics from Colonel Galen Haralson, the world's most renowned expert in counterterrorist operations. Haralson had trained the agents of Israel's Mossad. It would not be a walk in the park, he promised the men.

Refreshed and raring to go, Rockham viewed his troops with satisfaction when they arrived: four squads of the Fourth Platoon, veterans intermixed with the successful candidates, as well as men from the First, Second, and Third Platoons and of Team Two. His command assembled and ready, he turned the podium over to Colonel Haralson, whose upper-class British accent floated pleasingly to his audience.

"Good morning, gentlemen. We are about to embark on a rigorous training schedule"—he pronounced it *shed*-jewel—"which is designed to turn you into terrorist terminators. What I mean by that is, when you encounter terrorists and assault their position, you do not leave any survivors. Remember, gentlemen, the only good terrorist is a dead terrorist. By their own choice they have put themselves beyond the pale as regards routine jurisprudence, the Geneva Convention, or the rules of war. In other words, they are *not* recognized military combatants, nor common criminals—as some want us to believe—not insurgents or 'freedom fighters,' nor even prisoners of war or bellicose detainees. They are vermin and must be exterminated like the filth they are. Think of them as *targets*! Shoot first and ask questions after the last one has fallen dead."

Paul Lederer snapped to attention and raised a hand. When acknowledged by Haralson, he spoke loudly enough for all to hear. "Pardon me, Colonel, but that is in direct opposition to the regulations governing the conduct of U.S. military personnel."

Galen Haralson produced a condescending smile. "Granted, but that does not apply to your newly authorized mission. You are going to be buried under so many layers of disinformation and misdirection that no one will ever know that you ever existed. So . . . to continue. The goal of this portion of your training is to prepare you to act independent of immediate orders when encountering terrorists in an operation. We will commence in half an hour. Load live ammunition and be prepared to sweat your bums off."

It would take three weeks, Greg Rockham reflected, to complete this phase of the training, given the need for daily distance runs, PT and classroom instruction, reading, writing, and speaking in both Arabic and Tamil. No telling at this point where they might end up fighting their enemies. A basic vocabulary of a couple thousand words would help their cause. To that end, Rockham decreed that all casual conversation would be conducted in the two foreign languages as their knowledge and facility increased.

Lieutenant "Mr. Bill" Rogers conducted the boat drills every morning. He was lean and brown-haired—his exposed skin mahogany colored by the sun—with hazel eyes and a light brown mustache. The SEALs loved it, because most often six of them or more wound up in the water—which they considered their natural element.

"Gentlemen, I was recently informed that we will be using a Swift Boat for our final exam exercise. In my book they are BMMFs."

"He means 'Big Mean Mother Effers,'" John Grant whispered to the others assembled on the dock at Little Creek Amphibious Base.

"I heard that, Cochise," Rogers growled. "If you don't want to find a comment on it in your 201, I'd mind my tongue were I you. But he's right," Mr. Bill went on. "The PCFs can be considered Big Mean Mothers. They're fast and almost invisible to radar due to their low profile. Their highly muffled engines give very little signal for enemy sonar to detect. One of them can hold all of us and our gear when we make a run-in on a moving vessel," he went on, describing the advantages they would enjoy. "Aft on the main deck we can lay out our Zodiacs—not inflated, of course. So, we'll have to get used to rather close quarters or wear a lot of deodorant. Actually, small boat handling is not that big a deal. You can pick it up rather quickly. We'll begin with a review of the principles of seamanship."

SMD SEALs worked for eleven days on the rigors of how to handle a small craft in waters of the bay, and then out in the open sea. They sweated and cursed and found ample reasons to take some time off at the Iceberg. Their former brother-in-arms served the beer in foaming pitchers, and glasses were quickly filled. The first one went down fast and clean and made way for slower contemplation of their new situation. Before long Mike Ferber made bold to ask Shaun Daugherty a pointed question.

"Just why are we going into such detail about boarding a moving ship? Didn't we already do that?"

"Some of us didn't participate, remember that, Mike?" Daugherty replied. "As to why Mr. Bill is harping on the finer details, I can't begin to tell you. There's always scuttlebutt; rumors fly thick and fast. I've heard everything from our being used to take the *Britannica*—the yacht of the Queen of England—back from terrorists holding her hostage, to our taking over a rogue Russian-built nuclear aircraft carrier. That last I think we can totally discount; no way in hell twenty-four of us are going to take a ship with a crew of six or so thousand."

Chief Monday agreed. "Yeah, we ain't got a clue, and we won't get one until the brass hats decide to tell us. Let's just forget about it, drink beer and eat Philly cheese steak sandwiches. You can count on there being more crap to crawl through next week."

Prior to their departure for the Caribbean, the SMD did another take-down operation. They were informed it would be a dress rehearsal for their final exam. For all of that, it didn't excite them much. The ship's crew, they were warned, would not be aware of the fact this was an exercise.

After swimming underwater up to the anchored cargo vessels in the roads in Norfolk Bay, Sukov, Hunter, and Mainhart—who served as hook men—took bear claw magnets from their pockets. They attached them to the hull after using scrapers to remove barnacles, paint flakes, and scum from three areas. The refuse formed a nasty, discolored cloud in the relatively still waters of the bay. Next each placed a magnet, to which they attached a length of fourteen millimeter derigging line, securing one end to each of the two-by-six-inch magnets. They then swam beyond their respective squads and secured the other end of the line to the next bear claw in order. The three hook men secured their painter's poles, with the hooks attached, and let them dangle by lanyards down from the derigging line.

While the squads began to squirm and wriggle out of their swim gear, the pole men made ready to ascend when the caving ladders were put in place. The three breachers who carried the caving ladders moved to the center to prepare to derig and assist the hook men. Rockham, Daugherty, and Jorgensen sent squeeze signals back down the line, and the SEALs performed a weird, puzzling ballet for the fishes, removing their swimming gear in a gray-green underwater world.

Only a few feet underwater, they had to take extra care not to broach the surface and compromise security. Finally, the end man in line sucked his Draegar breathing apparatus dry of gas and secured it to the derigging line. At once, he headed for the surface. He stroked with his legs, reached out to grab the shoulder of the man above him in line and drew him upward. Using that technique, repeated by all the swimmers, all of the SEALs broke surface at the same moment. Streaming upward in a shower of bubbles, Lieutenant (jg) Pauli Jorgensen considered what had brought him to this unexpected career.

He saw himself as a typical square-headed Nordic type with pale blue eyes, unruly blond curly hair, a lopsided grin, and large, powerful hands. At six-foot-one and 180 pounds, he was hardly the largest SEAL, but his thick-muscled, carpenter's square torso quietly spoke of enormous strength. Jorgensen, who believed he'd been brainwashed from kindergarten through his third year at college, found it funny that he had nevertheless become an officer in the armed forces of the United States. His teachers, and later his professors, had always considered it the most disgraceful of all occupations. Or so he thought. At the age of twenty-six his recollection was still recent enough to vividly recall, and he reached his gag point.

He'd been in his junior year at Yale when he realized how much disgust he had developed for several of his professors—those who seemed to be obsessed by a radical left-leaning agenda. He thought their view of reality was twisted. He considered them arrogant, believed they had an unquestioning allegiance to Marxism, which revolted him. Jorgensen had had enough. He quit school to enter the Navy. Following boot camp, a chief who felt as he did credited his three years of college as sufficient to earn him a commission.

Jorgensen had then taken the required Officer's Basic course and became a "mustang"—a sailor who had "come up through the hawse hole" to become an officer. Not long after completing a tour at the Language School, Ensign Jorgensen had applied for the SEAL program and was accepted. He graduated from BUDS second in his class. He did a tour with the Teams, and had only recently been promoted to Lieutenant junior grade. The change in his status compelled him to apply for a slot with SMD One. He was currently in charge of third squad of Gold Platoon. And he couldn't be happier . . . except he still experienced a bit of claustrophobia when swimming long distances underwater. And now he silently prayed that he would do well in this exercise and later distinguish himself in the actual operation—it was necessary, he understood, in order to make rank in the closed circle of Special Operations, and the Special Materials Detachment in particular.

His reflections abruptly ended as his hand found the trailing end of the caving ladder and he looked to make certain his shooting partner was at his side. Ahead of them, the first pair up the ladder had already gone over the swell of the hull. They had disappeared into the darkness of the night. Jorgensen received his tap-out and began to climb, his partner, Leroy Mercer at his side.

"We've gotta be quick as bunnies, LT," Midnight Mercer whispered to his officer once their heads had cleared the surface.

Always concerned about his men, Jorgensen agreed with that advice. He knew Mercer would have a round in the chamber. The paint ball rounds they would be using were considered a kick in the butt. His major concern was that his squad didn't collect a whole lot of them. The idea was to make the other guy take more hits than anyone on their side did.

"Keep a TA and watch for the bad guys," Jorgensen said. "The security boys have got plenty of those paint balls."

Mercer scratched his close-cropped hair in a parody of a dull-minded individual. *Keep a tight ass,* he thought, *You got it, LT.*

* * *

Already up the curvature of the port hull, the shooting team of Ryan O'Leary and Jay Hunter hung on the top rung of the caving ladder while they checked out the weather deck of the cargo ship they were boarding. Jay considered himself a reasonable, sane, and stable person. He had been born and raised in Tahlequah, Oklahoma, and educated there through a year of college. He had married his childhood sweetheart, Jane Pulte, right out of high school. They had a four-year-old son, Bobby. From his own boyhood, Hunter had been a natural shot. He easily qualified as expert in every weapon used by the SEALs. Now he looked forward to engaging a real enemy with live ammunition.

Hunter brightened as he took stock of himself and his partner. For once, he had not experienced the usual bout of motion sickness as he climbed the caving ladder. Why was that the only circumstance—other than a violently heaving storm at sea—that caused him to be overcome by terrible *mal de mer*? His mother had offered one reason that seemed to fit. Following the "Removal," the Cherokee had been landlocked for over 150 years. Quite naturally, they had lost any affinity with large bodies of water. On the other hand, he preferred a theory that included something about a small malformation of the inner ear. Neither his mother nor their old *Didahnvwisgi*, or medicine man, John Sixkiller thought very much of his "white science" explanation. That notwithstanding, Hunter placed more faith in his fellow SEALs and the excellent training they all received than in the traditions of the Old Ways and the spiritual efficacy of *Unehlanvhi*—God.

Hunter's partner, Ryan O'Leary, did not let worries about what anyone outside the Teams said effect his actions or determination to always come out on top. He was a sincere, practicing Catholic, a member of the Knights of Columbus, who had served as an altar boy from the age of nine to fifteen. Although he did not take an overserious view of his faith, he found it comforting, and when it came to the Muslim terrorists, a bulwark against despair. O'Leary was aware that it had been a strongly stated desire of those above him in rank that the efforts to combat terrorism not become confused with a religious war. Well and good, he thought. But if the effers took a shot at him, he'd damn well shoot back. Considering who his shooting partner was, he had no doubt as to the outcome of any encounter.

O'Leary's favorite line of movie dialogue came from Clint Eastwood, as Inspector Harry Callahan in *Dirty Harry*: "Go ahead, make my day." Imbued with that philosophy, he tensed himself now and raised his head entirely above the portside gunwale and railing. Not a soul in sight. He breathed harshly in relief. From an open hatchway, toward amidships, came the thump and thud of sub woofers and the discordant wail of an electronic keyboard, both recorded on a CD. O'Leary made an unconscious grimace and carefully swept his gaze across the open deck.

Nothing and no one moved. Satisfied, he leaned down, tapped his partner, and proceeded to climb over the combing, rapidly darting to the rear of the superstructure. Hunter came right behind him. Already in position were Rockham and Ferber, as well as Daugherty and Bryant. Quickly, the other pairs came up the three ladders and spread out to totally secure the deck.

From belowdecks, the men of Gold Platoon heard the steady thrum of the generator operating to provide anticollision lights on the foreshortened masts, fore and aft white lights, and colored port and starboard running lights of green and red. They also noted the internal illumination for those on duty watch, who were relaxing with a good book.

Following silent commands given by hand and arm signals, Rockham conveyed the start of the initial phase of the takedown. First squad of Gold Platoon would take the bridge deck, including the radio room. Second squad headed along the weather deck corridor to the ladder leading to Engineering. There, they would swiftly descend to take control. Third would take the crew quarters and galley. At a curt hand gesture from Rockham, the takeover began.

A third of the way up the bridge deck ladder, the men of first squad encountered a sailor taking a cigarette break on a landing. A paint ball

quickly "smoked" him—their briefing implied
that there were no civilians or noninvolved personnel. Every target would be considered a bad
guy, so there was no such thing as collateral damage. They ascended quickly and formed their train
outside the radio room. The breacher set his hooligan tool in the doorjamb and gave a quick yank.
The unsecured hatch popped open without damage to the mechanism. The two men in the compartment rose immediately, and one drew his
modified Glock pistol. Before he could fire, a trio
of paint capsules splattered in a diagonal line
across his torso. His own weapon spat harmlessly
into the overhead. Rockham and Ferber, as the
first shooting team, searched the room while the
train moved on to the next hatchway.

Their breacher had already leapfrogged, and
now set his hooligan tool in the thin opening under the lip of the hatch to the navigation station.
At a signal from the shooting team, Dan Able
flexed powerful muscles, and the door to the compartment opened abruptly with a loud pop, like a
gunshot. Grenadier Ken Fleming and Corpsman
Jack Tinsley snapped into the compartment,
weapons at the ready as they spun left and right
and covered what proved to be empty space. From
the corner of one eye Fleming caught a flicker of
movement, and he swung his H&K MP5-N to his
left, where the frightened chief engineer—who
doubled as navigator—rose up, hands trembling,
and begged silently not to be shot. His weapon on

single fire, Fleming double-tapped the trigger, and a pair of red paint splotches appeared in the center of the chief's chest.

Meanwhile, Daugherty and Bryant performed a similar maneuver at the captain's cabin, their shooting team functioning with well-oiled precision. Since the scenario for this training op indicated that all aboard would be "enemy combatants," Daugherty wasted no time before he theoretically rendered the captain helpless by the simple expedient of kneecapping him. They needed someone who had expert knowledge of the ship, and Daugherty had decided that the captain fit the role perfectly. In no more time than it took to render the captain helpless, Daugherty heard the forced entry to the bridge itself. Faintly, from down below, came the sounds of the remainder of the crew being rounded up.

"Is that it, then?" the redheaded Irishman asked, speaking softly into the mike at the left side of his lip. His voice was rich with the tones of County Cork, yet larded with the harsh consonants of Ukraine. Daugherty had grown up speaking fluent Russian, and he cursed in Gaelic. His very youthful, cherubic features with a shotgun pattern of rusty freckles favored both parents—he was a first generation American.

"Roger that, Red," Rockham acknowledged. "The engineering spaces went down as we reached the bridge."

Daugherty replied with sardonic humor, "That's

cool, but do you think for a moment the actual operation will go this smoothly?"

"Slick as a whistle," Rockham said through a chuckle.

As though by prearranged cue, an umpire's shrill brass whistle sounded to signal the end of the operation. At once, the SEALs ceased their actions, and, in accordance with the plan, assembled on the fantail as silence settled over the ship.

Made brassy by the bullhorn in his hand, the voice of Colonel Jerry Wharton blared over the afterdeck of the Navy cargo ship. "Gentlemen, you did an excellent job. I wish to express my appreciation of the professionalism and swiftness of third squad. Lieutenant Jorgensen, your men did an outstanding job of seizing the engine room with zero losses. Given all of the open spaces and exposed ladderways, I think the other squad leaders will agree when I say that you and your men earned the 'All you can eat and drink' party at the Chiefs' Club when we return to Little Creek. After all, the other two squads have done this before—under combat conditions, mind you—so they don't qualify for the prize, unless you guys had screwed the pooch really big time, which you didn't do. Remember one thing," he cautioned. "That party is for only two hours."

Laughter answered him, and Henry Limbaugh's voice rose above the general roar. "Why's that, Colonel? You cadre types can't stay up late or are you afraid we'll bankrupt you?"

"No, it's all about the fact we have to return to the regular training schedule the next day," the colonel replied. "No complaints, no hangovers."

Hunter banished his usual reticence for a moment to ask, "Whadda we do next, Colonel?"

"Final exam is on the way, SEAL. Are you ready for it?"

A thunderous reply answered him. "Hooyah!"

CHAPTER 3

★ ★ ★ ★

Lieutenant Commander Oscar Leavitt, captain of the LST bearing the high-speed boat assigned to Gold Platoon of SMD One, lowered his naval binoculars—made of excellent quality, gold-coated optical lenses and mirrors, and pure, flawless crystal prisms, with a one-to-ten focusing capability—and turned to the seaman manning the intercom enunciator.

"Commander Rockham to the bridge," Leavitt ordered.

"Commander Rockham to the bridge," the seaman repeated, and then spoke into the microphone that he removed from its bracket. "Now hear this, now hear this, Commander Rockham to the bridge."

Rockham had been pondering the purpose of this exercise. Another ship boarding seemed unnecessary. Granted, this time they were to locate and dispose of some containers of unspecified size, yet it still seemed excessive. He abandoned his speculations and climbed to the bridge. There, he spoke crisply. "You sent for me, sir?"

"Aye aye, Rockham. Take a look over there at the radar scope." The powerful EN-414 radar sweep sent its yellow phosphor line around the disk of the radar scope. The Mirage Over-the-Horizon, surface search radar had been in use in one form or another for thirty years. The modern, all solid-state model on the *Bataan* operated with laudable efficiency. Suddenly a blip appeared. "That's your target, Commander. That's the *Orient Trader*, right enough. They're out of Miami, bound for the Canal and on up the coast to San Diego."

"Did you obtain that information from Naval Intelligence?" Greg asked.

"Nope. I went to the Maritime Registry website."

"And that's the baby we're to board?" Shaun Daugherty asked—more of a statement than a query.

Leavitt nodded and handed Rockham the binoculars. The lieutenant commander studied the far horizon, delineated by a wide gray-white line. To his disappointment, he saw nothing of a ship. He continued watching, then turned to the radar console. Leavitt noted this and quickly appraised Rockham of the situation.

"We're a bit over the horizon from the *Orient Trader*. We'll keep station here and close in after full dark."

Rockham nodded thoughtfully. "Sounds like a plan. I'll have my number one coxswain, Ed Lopez, make the speedster ready."

Leavitt shrugged. "Shoot, Commander, that thing's hardly more than an overgrown cigarette boat."

"But big enough to handle four SEAL squads and their gear. Once you open the rear ramp and flood the stern, we can scoot out and close with the *Orient Trader* within ten or twelve minutes, depending on the height of the seas."

"Very well, Commander. We'll notify you on the squawk box when we are ready to drop the stern ramp."

Rockham turned to leave, then spun back on one heel. "Do the captain and crew of this *Orient Trader* know we're coming and that it is only a final training exercise?"

Leavitt hesitated, apparently uncomfortable with the answer. "Uh, I don't believe they do, Commander Rockham."

Rockham's expression turned grim. "Which

means that any security forces aboard will be using live ammunition. I don't like that a whole hell of a lot."

Although he agreed wholeheartedly, Leavitt had been given his instructions. "Which means you'll have to exercise special care to roll up any resistance before anyone gets hurt, right, Commander?"

Powerful engines drove the *Bataan* through the water in a southwesterly direction parallel to the freighter that would soon be invaded by four squads of SEALs, determined to take control of the bridge, crew quarters, engine room, and galley swiftly and efficiently. They had done it before a hundred times on ships at anchor in Norfolk Bay. Yet only once—and then only first and second squads of Fourth Platoon—had they boarded a ship under weigh. That had been off the coast of Sudan. Hopefully, their experiences, shared with their brother SEALs over the past few weeks, would serve them all well when it came time to climb the heaving side of the *Orient Trader*. Down on the vehicle deck of the Landing Ship Tank *Bataan*, Rockham went over the plan once more with the eager men of Gold Platoon.

Nestled in its launching cradle was a Swift Boat Mark One, a PCF-96. It had been loaded with the bow aimed at the stern ramp of the LST. The improvised driver ram could slide it into the water and reverse the cradle after the boat got under way. Rockham climbed the trailing ladder to the main deck and went aft to the vessel's stern rail, where he looked down on his assembled men.

"Listen up, men. Make damn sure you hear and understand everything now, because even with the submersible exhaust system and the added sound blankets, those Detroit marine diesel engines will make conversation difficult."

One SEAL—a new man, Hunter—raised his hand among the sailors below. "Excuse me, sir, but I'm not familiar with these boats. Isn't this a mighty large craft to use to 'sneak up' on an unsuspecting enemy?"

Rockham kept a neutral expression while he responded. "We'll be low and close to the water, giving us a very low profile. The overall full load draft is designed as three feet ten inches, but our Mark One is equipped with skegs, which puts us at four feet ten inches. Our overall height above the waterline is only eleven feet five inches. We still have almost zero radar image. That makes us pretty compact, wouldn't you say, ah, Quartermaster Hunter?"

Hunter produced a rueful grin. "Aye, sir, she looks a whole lot bigger than she is, I guess."

Senior Chief Boatswain's Mate Monday produced a friendly chuckle. "That's because she's out of the water, sailor."

Hunter blushed furiously. "Uh, I forgot about that, Chief."

John "Cochise" Grant from SEAL Delivery Vehicle, Team Two, clapped Hunter on the shoulder. "Take it easy, brother, no harm, no foul, right, Crazy Horse?"

The only other Native American in the ranks of SMD One, he had formed an immediate bond with Hunter and used his operator's name without self-consciousness, given the one hung on him by "Mr. Bill" Rogers, his Team OIC. Never happy having an Apache operating name—Grant was Southern Cheyenne—in retaliation he sometimes used the operator's name Mr. Bill loathed: *Mr. Rogers.* "Hell," Lieutenant Rogers frequently reminded the few who dared use that sobriquet, "I don't even have a garden, let alone a neighborhood."

"Yeah, I guess you're right, Cochise. What do I know about boats? Me, I'm just a landlubber from Oklahoma."

"'Where the wind goes sweepin' down the plain,'" contributed a pickup chorus of Leroy Mercer, Aaron Cohen, and Larry Stadt.

"Belay the bilge water, you clowns," Chief Monday growled.

Rockham continued at once. "Let's go back to your briefing, guys. What I was pointing out is that our low profile will make us invisible to radar, because the radar mast of the *Orient Trader* is so high above the water that they can't see anything within twenty-five miles at sea level. At night, human visual acuity is not good enough to spot us, since we're painted gray with splotches of black added randomly. On the other hand, we can keep in touch with them all the way in with our D-202 X-band three-centimeter surface search radar.

"So, Lopez will be our boat driver. He'll take the 96 boat in to within five hundred yards of the *Orient Trader*, where we'll transfer to the Zodiacs. That way it'll keep 'em from hearing your approach. Lopez will bring along an HST-4 satcom unit with a KY-57 encryption set, as well as the usual MX-300R Motorola UHF radio. That'll make it easier to relay information back to the *Bataan* in the event we fuck up big-time. He will have hove-to in the area and put out a sea anchor.

"Grant and Handel will operate the Zodiacs into the target. Sukov, Midnight Mercer, and Mainhart will be the hook men." Quickly, he named the other elements: point men, breachers, and shooting pairs. Then he added the final element. "Security on our six will be Tinsley, Limbaugh, and Maldonado."

Taco Maldonado made a face. He wanted to be included in the shooting teams despite being—like the other two—a rated hospital corpsman. HM-1 Maldonado spoke his mind. "Why are we suckin' hind tit again, boss?"

Rockham spoke candidly. "Because you guys do such a good job as prisoner holders. Any survivors will be mighty pissed, and we need you three to calm them. Remember, they're Merchant Marine dudes and we're interrupting their schedule for our little war game. If the captain got torqued enough, he could have us charged with piracy on the high seas."

"That sucks," the gravel voice of Henry Limbaugh advised. Joking, he added, "If we got busted, maybe I could get my cousin to stir up some support for us on his radio talk show. The Army's green beanies impressed the hell out of him. He ought to go ape over SEALs."

"Don't go overboard on that, Doc," advised Aaron Cohen. "Not everyone likes that guy."

Rockham gave all his troops a stern examining gaze. "I think we'd all be better off if we relied on our own resources while we carry this out. Let me remind you we'll be subjected to live fire from guys who won't know who we are and won't give much of a damn either. We'll have to make the takedown fast and clean. I'm counting on you guys to get me home to Sharon so we can make a little brother for Matty."

Under the shadow of this revelation and the threat of a charge of piracy, Rockham went on to give every small detail of the takedown. The big deal was to keep all of their bodies from being perforated by hot lead from some overeager Dirty Harry among the crew. When the final point had been made and the last question asked, Rockham dismissed the men to have a hot meal and make last minute adjustments to their gear.

Everything was going according to plan, noted Lopez as he steered the Swift Boat toward the invisible initial point on the surface of the deep waters of the Caribbean Sea. Far off to his starboard the lights of Kingston, Jamaica, glowed softly. To the port side, as Lopez ran in toward the coast of Panama, the beacon at Barranquilla, Colombia, warned sailors of dangerous shoal waters. Save for the heavily muffled engines of the Swift Boat, silence lay over the narrow passage that led to the Panama Canal. The small, speedy vessel handled beautifully, Lopez thought, as the powerful, counterrotating Detroit marine diesels drove the vessel at 23.5 knots. He considered their fuel consumption per hour. It gave them a range of only 250 miles. He felt comfortable with the armament sported by the compact speedster.

His primary long-range weapons came in the form of twin .50-caliber Browning machine guns, with bull barrels, on a manually operated, twin-scarf-ring mount. The cyclic rate of fire for those beauties was 450 to 550 rounds per minute. Equipped with ammo cans containing five to six hundred rounds per gun, he considered them formidable. Lopez let his eyes dwell on this weapon powerhouse, located in the gun tub atop the pilothouse.

"Hey, Ed, there she is. See the smudge on the horizon?" Jay Hunter yelled, excited at his first deployment.

Lopez nodded and returned his thoughts to the machine guns. Their maximum range was 7,000 yards, but he knew they worked best at less than

2,000 yards. To his satisfaction, Lopez learned that 20,000 to 25,000 rounds of .50-caliber ammo were carried aboard every PCF.

Daugherty edged up next to Lopez in the pilot house. "This baby's sure as hell got enough fire-power, eh, Boats?"

"You can say that, LT. Not only those MGs on top, but add to that an eighty-one millimeter Mark Two, Mod Zero trigger-fired mortar." Lopez grinned wickedly and pointed to the weapon. "It has a .50-caliber, Browning heavy barrel machine gun fixed atop it for target acquisition." Proud of his knowledge of weapon nomenclature, he paused to make a correction in his steering, and then added, "And there's more."

Lopez meant a retrofit that had been done in November or December of 1995, which added a 40mm, belt-fed machine grenade launcher. "Oldies but goodies," the permanent crew had de-scribed them to him.

Daugherty had more questions. "Just how pro-tected is this craft?"

"It's damn safe, sir, if you'll pardon my French. In an effort to provide protection for the overhead mount and fantail MGs of the PCFs, they added three-eighths-inch thick, fiberglass/ceramic armor. The guys in drydock added bonded woven roving also."

Even though Lopez would not need these ad-vantages on this practice takedown, the improve-ments would come in handy when they did the

real thing. When the GPS beeped, Lopez interrupted his reflections on his boat's capabilities and
signaled the squad members involved with inflat-
ing the Zodiacs and making ready to load and
shove off. From here on, Lopez realized, no matter how well they had prepared, all hell could
break loose and they'd be in some really deep
pucky.

Lopez throttled down, prompting the guys on deck
to move into position, and finally breathed easily.
So far they had escaped detection. On the horizon,
Lopez could see the superstructure of their intended target through his powerful naval binoculars. This was going to be one hell of a mix-up.
Was it true, he wondered, that not even the ship's
captain knew of the exercise being conducted on
his vessel? How could they get away with that?

He jumped when the compressed gas hissed
into the sidewalls of the Zodiacs and they began
to fill out. It seemed no time at all before the sleek
pontoon-style boats went over the side. Half the
SEALs boarded and began to take on the gear for
each squad. Quickly, they cast off, the soft purr of
the electric motors fading as the small boats drove
toward the *Orient Trader*. Behind them, Lopez
pointed the nose of the Swift Boat toward the co-
ordinates for the pickup and set the powerful engines at one-third ahead. A soft, red light winked
on the communications console, and he gestured
to his radioman to hand him the mike.

"Speedy here, what have you got?" he asked.

"This is Big Mother," came the reply from the LST *Bataan*. Then the radar operator gave them their location in latitude and longitude. He concluded with a curt, "Confirm, over."

"Roger that, Big Mother," Lopez replied. "We are about to make contact with the Sharks. They are currently at eighty degrees west by ten degrees forty minutes north. It's gonna be close."

"Yeah, maybe too close. If those merchant sailors get off a Mayday, we can be in some deep stuff," Captain Leavitt reminded them. "We're not supposed to be here, and if any of those banana republics send out any *Guardia Costal* units, it would blow your whole operation."

"Yeah," Lopez agreed. "The powers that be above us would not be happy."

"We'll keep in touch with you and monitor their frequency as well. Hang in there, sailor."

"Aye aye, sir," Lopez signed off.

None of that comforted Edgar Lopez in the least. Their passage had taken them from close to the tip of Cuba to damn near the Panama Canal. Fortunately, thanks to SEAL planning, the most heavily armed would be closest to the action. Not that they would use live ammo on these civilian seamen, but a few bloody spots from paint balls should tend to slow them down a bit.

Captain Norbert Settle had retired to his quarters. He peered through his granny half-glasses at the pages of a Robert Ludlum novel. It held his attention as the *Orient Trader* rolled and wallowed on the indeterminate sea run off the coast of Panama. He felt satisfied that they would be first in line to enter the canal on the morning. Settle loved Ludlam's many best-selling novels and read them avidly whenever he had time. His career future seemed guaranteed. On the wall to his left— framed in silver—hung his sailing master's certificate. Next to it was his navigator's license and a cargo master's ticket. Whatever the future held, he had a job he could fill. Unless, of course, he became crippled or otherwise disabled. Sighing, he put the book aside and stepped to his railed built-in shelf. He poured himself a big mug of coffee and added a dollop of *Tuaca* liqueur. Thus fortified, he returned to his comfortable chair and settled in.

He had read only another page when the sound of a faint, distant thump reached him. Only because the lower vent system was open and air-conditioned breezes cooled the ship was he able to hear even that tiny disturbance. *God, don't let it be a dolphin we hit*, he prayed silently. *The fish-kissers would crap if they found out.* Two more soft thumps followed. Perhaps it came from floating palm logs. The ground down here was sodden year-round, and any big blow ripped trees from the ground and hurled them into the sea. And they had seen a huge storm on radar the previous day. What Captain Settle failed to hear was the scrape and crunch of three caving ladders being attached to the main deck.

With a final tug and twist, the painter's poles were released from the securing hooks and the caving ladders hung free, the bottom rungs level with the surface of the sea. The point men quickly scrambled upward. Jay Hunter's head cleared the weather deck first, and he made a quick check of the fantail area. Nothing and no one moved. Seconds later he was joined by Bryant and Marks. They spread out to cover the entire area of the *Orient Trader*. A quick check showed the second shooting pairs on their way up.

Ryan O'Leary had plenty of upper body strength, but his short legs hindered him in navigating the treads of the metal caving ladder. Halfway up the side of the ship his foot missed a step and he slipped, hanging by only his arms. He did not panic, but had to stifle a groan when the seventy-pound pack on his back began to strain his shoulder joints and muscles. *Pull-ups, it's just like doing pull-ups*, he assured himself. Exerting every ounce of energy in his five-foot-eight body, he hauled himself upward. His eyes came level with the step above him and he urged himself to give even more. Only the "more" wasn't there when he needed it. His arms gave out and he dropped back once more. Would he fall into the sea and drown? Or be cut to chum-sized pieces by the turning propellers of the *Orient Trader*?

No! He wouldn't allow that. Once more he began the struggle to climb upward. His knees quaked and he suddenly realized he was going to lose again.

"Slide down one," Leroy Mercer whispered harshly to him. "I got you."

O'Leary felt a hand grasp the outside of his right thigh and steady him as he slid down the ladder. His foot touched the non-slip-covering of a lower tread and he righted himself. Panting, he nodded his thanks to Midnight Mercer and slowly, with locked-in determination, began to ascend once more. What he failed to see was the cost of his rescue efforts to Midnight.

A rising swell struck the burly black man and knocked both feet and one hand off the ladder. For a long ten seconds Mercer held on with a death grip to the ladder rigging. He drew deep breaths and flailed in an effort to connect once again with the spiderweb of ladder that hung down the side. It quickly came to him that if he did not lighten his body in some manner he would indeed fall into the water and drown. With a swift motion, Mercer unsnapped the chest clasp of his pack and switched hands on his fragile grasp to release the burden and let it fall into the sea. He'd be short as hell on ammunition, but at least he would be alive and breathing and solidly on deck.

From his position on the Zodiac waiting for his turn to climb, Rockham observed the two men's mishaps and glanced up to note that Mainhart had seen it also. "Take it up with them after the operation, U-Boat," Rockham advised him.

"Aye, sir. We lost a whole lot of gear in that little screw-up," Mainhart replied, stating the obvious.

"Gear, we can easily replace. Men don't come so easy. See to it they learn from this. Got it?"

"Oh, yeah, no problem there."

When the last shooter pair reached the deck, the squads quickly formed their trains and began their preplanned approach on the sensitive areas of the ship. First squad took the starboard side ladders up to the bridge deck. There, they set up to take out first the radio shack, then the pilot house. Dan Able set up to breach the radio room with a stick of two shooters behind him. Roger Kurkowski took the door to the captain's quarters, and Aaron Cohen made ready to break open the hatch to the bridge. With their weapons at the ready, the shooters stood close behind their breachers and waited for the signal.

Rockham gave a nod from his position at the door to the captain's cabin. At once, the breachers fitted the blade edges of their hooligan tools into the space between hatch and bulkhead and reefed on them powerfully. Metal screeched against metal, and as the hatches peeled away to the side, the men in the trains rushed into the compartments.

In the radio shack, the two men at the console spun on their swivel chairs in astonishment as the strange pair entered rapidly. Soft plops sounded as the shooters fired paint balls at the surprised occupants. The chief radio operator and his second looked in horrified surprise as the red jellylike substance spread on their chests.

"You guys are out of it. Just sit still and keep quiet," Monday growled. "We're SEALs and we're on an Field Training Exercise. Somebody high up in your company knows about this, but no one aboard does. Keep your cool, there's nothing to worry about."

"What the hell!" Captain Settle barked as Lieutenant Commander Greg Rockham entered, his MP5-N aimed at the center of the captain's pajama-clad chest.

"Sorry, Captain," Rockham said tightly. "Get on your knees and keep your mouth shut. I'll ask questions, you'll answer them."

"Who the hell are you?" Settle snapped, his British accent more pronounced with each word.

Rockham glowered at him and delayed his reply. "We won't be here long. Now, where is your second in command?"

"He's on the bridge," Settle answered tightly.

The sound of rubber-soled shoes informed Rockham of his men's progress. "Okay, then he's neutralized by now. Next, is there any other communications equipment aboard and who has access to it?"

Settle produced a rueful smile. "If I were really the enemy, I would not tell you."

"Okay," Rockham agreed, then fired a suppressed round. The discharged paint ball smacked a red smear on the captain's right shoulder. "So then I'd shoot you."

Settle stared unbelievingly at the thick ooze of red. "This will get you nowhere."

Rockham was relentless. "Now, tell me about cell phones or other communications equipment."

"And if I don't?" Settle asked.

Rockham had to admire the courage of this man. A small pain stung the area of the captain's left knee cap. "Then I shoot you again."

That brought forth the information Rockham wanted, and he relayed it by closed radio net to the men securing the crew quarters. On board the Swift Boat, Lopez also heard the rundown and activated the jamming equipment.

Rockham relented and informed the captain of what was actually going down. "I'm a Navy SEAL, a lieutenant commander by rank. My platoon is conducting a field training exercise using your ship. You and your officers were not informed because the goal was to elicit as accurate a response as we might expect from the real enemy in a similar situation. We'll inventory any physical damage to your ship and the Navy Department will pay for repairs."

Staring at the spreading paint stain, Settle worked his mouth silently awhile before he could speak. "Jeez, do you mean our troops are allowed to do things like that?" Doubt colored his words.

"We're training to fight terrorists—men and women who are not in anyone's official army—Captain. In these circumstances, as far as we're concerned, the Geneva Convention goes out the window."

A peaceful smile spread on Norbert Settle's lips. "Then I won't interfere, Commander. We in the merchant fleet live in constant fear of those fanatic Muslim bastards. If you're getting ready to take them down, more power to you. Just be careful not to injure any of my men."

"Deal. By the way, what is your name, Captain?"

"Norbert Settle. I've been a ship's master for fourteen years. This is the first time that something like this has happened on any ship I've served in."

Rockham reached out and shook Settle's hand. "Then keep cool and we'll be out of here within fifteen minutes."

Settle frowned in deep thought. "And if this were the real thing, what would happen then?"

"We would have killed all the terrorists and the ship's crew. Then we'd photograph any illegal arms or weapons of mass destruction aboard. Next we'd prepare explosives to blow the keel out of the ship and sink it by remote control after we shoved off."

"So the bad guys disappear without a trace."

Rockham grinned. "You got that right, Captain. I'll take you at your word not to tip off anyone aboard, and that'll give me one more man for

the op." He had no need to mention that had this
been a real operation, the captain would have died
a second after he answered the last question.

Every man in the engineering space froze in place
as the SEALs clattered down the steel ladders with
their fire-escape-style landings and fired weapons
that silently spat unidentifiable projectiles. One of
the younger engine tenders looked at his undam-
aged body in wonder and gasped out an answer
for them all.

"Paint balls, for God's sake. What the hell is
this?"

"Shut up and play dead, *amigo*," Taco Maldonado growled. "You'll find out what's going down
when we're ready to tell you."

Even over the rumble and hiss of the engines
and their auxiliary parts, Maldonado and the
other SEALs clearly heard the familiar crack of a
pistol discharging. "*Jesus, Maria y José!* What the
hell was that?"

Eying Maldonado's MP5-N, the youthful engineering tech swallowed hard. "It must be one of
the security men that boarded us off Miami. The
captain requested them."

"That could really screw the pooch. Hang on,
my friend, while we play a little game of rig the
ship to sink. And we'll all hope that dude can't hit
what he's shooting at."

*   *   *

A hand and arm preceded the burly man out of the hatchway to the portside crew's quarters. That hand gripped an H&K 9mm pistol. When the security guard stepped into the corridor, he instantly saw the automatic weapon in Daugherty's hand and he snapped off a hasty round.

Captain Settle had played the game well, omitting any reference to the security team he had summoned aboard from a fast motor cruiser. Settle was convinced that things were not entirely kosher in the Canal Zone due to the presence of technicians from the People's Republic of China and their Revolutionary Army thugs. Every time he'd made passage lately, Settle's skin crawled at the proximity of the Communist Chinese. He clearly recalled only too well that his father had fought in Korea against these beasts. He'd been captured and came home crippled and deformed by their torture. So Settle kept secret the presence of the strictly unauthorized security people. Besides, he reasoned, it would lend a little more realism to the SEALs' training operation.

Jude Trudeau prided himself on his marksmanship. Back home in the bayou he could take the head off a squirrel at a hundred yards with a handgun. On board a ship, things were somewhat different, he learned as the *Orient Trader* lurched in the swell. With no one at the wheel, the ship had turned sideways to the tidal flow and rolled randomly. As a result, his shot went wild, producing a ringing echo along the passageway as it ricocheted off the steel bulkheads.

Daugherty could not wait to reason with an armed man. Swiftly, he reversed his SMG and butt-stroked the surprised security man. Blackness swarmed over Jude, though he fought it and managed to trigger off another round that slammed into the metal decking at his feet before he dropped to the deck unconscious.

"Son of a bitch," Daugherty swore. "They said there would not be any problems like this."

"And you *believed* the brass hatters?" Lutz asked sarcastically.

"We're clear topside," Rockham said, making a crisp but faint report from the bridge.

"Clear in Engineering," Jorgensen declared. "We're nearly through planting the fake charges."

"Roger that," Rockham acknowledged. "How are things among the crew?"

"Someone took a shot at us," Daugherty reported flatly. "I thought that wasn't supposed to happen."

"Anyone hurt?"

"No. Only the guy with the gun. Him I cold-cocked with my H&K."

"Okay. Finish up everyone and let's make like a shepherd."

"Yeah," Monday added, "we get the flock outta here."

* * *

Back aboard the Swift Boat, Mainhart called O'Leary and Mercer aside and spoke earnestly to them. "I got this chore because I managed to save my shooting buddy in a similar accident. So listen up, guys. By now you are aware that the biggest problem with mounting a caving ladder at sea is the difficulty of maintaining your balance. All other considerations aside, that's the worst you will probably deal with. The danger should be obvious: you fall off—you drown. In my book that's damned serious. Midnight, you did right by dumpin' your gear. The operator who wants to cling to his stuff until the bitter end usually ends up badly. Stay alert, make use of the resin bags to improve your grip, and if possible keep your shoe soles dry. Caving ladders are deadly objects as well as a quick way to board a ship underway. Think about it, and if you have questions, ask them now."

Both SEALs examined their memories of the event and decided they had nothing they wanted to ask. Sobered by the near tragedy, it only deepened their commitment to do the drill right and do it that way every time. The Swift Boat made quick progress back to the LST *Bataan* and cast lines and fenders over the stern. Willing hands made fast the small, speedy boat, and those aboard climbed wearily up to the narrow weather deck forward of the superstructure. Behind them, winches whined as the Swift Boat was drawn inboard and secured.

Without delay, Rockham took Daugherty aside. "That situation could have turned bad in a hurry. The armed crewman was an unexpected menace, but you handled it okay. You literally saved lives. If someone had been hurt, I know our guys. One of them would have taken a K-bar to that dude and spilled his guts all over the deck. It could have turned into a massacre, and it would have been our asses in the end that got keel-hauled."

CHAPTER 4
★★★★

Four days after their unexpected adventure aboard the *Orient Trader*, the men of Gold Platoon, SMD One, had been debriefed and lectured on the hazards of their profession yet again. At last they staggered into the rear section of their combination barrack and headquarters. A plain white envelope rested on the foot of the bunk allotted to Sid Mainhart. He snagged it, slit it open with a finger, and quickly he read the message written by the duty yeoman.

"Holy Hannah! Hey, guys, get a load of this. I'm a daddy. And . . . and it's a boy! I've got a son."

Everyone in Gold Platoon gathered around and offered congratulations. Mainhart beamed. Later, no one recalled who it was that declared this enough of a special occasion to head for the Iceberg, but everyone, including the officers, went along gladly. Laughing and joking, they swarmed into the back room, which had rapidly gained an off-color reputation among non-SEAL habitués of the saloon and eatery. Today proved no exception.

Gold Platoon hit the Iceberg shortly after 1530 that afternoon. They shouted orders for burgers, popcorn shrimp, french fries, onion rings, and other high carb delicacies. They summoned up pitchers of beer and frosty mugs. With strong arms from two Teammates around his neck, Mainhart was led into the rear "banquet" room and the old rubber swim fin—a fifties era "Duck Foot" sign—went on the doorknob to indicate the occupants' desire for privacy. Now, not even the head waitress would enter. As requested, the beer came first, and willing hands took them at the door.

Chief Monday hoisted his foam-capped clear glass mug and outshouted the frolicking SEALs. "A toast! To our new daddy, Mainhart."

A deep rumble filled the room. "To—Sid! Hooyah! Hooyah!"

Suddenly, the door flew wide and a burley Hollywood stereotype of a truck driver filled the opening. His hairline grew low on his brow, his eyebrows thick tangles of wiry, unruly bristles. Tufts of hair sprouted from the V-neck of his T-shirt and on thick arms. He had a pugnacious jaw and a nose that had obviously been broken more than twice. Insolently, he glowered at the SEALs, either too drunk or too ignorant to sense the awesome power in the room.

"Hey!" he bellowed. "Cut down the damn noise. We don't need it out there."

Most of Gold Platoon felt only mild annoyance. Rockham let some steam build as he stepped quietly from the table where he had been seated. "This is a private party," he said. "I'd suggest that you apologize for your rudeness, close the door, and leave."

"You don't tell me what to do, swabbie. I say it's time all you trash leave here."

"I told you to bugger off," Rockham slowly repeated. "Don't make it worse." In response to his remark a menacing rumble rose among the SEALs.

Taking it in, the thick-muscled intruder backed down. He slammed the door in an effort to vent his anger and stalked back to the bar where his cronies waited. Their remarks could be clearly heard through the door to the back room, but the SEALs chose to ignore them. Their conversation returned to Mainhart's newborn son.

"Have you chosen a name for him yet?" Henry Limbaugh asked.

Sid bloomed with a new grin. "Yeah. Regina and I decided on it before I left for this cycle of training. If it was a girl, we were going to call her Emily Sue, and for a boy, Peter James."

"*Oye!* PJ, that's cool," opined Taco Maldonado. "A word of advice—don't let others get away with calling him Petey. That sounds sissy. PJ will make him *muy macho*."

"A lot of man, eh?" Mainhart speculated aloud. "Thanks, Taco, I appreciate the input. Actually, the choice was a lot simpler than that. Regina's grandfather's name was James. My uncle Peter was the man who raised me when my dad was away in the Army." He shrugged and grinned. "So we get Peter James Mainhart."

Off to one side, a group from first squad worked on a gag baby shower for the new daddy. Ferber had paused at the bar long enough to ask Moira—the dayshift cocktail waitress—if she had a baby bottle and nipple along. She had one, and Ferber asked her to fill the bottle with draft beer. Now, he produced it along with a stack of bar towels, which they folded into the ready-to-use diaper shape. Frank Monday produced a handful of number four buckshot, and laughter erupted from the plotters. Jack Tinsley slipped out of the back room and used up three quarters in order to snag a large plastic egg from one of the novelty arcade games that lined one wall, along with a pinball machines and a dart board. He emptied its contents and brought it back into the banquet room. Chief Monday quickly filled it with some of the buckshot and sealed the egg with tape. Attaching a corn dog stick with more tape, the SEALs of first squad now had a passable baby rattle. Their high jinks concluded with the addition of a bottle of olive oil. The rest of the celebrants were invited to observe. Snorts and bursts of laughter erupted.

When everyone but Mainhart had been let in on the joke, Chief Monday winked at Rockham, who took Mainhart by one elbow and steered him toward the table. "C'mon, buddy, it looks like the guys have gotten some stuff together for you."

Expecting something special to eat or perhaps a cash bag, Mainhart walked across the parquet floor to the table. His eyes widened with surprise as he took in the objects resting there. There was even a miniature rocking cradle made from a "strike anywhere" match box, with bent burned matches forming the rockers and a bow overhead with a canopy made from a handkerchief.

Lutz stepped forward, offering the baby bottle. "Here, have a drink on Baby PJ."

Mainhart produced a scowl for a moment, then relaxed into a broad grin. "You guys are nuts, you know that? Whatever, your hearts are in the right place. Thanks, guys. Now I know I'm really at home. I would never want to serve with any other bunch of hammock rats in this man's Navy. I, ah . . . I, ah . . . "

"Go on, say what you want," urged a couple of third squad guys.

"I can't go on. You got to me big-time, buddies. Thanks again, guys." He lifted the baby bottle to his lips and drank the beer.

After the laughter and renewed congratulations went the rounds, the food arrived, along with refills of beer. Quickly, the SEALs settled in and began to wolf down their various orders. Daugherty dug into a super-size bowl of smoking chili. The rich, sweet aroma that wafted over them told the more knowledgeable among the SEALs that the meat base was either bison or elk. Several sniffed deeply and glanced at their selections, wishing they had thought of the thick meat-and-bean stew.

Ken Fleming, proprietor of the Iceberg, joined them after a while and placed a plate of fried mushrooms and calamari rings—a house specialty—at the head table. The calamari, dripping marinara sauce, went down rapidly. He joined in the lighthearted banter, then changed the subject to a more serious vein. "You know, life in the Teams is really great. I'm still sick about blowing out that knee." It had forced him to take a medical leave. "But you know, the Teams put a hell of a strain on the wives and kids of the members."

Several around the tables frowned. "What are you getting at, Dolphin?" Chief Monday asked.

Fleming had a big nose, and had never outlived his operating name that derived from it. He had made sure his old Teammates from Fourth Platoon—now enlarged into SMD One—had a private place to hang out after duty hours, where they could talk freely among themselves and not worry about being overheard by those not entitled to know. Most of the customers and the wait staff knew the SEALs well, and wisely gave them a wide berth. Usually only the head waitress served them. This afternoon the task fell to Moira and their host to provide service.

Moira figured maybe some of the younger guys would smack her bottom once or twice or do some flirting, but nothing heavy. Now, she wondered what caused the sudden silence as she rapped on the door to signal the arrival of another round. Three men relieved her of the burden and one signed the tab. After she departed, the conversation returned to what life in the Teams meant to the families of the SEALs, especially those in SMD.

Bryant ran blunt fingers through his thick black hair. "I know what you mean, Dolphin," he began, returning to the topic prior to the interruption. "Last time I had more than twenty-four hours off, my kids didn't even know who I was. True thing," he went on. "My little girl started to cry when I knelt down to take her in my arms, and she ran behind her mama's skirt to hide."

"Yeah," growled Maldonado. "One time when I had been off to Language School and then came home, Tomas and Alberto would not come into the same room with me until I'd been back three days."

Then Daugherty spoke, softly, hands extended, palms outward in self-depreciation. "I'm not talking as an officer now, guys. I've seen this from personal observation. Matty has no confusion about who Greg is. The boy worships the ground Greg walks on. His happiest moment is when Greg swoops down and picks the boy up to put him on his shoulders."

"Hey, the kid's nearly nine. Isn't that a little old for that sort of thing?" protested Jorgensen. A relative newcomer to these get-togethers, he had yet to become familiar with the off-duty lives of all the SEALs in the SMD.

A different opinion was offered by Platoon Chief Monday. "Hey, guys, I don't agree with all that. Like Matty Rockham, my kids have no trouble knowing who I am. The fact is, I think our families have it a whole lot better—those of us who are married, that is—than other service families. For security reasons, they live anonymously off the base, they are relatively close-knit, and they are fully aware of the importance of what we do. I'm not trying to lean on you guys—I respect your opinions—only offer a different view of the same situation."

Hunter, a confirmed bachelor, shrugged. "That's cool. Things can turn crappy, but that goes for civilian families as well. I say it's *our* job to make sure our families understand what it is we're risking our lives for. They have to accept the risks involved, the inconvenience of being apart for long periods of time, and of maintaining a family structure while we're gone."

Jorgensen shook his thick shock of curly blond hair. "Where do we get this 'we,' redskin? You're not Western European and you are a bachelor."

Crazy Horse flashed a big, white smile. "Take it easy, Hagar," he urged Jorgensen, using his operator's name. "I may not have curly blond locks and a wife and kids, but I do know about the need to keep things within the family on an even keel. You married guys have it rough, no denying, but growing up on the south side of Tellaquah, Oklahoma, one of five kids with a single parent, isn't exactly a fun trip. I learned a lot about families under stress. I still have four brothers and sisters, only one over eighteen, and two under fourteen. It is our responsibility to ensure that the ones like these are spared anxiety and undue worry. I'd say that you should be grateful to have families to worry over you. You should cherish every minute you're with them and make the most of it."

Several of the SEALs applauded that statement, and the officers exchanged glances that said they accepted the bitching and moaning as healthy. It was a blowing off of steam that kept the guys on an even keel.

Well fed and satisfied, the SEALS were about to depart the Iceberg when Chief Monday reminded them of a longstanding ritual. "Time we had a final toast to Sid and his new son. Bring on the *Southern Comfort.*"

Cohen made a face. "Why did you ever settle on this particular poisonous potion?"

Tinsley answered him. "I'm not really sure, it just seems we always had a shot of *Comfort* at the end of our get-togethers."

"Hey, Jack, every horse-racing gentleman uses it for his mint julep. The Green Berets drank lots of it. Especially when those guys had spent all of their bread and got in the shorts around the end of the month."

"Oh, yeah, that's right," Tinsley agreed. "It was cheap and powerful. The only thing cheaper and higher proof came in quart mason jars from those little unpainted shacks out in the woods. Cost a buck a jug."

"You guys are dumpin' on me, right?" A former headquarters desk sailor, Cohen didn't yet fully realize the nature of life in the Teams.

Laughing, Rockham called for the round of liqour and told Moira to put it on his tab. When the drinks arrived, the SEALs downed them amid much laughter and made ready to leave the bar.

Half a world away, Grigoriy Rostov, Ivan Tsinev, and Vladimir Frolik celebrated for a far different and sinister reason. The first payment had been made, and the Taiwanese eagerly expected their purchases.

"This is a great day, comrades. We are on the edge of uncountable riches to be had from these Chinese."

Former Senior Lieutenant Tsinev frowned in puzzlement. "But are they on the side of our fellow Marxists, the People's Republic of China? Or are they on the side of the government in Taiwan?"

Rostov made an expressive shrug. "Who gives a

damn? But to ease your mind, Ivan Arkadyvich, they have been recruited by the Black House people for some purpose of which we have as yet to learn the details. What is important is they have U.S. dollars and they all spend quite well. We can milk this, ah, client for all we can get, and then . . . then perhaps we will get even more money for turning them in."

Tsinev looked uncomfortable. "Won't that damage our reputation as arms dealers with other clients?"

Rostov smiled jovially. "Not really. We can do it in a manner that hides the identity of whoever it was who betrayed them. We'll be in the clear, leaving all those hungry terrorists and malcontents out there who will still want to buy from us in the future. Drink to our continued success, gentlemen!" Rostov raised his small glass in salute, and the others joined him.

Following their unofficial closing ritual, the members of SMD walked out into the main bar room to settle up their tabs. The trio of truck drivers stood across the room along the mahogany slab of the bar. It had a highly polished granite inset for opening and rinsing clams and oysters. Standing unsteadily before it, it was clear that the burly men had been hitting the booze heavily. They turned awkwardly and swayed as they flexed over-muscled arms.

"Well, lookie here, Jeb, Marty—it's the damn

squids. Whasamatter, y'all too stupid to understand plain English? Jeb tole you to haul ass, your
kind ain't welcome around here."

Fleming spoke to Blaine Holley quietly from behind the bar. "I think you have it a bit wrong,
feller. Don't take this any farther or you an' your
friends'll be the ones eighty-sixed outta here."

Too drunk to think straight, Holley snarled,
"Stickin' up for the fuckin' squids, huh? C'mon,
Jeb, Marty, let's kick some swabbie butt!" He
turned back, grabbed a beer bottle by the neck
and broke off its bottom. Off balance, he took a
swipe at Fleming. The former SEAL's reactions
were far better than the drunk menacing him, and
he snapped back quick enough to receive only a
small nick on the tip of his nose. That was all it
took to unleash the fury of the SMD men.

Before the trio of drunks realized what was
happening to them, two very pissed-off SEALs
swarmed over them, so jammed together that not
all of their blows landed on target. Enough did,
though, to turn an afternoon of leisurely drinking
into a pool of misery for the truckers, who managed to tag the sailors with a few of their own.
Not enough, however, to prevent the awful pun-
ishment that rained down on them.

Eyes blackened, nose bloodied, the first to fall
rocked off the brass rail of the bar to a tattoo of
well-aimed fists until his knees went slack. He
slowly slipped to the floor moaning in semicon-
sciousness. The next to go down, with lips split

and a few ribs cracked, had been badly battered by the angry fists. Before long all three drunks went sailing out the open door to land hard on the pavement near the curb.

Still on their feet—and hardly ruffled—the SEALs walked out and past the fallen men, heading into the parking lot. A loud sound of crunching gravel from behind halted the SMD men. It was followed by the metallic sound of a cocking pump shotgun, which froze everyone in place momentarily.

Well trained, the team moved with precision an instant later. First to respond to this new threat was newly promoted Lieutenant Daugherty, who slid a Sig P-220 out of his shoulder holster and released the safety as he faced the charging, furious trucker. He fired only once—that was all he needed.

A fat, .45 ACP round smashed into the receiver of the sawed-off shotgun. The semijacketed hollow point expanded and drove the weapon backward into the man's grip. Howling in agony, the trucker quickly released his grip on the weapon and it fell to the ground. Immediately, Greg Rockham pointed at him, his voice ringing with authority.

"You! You're staying until the police arrive," he barked. "And you two—haul ass if you don't want to fall on a gun crime charge along with him."

His two companions departed with alacrity. Behind them, the fallen man whined pitifully. "You ain't gonna turn me in, are you?"

"You can bet your ass I am. A shot has been fired, and we'll have to explain that to the cops and to the Navy." Rockham frowned and gave him a cold smile. "Assault with a deadly weapon and attempted murder are not things taken lightly in the Commonwealth of Virginia. You're in some deep shit. And you're going to have to fight it on your own."

After the man had been carted off by the Virginia Beach police, the SEALs went home. On the way, Rockham's pager beeped, and the message instructed him to contact headquarters.

When he did, he received an expected summons. "There will be a meeting tomorrow at 1100 hours in Room 3D526 at the Pentagon. Subject will be promotions and manpower movement in SMD. Please be there on time."

Sharon met her husband at the door. She rose on tiptoe and gave him a big smooch. "Hi, big guy," she said breathlessly when their kiss ended.

"Hi yourself, sweetheart. I've got some bad news. I have to go to Washington tomorrow. We have a meeting at the Pentagon."

"Oh, honey, I hope it won't mean you'll be going somewhere again soon."

Rockham looked uncomfortable. "How can we doubt it?"

Young Matthew Rockham tugged at his father's pant leg, knee high, with a strong grip. "You goin' away again, Dad?" trying not to cry.

His father bent and embraced his son. "Don't worry, buddy. I won't leave you forever. Count on it."

"Please, Dad, I don't want you to go at all," Matty said, his big blue eyes filling with tears that he refused to let fall.

Rostov wore a frown as he entered the room where his underlings waited for his briefing on gaining more control of the illegal arms business inside Russia. Rostov's displeasure was readily recognized by Frolik and Tsinev. They exchanged covert glances, expressing their puzzlement.

"It appears that we have come to the attention of the Americans," Rostov said.

"What could they possibly know?" Frolik said dismissively. "And, more so, why would they care?"

Rostov's tone of voice came just short of being patronizing. "Vladimir Konstantinich, I am astounded. Surely you are aware that the Americans are the only remaining superpower. Anything that involves the distribution of weapons interests them.

"Consider this," he went on. "It is unlikely that the Americans would operate against us here in Russia, but say the Americans manage to determine the identity of our customers, and then manage to disrupt whatever those customers might be planning. A series of such disasters would create an unfavorable reputation for us, would it not? If everyone who purchased weapons from us got caught by the authorities in their countries, with the help of the Americans, how long could we expect to remain in business?"

Tsinev frowned and Frolik swallowed hard. It was the former senior lieutenant who spoke first. "What can we do about this?"

For the first time, Rostov smiled. "Some of our assets inside the United States have identified one particular man as having a great interest in our sales activities. He is a colonel in their Army intelligence—the counterintelligence division. He is also known to be liaison officer to a highly dangerous organization called the Special Materials Detachment—it is a new unit of the notorious Navy SEALs."

Frolik thought little of that. "How do a lot of supply people represent a threat?"

Rostov's voice rang with the sound of doom. "Like many things the Americans do, the name is a misnomer. They are in fact a highly professional group of warriors—you could call them killers, in fact. This colonel—his name is Wharton—is closely involved in any operations undertaken by these SEALs. Wharton has made inquiries about who is the most active in illegal arms sales worldwide. Since we are in the process of removing all competition from other arms dealers, we can be sure that our names have come up, and that this Wharton is aware of our ambitious program."

Frolik asked the obvious. "Why do we not simply have him killed?"

Rostov shrugged. "It is not as easy as it sounds. His office is in the Pentagon, so he is well-protected from an assassin's bullet. But rest assured that I am working on it. Some of our friends in Al Qaeda are aware of Wharton's interest, and I have arranged for them to send a team to dispose of this irritant. In fact, they should be close to consumating his removal as we speak."

CHAPTER 5
★★★★

Nothing had changed in the room, Rockham noticed, except perhaps the custodial staff had forgotten to dust the low bookshelf along one wall.
The same coffeemaker gurgled and hissed on a
counter to one side, and the long, oval table held a
high shine. As the ranking officers concerned with
the topic of this meeting took their seats, aides
brought them steaming cups of strong black coffee. Rockham had once been told that Admiral
Cromarty preferred French Roast blend coffee
from freshly ground beans. When in a jovial
mood, the admiral called it, "Frog brew."

Cromarty cleared his throat to call for silence.

"Gentlemen, as soon as General Warburton arrives, we can begin.

Two minutes later the general entered the room. Cromarty waited until the Army COS settled with coffee and a large cinnamon honey bun. "Now, gentlemen, I wish to open this general meeting on the personnel problems attendant upon the continued existence of the new Special Materials Detachment. Let me introduce to you once again Lieutenant Commander Greg Rockham. At present he is CO of SMD and in a position to best describe what problems exist. Commander Rockham . . ."

Rock came to his feet and hastily marshaled his thoughts. "It has become apparent to me since taking command of SMD that there are enormous problems with opportunities for promotion within the structure of the SMD. Example: current plans for enlarging SMD to have two or even three task units of Special Operations company strength. If this is accomplished, it will be a good thing, provided we are able to promote from within. At present there are no promotion possibilities that haven't already been filled. There's not a man in this room who can honestly say that promotions don't matter. Just so long as *we* continue to climb the ladder from jg to Admiral or shavetail to General it's 'business as usual.' I cannot keep men—nor can any other commander—if we are not able to promote the deserving ones." He paused and took a deep breath before continuing.

"If some of my current people can move over and obtain promotion by filling a Table of Organization slot requiring a higher rank, then I say well and good."

"For the sake of argument," Colonel Jerry Wharton interrupted. "Let's say that as it stands the personnel people here in the Pentagon insist on accepting only SEAL-qualified transfers from the surface fleet or newly graduated candidates from BUDS."

Rockham looked at the man as though he had suggested they develop plans to surrender the country to one of their enemies. There was much he had yet to learn about this Special Ops intelligence liaison officer. Rockham's lack of knowledge brought a frown to his brow.

In fact, Wharton was a graduate of West Point who had attended the Intelligence School at Fort Belfore, Maryland. After that, he went to Ranger School, followed by the Army Language School at the Presidio in San Francisco. He rose quickly through his assignments to a slot in a Ranger Battalion as S-2. In that position, he had served in a line outfit during Gulf One. Then he attended advanced intelligence training, after which he was assigned as aide to ACOS, thus his rank of Colonel.

It had not been a coincidence that Rockham accepted the new colonel without question upon first meeting him. Wharton was six-foot-one, 178 pounds, lean and hard. He was married, the father of two boys—ages eleven and eight—and a daughter, who was six. His wife Judy was from a family of lawyers, two of whom had served with JAG. Wharton's boys had taken to Matty Rockham like a long-lost brother. Now the colonel suggested that exceedingly rough times might be ahead for SMD.

"Begging your pardon, Colonel," Rockham began. "Why would the personnel people do such an unlikely thing? People fresh out of BUDS don't know their ass from an acorn. There isn't a man in SMD who hasn't run ops independent of their current assignment. Don't any of these bean counters know the definition of the word 'experience'?"

Wharton produced a rueful grin. "We all know about what is called 'interservice rivalry,' right? Well, Commander, you should peek into some of these offices and see the high degree of jealousy possessed by desk sailors for Special Operators and for the guys in your Teams. Which attitude goes for the other services as well. They hate the existence of any unit that is called 'elite.' It implies that they don't measure up. Believe me, I've gotten an earful."

This put a whole different light on things for Rockham. He paused in his presentation a long moment, furiously redesigning his method of approach. "Not only do we need to enlarge SMD as per plan, creating SMD Two and SMD Three, but also to make certain it grows. Only so long as it reflects an increase in suitable operators. To be brief, I for one visualize our needing more, not less, men."

"How is that, Commander?" Wharton asked.

Rockham gave him a brief smile. "I'm glad you asked. I can clearly see the mission parameters of SMD increasing rapidly. Specifically: we're all aware that a certain Captain Rostov has set up as an arms dealer in Russia. We are fairly certain he has access to WMDs and is offering them for sale. Further, the ayatollahs are still working on developing nuclear weapons in Iran. The time is coming when we will have to take out their facilities." He went on listing the ways that could be accomplished. "We could bomb hell out of them—ask the Israelis about that. But the fact is, ensuring the security of any piece of ground falls to the grunts and the armor. That calls for troops, if we choose to occupy, to Special Operators, if we choose to sanitize and withdraw."

All of the ranking officers around the table settled into thoughtful poses. At last Admiral Cromarty broke the silence. "Go on, enlighten us," he said dryly, well aware of Rockham's thoughts.

Rockham acknowledged the directive with a nod. "Admiral, gentlemen, we well know that the list of enemies or potential enemies is quite large. Add Iraq to Iran—Saddam Hussein is one nasty bastard who has already used biochemical weapons against Iran's army and civilian population, and his own people as well. Then there's the Abu Sayyef in the Philippines, head-hunting Muslim murderers with the moral values of cavemen." He went on to name the Islamic Defender's Front—*Darul Islam*.

"Add to them our old friend, Osama bin Laden, who financed and helped organize the Al Qaeda terrorist network. There are also Al Qaeda cells in Kenya—led by Khalfan Khamis Mohamed and Mustafa Mohamed Fadhil—and in Somalia."

"You seem rather well versed on terrorism worldwide, Commander," General Ashton Bancroft rumbled, stung by the revelation of a couple of terrorist groups he was not familiar with.

Rockham had the good grace to blush slightly. "Special Operators live or die by the maxim, 'Know Thy Enemy.' Beyond my other qualifications, which you *do* know, General, I've made my specialty terrorist organizations. In so doing, I would be tempted to add the Muslim extremists of Bosnia and Chechnya. Granted they're not Semitic Arabs, but they are Muslims. I consider all of them a potential threat to the entire civilized world." He paused a moment and went on apologetically, "I know it is not politically correct to condemn Muslims out of hand, and particularly those with round heads, blond hair, and blue eyes. But, gentlemen, I have read the Koran—twice. Are you aware that there are over thirty references to the rewards waiting for those 'believers' who kill an infidel? There's even a rabble-rousing prayer exhorting those who take up the *jihad*—the holy war—to cut off the heads of the infidels. In my opinion, that's the heart and soul of the so-called 'Religion of Peace.'"

Several of the officers present let out their

breaths in a gush. "Those are strong words," Air Force General Rashid Odeh declared in a serious tone. "They could prove an embarrassment to the Navy and a danger to you."

"Sir, I am fully cognizant of that," Rockham replied, recognizing the implicit threat in the general's words, "and I accept your caution in the spirit I'm sure you intended it." The proverbial butter would not have melted in his mouth. "I am also aware that once SMD Two is up and running, I shall be 'bumped upstairs,' which is to put it delicately. I will possess too much knowledge to be allowed to operate in the field. At that point I'm inclined to say let the chips fall where they may. Now, may we move on to my next point?"

"Yes, please, Commander, do so," Admiral Cromarty prompted.

"Another area in which we can be most effective is operations to secure sites where WMDs are stored. These are prime targets for terrorists. I believe it is idiocy to consider that terrorists can be dealt with solely by our civilized legal system. They do not and should not ever be granted the rights and privileges of American citizens under our Constitution and our justice system. Lawyers, judges, and many cops are not equipped for even brief combat situations. They cannot properly deal with madmen who routinely slaughter women and children as training exercises. Their barbarity is beyond the pale, and the only answer we need give them is from the muzzle of an H&K

MP-5 or a twelve-gauge shotgun. Our nuclear power plants and our stores of nuclear and chemical weapons are prime targets for terrorists. SMD has the weapons and the skills necessary to protect these sites in the style of Rick Marcinko's Red Cell."

There followed a series of disgruntled *hurrumphs* around the table. Particularly embarrassed, Rockham noted, were the officers of flag rank. Rock knew and liked Commander Marcinko, the former CO of a special counterterrorist unit, SEAL Team Seven. He recalled that back in early 1984, Marcinko had been summoned to the office of Vice Admiral Lyons, Jr., who was then Deputy Chief of Naval Operations.

Admiral Lyons explained his concerns over the accessibility of U.S. military bases to terrorist attack. Marcinko agreed and was directed to draw up organizational plans for a new unit. It was to be one specifically tasked with testing the security of U.S. Navy bases. This was not to be the only mission of the new team. Actually, testing of naval facilities would primarily be a cover for the unit's actual function—covert counterterrorist missions around the world.

Following this plan, a portion of the unit would deploy overtly to a base to carry out its security mandate. Meanwhile, a small part would proceed to a foreign nation to carry out the indicated counterterrorist activity the situation required. Their operation would be closely in line with the principals of aggressive neutralization of enemy elements as carried out on a regular basis by nations such as Israel and Greece.

Opinions of Marcinko's command and operations style varied. It included many who wanted his scalp. Others swore by the benefits they and their men derived from the lessons he and his team taught. One retired SEAL officer summed up the pro-Marcinko faction position by saying, "When you get right down to it, the concept is brilliant. Timid bedside manner is what killed it. . . . My understanding from the bubblehead admiral who headed the inspector general team was that too much had happened. It went to, 'kill the name, remove the shame' type of thinking. The sad fact is that Dick's guys did some great penetrations, but the value of the lessons got lost in 'the cult of personality.'"

Rockham agreed, and so now said cryptically, "To me, it all seems to fit. Red Cell had a hell of a thing going. We would do well to emulate them, at least in the tactics of penetration operations and protecting sensitive sites." He paused to take a long swallow of water from the glass at the edge of his green blotter.

Colonel Wharton leaned over and whispered to him, "Jeez, that's some speech. I didn't know you were an accomplished public speaker. Keep stickin' it to 'em, boy."

Rockham glanced down at the trident badge

that denoted a SEAL. "I'm not blowing wind like some friggin' politician, Jerry. I'm dead serious."

"I know, and I love it." Wharton leaned back, sipped from his own glass and smiled around the room.

"Another reason our operators are ideally suited to this sort of task," Rockham went on, "is that we have received the special training to handle the necessary weapons and protective equipment." He paused and gave a low chuckle. "Even our tactical uniforms are designed in such a way as to constitute protective suits for chemical and biological weapons—ours or theirs."

"Are there any other ways you foresee employing the Special Materials Detachments?" General Warburton asked. "I assume we are in agreement to the enlargement of the Table of Organization and Equipment for SMD, gentlemen?"

Nods of agreement followed, while Rockham prepared to elaborate on his dream organization. When everyone directed their attention his way, he spoke again. "Someday we will have to confront the dangers presented by North Korea, Iran, and Cuba. Granted these are all 'nation states,' and as such we cannot conduct acts of open warfare against them without a declaration of war. But God help us if they ever develop nuclear weapons or other WMDs. Then it might well be necessary to send in SMD to mess up their playground."

Unhappy, General Odeh grumbled. "Do you mean covert operations in platoon strength, Commander?"

"No, sir, I'm talking company size if necessary, like for North Korea."

"Our bombers and the Navy's Trident missiles can handle that problem," Odeh boasted.

"Not if the installation is more than five hundred feet underground. Am I right, Admiral?"

Cromarty agreed. "We have nothing short of the nuclear arsenal capable of that. And, as you pointed out, Commander, if we're not at war with them, we'd take hell trying to explain why we popped a nuke."

Colonel Wharton said he was buying, and Rockham readily accepted the invitation to a late lunch after their meeting concluded. At least, he thought wistfully, he had achieved nearly everything he wanted. He also knew that his plans for the future of SMD would be given thoughtful consideration. Revising the project and objectives of Red Cell might be risky, but he felt the concept worthy of implementation. Only this time they'd do without the cowboy attitudes.

Wharton chose *Andale*, at 401 Seventh Street NW, listed as one of the hundred best restaurants in D.C. They sat down at a table featuring large fan-back chairs made of split palm fronds and bamboo and contemplated the menu. When a slim, smiling waiter appeared, Wharton ordered a pitcher of margaritas. "That all right with you?" he asked Rockham.

"I'm a SEAL, remember. I'll drink anything except kerosene or torpedo propellant."

After the level in the pitcher had lowered by half, Wharton indicated the menus. A loud stomach growl reminded Rockham of how long it had been since he'd eaten. Like Wharton, who had a reputation for a prodigious appetite, Rockham ordered a lunch menu item called a *Combinacion Grande*. The description in English implied that the platter came with every Mexican dish in the cookbook. While they waited, the two men finished off the remaining margaritas.

When the food arrived, Rockham was certain that the claim was not an exaggeration. The plate held a shredded beef taco, a chicken tostada, a pork tamale, and a chile relleno, along with the ubiquitous rice and beans. As he dug in, he wondered if they provided bowser bags. Wharton called for a round of beers to accompany the mountain of food and set into it with gusto.

After the two men had demolished about half of their huge repast, Wharton asked Rockham pointedly about Red Cell. Rockham quickly replied, "Rick Marcinko named it that within days of receiving orders to organize the unit. He said it was an 'up yours' to the communists. Despite the destruction and havoc they created, they created a lot of useful information about protecting static installations.

"Only one big problem stood out. It seemed that everyone who'd transferred over from Team Six engaged in a *macho* contest. From what I've heard, things were sort of wild from the git-go. Rick used to show up for morning formations and briefings half drunk, wearing canvas shorts and flip-flops. Things sort of went downhill from there." Rockham shrugged, attempting to make a better case. "For all that, they turned in some damn good results. A lot of their security techniques are still in use."

"Yet you want to create another outfit like Red Cell?" Wharton asked incredulously.

"Uh . . . no, not exactly *like* that. But some outfit to do the same thing. You know, check up on our WMD sites and be able to take out those that belong to an enemy or potential enemy."

Wharton eyed him over a mouthful of savory taco. He chewed industriously, swallowed, then asked his prime question. "How large do you want this unit to be?"

For a moment Rockham's eyes would not meet Wharton's, then he looked up and stared hard into those blue orbs. "I would say start with a company in strength. Not a SEAL company, but an infantry company—say a 112 enlisted, five officers, a first soldier of some sort, five RTOs, and attached transportation."

Wharton whistled softly. "That's one damn tall order, sailor. To put it frankly, the brass hats would crap their drawers over such a proposal."

Rockham winced. "You mean I don't stand a snowball's chance in hell to get it?"

Wharton forked up some tamale, chewed and swallowed. "Not that size. Try a reinforced platoon for starters and I'll back you one hundred percent."

Taking a long, deep gulp of his *Cerveza Pacifico*, Rockham had a light of anticipation twinkling in his eyes. "You're serious, aren't you?"

"Darn right I am. If I had known about Red Cell and what their mission was, I would have been beating the drum for a similar unit from the day I got here."

Rockham extended his hand and shook that of his Pentagon liaison officer. "I think we're going to work this out perfectly, you and me. Moisen was a bit too doctrinaire for my liking. 'Don't make waves. When you make waves you stand out and become a target.' That seemed to be his credo."

Wharton laughed out loud. "You can bet your ass it's not mine. When you get a chance to get back up here to D.C., let's get together and work out something solid. Bring along your ideal T.O.-and-E for a reinforced platoon-size unit. My people in Special Forces will be most interested in the concept. And I'm willing to bet that Force Recon will be hot for it too. A combined, highly skilled unit—led by SEALs, of course—could bring down a lot of scalding pee on the likes of Muammar Gadhafi."

Rock was puzzled. "Why do you want to open this up to other services?"

"You're talking about the '*blanketheads*'— that's what you SEALs call us, right? We have some talents and areas of expertise that you guys don't. At least more developed, like ground warfare. Also, the Air Force has some pretty bad-ass Special Operators who can also fly airplanes. If we keep it all in the family, the brass hats will find it much harder to screw us."

Rockham beamed. *Wharton had said us.* That put him in the mix up to his ears. Nothing helped more than total commitment. "I like that. You'll have your T/O within two weeks. Now, what would you say to some *sopaipillas* for dessert?"

Wharton shook his head. "I'm more of a Mexican fried ice cream guy myself."

"So let it be."

Seated two tables away, two men ostensibly pored over that day's edition of the *Washington Post*. In fact, one of them industriously worked a tightbeam, highly sensitive parabolic mike. The unit was so tiny it was invisible to the casual observer. The pair had followed Colonel Wharton from the Pentagon and set up their surveillance post after the two officers settled in with their drinks. They neglected their lunch.

One of them, Saif Daoud Saddiq, nodded to the other as Wharton and Rockham made ready to leave. "The doctor will be pleased with what we have learned, Fazoul." He referred to Ayman al-Zawahiri, top lieutenant to Osama bin Laden.

"Yes, it is so, Saif Daoud," answered Fazoul Mahmoud Hamza. Both men were members of a sleeper cell of Al Qaeda, located in the Tidewater region of Virginia. It was one of many under the control of Ali Abdelseoud Mohamed, a native Egyptian who had become a naturalized citizen of the United States before assuming his duties as a top leader of Al Qaeda. His allegiance to Osama ensured his loyalty to the cause.

"They are leaving. Take the car, Saif, and follow the colonel. He is the more important one. I will go back to our safe house and use the computer to get an identity on the other. We have his name, so it should be easy."

"Yes. I suspect the colonel's guest is the other one we were told about. Perhaps he will prove worth looking into," Saif agreed. "When will we strike directly against the Great Satan, Fazoul?"

"If you mean the men we are watching, soon, I believe. Also, we are told to be prepared to receive some of our bravest warriors for a special cause."

"What is that?"

Fazoul hesitated a moment, then went on. "They are to take flying lessons, earn commercial licenses, and then go on to bigger aircraft."

Saif frowned, confused, as he prepared to follow

Colonel Wharton. "But how will that harm the Great Satan?"

With a shrug, Fazoul Mahmoud Hamza replied, "I do not know, but we should not question the wisdom of al-Zawahiri and the prince."

CHAPTER 6

★ ★ ★ ★

Thick smoke from the strong, black-paper-covered Russian cigarettes filled *Relykey Medrad*—the Great Bear—making wavy beams of the dim lighting of the bar and grill. Rostov and Tsinev sat at a small table in one corner, large bowls of borscht cooling in front of them, the dollops of sour cream already melted into a whitish film over the red soup. On a postage-stamp stage a young woman—thin to the point of being unhealthy—sang into a microphone. Her effort to produce a current favorite, "My Butterfly," seemed to drain her of all energy; standing upright, she still seemed to languish.

"*Borge moi!* She is awful. Can they not find better talent than that?" asked Tsinev.

Rostov smiled ruefully. "All the good ones are in Moskva and Leni—er, Saint Petersburg. But we must be here. Arrangements have been made to ship the first order from Saint Petersburg to our Oriental friends. Have you made contact with the office of the shipping company here in Vladivostok?"

Tsinev snickered. "If you can call a back-of-the-hall, dingy room an office, yes. I have made arrangements for them to prepare shipping manifests as we require, and our future clients' orders will go out on one of those horrid old rust-buckets they call cargo vessels."

"Excellent. And I have paved the way for us with the customs people. Also, I've greased the palms of the harbor officials. Both expect a monthly stipend. They're greedy bastards, the lot of them."

Tsinev frowned. "What about the future? How will they all react when we need a regular schedule of departures?"

Rostov laughed. "They will ask for more money, of course. Much of our success is due to you, Ivan. Your experience and knowledge in communications and electronics has made it easier. We now stand on the brink of enormous wealth and lives of utter comfort."

"What about additional clients among the Asians?" Tsinev asked.

Rostov frowned. "There's no lack of them. Abu Sayyef in the Philippines wants WMDs. So do the socialist revolutionary organizations in Indonesia. You will find Al Qaeda in Malaysia, Southeast Asia, Central America, South America, and even the United States and Australia. They all want the same thing."

Tsinev knocked back another shot of vodka. "Oh, yes, I am certain of that. They all seek weapons of mass destruction. Are we able to satisfy their demands?"

Rostov shook his head. "Regrettably, no. They are not available in sufficient quantity at the present time." He sighed heavily. "What truly upsets me is all of the legends flying around about the supposedly missing backpack nuclear weapons. To the best of my knowledge, they are all accounted for. That is too bad, because the sale of them could have brought us billions of American dollars. Curiously, many of these terrorists are not from the 'have not' class, but are fabulously wealthy. Bin Laden is rich beyond all imagining. Saddam Hussein could buy those weapons, provided we could get our hands on one or more of them, and not notice the drop in his bank balance."

Tsinev frowned. "Hussein would only sell them to some terrorist group, correct?"

A faint smile flickered below Rostov's mustache—a new, Stalin-style addition to his changed appearance—as he considered his electronics expert's observation. "Yes, he has little choice, actually. For some reason, he insists on maintaining the fiction that he and his regime have nothing to do with terrorism. Sometimes, I suspect his only goal is to increase his financial assets. He wants to become the richest man in the world. And, in order to achieve that, he has no objection to taking bin Laden's money to have the Republican Guard's crack cadre train Al Qaeda terrorists. I learned recently that Hussein purchased a Boeing 737 and stripped it of its wings. It is set up in a remote Al Qaeda training camp in northern Iraq. For what reason, I cannot guess, but I surely would like to have been in on the sale."

Tsinev nodded agreeably. "Those planes sell for over seventy million on the open market. A covert, illegal sale would be worth at least a quarter of that more."

"How true, Ivan. Then there's another rumor that went the rounds about a fake nuclear artillery shell supposedly sold to our Soviet masters by a disgruntled American artillery officer. I detest turncoats. Our leaders should have known better than to trust him. Provided that story is true, of course. It is difficult, nearly impossible, to tell a fake from the real thing. The only test to prove the authenticity of such a shell destroys the product along with a good piece of real estate. For all the eager buyers, with huge bankrolls to purchase such sophisticated ordnance, it is still better to build a very large bomb. Say, for example, the large cylinder of a cement mixer filled with diesel-fuel-saturated ammonium nitrate, triggered by a kilo block of Simtex. Or use a propane or natural gas tanker truck. Better still, since they operate in three dimensions, an airplane loaded with fuel." Rostov smiled. "That last is a favorite of mine."

"I understand why. But, Grigoriy, it would have to be a big airplane to do much damage."

"Without a doubt. I visualize a large cargo craft like the Antonov 144 or a passenger liner. Think of it, thousands of kilos of jet fuel."

Tsinev got into the spirit of the game. "And thousands of metric tons of explosives could be placed inside if one used a cargo craft."

Rostov rubbed his hands together. "Exactly what I had in mind. Unfortunately, most of those items are readily available in the countries where these Asians are planning to operate."

"So? We do not sell them those things. Knowledge is golden, as you well know. We teach them how to make the bombs, and we provide the Simtex, and reap a reasonable profit for doing so."

Rostov chuckled. "You make it sound so easy." He clapped his hands together and abruptly changed the subject. "Now, we must make ready to meet with our new client."

"Another eager Asian, yes?"

"*Da, sto vi doomat?*" He repeated his words sadly, "What do you think? This one is a pushy bastard."

Tsinev raised an eyebrow. "How did you determine that?"

Rostov frowned. "He insisted, no *demanded*, that we have the meeting at the Sunrise Tea Shop."

"How stupid!" Tsinev exploded. "He might as well suggest we meet at the Vladivostok City Police Center. How can we discuss business in such a popular place?"

Rostov patted Tsinev on one shoulder. "Do not trouble yourself, comrade. I will find a way. Trust me on that." Then he added as an afterthought, "Oh, for your information, remember our earlier Oriental customers? Well, as predicted, the Chinese security service caught them and they disappeared into the Black House, never to be seen again."

"What a pity," Tsinev responded without real concern. "I do hate losing good customers."

Over the ornate Romanoff-era entranceway and gingerbread door, a large sign in bright colors read SUNRISE TEA SHOP. Inside, Rostov and Tsinev discovered that their eager client had the forethought to arrange for privacy. He had reserved one of the small, private alcove rooms off the main floor of the upscale café. He bowed graciously and indicated their meeting place with a wide sweep of one arm. Dressed in a luxurious blue silk suit, albeit cut in the Mao style, he shimmered in the sunbeams that shot through the cupola of the large central rotunda.

"I am overjoyed to see you again, Captain," the Asian said to Rostov after closing the gold-colored curtain and the pocket door.

Rostov managed to hide his surprise at finding at least one of their former clients alive and well, and here in Vladivostok. "Thank you, Mr. Youang. This is my electronics and explosives expert, Senior Lieutenant Ivan Tsinev. May I order us a round of *grooshu* liqueur?"

"Yes, that would be most agreeable."

Rostov pressed the button above the wainscoting near the doorjamb.

Youang continued, eyes alight with anticipation. "Now, have you found one of the missing backpack weapons?"

Rostov paused when the door opened and their waitress entered. She wore a typical English maid's uniform of white bonnet, white blouse with a small, symbolic black tie, and a black pleated skirt. He placed their order and Youang added a pot of the house's best tea and a plate of butter cream sweet rolls. After she departed, Rostov answered Youang's query.

"You have been the victim of rumors and legends spawned out of the breakup of the Soviet Union. I have searched exhaustively and I am sorry to say I can find record of no such items."

Disappointment clouded Youang's face momentarily. "But we must have some weapon of mass destruction. I cannot go home as a failure. Not after the tragedy that befell my former colleagues. It would be terrible. The loss of face—it would prove unbearable."

Rostov expressed his sympathy. "I am truly sorry you must return home in disgrace, Mr. Youang. I would like to help, but it is not possible. I assume you have new associates to bring forward your plan?" he probed. At Youang's nod, he went on, "If you are willing to forego a nuclear weapon, there is, perhaps, something I have in mind that might fit your needs, and help you save face."

Eager once more, Youang leaned forward as the door slid open and the waitress entered with their order. The three men drank off a third of the small glasses of pear liqueur, biding their time until the waitress departed. "Tell me what that might be, Captain."

"I have recently learned of several biological weapons that have come on the market. They are filled with augmented anthrax."

"Magnificent!" Youang enthused. "Several vials of that would do a great deal of damage. We could wipe out the entire population of Taiwan, and there would be not the least connection to the People's Republic."

"They are not vials of liquid or even solids. They are 122 millimeter rockets, each fitted with four modified SS-18 biological dispersal submunitions. The submunitions are filled with an active agent of 45.9 kilograms of weaponized anthrax spores, milled and treated to a sub-five micron powder. We would, of necessity, leave the distribution method up to you. One, perhaps two warheads should be sufficient to eliminate your—ah, enemies. But let me caution you, Mr. Youang, they would be very expensive."

"You never cease to amaze me, Captain Rostov. You speak of them being expensive, a relative term. Exactly how much are we speaking of?"

Rostov had already calculated what the traffic might bear. "We will need two million dollars for each warhead—a total of four million."

Youang prompted him with a tantalizing idea. "And if we wanted an entire launch system?"

Rostov considered that a moment. "I am afraid your principals could not afford that sort of expense. The total would be $110 million—eighty million for the warheads and another twenty million for rockets to deliver them, and for the BM-21 rocket launcher, another ten million. If you also wanted the vehicle to transport the unit, the Ural-375 truck would be another forty thousand—trucks are cheap in Russia today."

Youang swallowed with obvious difficulty, oblivious to the sarcasm in Rostov's remarks about trucks. "It is an attractive figure, though somewhat excessive. I will have to contact my superiors to obtain permission to go that high. When could we expect delivery?"

"Within two weeks, with my usual caveat to a transaction," Rostov answered simply.

Youang's broad, flat face reflected his disapproval of another item in Rostov's presentation. "The BM-21 launcher and the Ural-375 are quite old, are they not?"

Rostov shrugged. "So? They have been well-maintained, and the rockets themselves are new, assembled only a year ago. The submunitions are of recent manufacture and are duplicates of our most virulent and effective biological weapons."

For the next five minutes Youang haggled over the price, always going back to the age of the launcher and the truck. Bargaining for any- and everything was an ancient tradition with the Chinese, so Youang felt it was part of the buying process. Rostov, on the other hand, was a "one price only" merchant.

At last, his patience worn thin by this bickering, Rostov raised both hands in mock surrender. "You have the better of me, Mr. Youang. I have other clients to whom I could sell this package, and in fact I have an appointment with one of them in an hour. But because I like you personally, and admire your desire to eliminate the nuisance on Formosa, I am willing to reduce the price by a million U.S. dollars. It must be a terrible threat to face to have these stubbornly antisocialist recalcitrants literally on your doorstep. So, if my sacrifice of profit will aid you, I will be pleased."

Insincere bastard, Youang thought. *One had to*

expect that, though, when dealing with the quai lo. Foreign barbarians were difficult. He forced a smile. "You are most generous. I will convey your willingness to be accommodating to my superiors. Now, good day, Captain Rostov."

Asians! They all wanted to twist and turn and drive down the price. Fortunately, he had made preparations for this event by raising the final price in advance by two million. He had exhausted his patience yet again with his other prospective client. This one, like Youang, wanted a large price-cut for twenty crates, each of nine cases of AK-74s—under the mistaken belief that they could use the American-manufactured 223 ammunition. In fact, the latest model Kalashnikov assault rifle fired 5.45mm rounds, not the American 5.56mm. A small detail, but one that inspired heated bargaining on the part of Amahl Abdullah Thalib—the chief financial officer and brother of the leader of *Laskar Jihad*. He insisted on a fifty percent reduction in the price of the weapons. Granted, the Indonesian terrorist organization was poorly financed and had rejected overtures from Al Qaeda to send elements of bin Laden's Afghan mujahadeen to intermingle and train *Laskar Jihad* operatives. Ja'far Umar Thalib had made public statements to the effect that *Laskar Jihad* did have links to the Kumputan Mujahadeen Malaysia and to other international terrorist networks.

It was amazing, Rostov reflected, how conversant he had become with international terrorist organizations. He owed it all to an old schoolmate and fellow climber up the ranks of the officer corps, Yuri Nikolia'ich Bassov. Yuri had chosen the KGB path to higher rank, and by the time the Soviet Union came crashing down, had earned the rank of Colonel on the staff of the First Directorate for Foreign Operations of KGB. Grigoriy Rostov had heard rumors that Yuri had also worked briefly in *Otdil Chihtv'ohti*—the dreaded Fourth Directorate, which was dedicated to *mokriyee delah*—wet affairs—sabotage and assassinations. Whatever the case, they were once again brothers in arms—in this instance, illegal arms—and Yuri had given him an excellent briefing on those he might expect to encounter as clients.

"Captain Rostov," his Malaysian customer said now. "I am sure you know there are tens of thousands of these assault rifles for sale worldwide. There is a phrase the cursed Americans use that fits quite well. 'They are a dime a dozen.' Why should we pay the outrageous price you demand when we can get them much cheaper elsewhere?"

"If that is so, comrade, why then, good fortune to you. Go and get them elsewhere. But, let me advise you that our goods are of the finest quality. Bulgarian-made Kalashnikovs are highly accurate. Also, bear in mind that we are the only exporting company that can get them delivered directly into your hands in Pamekasan harbor without interference by the authorities. And I mean all twenty crates at one time, on one forklift pallet."

Not as accustomed to holding a blank expression as Orientals, Amahl Talib's eyes opened wide and his brows rose sharply. "You can do that? We are fortunate to smuggle in one case at a time, twenty assault rifles."

Rostov smiled a shark's smile. "It is for that after-sale service that you pay the higher prices. By the way, we also have an ample supply of ammunition for the AK-74s. We can sell and ship it in fifty thousand round lots. Would that be helpful?"

"And what is the cost?"

Rostov took a calculator from his jacket pocket. "Let me check." He punched buttons rapidly. *Um-hmm.* "Ah . . . yes. If we were to ship at the same time, it would cost you one and a half U.S. dollars per round. I make that a total of $75,000."

Talib began to sputter. "But—But, I can walk into any WalMart gun counter in the United States and buy a box of twenty rounds for five dollars American. Why do you charge this excessive price?"

"I can give you three reasons. First, you are not in the United States. Second, American 223 rounds won't work in an AK-74—they use 2.45. And third, one must figure in the value of the guaranteed trouble-free, undetected delivery."

Amahl leaned forward in exasperation. "Is that not somewhat excessive, even for this—ah, service?"

Grigoriy shrugged his wide shoulders. "Not when I have to pay off the harbor master, the costal patrol, and half a dozen others here, *and* on the other end, and some of them can be quite greedy. It is not too much to ask. This is a simple deal, as you say. These goods are available elsewhere. You might like to deal with our Chinese comrades. They are most eager to sell their Type 51 copies of the Kalashnikov. Of course, you cannot obtain replacement parts for those, but . . ." He let the thought hang.

"Very well," Talib relented. "You have convinced me. I would ask only one thing more. Can you provide anyone to give expert instructions in the care, maintenance, and marksmanship of your excellent weapons?"

Rostov's forehead wrinkled in consternation. "Do you expect this training as a free service?"

"Yes, of course."

"Sir, although we might be brother socialists, I am in business now in a capitalistic society and nothing I provide is free. For a thousand dollars each per month, I can provide you with two superior instructors who originally served as arms instructors for our Spetznaz forces. If that is not acceptable, you must look elsewhere."

Sighing, Talib considered the limited funds of *Laskar Jihad*, then shook his head and gave in again. "Very well. How soon could they come to Indonesia?"

Rostov rose from the table, folded his napkin

and started to leave the restaurant. "Say, five days to a week? Would that be satisfactory?"

Amahl Talib nodded enthusiastically. "Oh, yes. Quite so. Thank you, Captain Rostov. Your money will be delivered as per our agreement to the numbered account in Switzerland."

Grigoriy departed humming a happy tune. The bill for their expensive dinner—caviar and escargot for appetizers, borscht for the soup course, a whole, steamed Pacific salmon with the inevitable boiled potatoes and beets—would be paid for by Amahl Talib and the *Laskar Jihad*. The cost of the champagne alone would probably send the kopek-pinching Indonesian into a deep depression, but so what? He was ready to buy, and the AK-74s had been in the warehouse for two months now. Time to move them or they would become a liability. All in all, a satisfactory day, Grigoriy Rostov decided.

CHAPTER 7

★ ★ ★ ★

2200 ZULU
Al Qaeda Safe House
Alexandria, Virginia

Saif Saddiq returned late to the safe house. He
smiled with satisfaction about his accomplish-
ment, but not for the results. "We have little to tell
our Russian friends," he complained. "The colonel went back across the river to the Pentagon, Fazoul. He is so predictable."

Fazoul spoke gruffly. "Do not fall into the trap
of believing he will always be that way."

Saif frowned. "How do you mean?"

"He is an intelligence officer," Fazoul explained. "He knows how to detect surveillance
and to recognize a vehicle following him. He can
discover a person on foot even faster. Now, did he
meet with anyone else?"

"No, Fazoul. He drove directly to his office."

Fazoul smiled with satisfaction. "Very well. I too have news. The man he took to lunch is a naval lieutenant commander named Gregory Rockham. He is stationed at Little Creek Naval Station, which means he is a SEAL. He commands a highly secret organization and travels frequently."

Eagerly, Saif asked, "What organization?"

"It is so secret I could not learn the name. The SEALs are Special Operations forces, however. I fear this Rockham might prove to be a danger to Al Qaeda, which means he is a threat to our Russian friends as well."

"And therefore Rockham's unit must also constitute an immediate danger to us," Saif summed up. "Should we kill him?"

Fazoul shrugged. "That is a decision to be made by Ali Mohamed or al-Zawahiri. We cannot take it upon ourselves to proceed. We have an assignment of more immediate nature. Our first volunteer martyrs will be here in a week, the time has been moved up. We are to take them to Florida and get them into a flight training school."

Saif Saddiq looked eager and excited. "Is it the crop sprayer project al-Zawahiri suggested?"

Fazoul could not hide his exasperation with his subordinate. Sometimes Saif acted more the child than a twenty-year-old man. "For the last time, I—do—not—know. Let me explain it this way: we are but cogs in a gigantic wheel. The hub is Osama; the axle is made of Muhammed Atef and Dr. al-Zawahiri and others of their rank."

"I . . . see." Saif hesitated, then drew a deep breath. "Will we ever know what their mission is to be?"

Fazoul pursed his lips. "I doubt it. Now, I must contact our superior and have them get authorization from the Russians to take out this Lieutenant Commander Rockham."

Saif sounded pleased at the prospect. "When will we find out about that?"

"Soon, I pray to Allah, very soon."

Later, Pyotr Adamenko, who served as Grigoriy Rostov's communications officer, brought a message slip to Rostov, who read it with interest. "This is most disturbing, Pyotr. The American aiding our Colonel Wharton is none other than an old adversary; Lieutenant Commander Gregory Rockham. This calls for immediate action."

"Why is that, Grigoriy Mikhailavich?"

Rostov seemed genuinely surprised. "Do you not recall that we learned that the man who disrupted our last operation for Spetznaz was this same Rockham? He is a dangerous man and his involvement with Wharton makes us vulnerable. I think it is time we deal with our threat from America. Notify our liaison with Al Qaeda to see to it, eh, Pyotr?"

The field telephone on his desk beeped politely, and Rockham reached for it, expecting a contact from the chief umpire. The men of SMD were conducting a Field Training Exercise on the huge reservation known as Fort Carson, Colorado. It seemed that no matter where they were recently, their Field Training Exercises had come one on top of the other. Rockham had the feeling that they were slated for another major operation, and damn soon.

"Yeah, Rock here. Speak to me."

Long ago, the formal radio and telephone protocol had been abandoned in an effort to shorten and make the delivery quicker for any communications that might be overheard by an enemy. The use of operating names and curt comments would baffle any non-native speaker of English. Rockham knew that the straight-laced "by the bookers" with the iron rods up their butts were horrified by this informality, but he and his boys frankly didn't give a damn. It worked well around the Arabs, and that was what counted.

From the other end of the line came the voice of his immediate superior, Colonel Abraham Grenville. "I don't know how much pull you have with the big man, but you got what you want, Greg," Grenville said, sounding impressed. "I received this communication only this morning. Frankly, I'm mystified, so I'll just quote it to you and maybe you can figure it out. 'By order of the President of the United States: Be it known that holding great confidence in the following named officer, Lieutenant Commander Gregory Rockham is to be retained in his current assignment for a period of not less than one year nor more than three.'" He went on to read the rest of the presidential citation while Greg grew more amazed with each phrase. At last he came to the final paragraph. "'Any questions regarding this directive should be addressed to this office, the Navy Chief of Staff, or Admiral Cromarty of SEAL Command. Signed this,' et cetera, et cetera, et cetera," Grenville concluded. "That's callin' in some mighty big guns, ain't it, Rock?"

"I guess so, but I didn't have much to do with it. All I did was ask Admiral Cromarty for an extension of my command function for at least a year, until all three new platoons are trained up to their peak and ready to go no matter who commands them."

Grenville snorted into his mouthpiece. "I'd say that got the job done. How's the FTX going?"

"Smooth as glass, as far as I can see. We're due to enter phase two this afternoon."

Genuine concern could be heard in Colonel Grenville's voice. "That's the part that includes a trip through the extended-length gas chamber, right?"

"You got it, boss."

"Make damn sure everyone has their autoinjectors along. That VX gas is deadly stuff. The protective clothing will take care of anything else. How do you plan to deal with a biological threat?"

"Extremely carefully," Rockham responded,

and he didn't mean it as a joke. "Actually, from what we have been trained to expect, whenever we go in, the bioweapons will still be in their containers, probably artillery shells full of small, hollow bombs. The most practical plan is to gather them all up, remove the explosive detonators, and bury them in a deep pit. Then saturate the whole mess with diesel fuel and ignite it with a thermite grenade. More likely, since they're inside the enemy's country, we'll probably leave them where they are, rig a delay igniter of some sort and get outta Dodge."

"What about collateral damage?" Grenville asked.

Rockham looked grim as he answered. "If it's in Libya, or say Iran or Iraq, or any other Islamofascist country, I frankly don't think there are any innocents to become collateral damage."

Grenville swore silently a moment then spoke gruffly. "Damn, that's cold, Greg. You know there are hundreds of thousands of innocent people who have nothing to do with the fanatics and terrorists. I hope you never let that position go public. I'm sure you know the popular opinion among Americans of our current President's persuasion."

Rockham's kept his reply carefully neutral. "Whatever. One of my platoon chiefs has a response for their kind. It involves letting God sort them out."

Grenville sighed heavily. Would Rockham ever

learn to speak in the politically correct way the brass hats expected? Probably not, he admitted. "All right, that's enough. Good luck this afternoon."

CHAPTER 8

★ ★ ★ ★

Fyodor Ivanovich Sarinov paced the floor of his luxurious apartment on the top floor of a prestigious residence hotel on Boris Godinov Street in the center of Volgograd. The view from two walls of picture windows showed the snaky course of the Volga River. His feet, clad in the finest Italian leather—black Gucci tassel loafers—were small, only size 41 narrow in Russian shoe sizes. He trod across the rich, thick Oriental rug oblivious to the quality of the century-old carpet. Only five-foot-seven, for a short man, Fyodor wore his clothes with the élan of a far taller man; a pastel blue blazer, off-white shirt, a paisley foulard tie, and gray slacks. A leonine mass of glossy gray hair rose above a high forehead, and his fifty-three-year-old face remained free of lines or other marks of age. His left hand sparkled in the sunlight reflecting off thick gold bands and flashy diamonds. A decidedly masculine necklace of precious stones slid out from under his collar and lay across his upper chest, a two-karat sapphire nestled in the foulard tie.

Sarinov was one of the fortunate in this new capitalist Russia. The local and national *Prestooplenek Poletsiy*—the Criminal Police—saw him as a major chieftain in the Russian mafia. He was a deadly, dangerous man, dedicated to making a fortune off the sweat and efforts of others—not by employing them, but by stealing money from them. Sarinov presided over a gambling syndicate that controlled the casino action at the resorts on the Black Sea at Dnepropetrovsk and Odessa. In addition, he operated the nationwide Russian version of the numbers racket.

He also made loans to those unable to secure one through ordinary means, charging an exorbitant rate of interest. Further, he had control of three chop shops that created "new" automobiles out of the parts from stolen Mercedes-Benz, BMW, Jaguar, and other luxury vehicles. His "family" was also involved in the illegal arms business—primarily as a supplier to the lower-level dealers. Now, he had a new idea working in his agile brain, and waited impatiently for the arrival of two men who had the ability to accomplish his desire.

Voltan Korievski and Mikhail Gorodinoff were subchieftains in Fyodor Sarinov's crime family. Both men were huge, transplanted Cossacks, each standing well over six feet tall and weighing in around 100kg, without an ounce of fat on either of them. They had rapidly come up through the ranks, beginning their criminal careers in childhood as petty thieves. When the USSR ceased to be, they soon extended their resumes to include head knocking and bone breaking. They then expanded their "business" again adding extortion to the list, which took them into the ranks of mob enforcers.

Killing came easy to Korievski and Gorodinoff. They waded through rivers of blood on their way up to becoming captains in the family of Fyodor Sarinov. Along the way, they had accumulated obligations—*blagoskbnnosti*, or "favors"—some of which were about to be called in.

They arrived separately, ten minutes apart, each accompanied by a bodyguard and their principal lieutenant. Fyodor greeted them warmly, clasped their hands in vigorous shakes, embraced them, and kissed each on both cheeks.

"Welcome, my loyal and trustworthy friends. Come, sit down, Voltan Tarussinov, Mikhail Nikolich. Will you take tea? Or maybe vodka, *da*?" When both indicated the clear, strong spirit, Fyodor rubbed his hands in appreciation. "Good,

good. Boris, bring the last bottle of Kremlin Krasnaya." Although it was not true that this was the last bottle, *Red Kremlin* vodka had become exceedingly rare in these days of the Republic. Sarinov sought to use this ploy to impress his underbosses. He had been fortunate enough to obtain twenty-five cases before it disappeared from shelves across the nation. Eighteen of those remained.

Always the good servant, Boris quickly brought out a silver tray that held three tall, slender glasses with gold rims and a bottle of rare 110-proof vodka. Each 7.5-centimeter glass bore an etched image of the onion domes of Saint Basil's Cathedral soaring above the high walls of the Kremlin. Silently, Boris poured, and then departed for the kitchen.

Sarinov distributed the drinks and raised his in a toast. "To our continued profitability and power."

"To your good health!" the two men toasted their boss.

Smacking his lips, Sarinov set his glass aside and resumed his seat in the big, plush Edwardian chair. "Now, to the matter that brings you two here. I have a desire to broaden my base in the arms business. I have learned of a very large deal that is in progress. It will be a cash sale and involves an enormous amount of money. I wish very much to be a part of this transaction, to—ah, get a piece of the action, as my American counter-parts would say."

Voltan did not understand. "Then why do you not buy into it?"

Sarinov did not wish to discuss the embarrass-ment of failure.

"It is not as simple as that. The man in charge of this sale to a foreign party is not one of us. He is an independent and he has twice refused my overtures to become his silent partner. I intend to call him now, with you two present, and make an-other offer to be a party to his negotiation. He must understand how advantageous this is to his business."

The eyes of both Korievski and Gorodinoff lit up as they realized the possibilities for mayhem inherent in the implied threat.

Sarinov picked up the French-style telephone handset and used the old-fashioned rotary dial to reach the number. "Ah! Do I have the honor of speaking to Captain Grigoriy Mikhailavich Ros-tov?" He waited for a reply. "Yes, yes, this is Sari-nov. Have you considered my offer?" A longer pause followed. "Truly, it would be to your great-est advantage to incorporate my family in your transaction. I can promise you that the benefits are limitless, if you associate your organization with mine."

This time, Rostov's reply was loud enough that both men were able to hear it clearly. "No, Comrade Sarinov, I have no intention of subordinating myself to the *Mafiya Russiya*. I am an *in-de-pen-dent* dealer." He exaggerated the syllables. "And I intend to remain so. Thank you for your offer, but I have my own men, my own organization to look out for, and although I appreciate your overture, I must decline. Now, a good day to you, *doz v' danya.*"

For the first time in many years, Fyodor Sarinov came close to losing his temper in front of his subordinates. After hanging up, he cursed Rostov in harsh syllables under his breath. "That stupid bastard! He badly needs convincing of the error of his ways."

Gorodinoff smiled, relaxed and eager to carry out any command his boss might give "That should be an easy matter, Fyodor Ivanovich. Am I not right?"

A sad smile crossed Sarinov's face. "He shows all the class and gentility of a typical Great Russian, yet he has some very rough men around him. They might prove a problem."

Korievski offered a simple solution. "We can always take along some of our *cheloveki*"—our people. "That way we can take out this problem and all his men. Who is he, by the way?"

"A relative newcomer to the trade. Captain Grigoriy Mikhailavich Rostov. I know nothing of his previous service. In fact, I can find no reference to him in military journals or records."

Mikhail looked uneasy. "He could be Spetznaz. That might create a larger problem than we expect."

Sarinov thought a moment, then dismissed it. "Whatever the case, he is but a man. One man alone should not be that difficult to convince. See to it as soon as possible."

"Very well, Fyodor Ivanovich, we owe you for many favors, and this will help repay them," Voltan replied. "Where do we find him?"

"He occupies a small apartment in Novosibirsk. Find him and do whatever it takes to change his mind."

Improvements had been made to most the major highways in the Russian Republic. The journey from Volgograd to Novosibirsk took only two and a half days, an uneventful experience for Voltan Korievski and Mikhail Gorodinoff. With them came two of their most adept muscle men. They drove in two separate cars, the older of which had been stolen and would be abandoned after the job was completed. Korievski thought that four men could easily handle the obstinate Captain Rostov. It took several minutes to locate the street and the correct address, but the Russian mafiosi found it eventually, driving slowly past in the stolen car.

"It is back from the street, I see," remarked one of the gunsels in the front seat. "Those fir trees make a good screen."

Gorodinoff grinned boyishly. "Fortune smiles

on us, my friends. We can park on the street behind, come in through the back, and not be seen by any of the neighbors or anyone here on Pushkin Alley."

Korievski nodded agreement. "Yes, this looks even easier than I anticipated. We go in, kill this man, and get out."

"Fyodor Ivanovich said to convince him of the error of his ways, not to kill him," Gorodinoff objected.

Korievski smiled condescendingly. "It is so simple, my friend. First, we force him to give us all the details of the transaction. *Then* we kill him. That way there will be no interference when our family takes over the deal."

"You have a marvelous mind, Voltan Tarussinov," Gorodinoff declared with genuine admiration. "A truly devious mind, but a marvelous one."

They parked under the street sign that read OOLITSA PROSPEK—Prospect Avenue—four doors down from the apartment house directly behind Rostov's residence. The four men shut the doors quietly and walked without speaking to the narrow alleyway between buildings. Once out of sight from the street, the thugs loosened their Tokarev 9mm pistols in the shoulder holsters under their left arms. Crushed rock crackled under the leather soles of their shoes as the four men advanced on their target. According to the quick plan developed after scouting the Rostov residence, three of them waited while Korievski rounded the corner and climbed the short flight of steps to the front door. His knock was answered after only a short delay.

"Yes, what may I do for you?" Grigoriy Rostov asked politely.

"Senior Captain Rostov?"

Rostov hesitated, attempting to identify his visitor. "Do I know you?"

"No, I am sure you do not," Korievski assured the former Spetznaz officer, then he suddenly lashed out with both hands, planted them firmly on Rostov's chest and drove the slighter built man back inside his apartment.

Startled by this sudden attack, Rostov staggered backward, trying to remain on his feet. An instant later, as his unwelcome visitor pushed further into his apartment, Rostov heard the scraping of feet and in a moment, three other men crowded into his home. Two of them grabbed Rostov's arms and held tightly.

The young man who had summoned him to the door fitted a pair of brass knuckles onto his right hand and began slamming it into Rostov's chest. Fiery pain radiated from the point of impact and he faintly heard a pair of ribs crack. His assailant shifted his aim, and stepping back to deliver hammer blows to Rostov's stomach. The damage to his soft tissues hurt more than the ribs. Those he had experienced several times before and could ignore the discomfort.

A voice hissed in his left ear.

"You should pay attention when a man of honor makes a request. It is impolite to refuse a generous offer like the one recently made to you. Do you understand what I am saying?"

"Oh, yes, I understand perfectly. And you can tell *Guspodyeen* Sarinov to go to hell."

A soft sound, like a stifled cough, came from the direction of an archway that opened into a short hall. It repeated twice more before the assailant on Rostov's left collapsed, striking the tile floor with the back of his head. A second later, Tsinev fired another muffled shot, dead center in Korievski's left eye. The man shuddered, his limbs twitching uncontrollably, and fell in a heap, stone dead.

Instantly, Rostov spun and struck with lightning speed, breaking both collarbones of the closest thug. In an effort to keep from screaming in pain, the gangster bit his lower lip so fiercely that his teeth sliced through it. Blood flooded over his chin as he groaned and tried to deliver a back-fist blow to Rostov's face. The attempt made him gasp aloud from the pain in his shoulders. Switching tactics, he tried a roundhouse kick, which Rostov intercepted before heaving the thug off his feet, to crash down beside his two cronies. Rostov drew his personal sidearm— a Glock 9mm—and shot him in the head. The discharge of his weapon sounded deafening in the confines of the apartment. Three down, one to go.

"Ivan, take the one by the door," Rostov commanded as he turned to Gorodinoff.

Stunned by the sudden reversal, Gorodinoff's eyes widened in shock. "*Nyet, nyet, pazaliooshtu, tovarish.*" His pleading did little good.

"No? Please? Comrade," Rostov mocked the man. "Go to hell!" They were the last words Gorodinoff heard, as Rostov shot him twice in the heart and once between the eyes. Blood sprayed from the exit wounds onto the floor on walls.

"Now we are in trouble," Tsinev remarked. "People are bound to have heard the shots. The police will come."

"Not a problem, Ivan. I acquired this place through multiple layers of cover. It can not be traced to me. Hurry, we must gather my belongings and depart within an hour. Most people around here are at work this time of day. It is possible no one heard the shots. But we must move quickly."

When no traces of Rostov or any of his gang of arms dealers remained, the former Spetznaz officer considered his options. "Get Pyotr over here and have him remove the heads of these *loshbachoe detya* and box them up separately," he informed Tsinev. "Then I want him to post them to the home of Fyodor Sarinov. It is time to convince him that I and my men should be left alone. I need to prove to him that we are the strongest bears in the forest."

* * *

Fazoul looked up when Saif entered the safe house. "What information do you bring me, Saif?" he asked.

"The man Ali said we are to kill has not returned to his base in Virginia for the last three days. It is said he has gone to Colorado—wherever that is—for some sort of training. Now that we have been given permission to eliminate this threat, can we not do so in this Colorado?"

Fazoul thought for several moments. "Colorado is a mountainous state, according to the maps I have seen. It might be an ideal place to conduct a removal."

"Why is it that we must do this job and risk discovery by the Americans?"

"It is because our Russian friends want it that way. We need them to acquire weapons more deadly than rifles and rocket-propelled grenades." He smiled warmly. "You have done well, Saif. I am pleased."

Brightening under this unexpected praise, Saif offered an eager reply. "Then we shall go there and finish this?"

"Count on it. We will need at least two of our brothers to aid us in this endeavor. I will alert Abdullah and Salim. They are ideally suited for what we have in mind. Meanwhile, you must go to our arms cache and obtain two of those excellent Soviet-made Dragunov sniper rifles. They are most modern, and light—only four and a half kilos—with a superior range of thirteen hundred meters."

"You know, brother, that I fired expert with the SVD sniper's rifle?" Saif offered.

"That is why I suggested these particular weapons." Fazoul smiled again. "The PSO-1 scope sight is as fine a quality as the Americans' Redfield automatic ranging telescope. I am not positive, but it may be necessary that we take the most advantage of the PSO's range and accuracy. We may be on one side of a mountain and the target on another."

Saif's smile matched that of his superior. "Abdullah Muhammed Atef is nearly as expert as I with the sniper's rifle."

"Excellent. I shall see that they are prepared, and when you return with the weapons, we will depart for Colorado."

One by one, the members of Blue, Gold, and Green Platoons advanced across the open alpine meadow. At the far side, the black hole of a tunnel could barely be seen among the swaying limbs and thick leaves of aspen trees. The first shooting pair from Green Platoon took up positions to either side of the tunnel. An abandoned mine, the hole in the mountain had been converted to a far more sinister use. It now contained a storage area for cases of the empty, hollow artillery shells, which could be used for chemical weapons deployment, and a gas chamber designed to test the ability of men to escape harm from those same deadly weapons. The exercise called for the SEALs of SMD to enter and simulate rigging the stored shells—designated for the purpose of this Field Training Exercise as loaded—for destruction, having entered through the gas chamber and exiting the same way. Rockham and Daugherty had learned that neither the Army Rangers, the chemical teams from Special Forces, the Recon Marines, nor even other SEAL Teams had been subjected to such a rigorous phase of training. This was SMD's baby, and they had to figuratively learn how to change the diapers.

Rockham would have it no other way. If they were to maintain their superiority in the Special Operations family, they had to prove they could do what no one else could. It made sense. He and Daugherty had spent long hours with Colonel Grenville and Admiral Cromarty, going over the entire program of instruction. Their goal was to become expert on WMDs—especially those of the chemical and biological nature—and how to neutralize them.

For this phase, Green Platoon would function as the security screen, keeping at bay the Rangers, who would act as the aggressor force. Inasmuch as the Rangers knew this terrain like the proverbial backs of their hands, they had a distinct advantage. It approximated the knowledge of native residents of any of the many hostile nations SMD would enter in the future. Tonight's exercise would be proof of the abilities of all Special Materials Detachment SEALs.

What came after would be even more difficult. It would consist of a cross-country expedition—which meant climbing up and down mountains—to simulate a raid on a facility for manufacturing WMDs. It would be an exhausting exercise, and one that would seal their bona fides as *the* premier authority on weapons of mass destruction. From there on, it would ensure the future of SMD. Rockham broke off his reflections on what could and might be when Chief Monday came to him.

"We're all set, Rock. Green is across the meadow and deployed to prevent any interference by the Red Beanies—aw, hell, I forgot. Everyone in the Army has to wear those lousy black frog berets now. Somehow, I pity those unlucky sack rats. Anyway, Blue Platoon is ready to cross and invade the arms cache."

"Move 'em out, Chief."

Monday didn't bother to stiffen to attention or salute. "Aye, sir, they're moving as we speak."

Jorgensen led the first two squads of Second Platoon as they advanced across the grassy expanse. A soft breeze created a mournful sighing in the Douglas firs, piñon, and bristle-cone pines, whose thick resin scent wafted to the nostrils of the tense, alert SEALs. The men rushed forward in shooting pairs, one squad covering the other, until they disappeared into the trees and closed on the old mine. Third squad formed up behind and covered second, and fourth squad covered third, being last to cross and now assured of no nasty surprises.

Those first to enter the gas chamber noted the eerie hissing of the deadly nerve gas being released. Along with it came a volume of CN/DM— tear and nausea gas. With a mind to the passing seconds, each SEAL hurried through the air lock door to the decontamination chamber and removed a set of autoinjectors from the pouches of their gas masks. Pulling the safety caps off the ends of the "slap packs" armed them. The smaller syringes, labeled NO. 1, were filled with atropine sulfate; the larger number two injectors were loaded with pralidoxime chloride. Pushing the front end of the injectors against their thighs fired a twenty-pound spring that drove the needle deep into the muscle and injected the contents. The drugs would be absorbed through the capillaries and spread to the arteries to prevent sickness and death. Following the cleansing spray of the antichemical shower, they hastily exited and made a count as the others exited.

With nothing worse than a few headaches and some dizziness, they gathered around the racks of pseudo-WMDs and began to rig them for destruction. When this had been completed, they once more ran the gauntlet of the gas chamber and repeated the decontamination process.

Outside the tunnel, Jorgensen turned the handle on an electric firing device and a quarter pound of

C-4 went off, signifying the successful completion of their mission. At that point, they withdrew, and it became the turn of Daugherty's two squads.

Everything went well, until the SEALs of Daugherty's squads of SMD Gold Platoon removed some of their protective gear and exposed themselves to the deadly VX gas. Halfway though the chamber, Wilkes began to stagger and moan loudly through his gas mask. Ferber was at his side in an instant.

"What's the matter, buddy? You don't look so good."

"I—I can make it, don't worry about me," Wilkes replied bravely. But he was sweating profusely and his eyes had become dilated. Involuntary tremors wracked his body and a trail of foamy spittle that ran from one corner of his mouth.

"Corpsman!" Ferber yelled forcefully in the direction of Henry Limbaugh. "Get up here ASAP."

Limbaugh approached at a run and peered through the clear patches of the eyeholes in Wilkes's gas mask. "Oh crap! For some reason the atropine didn't take. He's reacting to the VX. We've gotta get him outta here."

"Forward or back?" Ferber asked urgently.

"Back the way we came. It's closer," Limbaugh decided aloud. "C'mon, Pete, hang in there. We'll get you out. Promise."

The forty-five-second window was rapidly closing, and the two SEALs hustled their friend out of the chamber, dragging him bodily the last few feet. Out in the decontamination center, while the chemical wash sprayed over them, Henry Limbaugh injected Pete Wilkes with another dose of atropine.

Time had run out before the medic estimated that the antidote had reached enough of Wilkes's system to have an effect. Wrong, or so Limbaugh was quickly proven when Wilkes began to kick and squirm and his color changed from pale to flushed exertion. So far they had made it. So far, Wilkes remained among the living. The only trouble was, if he did not make the final operation, he could not be certified and would have to do it all over again or leave SMD. As this realization came over him, Wilkes lost the flush of elation. It was replaced by deep lines of worry across his brow.

Ferber and Limbaugh exchanged worried glances. "What now?" Ferber asked.

Limbaugh looked closely into Wilkes's eyes. "Pete, I want the truth now. How do you feel? Are you ready to go on with the op?"

Instead of a quick, snappy reply, Wilkes considered it a moment. "Yeah," he replied in a breathless tone. "I think I can handle it. Just show me the way."

Ferber slapped him lightly on the back. "SEALs forever, right? Hooyah!"

Despite their worries, Ferber and Limbaugh stayed close to Wilkes and saw him safely back to where the others were already going through the motions of "destroying" the biological weapons.

Fazoul Hamza released a snort of frustration and impatience. He glowered at Saif and the two members of their cell who had come with them. "We are getting nowhere. I am beginning to believe that perhaps *Allah* is not on our side."

Saif looked horrified. "Do not say that, Fazoul Mahmoud. We are engaged in a great *jihad*. Naturally, *Allah* is on our side. To think otherwise is blasphemy."

Fazoul gave him a weak, smile. "There are some scholars, Saif, who say that taking the lives of infidels is blasphemy. But I digress. This is the second time our target has evaded his fate. Who is it that looks over this Gregory Rockham? Surely it is not *Allah*," he opined, mocking Saif's piety.

Saif shrugged. "Whatever the case, we have missed him again. I had his head centered in my sights when he turned away and went back in that mine entrance. We were fortunate to learn of his cell's journey here to Fort Carson."

"The Americans call them 'units,' not cells," Fazoul snapped. "Get used to that." He paused, thinking. "He has to come out of there sometime. Let us prepare."

True to his words, only three minutes went by before Rockham appeared in the rectangular entrance to the abandoned mine. Immediately, Saif and Muhammed Atef sighted in on his head. Oblivious of the danger, their target stood still. Carefully, Saif and Atef fixed the cross hairs on Rockham's forehead. Eager to rectify his previous failure, Saif fired first and hastily.

Saif's bullet flew fast and true, and a stab of excitement went through him. But through their scopes, the terrorists saw a disturbing thing. Though only a bit over a second separated the muzzle of Saif's weapon and the target, in that scant fraction of time, their enemy moved back one step. The crack of the large caliber round broke the air near Greg Rockham's head, followed by the noisy smack of impact when the steel-cored slug hit rock to his left. He dropped to the ground at once, as a puff of rock dust flew from an outcropping beside the place his head had been. With Rockham out of sight, the would-be assassins were left with nothing to shoot at.

Accustomed to shots fired in anger, Rockham made an immediate evaluation of the situation. "Son of a bitch!" he swore hotly. "No one was supposed to have live ammunition. Who in hell was that?"

From behind him, the calm, quiet voice of Frank Monday replied, "Don't rightly know, sir."

"Well, we're sure as hell going to find out, when we do, I'm going to chew him a new asshole." Rockham lay still while closely studying the opposite slope in an effort to find the hidden shooter.

A moment later, a darker, moving figure emerged in his field of view. He watched while the unsuspecting man worked his way sideways along the slope. "Goose," Rockham said softly to Monday. "Straight ahead, about four hundred meters up from that talus spill and to your left."

Monday studied the slope through his compact Nikon zoom binoculars, then stiffened and fixed on a moving target. "I got him," he said softly, and breathlessly continued. "No, wait, there's another—make that three others. Two have sniper rifles." At a thousand yards, they had a field of view of 288 degrees, and it clearly revealed the moving terrorists.

Monday replaced his field glasses in their case and positioned his weapon, a suppressed Remington-700 sniper's rifle. "It just happens that I brought along some live ammo too," he remarked as he cleared the magazine and inserted new ammunition. Ignoring Rockham's raised eyebrow he aimed carefully and gently took up the military slack in the trigger, maximized his sight picture, and squeezed off. One of the terrorists stiffened and then went slack, jerking into death. Seized by panic, the others leaped to their feet and began to run uphill—a foolish mistake.

Monday fired again. A second later Saif Daoud Saddiq went to meet Allah in person.

When the exercise ended, two hours later, Rockham addressed all three platoons. "Whoever it

was that took those shots at us, I have to go in to
Ranger School HQ and make a report. We have
no idea who they were—they didn't carry any ID.
I'm willing to bet that all kinds of hell will be
raised over this. This is one of the most secure military bases in the country, and yet these yahoos
get in here and take a shot at me. Worse, two of
them got away. Before I go in to report this, I want
you gentlemen know you did well, exceedingly so.
Get plenty of rest, knock off a couple of beers to
relieve tension, and make ready. Tomorrow we begin the biggest and final test we'll face. It'll be a
bitch kitty, I guarantee you—we're going into a
nuclear storage facility. I have every confidence in
you, so we won't belabor the point by another
briefing. I'll see you all at 0930 tomorrow."

When apprised of the shooting incident, both Admiral Cromarty and Colonel Wharton exploded.
A team from the Office of Naval Intelligence was
dispatched, along with agents of the Army's
Counter Intelligence Division. They arrived late in
the afternoon and grilled Rockham and Monday
thoroughly. Then they went to work on the
corpses and the scene of the shooting. They advised Rockham that the dead men appeared to be
of Arabic descent. Why the hell had they shot at
him? Rockham wondered.

Meanwhile, the men of SMD kicked back,
downed several beers each, and had a meal at the
NCO Club. Their mood was solemn, everyone

aware that somehow some kind of terrorists had managed to get on the base and take shots at their CO. Tomorrow would be hard, they realized, and the work still being done by the investigators would be no easier.

CHAPTER 9

★ ★ ★ ★

1600 ZULU
Tactical Nuclear Weapons Manufacturing Facility
Monte Casino Ridge
Fort Carson, Colorado

In spite of the bright, early morning sunlight, a chill remained in the air as the Special Materials Detachment assembled in the bleachers outside the access trail that led to the area of their day's operation.

Rockham addressed his men. "Gentlemen, this is the big day. Our objective is the nuclear weapons manufacturing facility located over that second ridge. In keeping with our normal operational procedure, we will be inserted by helicopter on the facing slope of Monte Casino Ridge, which masks the facility. We will then climb approximately a quarter of the way up the slope and crest the ridge to recon the area before descending to the target. As before, modified suppressed weapons will be used, incorporating paint ball mechanisms. We've done that part before, guys, so you know what to expect.

"Insertion will be at 1540 hours, so the sun will be in the eyes of any security units they have on the western slope. Once we're down, we neutralize any of the enemy present and move out. Are there any questions so far?"

"Yes, sir," Boatswains Mate First Class Paul Lederer said. "Will we be exposed to actual radiation?"

Rockham smiled encouragingly. "Negative, sailor. Although this is an actual storage facility for nukes, they are all contained and secured well beyond where we'll be operating. We'll be nowhere near the real thing. The minimal radiation we will be exposed to will be hardly more than a tooth X-ray. The worst that should happen is a touch of diarrhea."

Lederer made a face. "You've gotta be kidding. We're in for a dose of the drizzling trots for a lousy exercise?"

Rockham frowned. "Suck it up, SEAL. What is a little case of loose bowels if it teaches you what you did wrong and you learn to correct it?"

Lederer's chagrinned expression told it all. "Aye, sir. I guess you're right, Rock. We've gotta do this without any slip-ups or the death rays will get us for real."

"Bet on it, Tall Paul." Rockham referred to Lederer's operator name, earned by his exceptional height for a SEAL. He stood just over six-four and presented a formidable sight to any enemy unlucky enough to run into him. "I'm convinced that we will be inordinately lucky to get out of there without at least one or more exposures to the mild stuff."

Lederer produced a boyish grin. "Oh, boy! Mom, can I skip school this morning? I've got runny squats."

Rockham addressed all of the SEALs. "Get your joking over now. We have some serious practicing to do on rendering various containers inoperative, and I want you to go through several scenarios of explosives placement to make sure we get it all."

Mid-afternoon came entirely too soon in the estimation of a few among the SEALs of SMD One. The three platoons were trucked to the central helipad at Fort Carson and gathered around the CH-47C choppers that would take them to the insertion point. The lead crew chief briefed them quickly.

"You will unass our birds by fast rope. Keep your elbows in and your ankles locked around the slick line. Control your descent by slightly releasing your grip with hands and feet. I'm sure you've all been through this before, but for your own safety, keep in mind it is always important to cover every element of an insertion. Thank you for listening, gentlemen. You may board any time in the next ten minutes."

Before Rockham gave the command to board the two Navy CH-47C Seasprites, he spoke a few words. "The first three down from each craft will spread out and establish a secure perimeter. The remainder will descend and immediately disperse to avoid easy sighting by the enemy. From there on we follow the ground insertion SOP. Now, let's mount up."

The pair of multipurpose helicopters could easily carry the twelve squads of the three platoons, along with the command element and all the equipment. The loading process took less than four minutes, with all loose gear stowed. At once, the Chinooks spooled up their engines, the rotors began to revolve at increasing speed, and the CH-47Cs lifted off at their operating flight level of 150 meters above ground, nosing in the direction of the landing zone. They moved forward at 275 kph. The LZ had been carefully selected to take advantage of a shallow basin surrounded by thick stands of aspen, white pine, and oak. The SEALs would be left with a scant fifty-five-meter climb to the crest of the ridge. In less than twenty minutes, the Chinooks crossed the first mountain range and neared Monte Casino Ridge.

In his headset, Rockham heard the crisp voice of the pilot. "Chief, prepare to deploy fast ropes. Commander, have your men unstrap and stand up."

Rockham spoke tersely into the tiny boom mike. "Roger. We're more than ready."

With a soft chuckle, the pilot came back, "Don't forget to disconnect our intercom headset before you leave."

Two minutes later, the red lights came on over the side exit doors. The first shooter pairs stepped up fore and aft on the starboard side, and took hold of the dangling fast ropes. They gripped them tightly in a ready hold, eyes fixed on the light indicators. Thirty seconds later, the CH-47s descended rapidly to thirty feet above the ground and the green lights came on. The first two pairs stepped out and slid down their thick ropes to the ground. Four more men followed, and they spread out to secure the LZ. It took only seconds for the remainder to unload and slide to the solid ground. The choppers descended closer, and the SEALs equipment bundles were kicked out.

Willing hands dragged the forest camo green canvas packages off to the concealing trees and the men opened them. Small, duffel-style packs were fastened by two-inch-long snaffles to the bottoms of their backpacks, and the six Remington-7188 automatic, twelve-gauge shotguns and six sniper rifles were taken out and issued to the proper shooters.

In five minutes, the squads were ready to begin their climb, the containers buried and everything policed up. Taking the point for Gold Platoon, Shaun Daugherty led third and fourth squads, while Greg Rockham took position between Gold and Blue. Green again fanned out to serve as a security screen during the advance.

Everything went well for the first half of the climb. Then the soft *chuffing* of a suppressed MP5-N alerted the SMD troops to the presence of enemy forces. A short, swift exchange of fire ended it, and Rockham found the RTO's radio still on the supine—but still living—operator's back, the transmitter in the stand-by mode. That reassured them that the "aggressor force" on the other side remained unaware of their presence.

"Good work," Rock told the men of Blue Platoon. "Now, let's move out."

At the crest, the SEALs went belly down and took out field glasses to observe the downslope. Ten minutes of careful observation assured them that no organized resistance awaited them. Now, Blue and Green Platoons swapped jobs, and Green spread into a wide front that swept silently down toward their target.

Master Sergeant Arnold Prentiss had been in the Rangers since he graduated the school at the age of nineteen. Now, at thirty-one, he felt confident that he could take anything that an enemy or a clever operator of his own service could hand out. To Prentiss, the Rangers played as hard as any Special Operations troops. They often had live-fire FTXs, so he eagerly looked forward to this one. Piece of cake, he figured. How tough could a bunch of squids be? Especially when they were from an outfit that, according to its name, spent the days shuffling around equipment and other stuff for the SEALs. He was sadly underrating the abilities of the SEALs of SMD. So too was his commanding officer, Lieutenant Colonel Fred Hansen.

Hansen was at least aware of the nature of the FTX being conducted for the benefit of these Navy types who had come to Carson only a week ago. Somewhat ignorant of the full scope of SEAL training, and thoroughly indoctrinated in the superiority of his own service organization, Hansen truly believed the SEALs inferior to his own men. He was about to be violently dragged back to reality.

They came silently down the mountainside, slithered through the trees, and closed on the opening to the nuclear weapon facility, without the least incidence of detection. Not that Hansen's men were inept. They simply had never seen or experienced such highly skilled operatives before. Blue Platoon spread out to neutralize any "enemy" patrols lurking in the rarefied air of the Rockies. Their job was the most hazardous, Rockham believed, because they would be the only raiders constantly exposed.

Despite any misgivings, everything went by the book, right up through the actual penetration of the facility. None of the Rangers had been imbued with enough *esprit de corps* to cheat. When they were "shot," they went down and did not betray their "killers" to their buddies. Once penetration had been completed, Gold Platoon rushed the offices, laboratories, and barracks areas with the goal of taking down all the defenders. Blue Platoon, new to the actual mechanics of a takedown, went for the supposed warehouse area to secure the "nukes." Two guards blocked their access to the area beyond the working section of the facility. Chief Ricardo Ortiz zapped one with a short, three-round burst of paint balls to the chest.

"Ow! Shit," moaned the "victim" as the red dye ran down the front of his uniform shirt and flowed in copious quantity under his belt. "This wasn't supposed to mess up my love life, you know," he protested as his partner went down, paint-balled by Hugh Nakamura. Both SEALs rushed the entry, only to find it secured by a combination lock built into the edge of the double doors.

"C-4," Chief Ortiz snapped.

"Roger, that," Nakamura responded. He reached into a trouser leg pouch and produced a quarter-pound block of the plastic explosive. He cut it in half with his bowie knife and shoved a precrimped fuse cap into the middle. This he patted gently to cover the entire dial of the lock and then lit the fuse. He and the chef popped on ear protectors and clutched the silver crucifixes that hung from chains around their necks while they prayed to the Blessed Mother. They might have been half a world apart racially, but their religion gave them a common bond.

Ten seconds later, the charge went off with a loud roar, the doors thrown open by the concussion. Weapons at the ready, the SEALs rushed inside, followed by three more shooting pairs. What they saw upset them. Floor-to-ceiling racks of artillery shells, small hollow warhead rockets, and other delivery vehicles for tactical nuclear weapons. Suddenly, their radiation detectors went insane. Nakamura swallowed hard. If all of this stuff was real, it could kill nearly the whole population of a small country. The flashing light and buzzing alarms spurred them to action.

"Let's get a move on," Chief Monday urged from the other room.

Light charges, sufficient only for spraying powdered chalk over the assembled fake WMDs, were put in place and the detonators rigged. Within five minutes, everything was ready. At a signal from Rockham, all three platoons withdrew. Once at their extraction point, the radio signal was sent to set off the charges. Almost instantly, the CH-47s returned and lowered, to hover a scant two feet off the ground.

"C'mon, c'mon, c'mon," chanted the platoon chiefs as the men boarded with alacrity, eager to get out without being detected. So far, they had carried off a perfect raid. The experience would serve them well in the future. A somewhat closer future than they presently expected.

* * *

Twenty-five grim-faced men rode in canvas-covered trucks and solid paneled vans toward the first of several addresses in Volgograd that had been targeted by their boss. Grigoriy Rostov had taken all he could from the arrogant, bloody-handed *Mafiya Russiya*. The decision had been made: Fyodor Sarinov, local Boss of Bosses, and all his henchmen had to go. Sarinov had committed a terrible error in making an enemy of Rostov. Sarinov's arrogance and false sense of security prevented him from acting sensibly, even after he received of the heads of his henchmen. How big his error had been, Sarinov was about to find out.

"Over there," the passenger next to the driver instructed. "That is where they will be." He indicated a disreputable-looking building that housed a "social club" hangout for some of Sarinov's mafia soldiers. The façade and windows were grimed to a dirty gray-black by wood and charcoal smoke. Garbage and bits of trash littered the gutters.

Pyotr Adamenko wrinkled his nose as he gazed from the front of the second truck. "These men live like pigs," he observed disdainfully. "I thought they wore fifty thousand ruble Italian suits, cashmere topcoats, and silk scarves. No one who dressed like that would come within a hundred kilometers of this place."

Sergei Nemec leaned forward and spoke lightly. "Do not be so sure of that, Pyotr. Look, over there, the man in the gray felt homburg. That coat is camel's hair, no?"

"So? Our job is to eliminate them, not comment on their sartorial preferences," he said, though it was he who had brought up the subject of clothing.

Viktor Nosenko gestured for the first truck to stop and waved Adamenko's vehicle on toward the mouth of the alleyway behind the social club. Nosenko waited three minutes to give the other truck time to get into place, then stepped from the cab, opened the back doors, and let the hard-bitten former Spetznaz troopers out. No one spoke. It took only a jerk of his head for Nosenko to send them to the front. Two of Rostov's troopers carried a battering ram.

A loud, splintering sound announced the entry of the Spetznaz commandos. The rammers dropped their heavy steel cylinder and cut to the left and right with weapons ready. The mafiosi inside were suddenly confronted by the classic weapon of their Sicilian prototypes—*il lupare*—ten-gauge sawed-off shotguns. A blazing hail of #00 pellets sprayed into the occupants of the low-ceilinged, narrow room. It shred the flesh from their bones in bloody chunks. A head exploded in a red mist, flecked with gray brain matter. A huge hole opened in the abdomen of another mafia gangster. Two men managed to pull their weapons.

A MAC-11 380 machine pistol cut across the belly of one Spetznaz trooper before flying to the ceiling. It had been sent upward by the impact of four rounds from an ancient British Sten MK-V 9mm SMG. Across the room from the shooter, another Don Corleone wannabe fired three wild shots from his CZ M-75, 9mm pistol, then bolted toward the rear hallway. He made it halfway down when the door blew inward in a shower of splinters, and the light, high-pitched crack of an AK-74 spelled an end to the mafioso.

Upstairs, Voltan Korievski and three of his men lay in spreading pools of blood, while the attackers checked to make sure none of Sarinov's men remained alive.

Across town, in a far more upscale neighborhood, the staid, reserved residents were about to discover a few unpleasant facts about some of their neighbors. Two trucks swept through the open wrought-iron gates of 327 *Oolitsa* Boris Godinov and up the wide drive. One stopped under the portico at the front double doors. The other continued back toward the converted carriage house that served as a garage and servants' quarters. Strange men, whom no one on that street had never seen, jumped from the vehicles and spread out to cover every doorway. A dust-streaked ten-year-old Saab rolled through the gateway and halted behind the truck at the front.

Rostov himself exited the vehicle and led the tough young men to the tall front door. Two men forced entry with a tubular steel ram and hastened inside. Shouts, screams, and muffled shots came from the interior. Outside, the startled neighbors gawked and speculated as to what might be going on at *Gospodin* Sarinov's elegant residence.

Inside, a clatter of shoe leather on marble stairs preceded Rostov and his Spetznaz subordinates to the second floor. Rostov led the way to a tall pair of ornate doors at the far end of the hallway. Lavishly decorated with gold and purple-painted bas relief in the *Empire* style, they proved remarkably vulnerable to a stout kick by the knee-high boot of one Spetznaz trooper. The vast room beyond proved to be empty.

Rostov made a quick evaluation and decision. "His personal quarters are on the third floor. We go there now."

Two young men approached Rostov as he and his entourage reached the stairwell. "Ground floor is cleared. None of them were left alive," the first stated flatly. The other messenger advised the same for the second floor. Rostov only nodded in the affirmative and proceeded to climb to the top floor.

Up there, the doors had been secured against them. Silent shots from suppressed pistols shattered the lock cases, and vigorous kicks slammed open the portals one after another. Inside each room, a ranking mafiosi died quickly, several screaming defiance as they went down.

Rostov approached the portal that granted egress to the suite occupied by Fyodor Ivanovich

Sarinov. The former *starshii kapitain* swiftly
searched the interior. A large canopied bed, the
size of an American queen size, occupied a low
dais against the windowless rear wall. The large,
double sliding doors to the closet stood closed.
With a nod, Rostov sent one Spetznaz trooper—
who wore blue trousers with an open blue jumper
that revealed the horizontal striped shirt of a former Soviet sailor—to advance on the ominously
silent side of the room. Two others crowded into
the room and faced the closet, weapons ready.

"Seychas!" Rostov barked and then repeated,
"Now!"

Three suppressed 9mm Stechkin machine pistols, their wooden shoulder stocks in place,
opened up, chopping neat little holes in three distinct levels through the sliding panels, biting into
flesh beyond as three of Sarinov's ranking underbosses jerked and screamed in their death throes.

Suddenly, Fyodor Sarinov appeared from the
blind side of his canopy bed. Tears of terror ran
down his Botox-smoothed cheeks. His eyes were
those of a cornered small animal, highlighting the
fear that distorted his countenance. "Do not . . .
do not kill me. Wh-Who are you?"

"I am the man whom you plotted to steal from.
I am Grigoriy Mikhailavich Rostov. And you and
all of your mafia cohorts are dead men." With
that, Rostov raised his favorite P-220 Glock and
shot Sarinov between the eyes.

Moments later, a flurry of gunshots came muffled from a distance. Rostov looked up, startled by this first deviation from his carefully made plans to eliminate the entire mafia family of Fyodor Sarinov. Someone, somewhere, in this huge mansion was fighting back. "Find out about that," he snapped to Adamenko.

Adamenko took the stairs two at a time, and at a barked question was directed toward the open doorway to the full basement under this wing of the mansion. He quickly clambered down the stairs, to find five of his comrades crouched behind counters and shelves facing a closed steel door built into a side wall. One man lay dead before the thick metal panel. Adamenko took in the situation in an instant.

"Do any of you have explosives?" he snapped.

"No, Sergeant, we left them in the truck."

All business, Adamenko made his decision. "Go get them at once. I will relay the situation to our commander."

When Rostov learned of conditions below, he hurried to the basement. By the time he reached it, two of the enforcers for his illegal arms operation had returned with blocks of Simtex. Rostov and Adamenko exchanged words on the unpleasant surprise.

"We have to get in there," Rostov said. "I have heard by radio that the other locations are all secured. All opposition has been eliminated. These are the last. Does anyone have an idea who they might be?"

Ivan Tsinev spoke up. "No, sir, but we have all the remaining rats in a single nest."

"That is a pleasant condition to consider," Rostov said through a smile. "You two, rig charges on that door and blast it open. Meanwhile, everyone else will leave this cellar at once. Use electrical leads to set off your charges and get out of here."

Two minutes later, the explosives were in place and Rostov gave the signal to detonate them. The blast proved to be almost overwhelming even on the second floor, where all of the Spetznaz troops had withdrawn.

When the thick cloud of dust and smoke cleared enough to see, five men rushed out of the apparent bomb shelter coughing and gasping, firing their weapons wildly in hopes of striking their attackers. No such luck, they quickly learned as they died rapidly. Rostov and Frolik descended the stairs and looked the last two men in the eyes. Rostov produced a fleeting smile.

"You both know what comes next. If you give up any more places that belong to your boss, we might let you live. What do you say? By now all of your mafia brothers in Volgograd have been sanctioned."

The two thugs exchanged worried glances. One of them wet suddenly dry lips. "Impossible! You cannot have taken all of our people without enormous losses."

"Yes," agreed the other. "We know how many you are. A pitifully small number, we have assured our Boss of Bosses."

Rostov almost felt sorry for their ignorance. Obviously they had been badly misled. "You made a terrible mistake, comrade. You see, we are all Spetznaz. Our numbers are legion compared to you petty criminals. All I needed to do was snap my fingers. . . ." He demonstrated. "So! And the most highly trained combat operators in the world come running to my aid. I will, however, leave one of you alive to convey the message to your fellow mafiosi throughout Russia to leave my team and our business entirely alone." Then Rostov raised his German-made Glock. *"Dos v'danya."* Swiftly, with neat efficiency, he shot one of the men between the eyes.

The other mafioso was quickly blindfolded by three Spetznaz operators and hauled up the stairs and into one of the metal-covered vehicles. "Take him forty kilometers from town and dump him along the road. The walk home will do him good," Rostov instructed. "Meanwhile, we will clean everything up. Tell the others to make certain there are no traces of violence. Then meet me at our second warehouse."

Fazoul Hamza cursed the bad fortune that had befallen them. Not only had they missed their target again, but Saif was dead, which put a crimp in Fazoul's ability to operate efficiently. Saif had been a superb marksman. He could shoot out the eye of a bird at eight hundred meters. Worse, Fazoul felt certain the American authorities would be looking for him. And worse still, he had lost contact with Ibrahim Ataffah, the only other survivor of the disastrous encounter with Rockham. For some reason, Ataffah had been scared by the shooting of the broad-shouldered, muscular man with the scoped rifle. When they returned to the local safe house in Santa Fe, Ataffah had gone out—for a pack of cigarettes—and never returned. Fazoul knew he would have to find the man. He cursed hotly as he considered the lost time. Would he never rid himself of this wretched Rockham? The secure telephone rang, and Fazoul hastened to answer it.

"*Na'am. Tatak.*"

Having been commanded to speak, the impersonal voice on the other end spoke softly and succinctly. "They have gone to Idaho. You will find them in the Seven Devils Mountains."

"That is excellent. It leaves me only two problems," Fazoul said sarcastically. "I lost two men on the last effort. Also, where in these mountains will I find the man I seek?"

"I am not certain of the precise location. There is a chemical and nuclear weapons facility located there, on He Devil Mountain. Be sure you do not miss this time."

Not the least intimidated by the anonymous control agent's attitude, Fazoul asked forcefully, "What about my sniper?"

"You will have to ask Ali Abdelseoud Mohamed about that. He is the one in charge, is he not?"

"Yes. I will call him and see what can be done." Their conversation ended, and Fazoul immediately dialed a number in New York City. When Ali answered, Fazoul spoke rapidly. "Saif is dead, killed by the enemy. I need another qualified sniper."

After a long moment's thought, Ali answered. "I will have a man on an airplane within an hour. He will arrive at the airport in Albuquerque four hours later. That is the best we can do." The Egyptian native sounded distant and distracted.

Fazoul did not like that; his own voice took on an edge. "I appreciate it, Ali Abdelseoud. Thank you." He groaned loudly as he hung up, not feeling the least bit more relieved. He had no idea who had designated his cell to conduct this operation, but Rockham was proving a far more formidable enemy than anyone had estimated. And the men with him were like—like killing machines.

CHAPTER 10

★★★★

It seemed incredible. Yesterday they had been in Colorado, at the largest military reservation in the state. Now, at 1600 hours local time, they stood in tight circles listening while their platoon leaders briefed them. This was the final test, the big one that counted more than any other. No more simulations. The men of SMD One were headed for a supersecret storage site for many of America's WMDs. When the operation had been revealed, it elicited expressions of disbelief and shock on most of the SEALs' faces.

Daugherty's explanation was typical. "Gentlemen, not only were we attacked last night, but we let enemies get away. The evidence found by the

Criminal Investigation agents—and verified by agents of the Counter Intelligence Division—indicated four men were involved, and the two that Chief Monday killed turned out to be of Arab origin. They had been provided with false passports and other ID. The other pair got away, and damnit, I don't like that. That was a missed opportunity. Now, we are about to enter an active WMD storage site to check for weaknesses—and verify if any are located."

He paused and affected a shy grin. "That's the bad news. Now here's the good. If we are successful, our unit mission description will be expanded. It will include worldwide examinations of WMD stockpiles and filing of accurate reports with the NRC and with Special Operations High Command. Our operators will then have a green light on enemy storage facilities. As a direct result, our T/O will be expanded and manning levels and rank slots increased. Not to mention a whole slew of promotions without the necessity to transfer out of SMD." That brought on general whoops of enthusiasm.

Master Chief Monday—now Senior Detachment Chief—stepped forward and raised both hands above his head. "Now hear this! If we pull this off, no screw-ups, our officers have generously agreed to provide burgers and brats and a keg of Colorado's finest. And I'm now adding another keg on me. Good luck, guys. Get your squads together and study the maps and movement timetables of this facility. We gotta go in, kick ass, and take names and *didi* the hell outta there."

Given their remarkable expertise in all aspects of such covert operations, it took them only forty-five minutes to develop functional operating plans for the various squads. What they came up with pleased the officers and NCOs in charge immensely.

Beyond the still open door, Grigoriy Rostov stood in the hallway of his inconspicuous new apartment in Novosibirsk, an expression of surprise on his face. A uniformed messenger had just delivered a large bouquet of expensive orchids—rarely available in eastern Russia at this time of year—and a small mahogany coffer filled with neat stacks of small gold bars. Along with this display of power and wealth came an unsigned message, handwritten on thick, creamy paper, placed in a thick envelope of matching pure linen bond. Stunned by the implications of this gift, he seemed unable to move or to close the door. Once again he read the neat, precisely placed handwritten script Cyrillic characters, this time aloud in order that his trusted associate, Ivan Tsinev, could hear. Frankly, Rostov doubted that either of them would fully understand the import of the gesture from the hierarchy of the Russian mafia.

" 'Your message has been received and understood. To your good health and long life,' " Rostov read aloud. "Now who do you suppose might have sent all of this?"

Tsinev considered that a moment. "I can think of only one name. Aleksandr Victorivich Petrenko, Boss of all Bosses in Russia."

"It is sort of hard to remain anonymous when you are this ostentatious in your peace offerings. But, Vanya, that he even made this gesture has nearly struck me speechless." Rostov raised a hand to forestall a quick response. "The troubling aspect to all of this is that Petrenko, and whoever made this delivery, knows where I live. It may be time to relocate yet again." Rostov sighed heavily, considering his options. "So long as they honor Petrenko's decision, I shall not say anything nor take any further action against them." He made an expansive gesture. "After all, we are all just businessmen, no? There are many millions to be had out there. No need for anyone to be greedy."

Tsinev smiled. "Then we are through with our troubles with them?"

"Yes, at least so long as Petrenko remains on top."

A wide grin spread on Ivan Tsinev's face. "Do you think we might be influential in ensuring that?"

"Without a doubt, Ivan. Now, we have plans to make in order to satisfy our newest clients."

It proved to be one hell of a climb up the face of He Devil Mountain. The freezing rain at that altitude—the mountain peaked at 9,400 feet—did little to help. As the men ascended higher, the rain turned to snow. It fell in small, pelletlike flakes, few and scattered enough that their path was not obscured. Their major hang-up came from the slick leaves and pine needles underfoot. After a quarter hour of climbing in these conditions, the SEALs began to slip and stumble on the unsure footing. Their seventy-pound packs did not help the situation. Despite the discomfort and hazardous going, they managed to keep their target in mind.

Over a century ago a large, three-story building had been built into the mountain to serve as a tourist hotel. From above, all that could be seen was the copper roof, now covered with verdigris and green oxidation. It had to be huge, yet all three stories were concealed within the cut. To further disguise the WMD facility, the streets of the ancient resort town had been conveniently laid out in a manner that obscured frontal observation of the building, effectively rendering it invisible. It was within these buildings that the security force and laboratory workers resided. Only one road led to the area.

They would approach the town by means of a roadway tunnel dug into one flank of the mountain. The vehicles would be waiting for them just inside the western entrance to the passageway through He Devil Mountain. They reached it after another twenty minutes of floundering in the mushy sleet.

* * *

Gold Platoon had arrived in a small convoy of windowless panel trucks, painted black, with smoked glass in the front. Close examination would show that the windows were not glass but Lexan, thick enough to stop an AK-47 round. The walls of the paneled portion were reinforced with thick layers of Kevlar, making them impervious to all but armor-piercing 7.62 millimeter ordnance, or projectiles up to .50 caliber. They were professionals, and they appreciated that in an operation like this one, every base had to be covered.

Quickly, they located an empty building across the street from the hotel and entered it, descending to the cellar the old maps indicated. They would make entry through a long-forgotten maintenance tunnel that connected the hotel to some of the buildings on the opposite side of the street. This tunnel contained the sewer system and carried electric and telephone cables, natural gas and water pipes. Several older structures also had a vacuum tube communications system that paralleled the other utilities. Through these brass tubes money or messages had been transported in the late 1890s and early 1900s. Most went out of use after World War II, when the tourist trade dried up and the town was abandoned.

None of this mattered to the SEALs as they used one of the damp, musty-smelling tunnels to approach the basement of the apparently abandoned structure that housed a third of the deadly chemical weapons owned by the United States. Their thoughts were on the new occupants and the condition of the service tunnel.

Water dripped and rats scurried through the tunnel. First and second squads of Gold Platoon used night vision goggles to show them the way, confident that any light-sensing security devices would not detect them. Stinking, rancid water swirled around their feet as they took baby steps to avoid loud splashing, in an effort to foil audio surveillance pickups. Over the slight noise they made, the SEALs of SMD One could hear the loud *plink-plink* of drops of moisture that seeped down from the street and condensed on the curved ceiling. It clearly indicated that no one monitored audio sensors. No one would remain sharp enough to react every time there was a miniature rainstorm underground. Unfortunately, there was nothing they could do if the tunnel was protected by motion sensors. Considering the age and condition of this decrepit brick tunnel, now-platoon leader Daugherty, and Rockham, had taken the calculated risk to enter in this manner. Sediment and slime from rotting critters and vegetation made progress slow and hazardous. At point, Ryan Marks raised his sight line from the treacherous, shin-deep water and glanced ahead. His green-glowing circle of light picked out a rusted metal door ahead, and he raised his left fist in the signal to halt.

Instantly, the men stopped. Slowly, conscious of the mounting danger, Marks advanced. He reached out with a gloved hand and cautiously felt the edges of the old iron portal. He could detect no trip wires nor see the presence of a pressure release alarm. The condition of the door told him that no one had used it in some time. He removed a large squirt can of rust-dissolving penetrating oil from his pack and applied it liberally to the three large hinges that held the door in place. Mike Bryant, the other point man, came forward from his position and fitted the splayed dual flanges of his Hooligan tool under the lip of the overlapping edge plate of the door. Taking a deep breath, he leaned into it and applied all the power of his shoulders. The rusted metal of the hinges gave a low groan but would not yield.

Marks flashed a bright, white smile and made the hand signals for C-4 plastic explosive. He nodded enthusiastically to reinforce his suggestion. Bryant shook his head in the negative. He pointed to the oil can.

Marks let out a heavy sigh and then did as suggested. This time he soaked the hinges until the oil ran off into the water below. Gently, he tapped them with a rubber hammer. When he was satisfied, he gave Bryant a signal to try again.

This time both men put all their strength behind the Hooligan tool and heaved mightily. With a loud groan and a cloud of rust, the door began to give.

"More oil," Bryant whispered into Marks's ear. This time the penetrating oil soaked deeply into the loosened hinges. Mentally, Marks and Bryant counted down to one minute. Marks tapped the hinges with the mallet and hunched up to apply pressure along with his partner, then both men stepped back and lunged forward, muscles straining as the Hooligan tool did its work. Power and the rust-solvent properties of the oil proved adequate. The bottom and middle hinges yielded first, with shrieks that could raise the dead, followed by the upper hinge. Wincing at the sound, both men put their gloved hands on the outer lip of the door and heaved to open it wider. A curt gesture brought the rest of the squads forward.

One by one, night vision goggles searching the area, they slipped through the opening and gained access to the cellar and the stairs leading up to the first floor of the old hotel. They removed their boots and replaced them with crape-soled shoes. Silently, the SMD operatives moved up the stairs and into the darkened building that housed the WMD storage site they had targeted. For this critical final exam, they had dressed in civilian clothing. The only deviations were the black ski masks they wore and the tool pouches slung around their lean hips. As always, they carried sterile arms available anywhere in the world.

John Sukov, the radioman for first squad, edged forward and whispered to Rockham, "Rock, I've got contact with the squad on security at the far end of the tunnel."

"What do they have to say?"

Sukov sighed heavily. "Not a lot, Rock. They haven't heard or seen anyone except our own people."

Rockham frowned. "Why does that bother me? There are scientists and lab techs all over the place, not to mention their families and the security people. We should have had to take out some of the 'hostiles' by now."

Looking ahead of them down the long central corridor leading to what used to be the hotel lobby, Sukov spoke with a grim note. "I think we can expect that to end damn soon. Look down there at the front door."

In an instant, Rockham saw what Big Bad John—as they called Sukov—meant. A small field desk had been set up perpendicular to the large glass panes of the oak double doors. On it rested a standard telephone and a military field telephone set. Behind it sat a female soldier in forest camo uniform, the big, black butt grip of her 9mm Beretta pistol visible in a shoulder holster. Across from her, two more burly soldiers stood at parade rest. In a flash, Rockham knew they would have to be neutralized before the SMD could conduct its operation.

"All right, we take them out," he declared. He made a quick evaluation of the situation. To hit accurately with a paint ball gun, his men would have to expose themselves too long, which might result in someone giving the alarm. But they had another weapon that could come close to shooting around a corner. He turned to the men behind him. "Which ones of you have the blow pipes?" Four men raised their hands. "Okay, Kurkowski and another two of you get them out, assemble the tubes, and use the paint ball darts. All three of you fire at the same time."

When the training phase came around to the use of blow guns and darts, the men of SMD had thought it was a colossal joke. Not so, they soon found out. Grinning broadly, Jay Hunter told them that his Cherokee ancestors had used blow pipes for over six centuries. As a silent weapon, nothing could beat one of the five-foot-long pipes. A sharp-pointed dart dipped in nicotine sulfate could bring on paralysis in six seconds, death in a minute. They made ideal weapons for a covert Red Cell type unit.

Creeping quietly and slowly on their soft sole shoes, the trio of men from Gold Platoon advanced within range without being discovered by their intended targets. Each slid a slender stiff-wire dart with a dye-soaked cotton ball at one end and a glass bead base into the tubes of their blow pipes, lifted them as one, and on a silent count, puffed the projectiles toward the unsuspecting guards.

With almost as much coordination, the two men and the young woman slapped at the stinging sensation in their exposed necks and came away with red dye on their fingers. "Crap," groaned one of the muscular MPs.

"Yeah, they're here," replied the other. "But how in hell did they get past us or the guys back in the kitchen?"

That confirmed Rockham's suspicion that the tunnel and its entrance to the hotel were unknown to the current occupants of the town. He watched while the three sentries wiped off the small spot of water-soluble paint with facial tissues and proceeded to ignore any sounds from within the building, since they were, after all, "dead."

Quickly, Sukov extended the handset to Rockham, who called Shaun Daugherty. "Hey, Snake Eyes, send over the other two squads. You stay with Green. Have Blue Platoon take over security."

When the remainder of Gold Platoon arrived, the men spread out though the building. All of them had autoinjector Syrettes of antidote for chemical weapons ready. Quickly, they tagged cases of nerve gas, mustard gas, and nausea gas, indicating their theoretical destruction. They scribbled down notes on weaknesses in the internal security system and the lack of surveillance TV cameras in all four corners of each room. They recorded the absence in some rooms of bars on the windows and a lack of movement and voice-activated sensors to detect any intruders. In fact, it looked as though the guards at the front door and those watching the rear door were the only ones actively watching the place. Perhaps the brass believed that with the women working there, shopping at the grocery store and at the small department store provided sufficient cover to misdirect any potential invaders.

The only active alarm system they discovered was a centralized one, controlled by a circuit breaker in the Square D utility box in a closet under the front stairs. Flip the switch and the entire setup went down.

"Maybe they depended on the isolation," Daugherty theorized as the four squads completed their inventory of the facility and its defenses and Rockham reported the results to him.

Rockham snorted in derision. "That's like a high school girl relying on her lace panties to protect her virtue. Maybe if you add to that the likelihood that they sought to prevent drawing attention to their real function here by not installing cyclone fence and razor wire, spotlights and guard dogs, I might buy that. But I'd also call it foolish."

Jorgensen joined in with a wise remark. "It's the damn bureaucrats. Don't mistake what I'm saying. They're not afraid of spending money. Only they don't want to spend any on military activities and facilities. They want to use it to buy votes for themselves."

Rockham clapped him on one shoulder. "Spoken like a true cynic, Hamlet. Remember, we in the military are not supposed to have partisan political opinions. Confidentially, though, I agree with you. Whoever designed the security for this place was crazy or stupid. Other than the nukes being buried in underground bunkers, they don't seem to have done a thing. That, or they had the budget cut drastically by the bean counters."

"Speaking of nukes," Rockham's RTO remarked, "Blue has checked in to inform you that the heavy stuff is taken care of."

"That's cool," Rockham responded. He turned to the four squads assembled in the kitchen and back along the main hallway. "Okay, guys, let's *didi* outta here. All we have to do is get through the tunnel and back to the trucks for the exercise to be over."

Fazoul Hamza and his henchmen dragged their way forward, exhausted by the strenuous climb up the steep mountain slope. They assembled on the roadway that did not appear on any map. They knew it had to lead to the storage facility for a lot of the Americans' chemical weapons. They were unaware of the cached nuclear warheads. Fazoul theorized that the man they had been sent to kill would be using this road. During his last conversation that morning with Ali, Fazoul learned that some powerful men in Russia—friends of Al-Qaeda—wanted the colonel in the Pentagon and this man, Rockham, dead. Ali surmised that Wharton, Rockham, and the men in Rockham's unit represented a great threat to the Russians, who provided arms for Al Qaeda. That thought produced a grim smile on Fazoul's lips. All they needed to do was set up a proper ambush and the job would be completed.

He spoke to Ataffah, whom he had retrieved from the Greyhound bus terminal in Santa Fe the day before. "Move the van to block the road just around this curve. Then come back. Omar, Mustafa, go up among those trees above the trail just this side of the roadblock. Ibrahim and I will take this side. When the vehicle containing our target stops, Abdelmajid Maslam," he indicated one of the reinforcements from his cell, "will throw in a satchel charge and then we will all mop up any who survive."

Omar and Mustafa crossed the road and took positions where they could cover the entire area of the ambush. They waited tensely for the American infidels to come.

A seasoned warrior himself, Fazoul could sense the tension building in his men. He could easily visualize their condition: sweaty palms, harsh breathing, eyes darting from side to side. They'd try to moisten dry lips with their equally dry tongues. He knew only too well—it had happened to him the first several times he had met the enemies of Allah—but they would eventually overcome it.

His musing ended as he heard the sound of trucks or other vehicles starting up in the distance above and beyond their ambush site. The Americans would be coming any second now.

* * *

SMD One had quickly made it back to the vehicles after completing their dirty tricks in the old hotel building. It would most likely not be long before someone discovered the incapacitated guards at the front entrance and the kitchen. Rockham wanted them well on their way before that happened. So far, it had been like a walk in the park for them, he mused as the lead panel truck rolled down the road.

A grinning Daugherty spoke to Rockham as the second truck, containing them, moved onto the road and started down the mountain. "We did pretty good, huh, boss?"

"You bet we did," Rockham responded. "Now all we have to do is get out of here without being discovered. Piece of cake, right?"

Rockham had no idea how wrong he was.

Less than half an hour passed before Fazoul had his opportunity. Six large panel trucks sped down the road toward the hidden terrorists. The second truck in the convoy had their subject in the front passenger seat. Fazoul directed fire into the tires of the first vehicle, causing it to fishtail and emit blue-white smoke from the ruined tires. Immediately, the other panel trucks screeched to a halt.

"Son of a bitch!" Fazoul heard a man shout from the wounded vehicle. "What the fuck is this?"

"That's live ammo, open fire, damnit!" the driver shouted.

A moment later Ataffah pulled the ring of the igniter, which made a ripping sound as it struck fire to the fuse. He rose up to hurl the twenty-pound satchel charge, only to be blown away by a short silent burst from an MP5-D submachinegun. The explosive charge fell at Ibrahim's feet. He screamed in terror and jumped from concealment, to be literally cut in half by a pair of fast rounds of 00 buckshot from a Remington-7188 auto shotgun. Omar and Mustafa opened fire at once, which revealed their positions. Three more expert marksmen in the trucks returned fire. Omar and Mustafa swiftly died when the third vehicle stopped at the roadblock.

Only Fazoul Hamza, praying to Allah with greater sincerity then even during his childhood, managed to escape. He dashed downhill, gasping in great gulps of air and sweating profusely. From behind him he heard sporadic shots, no doubt the *coup de grace* for any who had survived the onslaught.

"What in hell is going on?" Daugherty demanded after the last echoes of gunfire faded from the mountainside.

"We were ambushed," Rockham said stating the obvious. "I'll get hold of Colonel Wharton, maybe we can get away without some of the paperwork."

"Don't make book on that, boss," Master Chief Monday added his two-cents' worth. "Jeez, who the hell were they?" he asked, still shaken by the suddenness of the ambush. Then, he spoke rapidly to the SEALs in the third truck. "You guys spread out, check them for ID, take photos with the Polaroid cameras in the lead truck. The rest of you keep an eye out for any survivors. Shit, we get shot at yesterday, and now this. If these dudes turn out to be Arabs too, the whole country could be in some deep crap."

His prediction proved correct. There was hell to pay among the brass. Admiral Cromarty and Colonel Wharton believed that these incidents had happened due to overconfidence on the part of soldiers stationed stateside who had grown lax in their duties. They vowed it would change—and damn soon. Worse, a search of the wider area around He Devil Mountain by units choppered in from Fort Carson produced no useful results. Only the dead Arabs remained to indicate that it had been a terrorist attack. But why, and for what purpose?

What made him and his men so important that what must have been a terrorist sleeper cell had been activated to take them out?

That was something Greg Rockham worried over as they journeyed toward Utah.

CHAPTER 11

Outside, the four rigs looked like any other long-haul tractor-trailer outfit. Inside, they had been converted into comfortable quarters for each squad in Gold Platoon. For all the comfort—thick bunks, a wet bar, a small kitchen, and bathroom, complete with shower—the men weren't happy about their circumstances.

"What the hell is this all about?" Hunter demanded. "I thought that our last op was the final exam. What we doin' this for?"

"That's what we're supposed to be planning while we scout out the terrain around the target," Monday informed them. "This is the largest WMD site in Utah. Colonel Wharton has told us that it will be the proof of the pudding. If we can remove some of these weapons undetected, we've got the ammunition to sell the idea to the Joint Chiefs and the Secretary of Defense of a special SMD unit to check our security and raid the enemy's."

"So what are we doing in these overgrown RV trailers?" Henry Limbaugh asked.

Lutz shrugged. "You've got me. They're sure comfortable, though."

Chief Monday opened one side of a truck's rear double doors. "Mount up, men. Enjoy this luxury while you can. We're on our way to a quiet meadow to jawbone about the target. Jump-off time is 1530 hours. By then, these trucks will look like military vehicles. We even have the paperwork to get onto the reservation."

"How do we pull that off?" Tinsley asked. "Making them into military trucks, I mean?"

From inside the trailer, Monday pulled out a gallon paint can. "Thanks to the Glidden Paint Company, we have this handy-dandy stuff called strip paint. All we have to do is put it on, and then to change back we find a high pressure hose and blow the OD coating off the sides and tops."

Bryant blinked owlishly before asking, "And when we get there, what happens?"

Monday answered in a bored tone. "If we're not found out as phonies, we use our eyes and ears to figure out the best way to infiltrate the place after dark and what would be the best things to take out. We'll cover that at the premission briefing. Now, let's get going."

Fazoul Hamza reviewed his seemingly endless history of failure. The fury with which the designated targets had reacted left him breathless. How could they have turned the tables like that? They were the targets, yet they destroyed the ambushers. Then the image of a large sign he had seen at the base where this Gregory Rockham was stationed flashed into his mind: WELCOME TO SEAL COUNTRY.

It provided chilling confirmation of his theory. These men had to be the dreaded Navy SEALs, not supply clerks. The notion would have paralyzed any lesser man with icy fear. But Fazoul saw them only as a greater threat, a challenge to his ability as a freedom fighter. Then a sobering thought struck him.

What could he report to his superiors? Especially Ali Abdelseoud Mohamed. He recalled the coolness in Ali's voice the last time he had called to report another failure and the loss of Saif. Sighing, he reached for the telephone with the scrambler circuit and dialed the familiar number in Hampton, Virginia. Fazoul stiffened when Ali came on the line.

"What is it?" the terrorist leader snapped.

"*Saba'a AlKair,* Ali Abdelseoud. It is I, Fazoul Mahmoud Hamza."

"Good morning to you, Fazoul Mahmoud.

May I inquire as to your success in the project you have undertaken?"

Coldness spread from his gut to his chest, clutching at his heart. He would rather have cut off his right hand than reveal the bad news to this fearsome man. Swallowing hard, he began, "I have had a terrible setback. My entire cell came out here when I needed them. Now I have lost them all. We set up an ambush and by some twist of ill fate were wiped out by our supposed targets."

Ali thundered his disbelief: "That is preposterous! How is it that you are still alive if the slaughter was so complete? Did you run like a frightened child, Fazoul Mahmoud? Or did you weep and beg for mercy and have now been turned so that you work for *them*?" He paused to gather himself. "Whatever the case, forget this phone number. Do not call it again."

Struck dumb, Fazoul hesitated before asking, "B-But what about me? What shall I do now?"

"Frankly, I do not care. You are damaged goods as far as Al Qaeda is concerned. You could run and hide somewhere, or you might consider suicide."

Shocked to the core, Fazoul could only stammer, "Th-The Prophet forbade suicide. It is in the *Q'uran*, called a deadly sin."

"That is odd," Ali said, sarcasm dripping from his words. "How would you judge our holy martyrs? Frankly, I never considered you to be a religious man." His mood changed rapidly. "Perhaps

I have been hasty. If you are truly zealous, I might find use for you after all. You will report to me at the safe house in Alexandria in two days."

Ali hung up without a closing salutation. But a smile returned to his lips as he considered what use he would make of Fazoul.

From his closet, Ali took a canvas and leather contraption that could be worn like a vest. It had rectangular pockets on the front, sides, and back. They were of a size to perfectly fit a quarter kilogram block of Simtex. He would take it with him to Alexandria.

Looking every bit like grass-covered mausoleums, the bunkers containing stores of chemical weapons filled a large area of the obscure military reservation in Kolob Canyon in southern Utah. The papers that were presented by Chief Monday, now wearing Army BDUs, with master sergeant's stripes, were readily accepted, the camouflaged trucks dutifully logged in and passed beyond the gate to the storage site. Approaching from the opposite direction, Blue Platoon would do an overall, long distance surveillance, using portable camcorders with zoom lenses. The digital video discs they made would provide excellent intelligence on their objective.

When combined with the on-site observations of Gold Platoon, it would provide a comprehensive understanding of the reservation. It would facilitate the removal of the designated WMDs while improving their chances of doing so undetected.

At the briefing earlier in the afternoon, the men of SMD had been told that they would covertly enter the desired bunkers, chosen during the site survey, and steal 155mm M-55 Bolt rockets with VX warheads stored there, prior to destruction. Beyond that, the SEALs received little intelligence about the site, so their current mission was to seek out accurate information and develop their own database for the raid. Just prior to departure for Kolob Canyon, Ferber put in his view.

"What frosts my fuzzy nuts is that we're going to actually take some of that stuff out of there. What do we do with them once we get 'em?"

"Damn if I know," Monday responded. "Someone who outranks me will no doubt tell us when the time comes. Now, let's check out these camcorders and the other gear we'll be using. And remember to be discreet."

"What's that mean?" Hunter asked.

"It means to not go in there and poke the lens in someone's face and say, 'Smile, you're on *Candid Camera.*'"

Daugherty approached then, overhearing what Monday had said. "Har-de-har, Chief. But he's got a point there, men. We don't go in there and take pictures out in the open. Sneak the shots you take. The only exception will be my guys in Blue Platoon."

Now that they were inside the reservation, among the bunkers containing deadly VX gas and other chemical agents, they found the task of photo-mapping quite easy. Small holes had been cut in the trailer sides, covered by movable flaps. They exactly fit the outer circumference of the DVD camcorders. All they needed to do was shoot and scoot.

Rockham disabused them of that idea quickly. "We need to check the color-coded ID tags on the bunkers to find the ones we will hit tonight."

"That means we go up close and personal," Wayne Alexander complained.

"You got that right, sailor," Rockham told him lightly. "Now, let's get a few people out there to do it."

On close examination, the SEALs quickly recognized the color code that identified the bunkers containing the M-55 Bolt rockets. Walking at a fast pace, the members of first and third squads, Gold Platoon, spread out and put markers of their own on the proper bunkers.

From a distance, located on a wooded hillside outside the military reservation, part of Blue Platoon provided their security screening, while the remainder operated the camcorders, set up on sturdy tripods. It would be possible to enlarge the image on a computer screen to five hundred percent of its original size. When the DVDs were shown, all of the SMD teams involved could see in exacting detail what the men of Gold Platoon had done among the bunkers.

Lieutenant Shaun Daugherty, who commanded Blue Platoon, mumbled, "I only wish we had infrared cameras so we could shoot the actual taking of the warheads."

"Well, sir, we can always video the rockets once we get them away from here," his platoon chief suggested. "That should be proof enough we did what we came for."

"That's a point well taken, Chief. But it would be fun to show the video to the CO of this storage facility."

Fazoul made preparations to travel to Virginia. He called an airline that served Albuquerque and made a reservation for the next day. Deep inside, he suspected that in leaving the area he would be giving up his last chance to redeem himself in the eyes of Ali Abdelseoud. Whatever he was going to do would not be pleasant, of that he was sure. With a reservation secured, Fazoul started for the airport.

While he made the hundred-kilometer journey, his nemesis and the men of SMD—barely three hundred miles away—went about detailing the physical layout of the WMD storage site. Had he known this, Fazoul could have contacted the Al Qaeda sleeper cell at the mosque in Denver and had some of the men meet him in Utah. Success would have put him in a far better light with Ali when they met.

Unenlightened, Fazoul went on to the Albuquerque airport on the northeast side of town and boarded his flight to Atlanta. There, he would change planes and fly on to Virginia. He would make certain to stay as far away from the safe house in Alexandria as he could until the time for their meeting. It was not a lot, but at least it would reduce some of the anxiety caused by the prospect of the confrontation ahead of him.

In Cedar City, the squads of Gold and Blue Platoons got together and began to create the database from the information they had obtained. "Listen up, guys," Chief Monday said. "This is the big one. If we succeed, we're good to go against the real bad guys. But keep one thing in mind. These guys out in Kolob Canyon are good—damn good. Word will have gotten around, and I'm sure the security people will be hyped and living on the edge."

"So what do we do?" Hunter asked.

"Study these photos until you know the layout by heart. We check the paint on the trucks just before dark and head out. When we get there, we go directly to where we want to be, do the job and get the hell out."

Rockham offered up a correction. "I think the trucks have already been seen too much. Going in at night would really make them suspicious, even if they are OD in color. We need to take some other sort of civilian transportation."

Jorgensen gave him an odd look. "What do we do, steal them?"

"No, Pauli, there's a used car dealership here in

Cedar City," he reminded the CO of Green Platoon. "I propose that we appeal to the owner's patriotism to obtain the vehicles we need. Under actual conditions we would steal them, but that's what got Rick Marcinko in trouble during Red Cell's training phase."

Larry Stadt asked the question on the minds of several Teammates. "How do we get past the gate guards?"

"We take them out like we would in the real thing," Rockham replied. "The way this is shaking out, it looks like Gold Platoon will take the bunkers of chemical weapons and Blue will take the nukes."

Jorgensen frowned. "And Green gets stuck with security again?"

Rockham smiled in an effort to soften the reality. "That, and guard our 'borrowed' cars. After all, we do want to get out of there."

Master Chief Monday offered a refinement. "Might I suggest we opt for pickup trucks and vans? They'll hold crates of VX warheads better than a passenger vehicle."

"Good, Chief, that's the way to think. CYA for all of us," Rockham praised him. "Remember this, gentlemen: if we get caught, the shit's really going to hit the fan. So, this is what we'll do. . . ." And using the computer module to illustrate what each man would be expected to perform, he continued laying out the basics of the planned raid.

* * *

Colonel Wharton stood before Admiral Cromarty's wide, highly polished mahogany desk. Wharton's posture and sagging jaw clearly conveyed his disbelief, even before he spoke a word.

"That is unacceptable," he snapped. "With all due respect, Admiral, I think your decision to move Commander Rockham immediately after this phase of training is ill-suited to the facts. Why? Because it seems that from the gate, you've been stabbing the man in the back. First you promise—"

Cromarty raised a hand in an effort to restrain the flow of angry words. "Just hold on a minute, Colonel," he commanded. "Don't overlook the fact that they have been shot at twice by terrorists. I'm convinced that Greg is competent to fill a command slot, but the safety of all of them is at stake here. After all, this happened on American soil. The FBI is working on it, as well as our service intelligence units."

Red-faced, Wharton barked back, "No, sir, I cannot 'hold on.' These assassination attempts notwithstanding, let me review what has happened so far. From the beginning, Rockham has been the best suited of all senior SEAL officers to command a combined force—one that involves special operators from several services—and has proven his theory of engagement to be first-class, if not perfect, for the missions undertaken. As far as the attacks on the SMD go, none of that outweighs the importance of consistency in this matter. We have established a terrorist threat inside our borders. Who better to deal with it than Greg Rockham?" Wharton let that hang before continuing.

"First you promote Rockham and give him command of SMD One, then you promise him overall command of all three SMDs, then you yank the rug out from under him and say he has to be bumped upstairs to a staff job with the CNO's office. What in hell use does the Chief of Naval Operations have for the best qualified field commander ever turned out by the SEAL special warfare school?" He was fully aware that his protests bordered on rank insubordination, but felt compelled to make the best case for Rockham.

Cromarty changed his iron-jawed scowl to a pleasant smile. "I hesitate to mention this, Colonel, but I am not going to live forever. And I *do* intend to enjoy my retirement. That leaves an opening at the top for a he-gorilla to become Boss SEAL. I happen to think that Greg would fill that position perfectly."

Colonel Wharton swallowed hard. "My God, I never thought of that possibility. That's brilliant, Admiral." He paused to seriously consider this new idea. As he did, a huge feeling of relief washed over him as he visualized Cromarty's plan. "First Greg gets high-level command experience," Wharton summed up, "and then serves with high-level staff, and after that replaces you. Way to go, Admiral. When do you intend to inform Greg of your plans for his future?"

Cromarty lit a Honduran Monte Cristo cigar and puffed it to glowing life. "I believe when they complete this phase of training will be the right time."

"Ah . . . if I may suggest it, Admiral, I think that after their next actual field mission would be a better time. I'm sure that Rockham, flushed with success, would receive the news with a great deal more enthusiasm and a lot less disappointment."

Cromarty considered this, then extended a hand for Wharton to shake. He spoke through a chuckle, "And it gives him more of that high-level command experience you mentioned, eh? You've sold me. We announce the news after his next operation."

When Colonel Wharton returned to his own office in a less prestigious ring of the Pentagon, his voice mail informed him he should call a Colonel Bryce Simmons at a phone number with a Utah area code. Wharton felt certain he knew the purpose of the call, and it amused him. Seating himself in a spartan wooden swivel chair, he picked up his phone and dialed.

A moment later a gruff voice came on the line. "Wharton? Where are those super warriors of yours? None of us has seen a sign of them. Odds are they got cold feet. But when they do show up we'll nail them, you can count on that." The man's laughter was discordant and raucous.

Wharton restrained himself from a caustic reply and spoke with extra precision. "Don't worry overly about my missing men. When they've come and gone, you'll know it. That, my friend, is not a promise, it's a friggin' guarantee." Wharton hung up before Simmons could reply. He stabbed a button on his intercom with a thick, long finger. "Sergeant Raven, bring in the secure sat-link phone."

"Yes, sir, right away," came the reply. Sergeant Lowansa Raven immediately retrieved the encrypted sat-link phone from its locked cabinet and took it into Wharton's office.

After she had plugged it in and departed, Wharton dialed a number that consisted of twelve digits. It rang four times before being answered. Since it wasn't a scheduled call, apparently no one was actively monitoring the sat-link. "This is Wharton. Let me speak with Commander Rockham."

Within seconds Rockham came on the line. "Rock here, speak to me."

"Rock, have you or have you not visited the target?"

Rockham's soft chuckle came through clearly. The encryption program could not distort it. "Oh, yes. We spent most of the afternoon there. Why do you ask? Who wants to know?"

"A certain Colonel Bryce Simmons. Did you ever hear of him?"

Rockham answered at once with a question. "That's the colonel who runs the target facility?"

Wharton didn't hesitate. "One and the same."

"And he had no idea we'd been inside already? That means the ones we neutralized didn't say anything." Rockham paused and considered. "They won't, they're good soldiers and will not cheat. Which makes me wonder if the good colonel is well-liked by the men who serve under him."

Wharton's chuckle was rich and warm. "It's a sure bet he'd never win a popularity contest. I just had the unpleasant experience of talking with him. He came on like an arrogant, officious ass. Did you leave anything behind to let him know you'd been there?"

"No, sir, not in this stage of the plan. I figured we'd do something to yank his chain when we go in to steal the shells."

"Okay, keep up the good work. And—ah, be careful tomorrow night. Oh, by the way, do you have a plan for getting in without being detected?"

"Oh, yeah, tomorrow's a big interschool rivalry for regional football championship. We found out a lot of the troops at the WMD facility will be going to the game tomorrow night. We'll go in through a back gate, do our thing, and skinny out of there before they have a clue."

"Super, Greg. I'm betting heavily on you and your men. Let me know when you finish the job."

CHAPTER 12

★ ★ ★ ★

1730 ZULU
Jack Fulton's Auto Circus
Cedar City, Utah

All three men entered the lot together and spent several minutes looking over the cars and trucks offered for sale. A number of vans and SUVs shined after the detailers had slicked them up for display. The SEALs also found three pickups with camper covers on their beds, another plus factor. A rotund individual approached, a large smile flashing small white teeth.

"Gentlemen, are you looking for something specific? What can I help you with?" He rubbed his pudgy hands together in eagerness to close the sale.

Rockham took the lead. "We would like to talk to the owner."

Their deal-hungry salesman looked stricken. "Wha-What do you wa-want to see him for?"

"Is he here?" Rockham pressed.

"Well—ah, yes, he—he is. May I ask if you are with the Department of Motor Vehicles or another regulatory agency?"

"No," Daugherty injected. "We're from the Better Business Bureau. We want to talk about his sales practices," he added with a mischievous twinkle in his eyes, his guess striking home.

All but uttering a groan, the flashily dressed salesman turned on one heel and headed for the small building that housed the office and the pressure cooker rooms for use on reluctant customers. He returned shortly with a trim, balding man with a luxurious fringe of silver hair and a brush mustache.

"This is Mister . . . ?" the salesman prompted Rockham.

"My name is Rockham. This is Mr. Daugherty and Mr. Jorgensen."

With a decisive step forward and in front of his flunky, he extended his hand. "I'm Jack Fulton. Glad to meet you, gentlemen. What is it you wish to see me about?"

Rockham smiled broadly and gestured widely to encompass the whole lot. "We're interested in a short-term rental, a rather *large* short-term rental."

Fulton's smile bloomed. "Uh, then you're not from the Better Business Bureau?"

Rockham suppressed a grim. "No. My friend here sees himself as a stand-up comic."

Rubbing hands together in expectation of some

added revenue, Fulton spoke lightly. "Exactly how large do you call large?"

"Enough trucks, vans, and SUVs to move 110 men from place to place and back again."

"My . . . God," Fulton gulped. "I don't know if I have enough."

"If you're short, could you get enough if you had twelve hours?"

Fulton cocked his head to one side, his dark black eyes darting along the lines of his stock in trade, his mind busy calculating. "Y-You're serious, aren't you?"

"Oh, yes, I can assure you of that. And figure the rental at a fleet rate, if you don't mind."

"For—ah, for how long do you want to rent them?" Dollar signs had replaced the dark glow in Fulton's eyes.

"Figure until sometime late tomorrow evening," Jorgensen injected, splitting Fulton's attention in yet another direction.

Fulton rapidly calculated the profit this would mean to him. "Umm . . . let's say forty-four dollars, ninety-nine cents a day for an SUV, thirty-eight a day for a sliding side door van, and twenty-nine dollars, ninety-nine cents a day for a pickup with a camper cover. Does that sound reasonable to you, gentlemen?" He had made a great effort to fill his voice with sincerity.

"Not really," Rockham told him blandly. "I think twenty dollars across the board would be

more realistic. After all, we'll need fifteen to six-
teen of them, depending on size."

Fulton all but whined. "But—But that's not
leaving me anything for profit."

Daugherty interjected, "How do you figure?
You already own these vehicles, they are up for
sale, and you'll still be able to sell them after we
use them. That makes whatever we pay you one
hundred percent profit. Unless you intend to split
it with your employees, that gives you—ummm—
I make it a minimum of three hundred dollars a
day pure profit to you."

Bristling, Fulton nearly shouted, "You can't say
that."

"I think he just did," said Jorgensen with a note
of finality. "What's the nearest good-sized town
around here?" he asked his companions.

"Panguitch is not so far away," Daugherty answered, "and it's closer than Kanab."

"Either one sounds good to me." He turned to
Fulton. "So, Mr. Fulton, you can take your overpriced rentals and shove them where the sun never
shines."

"No no no, please, let's reconsider it. Perhaps I
did sort of overestimate. Call it twenty-five each,
is that okay?"

Rockham turned on one heel. "I think not. See
ya around, fellah."

Half an hour later they were in Panguitch, a
scant thirty miles away. They had no idea how the

locals pronounced the city's name, but they had no trouble with Herb Brown's. His "Choice Previously Owned Cars" lot sported twice the number of vehicles as Jack Fulton's Auto Circus. Within ten minutes a deal was struck and the papers signed for the rentals. Representatives from each squad would pick them up at eight that evening.

Fazoul Hamza arrived in Virginia on schedule. He took a bus to the Sunset Inn, a run-down motel in a predominantly black section of the sprawling city. Fazoul knew that a large number of Muslims—mostly from Iran, Jordan, Syria, and Saudi Arabia—resided here, and that a mosque had been established in an empty old stone-façade store. The imam of this holy place had connections to Hizbollah, he knew, so he could expect a warm welcome and assistance, if required. The satisfaction of knowing that he could lay low here without worry of discovery by Ali Abdelseoud eased him as he entered the small, unwelcoming room, removed his shoes, and lay on the bed, conscious of the musty smell of mold and too many human misfortunes that had played out in this restrictive cubical. Before he took a shower, Fazoul poured a powerful disinfectant on the floor and sidewalls of the cramped shower stall. Hardly a Donald Trump palatial hotel, but it served his need for anonymity. After showering, he dialed the number for the mosque.

"*Na'am? Masa'a AlKair.*"

Fazoul responded by asking if the imam spoke English.

"Of course I do. Who is this?"

Despite this assurance, Fazoul continued in Arabic. "I bring you greetings from the prince. He is pleased with your work for our holy brotherhood."

Wonder filled the voice of the imam. "Al Qaeda is calling me? I am most honored. Tell me, have you seen the prince lately?"

Fazoul sighed, playing a role. "Alas, no, it has been a long time. Osama is busy planning something important. I have been here, like you, serving without being recognized by our infidel enemy."

"So, you are undercover, eh?" Suddenly he switched to Arabic. "*Ma ismak*?" What is your name?

Fazoul considered that this obscure mullah would not be aware of the fate of the members of his defunct cell, that debacle being so far removed from this Islamic community. "My name is Saif Daoud Saddiq," he answered in response, using the dead man's name for security reasons. "I am in need of protective color for the next few days. Is there anything you can do for me?"

"Oh, yes. Where are you staying?"

Quickly, Fazoul gave him the name and location of the motel. They exchanged parting pleasantries and he hung up. He had been told there was a suitable restaurant that served Arabic cuisine only three blocks from his present location. The *Gar-*

den of Allah would serve as a place to eat while Mullah Rashid Ibn Rashid made the required arrangements.

Mitchell Reid, an upper level agent of the FBI, cast a doubtful glance at the man from the CIA seated across from him in the coffee shop. "This is for real? It's not some BS story cooked up by your people at Langley?"

Sam Gibbs, from the Domestic Affairs section of the CIA, sighed heavily. "No, I guarantee you of that. Our director of domestic affairs received the audio tape only thirty minutes ago, after our Arab speakers translated it. This guy, Saif Saddiq, is for real. Our information is that he is a member of a sleeper cell of Al Qaeda that's been embedded in this country for some three years. Why they are here, we do not know. But since we're friends, Mitch, I brought it to you. I know that technically you feebies are in charge of internal security, so closing this one out is your job. But my boss says we should have a hand in it. He believes that there has been enough lack of interagency cooperation."

"He wants us to make a complete report on whatever we discover?"

Gibbs shook his head. "No, he wants *us* to do the interrogation—with you and your supervisor along, of course—and be able to act on whatever is developed. Some of our special operators have been attacked inside the country by terrorists, which means we have plenty of Al Qaeda types here."

Reid distractedly shredded his paper napkin while he considered that. "I'm not sure the Bureau will go along with what you want. But considering that there has been terrorist activity on our soil, we'll no doubt work it," he concluded.

"If not, the Bureau will have another black eye. We want in on this too," he added. "Otherwise, you'll have to find this Saif on your own and develop a case. We can save you a lot of time. Let us help. We can wring this dork out in no time."

"Damnit, Sam, you've got me between a rock and a hard place." He glanced around like a cornered rat. "How would we work it? I mean, how long would it take to get a joint arrest cleared?"

"It's already set up on my end. What I suggest is we go over to where this scumbag is staying and take him down right now."

Reid was astonished. "You know where he is?"

"Yeah, we know. We've had a tap on the phones at a mosque where the mullah is connected to Hizbollah. Our guy called him for help. After we get him, we drive him to Langley and run him through a few hours of sensory deprivation. When that's over, he'll babble like a baby."

Reid looked worried. "What if he won't?"

Gibbs gave him a cold smile. "Then we do a chemical debriefing."

A look of horror shot across Reid's face. "Sam!

You know that's totally illegal. We could not act on anything developed that way."

"No, I suppose *you* couldn't," Gibbs agreed. "But we could. Afterward, we would simply sanction him and everyone in his organization we could lay hands on."

"That's cold, Sam. Sanction . . . does that mean what I think it does?"

Gibbs made a gun with one thumb and forefinger and produced a popping sound with his lips. "Yep, you've got it. There's no need to turn it all into a big media event that would work to the advantage of terrorist scum like this Fazoul."

"Wh-When would we grab him?"

Gibbs made ready to rise. "What say you pay for our coffee and doughnuts? I'll bring my Agency car around and we can do it now."

Even as familiar with the city as he was, being the Deputy SAC for the Richmond office, Mitchell Reid had never been in this part of town. He found himself a stranger in a strange land. Everywhere, he saw men wearing traditional Arab dress—long, flowing kaftans; *kafias* and *agals*; and huge, neatly trimmed beards with mustaches like Saddam Hussein's. Here and there young men in the uniform of Black Muslims—black suits and bow ties, snowy white shirts, and highly shined black lace-up oxfords—strolled down sidewalks and exchanged small talk with black business owners. Idly, he wondered what the brown-skinned Islamists thought of these emissaries of Islam in light of the fact that hundreds, if not thousands, of Africans were taken forcefully from their homes every year to be sold into slavery to some Arab imir, mullah, or Islamic warlord. Reid had another, most unpleasant thought. What if the Black Muslims knew what their Arab brothers did to their fellow Africans and didn't care? Whatever the case, he acknowledged, he was committed, and despite his misgivings, they were about to fall on one of these terrorists.

Gibbs pointed out the Sunset Inn, and they pulled into the parking area outside the office. Another plain, government sedan joined them, and two CIA domestic desk agents entered to learn which unit the subject occupied and to ensure that no one in the office warned the occupant. The manager claimed that no one of Arabic descent was registered. Yet when Reid came in and flashed his FBI badge, the short, swarthy Arab said there was an Achmed Jamal in Room 17. They all headed for number 17 on the ground floor of the motel.

Fazoul had only just returned from his repast at the *Garden of Allah*. He could still taste the flavor of mint-seasoned lamb, rich, nutty couscous, and crisp, sparkling sherbet. When the knock came, he assumed it was someone sent by the imam. He hurried over and opened the door.

"Saif Daoud Saddiq?" Sam Gibbs asked in a low, calm voice, still unaware they had caught a bigger fish than he had expected.

Odd, Fazoul thought, this one was a white man, an infidel. "Uh—yes, yes I am he."

Suddenly, strong hands grabbed him and yanked him outside the motel room, while two men pointed pistols at him. Peripherally, Fazoul saw the bright glint of sunlight on distant glass, and then he felt a something strike his forehead. His head snapped back, body wracked in intense pain for a moment as it twitched and jerked violently before blackness swarmed over him.

"What the fuck!" Mitchell Reid yelled.

Gibbs took a quick look behind them, across the street, scanned the windows of the surrounding buildings there, and rejected them as the source of the bullet that had killed their only direct contact to Al Qaeda, then looked at a low hillside that rose about a quarter of a mile beyond. Some bushes vibrated violently, like the legs of the dead man, then stilled as the assassin hurried away from the scene of his kill.

"Oh shit!" Gibbs bellowed. "They got to him, took out their own man."

"But why would they do that? They didn't know about our operation, couldn't have. So why kill their deep-cover operative?"

Gibbs gave that some careful thought. "Mitch, I think this dude must be more important than we thought. He had to have screwed up big-time. He pissed off someone above him in the Al Qaeda chain of command. No doubt they had people watching, followed him here, and he got blown away for it."

"Why do you keep saying 'Al Qaeda'?"

Gibbs shook his head. "They're bad news, Mitch, ol' buddy, and we know this one was a member. If he's tied to the attacks out West on our special operators, we've got a real problem."

Reid looked blank. "So then why haven't we gone after them before now?"

A chagrined expression formed on Gibbs's face. "We tried to. But for some reason, every time we set it up, our beloved President refuses to go through with it. Don't ask me why. We at Langley have no idea." He looked down at the cooling corpse. "Now we're stuck with this dead man." He turned to one of his agents. "Ralph, get a meat wagon in here, quick, and let's take this one out without attracting a lot of attention."

The agent nodded curtly. "Gotcha, boss. Only, ah, I've got a feeling we are goin' to be found out damn fast."

Gibbs and Reid looked around to find clusters of the curious gawking at the pool of blood on the asphalt paving and the dead man. He spoke quietly. "Perhaps we should search the room, get us out of sight of these people."

Reid gestured and they walked inside, after the agent covered the body with a bedspread from the room. "How could we have screwed up so badly?" Reid asked.

Gibbs shrugged. "It's like I said earlier. Someone was watching this guy. They had orders, and obviously the necessary equipment to terminate him. Our arrival only accelerated their plans."

Their quick search of the room revealed a surprising thing. When Gibbs learned the actual identity of the dead man, he whistled softly. "This guy wasn't Saddiq. He's a big fish, all right— Fazoul Mahmoud Hamza. He's the cell leader, or was, at any rate."

"So, what do we do now?" Reid asked. "This is going to piss off my SAC mightily."

Gibbs produced a rueful grin. "Perhaps we should fall back and punt."

Rostov stared hard into the flickering flames in the marble fireplace of the seventh floor suite occupied by Comrades Youang and Han. He had learned that Han was yet another covert agent of the PRC in Taiwan. Their presence bothered him. He had hoped he'd satisfied Youang on the issue of nuclear weapons. Han took the initiative in asking questions, his voice holding the tone of censure.

"We are no longer seeking nuclear capability. However, we were not aware of your access to such marvelous modern weapons as these accurate, powerful missiles and their warheads. Why were we not advised of their availability?"

Rostov shrugged and knocked back his glass of vodka. "*Pahzahloostah sto grahmmahv vodkee tavo zheh sahmahvha.*" Another shot of vodka, please, make it a double.

The man had the capacity of an elephant, Han thought in consternation. *How could he drink so much?* "Of course," he said as he poured.

Rostov explained glibly, "You kept insisting on nuclear arms or the big rockets. I did not think you would be satisfied with these—ah, trinkets."

Youang took over. "I take it that they *are* available in quantity?"

Rostov smiled broadly and knocked down the double shot of vodka. He gestured with the empty glass to Han. "Another, please," he requested in English—which he would also use to facilitate this critical transaction—"and, yes, we have them in considerable quantity. Certainly we possess more than enough to meet your needs."

"How large an area does a single warhead contaminate?" Youang asked while Han refilled Rostov's glass.

Rostov hesitated, but acknowledged silently that he had to be candid or lose the sale. "If there is a wind blowing, then one shell will saturate approximately two hundred square meters."

Youang scowled at this revelation. "That is not very much."

"No, you are right about that," Rostov said dismissively. "What you must bear in mind is that the biological agent contained in these shells and spread over that size area is highly contagious and extremely virulent. Depending on population density and access to vaccines, the result from one shell could bring down almost everyone within a square kilometer." He smiled pleasantly at these arrogant Orientals whom he loathed thoroughly. "Does that reduce your requirements?"

Quickly, the two Chinese considered the limitations and possibilities. Formosa possessed an area of 13,885 square miles. It would be impossible to directly infect the entire island. They could, however, take out the entire city of Taiwan and destroy the military bases along the coast facing Kwanzeu and Guiangdong provinces. That would open the way for an invasion—couched, of course, by the American media and the politicians as a "humanitarian rescue mission."

Han spoke first. "I believe if you could provide us with a sufficient quantity of these self-propelled rockets and their bioagent warheads, it would suit our purpose."

"Consider it done, Comrade Han. All that is needed is to arrange a point from which to ship the merchandise, and a port to which to deliver it. And, of course, payment."

"Then we have a deal? We will be able to obtain these biological weapons?"

Rostov answered with lightness, colored by relief. "Yes, absolutely. We will provide you with a launch mechanism and forty rockets? Have your principals agreed on the fee?"

Han looked at Rostov. "Yes, as we understand

it, we are to provide you with $1,800,000. Not to worry, we have a free hand in making the financial arrangements."

"Excellent!" Rostov enthused. "Then we can proceed and finalize our transaction. Thank you, Comrade Han. I look forward to taking you to see your new arsenal of biological weapons."

After Rostov left the suite, he allowed himself a broad smile of satisfaction. This deal had gone well. He had grossly overpriced the product, but these Chinese could afford it. Yes, this would make him and all his close associates very comfortably rich.

CHAPTER 13

★ ★ ★ ★

2415/0230 ZULU
Mid June, 1997
3840 Jefferson Street, Alexandria, Virginia
U.S. Army Tactical Weapons Storage Facility,
Kolob Canyon, Utah

While FBI agent Mitchell Reid had worked to
mollify his superior's anger over the attempted arrest of Fazoul Hamza and their subsequent failure, Sam Gibbs and a forensics team from the CIA
examined the room that the dead terrorist had occupied. One of the discoveries they made was a
note in Arabic script with a name, date, and an address in Alexandria, Virginia. The name was Ali
Abdelseoud Mohamed, who was badly wanted by
the CIA for questioning regarding the attack on
the *USS Cole*. An Egyptian native by birth, he was
a naturalized U.S. citizen.

In preparation for confronting Ali, Gibbs took

along three other field agents in one of the CIA's Beechcraft Duke airplanes and they headed for the sprawling Virginia city. They landed in under an hour. A car from the motor pool at Langley waited for them. Gibbs directed the others to load their gear, and they headed for the Jefferson Street address. Seated in the front passenger seat, Larry Sanford perused a map and gave directions to Gibbs, who guided the car through evening rush hour traffic. No one else spoke. Due to congestion, the drive took a slow fifteen minutes.

Stunted, untrimmed trees masked the front of the house on Jefferson Street. Long, scraggly uncut grass and weeds had already turned brown in a yard that showed extreme neglect, and the windows were obscured by a thick coating of dust. To everyone in the CIA sedan, the place looked abandoned. Not so, though, Gibbs pointed out. Through a narrow beveled-glass pane in the front door he saw a weak yellowish light.

"Must be a twenty-five watt bulb," he guessed as he pointed it out to the others. "My bet is someone is there or is expected." He turned and spoke to a black field agent in the rear seat. "Ralph, we'll pull around the block and then you go up and check it out. Just about any cover story will serve, but say you're looking for an old friend who used to live in the neighborhood."

"Gotcha, Sam, though I like 'huntin' for an old girlfriend' better."

Gibbs shrugged. "Whatever suits, go for it, Ralph."

Fifteen minutes passed while Ralph Murchison scoped out the target address. He found no one home and no sign of anyone in back of the house. By the time he returned and reported, Gibbs had devised a plan.

"Okay, two of us go in by the back door. Justin, do you have your lock pick set?"

Justin Foster patted the inside breast pocket of his conservative colored blazer. "Right here, Sam. I'll have us in there within thirty seconds."

True to his word, Foster opened up the back door for Gibbs in twenty-eight seconds. They entered and the CIA field officer relocked it behind them. Gripping their weapons tightly, Gibbs led the way in a thorough search. He took a secure cell phone from his pocket and called Larry Sanford in the car. The agent answered at once.

"Yeah. What'd you find?"

"Not a lot, Larry," Gibbs said tersely. "Place is empty, but the fridge is stocked with fresh food and there's a tea set laid out, silver salver and all. It looks like someone is expected soon."

"So what do we do, Sam?" Sanford exchanged a glance with his partner.

"I'll wait here, Ralph and you two take up a place on the street where you can watch the front. Ralph will watch the rear. When someone shows up, we move in and take them."

"That'll work," said Sanford.

All of the CIA operatives settled down to keep watch, and hopefully remain undiscovered by the neighbors. Darkness had fallen before a chorus of dogs began to bank at one end of the alley behind the house. They fell silent when a dark form appeared in the backyard.

"Sam, we got at least one in-coming," Sanford declared into his radio.

Gibbs was determined not to blow this one. He spoke to the man in the kitchen. "Ralph, pull back to the living room with me. When he's all the way in and committed, we call in the others and scoop him up."

"What if there's more comin'?" the agent asked as he entered the living room.

Gibbs chuckled softly as Murchison entered the room. "That's why we call in Larry and his partner first. We'll tie them up and gag 'em, then wait for any others."

Sanford and his partner had heard the warning and slid low in the car seat while Gibbs and Murchison remained silent. When the two in the house heard footsteps on the back porch, Gibbs communicated his intention by hand signals, and Murchison moved into position to get behind their visitor as soon as he entered the living room. Gibbs felt certain that Ali Mohamed already knew that Fazoul was dead, but this might be yet another good-sized fish they could land. Both men tensed when a key rattled in the lock.

A hinge squealed as the door opened and the

visitor entered. He closed it behind him. Before he turned back to relock the door, he stiffened, sniffed the air in a determined manner, then flung the door wide, running out without closing it behind him. Gibbs cursed and hit the redial button on his cell.

Larry Sanford answered at once. "Yeah?"

"The SOB got on to us and ran like hell. Get around to the alley and check it out. We'll take the street and meet you at the far end."

"Gotcha, Sam. We're movin' now."

Everyone went into motion, Gibbs and Murchison exited the house from the front door and trotted to the sidewalk. They turned right and started toward the far end of the street, where they could clearly see the alley opening. From behind them the sedan roared to life, and they knew Sanford and his partner were on their way.

For all their abilities and experience, the unknown visitor escaped. Only Murchison offered a speculation. "I'm betting that since we eat pork and he doesn't, he smelled us. He looked a whole lot like Ali Abdelseoud Mohamed. That SOB is one handsome dog."

Gibbs's lament came loud and clear. "Yeah, and we missed him. He knows the area too well, and we missed one of his ways out. If he had a car parked somewhere, he's history. Odds are, the bastard will show up somewhere else in the world doing his dirty work. And it'll all be because we screwed up."

* * *

Darkness completely masked the terrain when two quad-ATVs with ultraquiet mufflers ghosted ahead of the convoy from SMD toward the back gate of the Kolob Canyon Chemical and Biological Warfare weapons storage facility. Mounted on each were two members of Blue Platoon. According to the plan worked out earlier that afternoon, their task was to be certain that the guard post was either empty or the occupants neutralized.

"No sweat," Kade Warner assured his new platoon leader, Lieutenant Shaun Daugherty. "I've been hunting game since I was nine years old. I can smell my quarry from half a mile away." It might have been a brag, but it came close to fact.

Shaun asked calmly, "Do you smell humans too?"

"I sure can, if they're Italians or someone who eats Southwest chow a lot. It's the garlic, you know."

No one laughed. They took him seriously. Now, Kade put his nose to good use and sniffed out the terrain around the wooded copse that extended out from the gate. He cut back on his throttle suddenly and braked to a stop. His head swiveled and he sniffed audibly.

"What is it?" Tyler Richmond asked. "Do you really smell someone?"

Warner nodded. "Sure do. There's someone out there, and there's more than one. We go in from here on foot. Bring the long-range rifle."

Fifteen minutes later the four members of Blue Platoon crept through the Douglas firs, the stunted *piñon* pines, and the whispering aspens. Slowly, the guard post came into view. Rockham was radioed and told about the situation they had discovered.

"Go ahead, Turquoise Two, do what has to be done," he replied. "Just make sure the door is wide open for us when we get there. This is Dorado One, out."

Dan Abel, automatic weapons man of first squad of Gold Platoon, peered out the square rear windows of the panel van he rode in. "There's sure a hell of a lot of difference between this place and the one on He Devil Mountain," he observed.

"You can say that again," agreed Fleming, the squad grenadier. "I'd hate it like all get-out if we were on a real op."

Ferber growled. "You'd damned well better think of it as the real thing, sailor, or I'll have your butt for a football."

Sukov spoke from the driver's seat. "You'd think we were on the moon, with all that pale yellow sand. It's almost white."

"Didn't you see the pictures sent back from the moon when you were a kid?" Tinsley asked. "The rocks were gray, like volcanic ash, and the sand white. A real scary place, you ask me."

Sukov's eyebrows shot upward. "And this isn't? From now on every time we get a runny nose or a sneeze, we'll wonder if it's from bugs inside this place."

"Are you afraid, Sparks?" Doc Tinsley asked, using the classic Navy nickname for an RT operator. For the Navy corpsman, the mysticism surrounding bacteria, viruses, and septicemia had lone since been dispelled.

Sukov shrugged it off. "Naw, not really, I'm just bitchin' a little. Germs and that kind of crap—I don't get along with them—ya know what I mean?"

Abel nodded enthusiastic agreement. "Yeah, I get you, Sparkie. We drop one of those things and it breaks open we're in some deep stuff."

Tinsley kept a poker face as he informed them, "Only that stuff don't smell like what you mean. A point in fact, it doesn't smell at all."

"Oh, wow! Doc, thanks ever so much. I feel so much better now," Abel answered sarcastically.

"Everybody keeps a T.A.," the voice of Chief Monday advised over the speaker unit of the radio set resting on the floor beside Sukov; a tight ass. "That supposedly unmanned guard shack at the back entrance is coming up any minute now."

A desert camo-painted pickup truck was parked beside the guard shack at the rear entrance to the Kolob Canyon WMD facility. A deep frown creased the forehead of Master Chief Frank Monday. "What the hell? We were supposed to find this place deserted."

Beside him, in the driver's seat, Ed Lutz, RTO for first squad, Gold Platoon, chuckled softly as he scoped out the situation. "I don't think it's going to be a problem, Chief. The guys playing point man took care of that."

"How do you mean?" Monday asked.

"There are four men lying in the back of that truck with riot handcuffs on their wrists and ankles. The guys neutralized the place for us and made sure no one would cheat. It's clear sailing from here."

Monday erased his scowl and beamed. "Cool, I like that. These guys deserve some brownie points for initiative. Keep it rolling, Sparks."

While the members of Gold Platoon drove directly to the bunkers containing the stored VX gas warheads, shell casings, and cases of detonators, Blue Platoon broke off and headed for the bunkers that had been identified the day before as containing stockpiles of small tactical nuclear weapons. This time it would not be low-level radiation they would be exposed to. Instead, their Geiger counters would be swinging dangerously close to the one hundred Roentgen red line. They conceded that there was nothing like that prospect to reinforce their pucker factor.

Daugherty, in the lead truck, kept a careful watch on both sides in search of any unknown roving patrol that might come upon them. Two men knelt in the foot well of the rear seat, windows open, weapons ready to take out any unexpected company. Kade Warner and radioman Kevin Wainer had rejoined Blue Platoon and Wainer kept Rockham advised of their progress. He also contacted Lieutenant Jorgensen of Green Platoon to get an overall picture of any enemy activity. Wainer was thankful that the state-of-the-art jamming equipment carried by all three platoons did not interfere with their own operating frequencies. Even better, he reflected, they sure did keep the other side in silent ignorance. He had barely finished a round of radio checks when his headset crackled.

"Turquoise One, this is Dorado One, over."

Wainer snapped back immediately, "Roger, wait one." He leaned forward and handed the mike to Daugherty. "It's the boss," he informed his platoon leader.

"Turquoise One here, whatcha got, Rock?"

"We're on site. What's your ETA?"

Daugherty made a quick glance out the windshield and made a calculation. "Say two minutes. We're just rounding the corner."

Rockham felt relief at this news. "That's cool, Dorado One, out."

A second later the Chevy panel wagon in which Rockham rode braked to a halt and the men spilled out the rear and side doors. Immediately, they began to silence the mechanical alarms with cans of quick-setting plastic foam. Behind them, the other vehicles stopped and disgorged their passengers. Quickly, the men of Gold Platoon fanned out and headed for preselected bunkers. Most of these would just be opened and tagged with tiny explosive charges—actually, electrically detonated M-80s, mere firecrackers—and packets of powdered chalk. Only from three bunkers would they take vials of actual VX gas. Along with them would go a representative number of M-55 Bolt rockets and their propulsion motors. At the forefront of his thoughts, Rockham visualized how Daugherty and the men of Blue Platoon would handle what they would face. He didn't envy them. Meanwhile, he had his own problems to solve.

"Okay, men, let's get in and get the job done," he told the platoon through their intercom radios.

Jerry Wharton was at a small dinner party in Fairfax, Virginia, with his wife, when the host's butler approached him discreetly. "Colonel Wharton, I am sorry to interrupt, but there is an urgent telephone call for you. You may take it in the library."

Wharton erased the frown that had come at the prospect of the interruption of pleasure with business. "Thank you, Stevens." He turned to his wife. "Please excuse me, dear, I have a call. I'll be right back." Then, to his host, "Sorry, Congressman, but it seems even *your* phone number is known to my boss. I have a call I simply must take."

In the library, Wharton dispensed with the formalities of any greeting. "Okay, give me the bad news."

A short pause followed, and then the distant speaker responded, "I wasn't aware it *was* bad news." It was Nathan Chambers, his deputy liaison officer.

Pressed by the exigencies of his present situation, Wharton all but snapped at his immediate subordinate, "C'mon, Nate, what the hell is it?"

"You asked to be advised when our boys were in the playpen," Chambers returned, conscious that neither of them was on a secure, encrypted telephone. "They went in ten minutes ago. Estimated time for extraction is fifteen minutes from now. Oh, and not only are the Roman candles the real thing, so are the luminous watches, just like we were told."

Live VX gas and nuclear weapons, Jesus! Wharton thought, once more deeply worried about the safety of the SMD teams operating in Utah.

"Not to worry. There are at least twenty layers of cutouts between us and our boys in the field and the people who make critical decisions on what intel we set."

Wharton had to snicker over that. "You've certainly found a way to overcomplicate a statement about everything going SNAFU."

Chambers laughed with his boss. "Yessir, and it sure fits this situation. Are you going to prepare some sort of intervention or protest, sir?"

Wharton considered this a second. "No. I don't think it will be necessary. Let's just let our guys shove it up the 'wiser than thou' gang's arse."

Pleased at that image, Chambers answered at once. "Count on it, sir. It's no secret that some of the big brasses—with offices on the other side of the Pentagon—are trying like hell to screw our boys and you. Let them explain away a huge success." Chambers left it at that.

"Jeez, will you look at those," Pete Wilkes said in an awed tone.

Swiftly, the men of first and second squads of Gold Platoon spread out and took test samples from the hollow warheads that contained the VX gas. Every sample came back positive and highly volatile. The squads quickly carried out the second part of their assignments. Ten of the heavy M-55 rockets, complete with warheads, were carried out and placed in the padded beds of several pickup trucks. They covered them with tarpaulins and layers of dirt taken from black plastic trash bags. The little squib charges and their bags of powdered chalk came next, placed in strategic locations around the breached bunkers. Cautiously, they secured the doors and moved on.

They knew what the next set of bunkers contained, and it made the SMD operators nervous as they headed for the bunkers that contained plague and anthrax cultures in refrigerated vials waiting to be loaded. None of these would be moved, only rigged to show the SEALs had been there. Within half an hour, their work was concluded, the two squads had returned to the vehicles. The other squads, which had provided local security, joined them.

Meanwhile, Blue Platoon went about the same sort of activity among the nuclear storage bunkers. They progressed even more cautiously than Gold Platoon. After all, if one of the tactical nuke warheads got ruptured, they would all die. Not at once, but slowly and horribly.

Kade Warner marked half a dozen nuke warheads designed for fitting on the nose of submarine-launched Trident and Tomahawk missiles. In several bunkers, they left markers to indicate they had been there. Always the joker, Kevin Wainer left behind a neatly lettered sign that said "Guess what, you've all been stolen."

When everyone reported back and the two platoons made ready to withdraw, the men breathed a long, communal sigh of relief. Their relief was premature.

A bright beam from a halogen spotlight washed over the vehicles of the two platoons, making black silhouette targets of the heads and shoulders of the occupants of the SUVs, vans, and trucks. "All right, no one moves. You are covered by weapons with live ammunition. Drivers, get out of your vehicles. Do not attempt to run."

His orders to the intruders ended suddenly in the soft *plops* of paint balls bursting on his body.

The other guards opened up with their own weapons. Green Platoon had come through, but not without some damage. Two men went down, chests splashed with red dye.

Greg Rockham breathed a huge sigh of relief. "Sorry, guys, it's all over. You're all dead. Now be nice and keep quiet while we withdraw from the scene, then go find a hot meal and a cold beer. You've just been invaded by the SEALs of Special Materials Detachment One." With that, the explosives men of each squad pushed the buttons on their remote detonators and triggered the planted charges. "Good night, gentlemen, I hope you sleep well."

Rockham and his men made a hasty departure. Laughing aloud, they left behind some exceedingly disgruntled Army guards, who fully realized what sort of chewing out they would receive. Their security unit commander summed it up for all of his men.

"Beaten by a bunch of damned swabbies. We'll never live it down."

CHAPTER 14

★ ★ ★ ★

Colonel Bryce Simmons sat behind his desk, a huge smile on his face. The hotshot SEALs had gotten in, right enough. But they hadn't taken a damned thing out. He had made a cursory survey of all departments. Everything remained untouched, except for a few guards. So he'd lost some gate guards and a security patrol? That was only, what—seven men? That was more a nuisance than a threat. His inflated ego blinded him to the possibility that all was not indeed okay. Simmons leaned back in his swivel chair.

He reached for his huge thermal coffee mug—decorated with the silver eagle emblem of a colonel—when the phone rang. His clerk informed him that it was the colonel from the COS staff, Wharton. Well, he'd have a few things to say to Wharton about his boys' failure. Grinning, he punched the button for line three.

"This is Colonel Simmons. Do I have the pleasure of speaking with Colonel Wharton?"

Wharton chucked heartily before answering. "Yes, you do. And boy, do I have the horse laugh on you."

Irritated, Simmons snapped, "What makes you think that?"

"It's simple, really. The SMD boys got in and took out everything they were supposed to. Your security sucks, Simmons."

"Nonsense," Simmons barked. "Your SEALs got in here, all right, and they did take out some of our security force, a couple of gate guards, four men in a patrol. But they could not have taken anything but dummy rockets and empty projectiles. Everything here is secure and locked as per the SOP. Besides," he bragged on, "it is impossible for them to have penetrated the multiple layers of the most sophisticated security systems in the world around the live warhead storage."

Wharton's soft, mocking laughter irritated Simmons even more. "Have you checked your security systems lately?"

Suddenly suspicious, Simmons frowned. "What are you getting at?"

"They got by every one of your warning systems. They got in and took out samples of VX and a couple of nukes."

"Bullshit!" Simmons thundered. "There's absolutely no way that could happen."

Again Wharton's chuckle grated on the distant colonel's nerves. "Go out there now. Especially check Bunker 2331. Then check the rest of them, if you like. *But do it now.*" Wharton added forceful emphasis.

Silence followed as Simmons considered it. "All right, I'll call your bluff, and then I'll have the last laugh."

Wharton's voice was droll and dry. "Oh, by all means, please do."

Morning brought a more sober outlook to the men of the Special Materials Detachment. The question on everyone's mind: why had it gone wrong at the end? Had they been sloppy? Two men dead was an acceptable combat loss, but they prided themselves on everyone coming back alive. The incident brought home to all of them the harsh realities of their chosen profession. Then there was the matter of what they had taken out of the facility. Bryant stared in consternation at the lead-lined crate resting in the back of one pickup truck. "Exactly what in hell are we supposed to do with this?"

Chief Monday looked at it also. "You mean the nukes?" They were packaged two to a crate. "We take everything back later today. At least that's what the old man says."

"We done good, huh, Chief?" Bryant asked him.

"You bet we did. Blue Platoon's guys are no slouches either."

Bryant looked at the nuke once again, wrinkling his nose. "Why can't we unload it now?"

Monday grinned. "Rock will have to make a call to the CO of that outfit and ask when he'd like his toys back. I'd like to be able to hear that conversation."

Daugherty approached with a worried expression. "Maybe not, Chief. If that colonel gets pissed off enough, he could charge us all with some sort of violation of nuclear security regulations. I have no desire to face a court-martial hearing."

Silently, the others agreed. Then Rockham, who had overheard their discussion, approached. "Not to worry, guys. Even Marcinko wasn't given a court-martial." He turned to Daugherty. "That's actually one of the fake ones, isn't it, Shaun?"

A rueful grin spread on Daugherty's face, along with a flush of embarrassment. "Yes, sir. I made sure that one of the practice weapons was taken. Only problem is, we rearranged things so Colonel Simmons doesn't know it."

A fuming Colonel Simmons, dressed in his chemical warfare suit, approached the indicated Bunker 2331. It contained, he knew, VX gas warheads. At his direction, a sergeant tapped out the numeric code on a key pad that opened the locked door and then pulled it wide.

"Better wear your gas mask, Colonel," he suggested.

Simmons disdained the suggestion. "They'd never release any of that in here."

His prediction proved correct—to a point. They soon found the spray of chalk dust that indicated the bunker had indeed been breached. Simmons gritted his teeth until a sound like rocks in a tumbler came from his closed lips. Growling, he moved on to one of the nuclear storage bunkers.

"I've got the Geiger counter, sir," his sergeant offered.

"Never mind," Simmons snapped, his fury escalating.

In close to a march tempo, Simmons boldly entered the bunker. A second after his eyes adjusted to the dim light, he stared in consternation, his jaw sagging. There, sitting in an empty space where a nuclear warhead had been, he found a bottle of the famous "Bad Frog" beer.

"What the bloody hell is that?" he bellowed, a shaking finger pointing to the offending beverage.

"Begging your pardon, sir. It looks like—ah, it looks like a bottle of beer. Sir."

The partially underground bunker formed an imperfect echo chamber, yet sufficient to create an eerie Doppler effect as Simmons bellowed in defeated rage, "Those baaastards!" He did not yet realize that this was only the least of what had gone wrong for his side.

Part of the baggage carried around by intelligence agents or deep-cover active terrorists was insipient paranoia. Ali Mohamed was no exception to this fact of life. He saw FBI agents and CIA operatives everywhere as he made his swift escape from the safe house that had become a death trap in his eyes. Always prudent in making preparations for a hasty departure, Mohamed had secure lockers in the airport terminal, the bus depot, the Amtrak station in downtown Alexandria, and three rental storage rooms. He headed for the nearest of these at once, for he realized he would have to completely change his appearance. Not only would he need a change of clothing, but his skin color would also have to be altered, likewise his hair. Everything he required he had stored in a small, attached, shedlike rental space.

Too bad he would have to abandon so many weapons. Most of the lockers contained handguns, and one held an unassembled SVD sniper rifle with PSO-1 telescopic sight and a long, bulky suppressor in place of the standard bayonet and flash hider. Maybe he would take that along. The long-range capability might serve him well. The ideal thing, of course, would be to escape this country and return to Egypt.

In fact, there were events forming with Al Qaeda in Yemen and Sudan that might well call for his abilities. He considered the cost of a normal airline ticket and dismissed it. If he went, he would have to go the same way he came—slow but safe travel on a Liberian registry freighter captained and crewed by his brother Islamists. They would hide his weapons and anything else he brought along.

Mohamed approached the long building with the garage-style, full-front overhead doors and a people door cut in the middle of each. Carefully, he examined the tell-tales he had put in place to determine if the door had been tampered with in his absence. They were undisturbed. From one pocket he fished out a key he had not thought about for at least six months.

He closed the door and locked it behind him before turning on the overhead light, then glanced around the room, inventorying the contents. To his relief, it remained exactly as he had left it. He crossed to a cabinet and opened the tall doors. From inside he took out a self-illuminating makeup mirror, a choice of male wigs, and a theatrical makeup kit. These he put on a low shelf along one wall and drew up a chair.

He removed his shirt, trousers, and shoes, then gave himself a critical examination in the long mirror on the inside of one cabinet door, evaluating what clothes would be most suitable. He settled on a pair of carpenter's jeans, a V-neck T-shirt, and a lightweight, flannel, long-sleeve outer shirt. Quarter-top work boots joined his other selections. From a chest nearby he extracted three more merchant seaman's costumes, this time two pair of white, long-sleeve shirts and black trousers as well and a dirty, scuffed duffel bag. After packing his new persona in the sea bag, he turned to altering his appearance.

First to go, Mohamed decided reluctantly, was his lush, luxuriant black mustache. Next went the Elvis Presley sideburns. An electric razor hummed to life and did its job on his face. He followed up with a closer cut from a straight razor. Now was time for the heavy duty work. The terrorist chieftain took an extra large jar of Nadinola skin lightener from his makeup kit and liberally applied it to his face, neck, arms, and chest. While he waited the requisite time to remove it, he worked on a laptop computer with an Arabic keyboard and font. He worked industriously to contact his superior in Al Qaeda. His e-mail message to Ayman al-Zawahiri was tersely to the point.

"I need to come in out of the rain. Everything is much too hot over here. Please advise. Ali."

After he posted the message, he went on to contact yet another ranking Al Qaeda leader. To Wadih el Hage—bin Laden's personal secretary—he sent a longer, more detailed message: "Tell the prince that our operation here is compromised. The FBI is looking for me and they have penetrated our safe house in Alexandria. I must return to my native Egypt at once. One man failed utterly in his assignment, lost nine men and was taken

care of on my order. I am unable to expose myself
in such places as banks; I will draw the maximum
from my three ATM accounts, but will still need
funds to return to Cairo. Please ask the prince to
authorize travel expenses for me to cover passage
on a friendly cargo/passenger freighter. By the
mercy of Allah, I remain your loyal servant, Ali
Abdelseoud Mohamed." Both messages had been
sent on a secure, encrypted line.

That accomplished, he removed the skin light-
ening compound from his face, arms, and chest.
Satisfied with the image in the mirror, he did the
necessary contortions to do the same with his
back and his legs below his jockey briefs. As the
chemical went to work, he produced a bottle of
silver-gray hair color and went to work on his
short-cropped mane of black hair. He had rejected
a wig. Perhaps that would come later. First, he
bleached his shortened locks with peroxide. He
rinsed thoroughly to remove any latent bleaching
agent, then applied the dye that would transform
him into an older, distinctive man with silver-gray
hair. When dressed, he could pass as a chief purser
or some sort of seagoing occupation. After clean-
ing off his back and legs, Mohamed set about creating false papers for himself.

"Who shall I be?" he asked the otherwise empty
room. "Perhaps I should be a Frenchman? Perhaps
I become one from the South of France. That would
account for the slightly darker complexion. Those
poor fool Americans. They have no idea of the con-

nections between the French and the Husseins, or Osama bin Laden. If they found out, things would not go well for the French." Mohamed stopped abruptly, aware that he had been talking to himself. That was an unforgivable sin for someone living an underground life. *But then,* he thought, *to whom else would it be safe to speak?* A tinkling sound from the built-in speaker of his open laptop summoned him.

"You've got mail," the inane AOL message in Arabic read on the screen. Could he not escape the banalities of the cursed infidel Americans even in the sacred language of the Prophet? He stroked a key, rolled the built-in mouse, and the message appeared.

"Do come home at once, all is forgiven. The Doctor will tend to your injuries."

It was not signed, but Ali knew the identity of the sender. Al-Zawahiri was frequently referred to as the "Doctor." So, he reasoned, there would be a place for him in Egypt. He'd have an assignment, some important mission. He needed that to wipe the taste of failure from his mouth. He would contact the Liberian shipping line at once.

Frownlines formed on the forehead of Chief Monday as the truck bearing the "borrowed" WMDs approached the main gate at the Kolob Canyon Storage Facility. "D'you think this Colonel Simmons is a poor enough loser to have us arrested for what we did?"

Rockham saw no need to spare his senior chief's nerves. "Well, we *did* steal weapons of mass destruction," he said, "including a pair of nuclear warheads, albeit simulated ones. That offense alone could get us thirty years in Leavenworth. That these items remained in the hands of U.S. military personnel is merely a formality. Simmons is a stuffed shirt. Worse, he's a political animal promoted to his position by the President. Given the current climate in Washington, it's not surprising he was rewarded rather than punished. He's a sour, vindictive, petty little man whose wife left him six years ago and took him for nearly everything he had."

Surprise and puzzlement appeared on Monday's face. "How do you know so much about him, Rock?"

Rockham smiled. "It's all part of 'cover your ass,' Chief. Once you get beyond JG in this man's navy, you learn to be nimble and quick on your feet in order to survive. It wasn't always that way, but it sure was in the seventies and it sure, by God, is now. In our business it pays to extend that caution of insider knowledge to officers of the other services, if at all possible. As it happens, I have friends in high places, as well as low, and when I learned who commanded out here, I did some checking. Taking a nuke bothered me too. That's why we took just practice rounds and let him think otherwise."

Monday was suitably impressed. "Wow! Here I

thought the chiefs' coffee mug network was good at those sorts of things. So the odds are he's going to raise hell, sir?"

"Count on it. But in the end we've got the right hole card. So if he does, I have some ideas that might work." Rockham looked up and gestured to the closed, barred gateway—something that hadn't been in place before that morning. "Check out the increased security, Chief. I doubt it will stop us, but it is amusing."

In ten minutes, Rockham and Monday stood before the desk occupied by Colonel Simmons. "Lieutenant Commander Gregory Rockham and Senior Chief Boatswain's Mate Monday reporting, sir."

Simmons scowled. "You don't salute a superior officer?" he growled.

"If you'll permit me, sir, let me remind you of your course on military courtesy. Naval personnel *do not* salute inside a building or within the bulkheads of a ship."

"So noted," the disgruntled colonel mumbled. "Now, where are my weapons?"

Rockham smiled. "They're right outside, sir, in our truck. We're ready to return them."

Simmons half rose, his mouth twisted into an ugly slash. "My men will handle that. For some reason, I don't trust you two."

"Hey, begging the colonel's pardon, sir, but if Chief Monday or any of my men or I were untrustworthy, we could have made a righteous amount of money selling the whole lot to some terrorist organization. I'm sure Hamas or Hizbollah would love to have them to use on Israel. Not to mention those lunatic Iranians, or the scumbags in the Philippines."

Still not satisfied, Simmons charged, "You seem to be well-versed on geopolitics, Commander."

Rockham shrugged. "It's our job to know the enemy. We're special operators, sir."

"And you stole my weapons." Simmons seemed determined not to let it go.

"Yes, sir, that was our job. It's sort of our final, final examination, in a manner of speaking. From now on we do it for real with the enemy, not against U.S. forces. Only I probably shouldn't have told you that, sir."

Simmons continued to be belligerent. "Your candor may not be enough to save all of you from paying dearly for this little incident."

Rockham shrugged that off. "Well, sir, as it stands now the only ones who know about this incident are Admiral Cromarty, our intelligence liaison Colonel Jeremiah Wharton, my men and yours. I'm certain none of the aforementioned will be talking about it. So, consider this, sir, and please don't be hasty . . ."

Rockham paused as though to marshal his thoughts. "Do you actually wish to turn this over to JAG and have the whole thing explode on the front pages of the *New York Times*, the *Washington Post* and the *Los Angeles Times*? None of these newspapers are kindly disposed to the military, let me point out. When they get done with you, you'll look like an incompetent idiot who cannot be trusted with our nation's most deadly weapons. And what about us? We'd no doubt be elevated to the ranks of such bold adventurers as Saladin and Robin Hood."

Simmons's chest swelled with a deep inhalation and his face grew ominously dark red. Would he have a stroke? A coronary? Both possibilities occurred to Rockham before the colonel finally answered. "I think . . ." He hesitated, then went on, "I think you deserve a reprimand for allowing your personnel to be exposed to the most deadly substances known to man. The slightest leak of the nerve gas alone could have killed all of you."

"Yes, sir. We were all well-aware of the situation. If you will permit me, let me take you out to our truck."

"What for?" Simmons snapped.

"That's where everything we used has been stored."

Out at the curb, Monday gestured to the back of the covered three-quarter-ton pickup. Simmons held back a moment then looked inside. He saw the protective chemical suits, the plexiglass-fronted helmets, a box of atropine autoinjector sets, gloves, boots, Geiger counters, dosimeters, the works. He had to struggle not to reveal how impressed he was. When he regained control, he spoke with reserve, his authority ringing in his words. "It would be expedient if the weapons were returned at once to their proper storage areas and the whole incident forgotten by all concerned." He sighed heavily. "Likewise, I would consider it advisable if you made an apology for your men's conduct in spreading chalk dust all over the other storage bunkers."

For the first time since entering the office, Rockham produced a broad smile. "Done and done, sir. Outside of those who need to know for our—ah, graduation, no one will ever hear a thing about this. If there is nothing else, sir, we'll take our leave." He snapped off a crisp salute this time.

Rockham and Monday left behind them a humiliated, sputtering Colonel Simmons. *To be outsmarted by sailors*, his mind raced. *Sailors, for God's sake!*

CHAPTER 15

★ ★ ★ ★

His pin-stripe Seville Row suit in sharp contrast to the drab garb of the other denizens of the popular bar on Victory Street, Aleksandr Victorivich Petrenko sipped at his *Chateau Santé Marc* VSOP cognac and waited for the man he had contacted to arrive. Gold-edged Cyrillic letters spelled out the name of the establishment GYERBYEEROE SGO'EYAHA, Heroes' Bar in English. Would the American be able to find it? The question came naturally to Petrenko. He had come up the hard way. In childhood he'd been skinny and gawky, a target of the bullies in school, and considered not too bright by his teachers. Not until he reported to do his mandatory national service in the army did he begin to blossom. He filled out, developed muscles through the usual regimen of the soldier and through a voluntary program of lifting weights. As a senior sergeant, he had participated in Olympic weight-lifting for the USSR. He had come away with a bronze medal and a burning desire to achieve even more in his closed world.

He attended Officer's School, and thanks to excellent tutoring by a friendly fellow candidate, managed to graduate third in his class. His absolute, doctrinaire belief in communism ensured his rapid promotion. All he needed to do was avoid stupid mistakes, kiss the right ass, and scowl as though the burdens of the entire world rested on his shoulders. Was it cynical? "Hell yes," he said aloud honestly. He had always remained rigidly honest with himself. He believed it was the only way to succeed and remain sane. When the Soviet Union collapsed, he found himself totally at sea. But not for long.

Using his experiences with brutality and murder in the KGB's *Mokkrye Della*, Petrenko shot, stabbed, and poisoned his way to the top of the suddenly revitalized Russian organized crime syndicate. Fighting dirty came as second nature to the tall, thick-muscled man. Now, the dulcet notes of an unseen balalaika player soothed his raw-edged nerves. He hated to have to do what he was about to do. Russians should remain loyal to Russians, he believed, yet this man deserved a lesson he would not forget. Perhaps an outside agency could accomplish the task cleanly and not reveal the involvement of his vast *Mafiya Simyou*, his mafia family.

While weighing the benefits of this, Petrenko looked up and affected a smile he did not feel. His guest had arrived. Then, Petrenko did a totally uncharacteristic thing. He stood up and extended a hand to shake in greeting.

"Ah, Mr. Frazier, I believe," he began in Russian. Then, for the benefit of his visitor, he added in English, "I am pleased to meet you. You are welcome here."

"Thank you, and how are you today?" Frazier responded in Russian. Petrenko's left eyebrow rose slightly, revealing his surprise at the American's flawless Moskovite accent.

To the mafia chieftain's delight, they continued their conversation in Russian. "I am very well, thank you," Petrenko replied. "Please, sit down. Will you take a cognac or tea?"

"Tea, please, if you don't mind. Perhaps some *petrovka* vodka later on," he added with a quick smile.

Petrenko uttered a sharp bark of laughter. "A man after my own heart, I like that. Napoleon brandy is a bit, as the French say, gauche for this time of day, so I shall have the *limonaya* vodka, and then, after we have ordered, we can talk seriously." He gave a sly wink. "I take it you are not actually the cultural attaché at the embassy."

"Oh, but I am. My parents were absorbed by opera, and I am a chess champion in my own right. When I was a small boy I sang in the chorus at the Metropolitan Opera. I can hold my own with foil or epée, and I studied the classic and renaissance painters in Paris." He made an elaborate shrug. "So you see, I am truly qualified to be a cultural attaché."

"My goodness, I am impressed. But your actual job is with the, ah . . ."

"As an ally, you may have a need to know. It's true that I do work for the Company. That is, however, more of a sideline."

Despite himself, Petrenko produced a shark-eating-fish smile. "Yes, of course."

They ceased speaking while a waitress in a black pleated skirt, lace-edged white blouse, and Mary Jane shoes approached and took Frazier's order. Both men remained silent until the drinks had been brought. Then Frazier touched on the cause of their meeting. "Your associate—or perhaps I should say employee—informed the ambassador that you desired to speak with us. May I inquire into what it is you wish to discuss?"

Petrenko sighed heavily. "Not unlike great nations, our association can be plagued from time to time by those who seek to not live by the rules. These, er, renegades persist in flaunting our civilized conduct for successful business."

Frazier feigned surprise. "What is it you are saying? I understood that you—ah, gentlemen had a foolproof solution for such situations. 'Screw us once, shame on us, screw us twice and you get whacked.' Isn't that about the way it goes?"

After a long swallow of lemon vodka, his gusty answer came. "Yes, that is the usual way. However in this case the one who has—how you say?—screwed us, has associates too powerful for us to handle alone without subjecting our association to unwanted government attention. Perhaps if your agency were to aid in the disposal of this man and his soldiers, it would be of mutual benefit."

Intrigued by this circumlocution, Frazier asked, "How do you see it in such a light?"

"Because this particular gentleman poses a potential—let me say an *actual*—threat to your nation and to your ally, Israel. He is a dealer in illegal arms and not too particular about whom it is he sells to. Further, some of my business associates have discovered that this former captain in the Spetznaz is planning on selling certain biological weapons to some worthy Oriental gentlemen who constitute a very real danger to the government on Formosa."

Frazier had to smile at the Russian mafioso's use of the old British Empire colonial period name for the Chinese, usually rendered as an acronym: WOG. He quickly regrouped his straying thoughts and spoke with ill-concealed urgency. "Do you have any solid proof of this? We would need to see documentation."

Petrenko shrugged in a typical Russian manner.

"What can I tell you? Surely you know that businessmen such as me and my colleagues are shy about committing anything to writing?"

"I quite understand," Frazier said. "If this is as threatening as you imply, then it would follow that we need something concrete to base any action upon. To operate openly within your country would require the cooperation of your government. To do so covertly would invite their extreme displeasure."

Spreading his blunt fingers on the white tablecloth, Petrenko sighed. "Our president, as you know, was once in the *Komitet*, as was I. I feel that it would not be difficult to obtain his approval for your people to take direct action against Captain Rostov."

"How direct?" Frazier wanted to know, fearing he already knew the answer.

"We are talking wet affairs. I'm sure you know the term."

"Oh, yes," Frazier admitted. "But we are all supposed to be good little boys and girls now and not dirty our hands with that sort of thing."

Petrenko chuckled softly. "And do your people always abide by these new rules?" He watched Frazier's eyes and saw him squirm a little. "I thought not. Neither does our new PGB—our Russian State Security. Odd how some things change so rapidly yet remain so much the same, eh?"

Frazier nodded agreement. "So, assuming what you say is correct, do we get any bona fides?"

"That, I think, you will have to develop for yourselves. You must understand that I cannot expose myself to a lot of public scrutiny. Were I to provide you with some documentation from some of Rostov's associates, would that suffice?"

"Yes, certainly," Frazier replied quickly.

"Well, then, excellent. If your government chooses to act on this information, please be so kind as to advise me. Otherwise, we shall probably not see one another again. Enjoy your pepper vodka, it is one of my favorites."

With that, the mafia kingpin rose and, clasping his gloves and homburg, departed.

"Da-a-a-ady!" young Matthew Rockham yelled gleefully when Gregory Rockham arrived at the low gate in the white picket fence—something that he had always considered a cliché—that surrounded his comfortable home. His wife Sharon stood in the open doorway, a dish towel in one hand.

"Greg? My God, Greg, why didn't you let me know?" she asked, her voice strained.

Passing through the gate, Rockham produced a huge grin as he inspected the copper-haired beauty he was lucky enough to have as his wife. Surprisingly not-so-small eight-year-old arms wrapped around his left leg and he surrendered to an old ritual, even though Matty had grown entirely too big for it. With feigned effort, Rockham continued toward his wife.

"Sorry, hon," he told her. "We were only told that we had completed all our training late yesterday afternoon and that we would be given leave as part of the graduation from the RC school." He could not even tell his wife that *RC* stood for Rick Marcinko's Red Cell. *What a hell of a world we live in as special operators*, he thought as he dragged his equally auburn-haired son toward the boy's mother. At last, he looked at and spoke to Matt.

"Hey, champ, you're gonna have to let go so I can climb the steps and kiss your mother."

Matty made a typical young boy's face. "Ugh! Kissing an' all that stuff. Do you *really* like it, Dad?"

Rockham chuckled. "You bet I do, at least when it's your mom." He ruffled the boy's longish hair and inspected the emerging plethora of freckles across his high cheekbones and nose. "Have you been standing behind a cow eating bran, Matty?"

Puzzled, Matty looked up adoringly into his father's face. "Huh? What's that mean?"

"Oh, it's an old joke my grandfather often told me. I won't go into the details."

Sharon responded, her initial shock and surprise fading. "I certainly hope not. He's already acquired an extraordinary vocabulary of four letter words. No need to give him encouragement."

Rockham embraced his wife. "You're sweet, button nose, d'you know that?"

"Greg!" she squeaked, embarrassed. "Think of the neighbors."

"To hell with the neighbors," Rockham responded, then his eyes went wide and he put a finger to his lips. "Oops! I forgot about the kidlet here. But seriously can't I kiss my wife if I want to?" Then he grinned mischievously.

"You can as far as I'm concerned, unless the feminists complain."

"Who?"

"We've had a couple of rabid feminists move in since you left for Colorado."

That surprised Rockham. "Two families?"

"No, dear, they live together. They bought the Kimbrel house."

Rockham groaned. "So we're stuck with them, eh? Did you take them the usual casserole?"

"I tried, but Butch told me Jane was not receiving that day." Sharon giggled. "Come on, let's don't just stand here. How long are you going to be home?"

"I don't know. We were given two weeks' leave, but I think that's someone's pipe dream. There'll still be station-keeping duties at the office."

"Whatever the case, I'm glad you're here." Sharon leaned close and whispered in his ear. "I've gotten *very* lonely with you so far away. Maybe we can have a party tonight?"

"Hon, I'm not in the mood to see a bunch of—"

"A party without guests," she said.

"Oh! I see what you mean. Sure, nothing more important on my mind."

Laughing together in anticipation, the two walked through the house to the kitchen in search of a couple of bottles of cold beer, the little boy trailing behind. What, he wondered, did Mom mean by a party without guests?

Peter Danzig sat staring at the fax sheet that lay on his otherwise uncluttered desk. As Deputy Director of Operations for the CIA, foreign intelligence and espionage were well within his purview. The counterspies and spies who worked for the CIA received their orders from him, no matter how many cutouts existed between his workmanlike desk at Langley and the field case officers who received them. Danzig had held this important position through the administrations of three presidents; Reagan, Bush, and now Clinton. He had watched with a worried eye the systematic slashing of the budgets of the military and the intelligence services under the present administration. Even so, this remarkable communiqué from Moscow Central, following so close on the heels of the assassination of an Al Qaeda sleeper cell commander, showed that they were at least able to function in some parts of the world.

Who would imagine it? Aleksandr Victorivich Petrenko, Boss of all Bosses for the Russian mafia, actually making initial contact and providing information to the station chief for Moscow Central. Something like this just never happened. Danzig carefully reread the communiqué:

Target individual is identified by source AV as former Naval Spetznaz captain Grigoriy Mikhailavich Rostov. Rostov is believed to be engaged in the illegal arms trade, stealing many of his products from the less-than-efficient New Russian Army. Recently, the source states, Rostov has sought to obtain weapons of mass destruction for his clients. Field case officers from this station have managed to verify this, also evidence of an internecine war between Rostov's gang of ex-Spetznaz troops and the Russian mafia. Information coming out of Rostov's organization, provided to us by source AV, indicates that a mafia chieftain and his entire crew have been wiped out at Rostov's orders.

"Well, what the hell's wrong with that?" Danzig asked aloud. He went on to consider the implications. This so-called Russian mafia was powerful and getting more so every day. Taking out a couple of dozen of them would seem a plus. Yet if it were true, it implied Rostov's group had become even more powerful and ruthless. How could the Agency deal with that? More important, and to the point, the reference by the godfather of the Russian mafia to Rostov seeking WMDs provided the necessary independent verification to allow them to act against Rostov. He would have to pass the word to Wharton and Rockham at once.

Danzig reached to his intercom-phone set and pushed a button. "Lucille, get me Colonel Wharton at the Pentagon, please."

Lucille, who had spent her apprenticeship as a field case officer, had a sixth sense about critical operations. "Is something hot coming up, Chief?" she asked.

"Let's just say that a pot that's been on simmer has just been put on the front burner."

"Screw that metaphor, Chief. I'm about as domestic as doing take-out at Applebee's."

Laughing, Danzig cut the connection and waited for the ring-through. It came after only a minute's delay.

"Wharton here, sir," the voice on the far end of the line came to him.

"Good morning, Colonel. This is Peter Danzig over at Langley. We've uncovered an independent source for our bad boy's activities. Can you come over and discuss it?"

"When?" Wharton asked, mindful of his enormous backlog of unattended tasks.

"Yesterday would suit," Danzig returned, then looked at his Rolex. "But what say you make it an hour and a half and we can have lunch."

"Got it, Mr. Danzig. I'll be there at 1300."

When Wharton arrived, Danzig met him at the

door to his inner office. "Come in, Colonel. Here, take a seat in that recliner. We'll do business first, and then have the pleasure of lunch."

"Call me Jerry, okay?" Curious, Wharton asked, "Where do you suggest for lunch?"

Danzig smiled invitingly. "How about we go up to our executive dining room on the seventh floor? We can have a nice filet and cherries jubilee for desert. Jules, our wine steward, will have the perfect wine for each course."

Wharton's eyes widened. "Do you people eat like that all the time?"

A chuckle accompanied the rueful grin on Danzig's face. "Not likely, Jerry. More often the choice is Wendy's for a burger or a chicken salad, or delivery from Papa John's."

"I'm relieved. I thought my escape from institutional Army chow was the only one to include such emporiums of epicurean delight," he said, making sarcastic reference to the fast food places. "Now, what is it you want from me?"

"Something has come up in Russia that I think is right up the alley for SMD."

Wharton nodded. "And that would be?"

"It involves illegal arms sales and WMDs, a rather troubling sale in particular. We have received confirmation from a—ah, rather questionable source that our rogue ex-military types—Senior Captain Grigoriy Rostov, to be precise—is in possession of a certain number of biological weapons with the means for delivery and proposes to sell them to some unspecified Oriental customers."

Wharton leaned forward. "Do you have any idea who the customers might be?"

"I'm pleased to say we do have a line on them. It seems that one of our field case officers discovered that some rather unexpected visitors recently came to the Russian Republic. They are—and I hesitate to mention this—supposed to be deep-cover agents of the PRC. They are actually citizens of Taiwan—turncoats, we'd say."

"Jee-sus!" Wharton gusted out. "You've gotta be shittin' me. I thought Russia and China were traditional enemies."

Danzig shook his head. "It's only window dressing at the upper levels of government, I'm afraid. We in the Company have said it often enough, only no one is listening. But I digress. The main point is there are still enough old-line Marxists in Russia to provide a friendly atmosphere for agents from the People's Republic of China."

Wharton shook his head. "I'll be damned. I thought we were the only ones who knew the Chinese were asshole buddies with the old Bolshevik types. But, you're serious? This involves bio-weapons?"

"That's what our contact told us."

"Would I be out of line to ask who that might be?" Wharton asked, pressing his luck.

Danzig smiled boyishly. "Oh, I *could* tell you."

"Yeah, I know, but then you'd have to kill me."

Danzig raised one hand from his desk, palm
out. "Nothing quite that drastic. In fact, since
your people might have to contact this individual, need-to-know dictates that I fill you in." He
drew a deep breath. "Our source is Aleksandr
Victorivich Petrenko."

"I don't believe it. He's the biggest kingpin in
the Russian mafia."

"That's why I say it's not entirely reliable. After
the little war between Rostov's Spetznaz buddies
and the mafia, it might be that Petrenko is only
trying to get us to do his light work for him."

Wharton frowned. "But if it's true, then every
nation on earth could be embroiled in another
world war, thanks to Rostov."

"My thinking exactly. I believe we have no
choice but to send in at least one platoon of the
SMD to find out, and if necessary, to stop it."

Wharton seemed to have shrunk into himself.
"And I have to concur. I'll get on the horn to
Rockham right now. He's not going to like this.
He and his men are only four days into a two-
week leave."

Rockham's cell phone and pager went off at the
same instant. "Rockham. Speak to me." He received the call the same afternoon on the golf
course at the O Club at Little Creek Naval Amphibious base. He had Matty along—the boy had
his cut-off set of clubs—and was teaching his son
the fundamentals.

"This is Jerry Wharton, Rock. Got a little job for you and your boys."

"Meaning?"

Wharton's response was cautious. "Are you on a secure phone?"

Rockham glanced at the pager and saw that it was the number for his office. No doubt Wharton had called there first. "No. I can be to one in twenty minutes."

"Do it. This is a priority one. I'll call in exactly thirty minutes." He ended without any closing salutation.

Which means, Rockham thought, *that the fit has hit the shan.* He spoke with genuine regret to his son: "Sorry, champ, but Daddy's got to go to the office for a while. We can continue later or maybe tomorrow."

"Daaad, this was supposed to be *our* day."

"Yep, but duty calls. Do you want to ride along with me in case we can finish our game after I find out what this is all about?"

"Yeah, Dad, yeah. I *miss you sooo* much."

Rockham barely seated himself at his desk when the phone rang. Wharton came on the line and explained the situation, then said to stand by for a call from someone at Langley. Peter Danzig handled that part himself.

"You guys are on immediate alert for a mission. Notify your personnel, and prepare to go into isolation by 0600 hours tomorrow. Your destination and the mission parameters will be given at your isolation site. If you will need the use of aviation and naval assets as well, you'll have 'em. That is being taken care of as we speak."

"Can you give me some clue as to what our mission will be?" Rockham asked.

"Sorry, that will have to wait until you go into isolation. But I can tell you it will be the biggest operation your people have taken on so far."

After Rockham cut the connection with Danzig, he thought of Matty, standing beside his desk. "Son, you'll have to go out and talk to Yeoman Murray for a while, okay?"

Matty shrugged and spoke in a matching soft tone. "Sure, Dad, but why?"

"I have to make an important call, son."

Matty grinned, wrinkled his freckled nose and skipped toward the door. "Okay, Dad, I'll go. Are we gonna finish our golf game?"

Rockham grinned back. "Bet on it, champ."

Rockham knew he had twelve hours to notify the members of his chosen platoon for this mission. He amended that order to include a backup platoon. This time, the often left-out Greens would go. He initiated the automated call system that would dial each platoon member's phone numbers and deliver the message he dictated to its voice cartridge. He would have to leave for the isolation cage at Little Creek well before midnight. From there, only God and the CIA knew where they would be headed.

CHAPTER 16
★ ★ ★ ★

Agents Han and Youang of the People's Republic of China were meeting with a new arrival, Chang Shee Tung. Chang bore a remarkable resemblance to Mao in his earlier years. Some in the government believed him to be the illegitimate son of the legendary leader. Now, they all sat in comfort in the delicate, Nicholas II era, white-painted cushion chairs, covered with heavy blue silk with wide red stripes, with white and gold. They drank strong tea from a large silver samovar on the sideboard and cast occasional glances out the tall, lead-glass windows. Lace curtains had been restrained by cream-colored velvet bands with gold hooks and fasteners, while drapes in the colors of old Imperial Russia graced the sides. The topic of their conversation was the tremendous success of Han and Youang in obtaining biological weapons.

"Let me assure you, gentlemen," Chang Shee advised them. "Your cover as 'super patriots' remains intact, as does mine. Some in the Beijing government consider all of us to be a bit extreme, but they applaud our efforts toward terminating the arrogant independent nation state on Formosa. Every day the politicians of your homeland talk of terminating any connection to Greater China. Secession would result in immediate invasion by our motherland, but then, face it, who wants to deal with over three and a half million people who have been conditioned to the concept of freedom?

"Your defection to our cause is in the finest tradition of Chairman Mao. It is likewise most timely. When an attack seems to come from the People's Republic, the army will retaliate, of course. Yet the best part is that, by significantly reducing the population, there will be little resistance and the problems our troops and administrators will face will be insignificant. When our *benevolent* medical personnel make available an antidote, the people will welcome us with open arms. That medication the People's Republic will only share with those Taiwanese willing to embrace the political necessity of realliance with the Mainland."

"You amaze me, Comrade Chang," Youang declared as he sat down his teacup. "Here we are on the verge of initiating a bloody, violent conflict between Taiwan and our motherland on the Mainland, yet you do not turn a hair."

"What is to worry about, comrade? With the transfer of Hong Kong to our nation imminent, the obstinate, pathetic holdouts will no longer have people there to rely on for support," Chang Shee riposted with a dismissive shrug.

Han joined in. "Yes, time is running out for them. Nineteen ninety-nine is not that far away. I feel it is providential, that you and Comrade Gao contacted and recruited us to serve the People's Republic. Otherwise we would probably die fighting a lost cause, one in which we did not truly believe."

Youang spoke slowly, a wide smile spreading on his face. "Now I clearly understand why it is that the People's Republic wishes to initiate hostilities at this time."

Chang leaned toward Youang and spoke in a conspiratorial manner. "Fortunately, the purpose for that is unknown to many. It all revolves around proper timing. For example, one of the terrorist organizations that the People's Republic—and the Russians—are supporting is about to launch a devastating attack on the United States, and it will surely paralyze them in regard to any actions directed our way."

Youang sighed, pleased. "One thing, however,

worries me, if I may? Is there not the risk that the Taiwanese army might procure some of the same sort of weapons and use them on the Mainland?"

Chang shrugged and produced a fleeting smile. "So? Gao and I are citizens of the People's Republic and the prospect does not bother us in the least. After all, we are nearly as overpopulated as the traitors on Taiwan. We could easily absorb a loss in our surplus population of say . . . ten to twenty percent."

His words disturbed Youang. "That is cold, Comrade Chang. Is there no room for compassion, no respect for elders, no love for children within the principles of communism?"

Chang's lips curled in contempt for the nature of the question. "Not much beyond the personal level of parents for their children, children for their parents. The way of Chairman Mao demands total dedication. On the Long March and for several years after, a great number of those unwilling to embrace the glorious truth of communism were, regrettably, eliminated. The same will have to be done on Formosa. The people of Taiwan are a thorn in the side of the Politburo. Simple as that, they must go anyway. Why not in a disaster that decimates the entire population?"

Han, usually the sour note of the pair of Taiwanese traitors, spoke up. "There is a possibility of the spores escaping and infecting areas outside Taiwan."

Chang smiled coldly. "It would be nice if it ran

rampant through the islands of Japan. There would no longer be bases for the cursed Americans then."

Han nodded thoughtfully. Until now, it was the close presence of the American military that had forestalled the People's Republic from invading and destroying the Taiwanese government. "That might not be in China's best interest," he suggested.

"And why not? It will take so long for the Americans to come after such destruction that they will simply turn their backs. It is particularly likely when we take into account the lack of principle and truthfulness on the part of their President."

Han continued his opposition to his superior's point of view. "There is no doubt that the use of weapons of mass destruction could bring the United States into the conflict on the side of its traditional regional ally, Taiwan. Such an event could usher in the next world war."

Youang smiled depreciatingly. "But consider this: the use of biological WMDs is particularly suitable for the high-population areas that are so common in our part of the world. Like us, all of Asia is critically overcrowded. Even if our initial release of the anthrax does not reach there, Japan will be particularly terrified of bioweapons being used on it by the People's Republic, especially if they believe it was China that attacked Taiwan. Let me remind you that the Japanese Unit 731 conducted such attacks against the Mainland during World War II."

Quickly Han interjected, "Yes, and they would be expected to put pressure on the United States to aid Taiwan. After all, Japan's interests would be immediately at stake in the face of such a war of reunification."

Chang interjected a stern reminder. "Remember what I said earlier about a terrorist attack on the homeland of the Americans? From what little we have been told, it will leave their financial network in gridlock, terrify the common people, and open the door for further attacks. Such a situation would destroy their will to fight if it happens soon, and prompt them to seek conciliation, if not outright surrender. Would that not keep America from any direct involvement?"

"True," Youang agreed. "Yet it would be advantageous to keep civilian deaths on Taiwan minimal," he ruminated aloud. "The good news is we will just 'happen' to have our own containerized shipment readily available in my Taipei warehouse when required. It consists of ample supplies of ciproflaxin and other prophylactic medical materials."

Their roles changed, it was Chang who made objection. "But will not the government seize this supply for the protection of the population?"

Youang replied with a lighthearted smile. "Yes, we can count on that. But the government cannot take this *privately owned* cache of medical supplies without adequate reimbursement for the shipment. Accordingly I expect to be more than generously paid, not to suffer the loss of such a valuable and timely commodity."

Uncharacteristic of his usual demeanor, Chang applauded this revelation. "Excellent. You surely haven't enough for everyone, so we will issue ours mainly for propaganda value. Please to have your container of supplies ready at least three days before the weapons arrive. Good work, both of you."

Captain Reigel Davis, recently appointed commanding officer of that portion of Naval Special Operations that contained the Special Materials Detachment, met for half an hour with Greg Rockham prior to the briefing session for SMD personnel after they had gone into isolation. In the meeting, Davis revealed that the chosen platoons—he readily accepted Rockham's assurance that two platoons would be required—would be briefed after they had something to eat and settled down.

"A midnight snack is being provided for the men, but sans the cold beer you all would have enjoyed at the Iceberg," Davis told him with a smile. "Oh, I know your favorite watering hole. Sounds like a good place to me," he added parenthetically. Then Davis concluded the advance briefing with a question. "Are you ready to go for broke on this one?"

"You've got it, Captain Davis. We're worried

about growing rusty with nothing but practice operations. It's time to get our feet wet again," Rockham declared.

Captain Rostov received the phone call half an hour after he returned to his hotel in Moscow, the Palace, which was even more opulent, if possible, than the Metropole. So far as he was concerned, living high was part of the persona that an arms dealer had to assume in order to be convincing to the customers.

"Yes. Speak to me," he demanded.

"Comrade Rostov, it is I, Mr. Youang. How are you this fine day?"

As usual, Rostov had little use for the refinements of Chinese conversation. His response was predictably curt. "If I am not mistaken, this is the same day on which we met several hours ago."

Only mildly irritated at the rudeness of this *quai lo*, Youang continued in a calm voice. "We have met with our principals and it is decided. We would like the full forty items you described to us. Also, we require the means to distribute them and their contents."

Billions of rubles spun in Rostov's head. No, he thought, make that hundreds of millions in American dollars. "That is excellent, Mr. Youang. Let me congratulate you on the wisdom of your decision."

"Thank you, comrade. We have only one question. Is there any way to test the efficacy of the nostrum that we will obtain?"

Rostov considered that for a moment. "I regret to say, Comrade Youang, that—"

Youang interrupted him. "It is vital that we know what we can expect."

"Comrade, I was about to explain why it is impossible to do as you wish." When Youang remained silent, Rostov continued. "Except under the most cautious, highly controlled conditions, it is not safe to use any of that substance for any reason whatsoever."

Youang's voice sounded strained. "That is your final decision?"

"Yes. I regret that it must be this way, but surely you understand. It will not affect our doing business, will it?"

Youang, who had the call on the room's speaker phone, glanced to the Black House agents, who reluctantly nodded approval. They knew they *had* to have the anthrax or the plan would fail. After a long delay, Youang replied to Rostov's question. "No, it will not cause any problems. I will contact you later at your hotel or in Novosibirsk when we can complete the transaction. And now, I bid a good day to you."

Rostov turned to his former senior lieutenant. "We should have destroyed the wretched Chinese and subjugated those who survived when we had the chance," he declared hotly.

Ivan Tsinev wrinkled his brow in curiosity. "What have they done now?"

"Nothing new, Ivan, they are just being themselves. They make the Gypsies look like rank amateurs when it comes to haggling. They wanted a test of the anthrax, can you imagine that?"

Tsinev's eyes twinkled. "And of course they would not be troubled by a few thousand Russians dying—is that not so?" Tsinev said.

"Oh, that's quite so, my friend—and the main reason I refused. They are still going to buy, so we can look forward to the flat-faces killing themselves off with a few liters of anthrax spores. Something I will anticipate with considerable excitement."

Tsinev frowned. "But won't that cut down on potential customers?"

"So what? There are plenty of others. Keep in mind the Philippines, Indonesia, bin Laden in Afghanistan, the Iranians, Sudan, even Libya now that they are under an arms embargo by the United Nations. Too bad Saddam Hussein is provided for by our generals, for he would make a great customer."

While Rostov and Tsinev gloated over their sale, Captain Davis stood at a podium, hastily erected in the small hangar inside the tall wire fence of the isolation area, before the assembled members of Gold and Green Platoons. He used three carefully positioned seventy-two-inch projector TV screens hooked up to a computer. Using a remote control, he employed a PowerPoint presentation to emphasize the salient portions of his briefing.

"Gentlemen, we have recovered a great deal more about your target. We might as well start at the top. This is Senior Captain Grigoriy Rostov. I am aware that you are familiar with this particular bad guy, but let's review for the sake of accuracy." On the screen, a class photograph appeared, revealing the graduates of the Naval Officer Corps of the Soviet Military Academy. Circled in white was the likeness of a handsome young man of medium height, relatively thin, yet with an athlete's muscular build. It was his eyes that riveted the attention of the assembled SEALs. Cold and haunting, the gray orbs seemed to glisten with malice.

"This is Rostov at his graduation from the Military Academy. And here." He keyed the remote and another photograph appeared of an officer in the white turtleneck, blue jumper, and trousers of a naval officer. Over the blouse was the typical wide lapel coat, but instead of the usual white "flying saucer" black bill hat, the subject wore a blue-gray beret with the insignia of the elite Spetznaz force. This snapshot revealed a marked reduction in the amount of jet-black hair Rostov kept closely cropped, and the addition of a thick, neatly trimmed Stalin-style mustache. Davis continued, "As you know, both the Soviet army and navy had special operations troops designated as *Spetznaz*."

Again the scene changed, this time portraying

Rostov in combat gear, his face notably older, deep lines around his mouth and across his forehead. He and three others, with parachutes back and front, wearing the soup-bowl-style gray and black Russian airborne helmets, stood ready to board an aircraft. Davis's narration continued. "Naturally your target is airborne qualified. His records indicate he had over 350 jumps, with an additional three rated as combat jumps in Afghanistan. He is also an expert marksman, a capable pilot, and qualified on Soviet-style scuba gear. The Agency has also discovered that Rostov was for a long time an intelligence officer with the Northern Fleet Intelligence Directorate's Third Division, as well as his assignment to Spetznaz. Despite his age, Rostov has kept himself in excellent physical condition." A recent photograph appeared, taken no more than a year earlier. "Taken all together, he is one dangerous SOB. He has just passed the age of forty-five and is believed to have surrounded himself with former Spetznaz operatives, all of whom are the best of the best the old Red Army ever produced."

"Sir, who's paying all of his troops?" asked Shaun Daugherty.

Davis clicked to another slide on his PowerPoint production. "We have very little information on that. Suffice it to say that he charges enough for his product that he can afford the payroll without external aid. It has been reported by our source that this is a loosely knit organization, with only six or eight full-time followers in Rostov's . . . call it a gang. They work at whatever job they happen to have and report for duty with Rostov whenever required.

"That, as you can see, obviously gives Rostov an enormous advantage in managing his criminal enterprise. He only has to pay them for each specific job they do."

"So that's the whole deal with him?" Rockham asked, clearly expecting more.

Davis took a deep breath. "That's it for now, Commander. We're awaiting further intelligence on Rostov, but until then, we go with what we have. Very well, we've come to the mission parameters. You will depart for the target area later this afternoon When you reach the near vicinity of your AO, you will go into residency accommodations at the nearest U.S. military installation to the target area. From there you will have a choice of conventional aircraft or helo for insertion. Preferred insertion method is either HALO from aircraft or slick line from semistealth choppers."

"Where will we be when we do this?" Rory Parker of Green Platoon asked.

Davis seemed almost blasé about it. "You'll be landing at an airfield somewhere in Romania. The exact destination will be radioed to your pilot after you refuel over Spain. From Romania you will go to the target area in one of the manners I described earlier."

"And where will that be?" Henry Limbaugh prompted.

Davis replied in an offhand manner. "Perhaps somewhere close to Novosibirsk in the Lower Siberia area of the Russian Republic. That's where Rostov is supposed to have his headquarters. Or near to where the shipment is believed to be departing from. You'll be advised of that location while in transit."

The SEALs eyes opened wide and eyebrows rose at this revelation. "Son of a bitch!" exclaimed Larry Stadt. "Why don't we just invade a nation relatively friendly to ours?"

Davis spoke with dry sarcasm. "Mr. Danzig at CIA and I doubt greatly that we would send you guys to kick ass in England or Canada. We might employ you in France, of course, or Germany, since there are a lot of Muslims in those countries, with terrorists among them, as seen by that bombing at the beer hall in Bonn. But we wouldn't commit you against our true allies anyway. Russia is in a state of flux. They haven't yet stabilized their government or the military. Things are pretty much in a condition of chaos. Organized crime—the Russian mafia—is into everything and has a death grip on some business enterprises. If it weren't for this Rostov screwing with some of the mafia's top people, we probably would never have learned of this until the stuff had been used."

Quinn of Green Platoon spoke up. "Exactly what kind of 'stuff' are we talking about?"

Davis didn't look pleased with the question, but he knew he would have to tell these guys the whole story. By the very nature of their training, SEALs had to be above average in intelligence. They would never buy the old line of "Just follow orders." He pressed his lips together and made a hesitant reply. "It's the same strain of anthrax that the Soviets produced back in the eighties. It is incredibly deadly and easily disseminated. In aerosol form, it is easy to spread over vast areas. Only a couple of spores are enough to infect a person. There are probably 150,000 lethal doses of anthrax in an aerosol container the size of a shave cream can. The weapons-grade anthrax in powder form can also be loaded into the warheads of small, easily transported and stored rockets, such as the 120-millimeter BM-21, or the BM-24, a 240-millimeter rocket system, and the obsolete BM-25 250-mm rockets. They have ranges respectively of about 21,000 meters, 11,000, and 30,000 meters. Given a country as small as Luxembourg, Sri Lanka—or Taiwan and Israel—and you can see it wouldn't take a hell of a lot to totally depopulate the country."

"Jesus," Jay Hunter of Gold Platoon breathed out, more than suitably impressed. "And this guy, this Captain Rostov, is going to sell some of that crap to some sort of terrorist bastards?"

"We do not know for certain exactly to whom he intends to sell these deadly bioweapons. Only that he is in the process of finalizing a deal."

"Do we stop the deal or do we stop the shipment?" Rockham asked, always quick on the uptake.

"Neither right away. First we want to verify who is involved on the buyer side and to what extent they will go to get what they want. We also want to stop the shipment at sea, before it reaches its intended operational area."

Rockham offered a protest. "This is all so . . . up in the air. Can't you give us more specifics?"

Davis paused, his gray eyes sweeping over the assembled SEALs. "Sorry, but that's the best I can offer you at this time."

"What specific weapons will we carry?" Rock asked.

"You should plan on taking your usual range of small arms. By that I mean your own personal sidearms, at least two sniper rifles for each platoon, all weapons to be suppressed. Also, you will have a lot of highly sophisticated surveillance equipment, including long-range parabolic mikes, special vision equipment, clothing and makeup to provide level two disguises, and enough rubles to buy a whole lot of stolen Russian weapons."

Rockham nodded. "Sounds encouraging. Why the heavy emphasis on surveillance equipment?"

Davis smiled. "The Company wants more for its

bucks than a standard raid. While you are tracking down Rostov and whoever is with him, you can do a little snooping for the boys out at Langley. At least in theory that's what you can do. For my own part—and I imagine yours, Commander—you'll get damned little sneakin' and peekin' done. What Rostov and his people are playing with is far too dangerous to have you distracted by an information-gathering sideshow."

"Roger that, sir. There's no way I'll divide my people or be distracted by trying to find out how often some Russian intelligence type takes a crap. Let the Agency send their people to do that. After all, that's what they're trained for."

Davis smiled broadly. "I like the way you think, Commander. Now, as to your extraction, we'll have to wing that. If you succeed in carrying out the operation at sea, you can use your own transportation to get away. If not, there's always the Trans-Siberian Railway. I've heard they have a new passenger train that has a dining car with a *cordon bleu* chef. How many of your people speak and read Russian?"

Rockham didn't need to think about it. "Count on at least fifteen. Not all of them fluently, and some have a slight Brooklyn accent. But we have enough to get by."

"Okay, so worst case scenario is you go by train and get the hell outta Russia. You can change trains in Gorki and go right into Turkey."

Rockham finished his statement, "And get out from one of our air bases."

"You got it," Davis agreed, and quickly went into the remaining details.

CHAPTER 17

★ ★ ★ ★

Grigoriy Rostov hurled the glass, an antique from an early Romanoff czar's collection, against a wall in the sitting room of the suite. It shattered into thousands of shards. "I do not give a damn about any of the grandiose plans of these Taiwanese turncoats. Their cabal is meaningless to me."

He had been discussing their recent sale with Ivan Tsinev and Vladimir Frolik. Once again, the subject of their conversation centered on the potential consequences of allowing bioweapons to get into the hands of fanatics.

Tsinev spoke calmly, seeking to erase Rostov's anger. "Tell me, Grigoriy Mikhailavich, why could they not get such weapons from China, if this is indeed a plot by the People's Republic to foment an excuse for invasion?"

Rostov paced the floor, stopped at the sideboard and poured another thimble glass of vodka. "Of course, my dear Ivan Arkadyvich, China has chemical and biological weapons. So does North Korea. But every nation that produces such deadly and dangerous weapons has provided certain microscopic tags—tiny identifiers that reveal who manufactured any given warhead."

"So then," interjected Frolik, "they seek to cast all blame on Mother Russia for when their terrible mass murder is discovered and the source of contamination identified?"

Rostov smiled for the first time in a half hour. "Excellent, my friend Vladimir Konstantinich, I see you have figured it out. That is one major reason why I want to know nothing at all about these flat-faces and their plot. They can kill one another in wholesale lots for all I care. So long, of course, that I get paid for the case of rockets, the launcher, and the carton of anthrax powder in its vials."

Tsinev spoke up. "I agree with you entirely. But tell me, I strongly feel that there is something else bothering you."

Rostov cocked an eyebrow. "How perceptive," he jibed. "Our plotting friends from China want us to be personally involved in this madness. We are to install the launch rack on shipboard, of an anonymous freighter, and fire the rockets from there."

"And where will this ship be at the time?" Tsinev asked.

Rostov made a sour expression. "In the Promansa Strait," he said bitterly. "They want us between Taiwan and Mainland China and as close to China as we dare go. So it will appear the missiles were fired from the People's Republic. We will be like—how do you say?—sitting geese."

Tsinev asked, "Do they intend to pay us more for risking our lives like that?"

"No, and that is what makes me so furious." Then Rostov lost it for a moment. "*Yob, byashka datdaka!*" Then he repeated it, his anger not yet dissipated. "Fuck your mothers!"

Unruffled by Rostov's outburst, Frolik offered a solution. "It is simple to handle, Captain. We meet with them, we take their money, and we kill them. The bodies can be dumped in the Volga or the Riga estuary. Let the sturgeons dispose of them. They should make tasty caviar."

Tsinev made a face. "That is disgusting, even though I never developed a taste for caviar."

Rostov looked surprised, although he felt relief from the rage that had been boiling inside him. "You were an officer of Spetznaz and you never liked caviar? For shame, I must devote time to educating your palate. Now, here is what I think we should do." He paused dramatically, then laid it out in detail, concluding with, "And then we tell them we cannot and will not deliver the rockets, the launcher, and the warheads unless and until they provide an additional fee for us to actively engage in the operation. When we pull this off, we can be assured that we will all have enough money to leave this business and retire, if any of us wish to do so."

"Yes, good, I like that too, Grigoriy Mikhailavich," Tsinev responded. "We should do just that."

Droning engines outside the pressurized hull in the passenger section of the C-141 Starlifter produced a soporific effect on the occupants of the abbreviated passenger deck of the huge transport. Eyes drooping, the SEALs of SMD slouched in their military-style bucket seats, their three-point safety harnesses in place and tightened securely. Down below, on the huge cargo deck, their Zodiac insertion boats and inflatable small boats—dubbed IBSs—waited. The twelve-foot-long, six-foot-wide IBSs weighed in at three pounds, and SEALs everywhere despised every ounce of them. In fact, the only concession to comfort was that all of their gear was also stowed below. Out the port and starboard windows, the members of Gold and Green Platoons saw nothing but blue sky, puffy clouds in the far distance, and, if they leaned close to the bulkheads, the glassy blue-green surface of a restless Atlantic.

Greg Rockham returned from the galley compartment aft on the passenger deck. "Relax, guys, it's going to be one hell of a long trip."

A relative newbie among the personnel assigned to Green Platoon spoke up. "When are we gonna refuel, boss?"

"Bean, weren't you listening when the pilot told us all about the flight?"

Andrew Bean blinked. "No, sir, I guess I wasn't." He flashed a boyish grin. "I always consider that chatter a lot of boring bullshit and snooze through it."

Rockham affected a scowl. "Well, mister, that crap doesn't work on a *military* flight. You always listen close, Bean, real damn close. Your life might depend on knowing where the emergency exits are, where we can strap on chutes and jump off the rear cargo ramp."

Looking chastened, Bean offered another question. "Are the flyboys going to serve mess or do we have to get our own?"

Rockham gestured with the thick rare roast beef sandwich in his left hand, his voice heavy with sarcasm. "Does this look like a love letter from your sweetie?"

Platoon Chief Reynolds chimed in, "Yeah, virgin, there ain't any mess deck on this here airplane."

Bean's lower lip slid out in a swift pout. "I ain't a virgin, Chief. I broke my cherry two years ago on that op in Thailand."

Reynolds's eyebrows raised closer to his receding hairline. "You were on that hairy operation? Jeez, that's some heavy stuff. Did you take a hit on that one?"

"Nope, I came out without a scratch. And I did three more ops after that. But hey, Chief, you've seen my personnel jacket. You should know all this stuff."

Reynolds blushed. "Yeah, yer right, kid. I just wanted the others to know you aren't some Nervous Nellie or a weak sister."

"Go grab something to eat, Bean," Rockham offered. "We've got to preserve our strength, right?" He winked broadly.

"Yessir! I'll do that, sir. What's back there?"

Rockham spoke lightly. "Just about whatever you'd want, Bean. The only thing we don't have is a couple of cases of that fantastic Alpine Brewery pale ale. Go for it, kid."

"Aye, aye." Bean disappeared aft.

A voice came over the intercom. "This is Lieutenant Colonel Holcomb speaking. We are half an hour away from the coast of Spain. Refueling will commence in forty-five minutes over the Med. Let me remind you that there is plenty of chow in the galley. Help yourselves."

"We know!" shouted the SEALs, most of them with sandwiches or cold fried chicken in hand. "Hooyah!"

Youang Fu Genn sat fuming as he and Han Dhao Ahn listened to Grigoriy Rostov's demands regarding their intended purchase. "Entirely out of the question," Youang snapped. "We are not—ah, what are the English words?—yes I have it, babes in the woods to be so foolish as to present you with a nonrefundable deposit on this purchase."

Rostov shrugged. The caustic words, intended as a sharp criticism, had not even bothered him. "I truly regret your obstinance, Mr. Youang." He turned to Han. "Surely you are a man with more exposure to the give-and-take nature of doing business in the outside world. As the owner of twenty *gohdowns* along the piers in Taipei harbor, you should be well aware of it. As a result of your business prowess, you are on a first-name basis with the governor general of Hong Kong. Your wife is a successful banking executive, as I understand. Your home is one of the former imperial palaces, and you employ two cooks and six other servants. Your children attend private schools in Switzerland. I would urge you to impress on your associate the necessity of being realistic. We are not in China. This is Russia, and we are now capitalists. And consider also, we have what you and your principals desire."

Han fought to keep his face impassive, shocked as he was by how much the Russian barbarian had discovered about his life. He tried to wet his lips, his mouth suddenly gone dry. He found it necessary to force the words from his throat. "Yes, of course. Comrade Youang is a university professor, truly a brilliant man to hold his position at such a young age. But like most academics he is totally oblivious to the—as you called it—give-and-take of the business world." He turned to Youang, leaning forward to emphasize the importance of his words. "Comrade, your dedication to socialism is pure, but you must be willing to defer to those who better understand commerce. It is my experience that although it is unusual asking for such a large, nonrefundable deposit, we are faced with a harsh reality—the law of supply and demand. We have an old saying born of wisdom; I am sure you recall it. 'Bend with the bamboo,' *heyah?*"

Youang gave him an irate look and uncharacteristically gestured in chopping, curt hand movements, speaking earnestly. "I can accept that in principal, but a nonrefundable deposit of fifty percent is totally beyond realistic consideration. Seventy-five million U.S. dollars is a figure nearly impossible to obtain. Even given two or three months, we will have difficulty coming up with the $150 million you are asking in total."

Rostov laughed softly. "Oh, my dear Mr. Youang, I doubt that greatly. I am certain the Black House has far more than that in readily available U.S. currency. I am equally certain that your Mr. Chang, their agent, can arrange to have that sum delivered wherever we designate. We have made suitable preparations for laundering the money you give us, using false names. So, if the government in Beijing and you gentlemen are so set on fomenting war with the Formosans, the money we ask will be forthcoming."

Moon-faced Han smiled contentedly at that.

"That is an accurate estimate of our intentions, Comrade Rostov. Yet, I find myself in agreement with my associate. Half of the total is a lot of money."

"Yet, according to you, your principals have agreed to the total price. Now, I have a further bit of news for you. If you wish a truly first-class result, then it is going to cost you another $700,000 for the seven of us who will do the job."

Youang all but exploded out of the chair. "No! We would not even dare ask for that now, in addition to the huge sum you have already demanded."

"Well," Rostov said with a shrug, "there it is. Either take it or leave it. And if you leave it, we will not participate in this operation of yours at all."

Youang and Han exchanged worried glances. Han saw the eyes of his partner waver. "Very well, we will ask for the extra funds," he said in surrender.

"Wonderful," Rostov enthused. "Then have the initial deposit ready to deliver five days from now. We must grease some noisy wheels in order to remove the missiles and the warheads from their present storage places." Rostov readily told this lie, since they already had what they needed, though the Taiwanese did not know it. "We will need to rent a warehouse, a *gohdown* to store the materials in. Also to make preparations for shipment when the transport vessel reaches the quay and we can begin to load."

*   *   *

Deep in the bowels of CIA headquarters at Langley, cryptographers busily worked to break down and prepare communiqués for the translators up on the next underground level. One, a fresh-faced young man, turned to his fellow crypto expert. "I can't believe the Russian Security Service is being so cooperative. I must have fifteen pages on this guy Rostov."

His partner, a sweet-faced, matronly lady with wide wisps of gray in her formerly rich auburn hair, smiled understandingly. "Oh, you'd be surprised how forthcoming they can be when it's in their own interests. Right now they are worried about traceable weapons of mass destruction escaping the country and getting in the hands of the fanatics. Too bad they're not so generous with information on this terrorist leader who is stirring things up in Afghanistan. They say he is training thousands of fanatic Muslim killers to strike all over the world." She paused a moment to take a sip from her mug of tea. "The Russians know them well from when the mujahadeen kicked them out of the country. If they wished, we believe they could provide us with valuable data on the internal workings of both organizations."

Her youthful fellow cryptographer shrugged. "I suppose I know about as much as anyone at Langley about the Taliban. Are they really just terrorists hiding behind the façade of a legitimate government?"

"Oh, yes," she told him without reservation. "And truth to tell, I don't think the Saudis are at all friends of ours either. Some of the intercepts I have seen—" She stopped abruptly, painfully conscious of the firewalls, cutouts, and need-to-know that governed the intelligence community.

Her partner turned back to his computer console. "Whatever, we've got work to do."

She nodded forcefully. "Yes, and we had better get to it."

Although they could not watch the aerial refueling from their seats, the SEALs knew it had gone well, as usual, and they were on their way. Where, exactly, they did not lnow, only that the first stop would be Aviano Air Force Base in Italy, to change into smaller aircraft for the flight into Romania. Senior Chief Monday summed up the thinking of many aboard when he addressed their staging area location.

"Hell, guys, it wasn't all that long ago that the Romanians were our enemy. They were part of the old Warsaw Pact. In fact, they were nothin' but puppets, and the Soviets called all the shots. There's no way in hell we coulda landed and set up a staging area for covertly entering Russia itself back then."

One of the new men in Green Platoon asked, "Will it be safe now?"

Monday chewed on that for a while. "It depends on several things. First, is where we'll be landing. And second, how the locals feel about us.

Best bet is to make certain no one even looks at a native, let alone talks to one. Third thing is how long we'll be there."

"We've gotcha, Chief," a couple of the old hands responded.

Another interruption came from the pilot. "We'll finish crossing the Mediterranean shortly. We'll be going by the French Riviera, so if you have some really good binoculars, you might catch a glimpse of some of those big-boobed French honeys cavorting naked on the beach."

"Yeah, right!" exploded five or six of the SEALs. Based on previous trips across the Med, the old hands were well-aware that the flight plan would keep them a good fifty miles off the coast of France. Fat chance that would give them to view any bare female flesh.

During the flight, Rockham and Pauli Jorgensen had been busy drawing up what would pass for an operations order, once they learned where and when the transfer of any WMDs occurred. Armed with the latest intelligence beamed by satellite to his laptop, Rockham began with a summary of what they knew.

"Thanks to the boys at Langley, we now know that the rumored transaction is real and already agreed to on both sides. The clients are believed to be malcontent Taiwanese who have gone rogue and allied themselves with the Communist Chinese on the Mainland. With the help of the Black House—the PRC intelligence service—they have devised a monstrous plot to foment war between Beijing and the government on Formosa. That will open the door to invasion and conquest by the People's Republic." Rockham checked the page of decrypted characters before going on.

"One of these traitors, Han Dhao Ahn, is incredibly wealthy, even by Western standards. The CIA discovered that his wife has family living in the PRC and most of his kids are in private schools in Switzerland. There's only one exception—his eldest son, a boy of seventeen, who became a drug addict. He started smoking opium, and graduated to heroin. The Taiwanese police arrested him when the boy attempted to smuggle a large quantity of opium, heroin, and cocaine into Taipei. He was tried and convicted, and is doing fifty years in a Taiwan prison. They take drug pushers seriously there."

"Okay, so we know why Han hates his own government," Jorgensen said. "What's the story on the others?"

Rockham scrolled down, read quickly, then replied, "Youang is a professor of political science at Taipei University. No surprise there, eh? The Agency believes he was the first one recruited by an agent from the PRC Black House. He has, of course, given glowing lectures on the brilliance of Chairman Mao. He also describes Marxism as the 'ideal political system—when directed by the intelligentsia elite—to govern the masses.' Frankly, I don't think it took a hell of a lot to recruit him."

"I'd say you got that right," Jorgensen opined. "What else have the spooks learned?"

Rockham frowned. "The control for the entire communist cell in Taiwan is Chang Shee Tung—believed to be the bastard son of Mao. He is a longtime agent of the Black House. He's dangerous, and he's far too intelligent for the liking of those who have crossed swords with him."

"Do the boys at Langley have any *good* news?"

"I'm afraid not, except NavSpecOps have cleared us to terminate Rostov when we find him. He is considered too dangerous to be allowed to run around free. And the Russians are corrupt enough to take a bribe to let him go. So it will be up to us to end his career."

Jorgensen grinned. "I like that. How do you see us going after him?"

Rockham pointed out the only sticking point in their planning. "It depends on which way he plans to take his stuff out of the country. If it goes by one of the Barents Sea ports, we go in by chopper, giving us a long ride north. If he chooses those on the Black Sea, we're going to be right on top of him."

"What about a Pacific port, like Vladivostok?"

"We'll have all of Russia to cross, and I don't like that a whole hell of a lot," Rockham remarked. "But contingencies are being made for that situation."

"What are those?" Jorgensen prompted.

"You know, Pauli, that's what pisses me off so much. Everything about this mission is cloaked in so much damned secrecy that our left hand isn't allowed to know what our right is doing. We won't know what is laid on for a specific operation until it becomes necessary to brief us on it."

Jorgensen made a face. "Pardon me, sir, but that really sucks."

Rockham chuckled. "You've got that right, sailor. You want the bottom line? Some of the big ticket people think we should not even go to Romania, that we should wait at Aviano until we know where we'll be headed. They don't like the idea of our chasing across half of Russia to Novosibirsk in search of Rostov. To be frank, I agree with them."

Jorgensen nodded. "And so do I. The idea of rubbing shoulders with a whole lot of former enemies doesn't sit well with me. At least at Aviano we've got friendly Italian air force dudes around us and a damn good officers' mess. The chow is incredible."

"I know. I was there often back when I was with the regular Teams. We had a number of ops originate out of there—Lebanon, Libya, once even into Romania to make a hit on Ceausescu's chief butcher. This dude was known to have tortured, raped, and murdered at least two hundred young women and girls—some as young as nine and ten."

"So, what happened?" Jorgensen prompted.

"We took him out with a long-range SR-700 Remington sniper's rifle, then moved in close, gelded his corpse and stuffed his nuts in his mouth."

"Jeez, that's cold, real cold," Jorgensen said softly.

"I trust it will go no further. The SEAL high command would not have approved. But when you think about some cute little button-nosed ten-year-old girl with rosy cheeks being ravaged by that son of a bitch, I'm sure you can understand why we did what we did."

Sobered, Jorgensen could only nod. After a pause, he asked for more details. "If we have to go into Russia after Rostov, what do we take along? We're packing a lot of sophisticated equipment that should never be at risk for falling into the Ruskies' hands."

"If we have to travel inside Russia, we can destroy any of the highly classified equipment. Keeping it out of unfriendly territory as long as possible is another reason I want to stay at Aviano."

"I'll certainly back you on that, Rock. Count on everyone else feeling the same way. At least my guys in Green will, when I get done politicking with them."

"Somehow I think I'll sleep better on the rest of the way to Italy." He stopped abruptly and returned to the initial subject. "Okay, Pauli, that's all

I know for now. I'm expecting a visit from our old friend, Jerry Wharton, when we reach Aviano."

"I hope he has more to tell us. It's plain suicidal to go into an op in total ignorance. I don't like that at all."

CHAPTER 18

★ ★ ★ ★

At 6:45 A.M. the phone beside the sturdy sofa rang. Ivan Tsinev groaned as the bell clamored for his attention, climbed from bed and padded barefoot to the living room to answer it.

"What is it?"

"Is this Ivan Arkadyvich Tsinev?"

"Yes, yes it is. Who are you? Why are you calling me?" Tsinev was agitated, since he had an unlisted number.

"This is Basil Sergeiavich Lubinov. You know me, Ivan Arkadyvich. I am a resident at the Odessa Women's and Children's Hospital."

Ivan brightened. "Yes, of course I know you,

Basil Sergeiavich. Have we not been friends for years? Did we not go to school together? It is good to hear your voice again. What is it you have called me about?"

A short silence followed, and a big sigh. "It is about your family. Your nephew, in fact."

Tsinev felt the color drain from his face. Little Josef Yurinovich Tsinev was the only other living member of his family. "Go on, Basil. What is it?"

Lubinov sighed heavily. "Josef took suddenly ill, Ivan. It was a virulent form of pneumonia. It is, unfortunately, one that moves so rapidly that it incapacitates a person within a few hours, and for which we have no cure. I am most sorry, old friend, but Josef died earlier this morning."

For a long while Tsinev could not answer. He could make no sound whatsoever. Tears coursed down his cheeks. He could not breathe. His knees buckled under him and Tsinev stumbled backward, falling into a chair. "My God. How could that happen?"

"We do not know. I hate to suggest this, but pending an autopsy, we can only speculate. It appears to have been the type of pneumonia that develops from exposure to anthrax spores."

"What in hell is this? Anthrax?" Tsinev bellowed as he sprang from the chair like a jack-in-the-box. "What the hell are you saying?" he repeated. Sudden terrible, chilling thoughts rushed through his mind. He knew that they had access to anthrax. Did someone else have it also? And why release it in Mother Russia? "Oh God, oh God, why did this have to happen to little Josef? Do you—if it is anthrax—do you have any idea of the source?"

Lubinov hesitated, conditioned by his service in the old Soviet army to be reluctant to reveal any weakness in the fabric of their *Rodina*. "Well, yes," he said. "I know of only one possibility. There was a small article about it in the local newspaper recently. There was a break-in at an old army storage facility. There were a large number of sophisticated weapons kept there, among them, chemical agents—VX, sarin, that sort of thing." Boris grunted his dissatisfaction. "They also had a large quantity of bioweapons. Among them were cases and cases containing vials of weapons-grade anthrax—do you understand what I mean? Our head chemist tells me the anthrax comes in powder form, which makes it easy to spread over a large area."

Overwhelmed with grief, blind for a moment to his possible collusion in this tragedy, Ivan Tsinev blurted out, "But how? How could Josef possibly have come into contact with it?"

Patiently, the medical expert, Lubinov, explained to his bereaved friend. "In its weapons-grade form, anthrax is a fine powder, an airborne contaminate. When the vials were stolen, at least two fell on the floor and broke. There was a wind that night; the spores could have blown anywhere."

"My God, where was this storage place?"

Tsinev asked, although he feared he knew full well. How had they missed any dropped vials? Why had none of them gotten sick? He realized, then, that Boris was speaking again.

". . . less than twenty miles from Odessa. The wind was blowing our way. They would have been scattered too far and too thin to have an effect in town. But I have learned that a group of scouts were holding a camp out gathering near the facility. They would have been in the direct path of the windborne pathogens."

A sudden, vital question occurred to Tsinev. "Have any of the other boys taken ill?"

"Well, ah . . ."

Tsinev yelled into the telephone. "Tell me, I want to know, I need to know!"

Ivan could hear the gulp from his end of the line. "So far, seven have developed anthrax-related pneumonia or other severe bronchial illnesses," Boris admitted sadly. "Two of them have also died."

Horror swept over Tsinev. For the first time in more years than he could recount, he felt an attack of conscience that threatened to overwhelm him. "I . . . see. Thank you for calling me, Boris. It is comforting to hear this from a friend, not some officious bureaucrat. I think I want to be alone for a while. Thank you again. When— When will the funeral be?"

"I will telephone you, Ivan Arkadyvich."

"I appreciate that. Good-bye now."

Alone in the silence of his apartment, Tsinev gave in to his raging grief. He cried, he howled, he moaned and beat his breast. Stumbling, he moved to a forgotten drawer and withdrew a sacred Russian Orthodox triptych, which he placed on the empty end table. Ivan quickly rushed to the kitchen to find a votive candle, then lit it and placed it before the three-panel religious icon. He knelt briefly and made the sign of the cross— backward, from the manner used in the Roman rite. "For Josef," he said softly.

Saddened beyond belief, he sat in a black funk and wondered how and when he, a young defender of the Motherland, had sunk lower even than a common mercenary soldier. Disgust rose up in him and he found himself vomiting the thin sour contents of his stomach, spewing it out over his chest and lap. *What had he done? What had he become a part of?*

Peter Danzig greeted Jerry Wharton when Wharton arrived at Langley in response to his summons. "Good to see you again, Jerry. I hope I didn't interrupt something important," he prompted with typical bureaucratic small talk.

Wharton's answer surprised him. "As a matter of fact, Peter, you did. Or at least starting about . . ." He consulted his three-dial, Omega aviator's watch ". . . ten minutes ago you did."

"May I ask what it is you should be doing right now?" Danzig smiled to show his sincerity.

Wharton spoke hesitantly. "You know that we're planning on expanding the Special Materials Detachment to something more like a Special Materials Battalion. I was scheduled to have a conference meeting with Admiral Cromarty and General McCallum from Army Special Warfare, as well as Admiral Victor Lyons, former Deputy CNO, and Captain Hal Hastings of SEAL Special Ops. I'm surprised you weren't invited."

Danzig cleared his throat. "I was and I am. They're delaying the meeting until we've had a chance to talk. We can go over to the Pentagon together."

Wharton relaxed. "That'll work for me. Afterward, we can hit that really cool Mexican restaurant you took me to. Now, what's so urgent?"

"In there," Danzig suggested, pointing to indicate one of the soundproof, certified bug-free briefing rooms maintained on the higher floors at the CIA. Once inside, he gestured to a chair, which Wharton took, and began speaking before grabbing a seat himself. "A couple of our cryptographers downstairs have come across some interesting information. Some of it was volunteered by a Russian security agency; other stuff came in the form of satellite intercepts."

Wharton found himself being blunt. "Meaning what?"

Danzig shrugged and made an open palms gesture behind the desk. "You already know about the intended sale of some WMDs? In sum and substance, there's been a recent theft of some small rockets—to be precise, a 122-millimeter BM-21 rocket launcher and a full compliment of forty rockets. There's no doubt that Rostov had his fingers in this disappearance."

Wharton lost his neutral expression in a scowl. "That confirms all we've heard so far."

"True, but when you add the fact that there have been some intercepts between their equivalent of our Centers for Disease Control and local health agencies in Odessa, it begins to take on somewhat greater importance. There have also been at least a dozen calls between officials at an elementary school on the outskirts of Odessa and several local hospitals and the public health authorities. In the 'new' Russia, media have not been kept completely in the dark."

Again Wharton looked concerned. "What bearing does that have on Rostov and his missiles, Pete?"

Danzig leaned forward, his words crackling with urgency. "The subject of all of those calls was anthrax. Specifically, a certain virulent form of the disease that the Russians are believed to have weaponized. Add to that a bit more military chatter between the commanding officer at a certain storage facility where chemical and biological weapons are stored and the same national disease control agency. The subject was a couple of stolen cases of anthrax toxin and the accidental breakage of a couple of vials."

"Go on," Wharton urged.

Danzig sighed heavily. "What it adds up to is our analysts—at least the experts on Russia and Russians—have put the anthrax together with the rockets and the launcher and got one hell of a headache for someone."

Wharton grimaced. "How dangerous was that spill?"

"Fortunately, it happened inside a bunker, and the 'theft' was discovered in only a short time. The bunker was sealed at once and decontamination procedures followed closely. But we'll have to accept that some of those kids at the school got infected; probably some died."

"Jesus, what do your Russian desk people say about that?"

"We're not posting odds just yet, but the prevailing opinion is that our boy Rostov is behind the theft of all this stuff. He's the only one we know of who's offering that kind of crap for sale."

Wharton pressed for more specifics. "Is there anything to suggest that this theft was a setup deal?"

"Oh, yes. The commanding officer at this facility—according to the Company assets who are in position to know the facts—is one Colonel General Sasha Voroshin. He is a big family man, with a reported eleven kids still living at home, all under eighteen. In the new Russia, such a family has to cost one hell of a lot of money. More than they're paying a mere colonel general, if he gets paid regularly at all. It could put him in tight corner."

"So it would not be impossible to offer him a handsome bribe to look the other way?" Wharton concluded. "Damn it! Where will Rostov take that crap? And when will he do it? Pete, I'm insisting that you find out, and do it yesterday. The guys have got to know what to expect and where to find it."

"You've got it, Jerry. I'll bend heaven and earth to get you the intel you need."

Wharton sighed with relief. "Thank you, Pete. We'll be grateful to you."

Aviano Air Force Base came as a big surprise to all of the SEALs who had not been there before. Andrew Bean's eyes widened in astonishment. "Why hell, this ain't anything but another U.S. military base."

"Wrong, buddy," John Sukov replied. "Only half the base is ours. The other half belongs to the Italian air force. And they've got the greatest noncoms' club. The grub is terrific. They make a pizza like you wouldn't believe." He referred to the fact that Italians did not heap three-quarters of a pound of veggies and meats on their original version of pizza. The dough was hand-tossed. After that the differences were marked. First the pizza crust was slathered with olive oil. Over that came a highly flavored tomato sauce with lots of garlic and sprinkled with a mixture of cheeses. If one asked nicely, the cook would add sliced mushrooms and Italian-cured olives. Meat was generally unheard of. Yet the influx of Americans had changed the style of the cooks at Aviano. All together, novice SEAL Bean was in for a surprise.

Their assigned quarters awaited them when the travel-weary SEALs entered the barrack. Neatly folded sheets and gray Navy blankets sat at the aisle end of each bed. Some of the more seasoned travelers among them headed to the Italian side NCO Club for dinner. Others waived dinner for sack time, falling fully dressed onto their bunks to snore away the jet lag.

Among those who chose to visit their Italian hosts were Shaun Daugherty and Pauli Jorgensen, with Greg Rockham declaring his intention to join them when his paperwork was completed. Chief Monday led the petty officers contingent. Many had been to Aviano before and had visions of succulent Italian dishes.

Left alone at last in the orderly room, Rockham sat at a small field desk and reviewed the information they had been given. The decisions were not hard to make. If they had to insert to take out the suspect weapons, and extract by way of the Barents Sea or the Kora Sea, then the IBSs would be used going in and out. They were big enough to carry all the gear and personnel required for the mission. And compared to the ones used in Vietnam, they were a whole lot faster. The present model could reach a top speed of twenty-five knots with a full load. One problem solved.

If they used the Black Sea, it would require the cooperation of the Russian government and the military. They could use the Zodiacs to go out, but entering by this means would be nearly impossible. One problem not solved.

That left Rockham with the Pacific option. Sea lanes were wide open, or helicopter late at night. Even going by submarine gave them an opening to enter Russia. If only Rostov chose the port of Vladivostok, on the sea of Japan, everything would be rosy for the SEALs. Think positive thoughts, Rockham reminded himself. This was another problem solved. Now for the next item on his list.

If the platoons had to travel any distance inland, transportation would be required. They could, of course, steal some trucks. Considering the chaos in Russia, it would be easy. But it would be better if they could be choppered in to wherever they needed to go. Rockham made a note to look into the possibility. Problem put on hold.

If Rostov managed to deliver his deadly cargo to an aircraft, they would have a hard time stopping it. Unless they hit before the plane took off. Another of his problems pending.

Then there was the prospect of Rostov beating them to the goal and shipping out by sea. A ship could be more easily identified and dealt with. Again, they would need to be on the ground and at the delivery site to make positive identification prior to taking action, but after that, easy money. Another problem checked off as solved.

Sighing, Rockham considered the required equipment. The simple answer was that the destination would dictate what the hell they had to take along. But SEALs were not trained to be satisfied with the simple or easy answer. Their mindset was to take the complex and turn it into the simple. What could they take and not invite the wrath of the Russian government?

Since their sniper rifles were Soviet-made 7.62mm SDVs for this operation, there would be little to worry about. A smidge of forethought would tell them to take along either AK-47, 7.62 assault rifles or the more modern AKS-74 in 5.45. U.S.-made or sterile arms would not suit. If everything could be traced back to the Russians, then no one would ever know who might have used them. And the Russian government would refuse any effort at a serious investigation. Their security service people had stated so when they first made contact regarding Rostov. The incident would be written off as a struggle between rival gangs of illegal arms dealers. He also made a mental note to have their issue equipment replaced with this special ordnance, including at least a case of Russian RGD-5 hand grenades. If they needed a means to reach out and touch someone, they might ask for a thirty-millimeter AGS-17 *Plamya* automatic grenade launcher. But then, the weapon had a reputation for premature detonations of grenades while still in the receiver. That was something they could not afford to have happen. Maybe they could take a risk on a Honeywell hand-crank multiround 40mm grenade launcher. They were never in widespread issue, and since they had not been deployed for use by the U.S. since Vietnam, they were not all that well known. Remove any identification of manufacture and it should work. If push came to shove, they could always dump the Honeywell over the side into a river, lake, or the ocean. Put another one in the "solved" column.

Rations and POL supplies came next. They could always use Russian-made field rations, but, dear God, they tasted like they had been predigested and deposited in plastic bags from the lower end of the alimentary canal. Using MREs was out, since they said "American made" loud and clear. Sterile rations? Whose? Maybe Polish would serve. At least *their* food tasted good. Would they need them at all? Borscht, blinis, and boiled potatoes would prove sufficient for the time he anticipated the men would be in-country. Yet another problem solved.

Fuel? Well, they would start off with full tanks and have enough to go out to any pickup vessel. Then he considered acquiring fuel for stolen trucks or large cars. That might prove more difficult. Once the vehicles were noted as stolen, they dare not hit a gas station. Were service stations still controlled by the government? If not, who did run them? How fast would the word go out about missing cars or trucks? Better to top off the tanks right after they got their hands on the vehicles. It weighed against using such means of travel.

What about communications? They had sat-link radio, computer links also, and internal intercom radio within each squad and platoon, plus a command circuit. They too could be dumped if need be. He'd be damned if they'd use internal Russian com systems. Local telephone lines were out, too. So, okay, problem solved. Rockham cracked his knuckles, leaned back and made a quick review of his strategic planning. It would work, but barely. It was time to get something to eat, have a couple of cups of coffee and get some sack time. He rose from his desk and started for the Italian Officers' Club, where the other commissioned ranks of his command waited, already at least two dinner courses ahead of him. Ah, the burden of command—shit! The necessity of command was how he saw it.

With a little luck they would come out of this one with minimal losses, and those only wounds. The next seventy-two hours would tell, he believed. Before he could get out of the room, the sat-link phone buzzed discreetly. He reached for the handset. "Rock here, speak."

"Rock, this is Jerry. We've got some news for you." Quickly, Wharton filled him in on the latest developments. He concluded with, "And check this, Rock. We have sat-phone intercepts that indicate some hasty high-dollar transactions between some Chinese at the Metropole Hotel in Moscow and the Black House. Also, our boy Rostov is on the move. Intercepts from inside Russia, made by the Company, indicate the likelihood of Rostov being behind the thefts I described. If so, things are imminent for your operation. Are you ready to be committed to this mission?"

"Within twenty-four hours." Quickly, Rockham read off the wish list of weapons and other supplies they would require for a safe, sterile insertion into the Russian Republic. Wharton agreed to get the gear to Aviano ASAP. It wouldn't be long before the shit would hit the fan.

CHAPTER 19

★ ★ ★ ★

Everyone—old salts and newcomers alike—agreed that the chow in the Italian air force service clubs was fantastic.

"Only in Little Italy," Green Platoon's Brooklynite O'Banyon said wistfully. Naturally, he was a rabidly loyal New Yorker and a Yankees fan.

"Only what, Blarney?" Tinsley of Gold Platoon teased.

Blarney O'Banyon—who'd earned his nickname honestly—frowned. "Good Italian eats, stupid. Whaddaya think? Man, down there in Little Italy you can find the greatest stuffed cannelloni—with meat and cheese and mushrooms. And Sunday morning after mass, the deep-fried cannoli filled with chocolate chips, sweet ricotta, and whipped cream. Man, I tell you they're to die for."

A grinning Henry Limbaugh, obviously a man who loved to eat, confided to O'Banyon, "Wait until you see their Sunday buffet. The only place that comes close that I know of is a restaurant in El Cajon, a suburb of San Diego, it's called *Three Guys from Italy*. I used to go there every Sunday when I was with the Teams at Coronado."

O'Banyon gave him a blank stare. "What was so great about that place?" the New Yorker snapped.

"Man, they have so many things piled up, it takes the whole buffet table, three round tables that seat twelve and another steam table for what they serve up. One thing they've got is a bank of ice with fifteen kinds of fruit alone. I tell you, these guys know their business. They learned as chefs at some of the fanciest hotels and restaurants in Rome."

O'Banyon challenged him, "You ain't ever been to Little Italy."

Limbaugh laughed. "Oh, yes I have. I can count at least a dozen times. Remember, Blarney, I was with the Teams at Little Creek for three years before I joined SMD. I always took my liberties to New York, to see the Broadway shows an' some of the off-Broadway stuff, too."

Paul Lederer snickered as he joined in, "Well, lah-dee-dah. We've got us a theater fan. I would never have suspected."

"Ah-ha! What have we here?" Limbaugh defended himself. "A crude popcorn-chomping devotee of the silver screen I've no doubt."

Lederer affected a hurt expression. "Hey, back off. I like my flicks. Especially those old ones from the thirties, you know, with Lon Chaney, Boris Karloff, and Bela Lugosi. And don't forget the kids from the *Our Gang* comedy shorts, Paul Muni, Elsa Lancaster, Hattie McDaniel, Fay Wray, and even the Three Stooges."

"Jeez, who are those guys?" Andrew Bean asked.

Lederer peered at him. "You're how old, Andy?"

Bean swallowed hard. "I'm twenty-two, Tall Paul."

Lederer became thoughtful. "That accounts for some of it, of course. But, me laddie, you're sadly lacking in the breadth of your education. Those people I mentioned were among the biggest stars Hollywood ever turned out. For their day, they made big money, more than anyone other than the Rockefellers and the Morgans. Hell, the Great Depression didn't even matter to them. And they had talent, man, *real talent*. They didn't mumble like Brando or mug the camera like James Dean."

"Who's he? James Dean, I mean."

Lederer threw up his hands in mock surrender. "Forget it, man, you're hopeless." He turned away and headed for the long worktable where the SMDs auxiliary equipment was laid out.

"Now hear this!" Chief Monday bellowed.

"The old man has something to lay out for us." He took a quick head count and turned to Rockham. "Commander, they're all present or accounted for."

Rockham faced his men with a neutral expression on his face. "The good news is the Company has found out where the bioweapons are being shipped from—which is Rostok Terminal in the port of Vladivostok. We also now know where the shipment is going. It is believed that it's headed for a small island off the coast at Fuching, China."

That confused Chief Monday for a moment. "I thought the bad guys were Taiwanese."

Rockham smiled at him. "They are, but they sold out to the PRC. On at least a Black House agent named Chang Shee Tung recruited them to work against their own country."

Bryant stood up. "Haven't we heard about these guys before?"

"Yeah, Mike, you sure did. Only now we have photographs of all of them and of some fifteen other Taiwanese turncoats. The Company also gave us physical descriptions and where they are presently located, which is the Metropole Hotel in Moscow."

"Well then, why don't we just send a black bag team to the hotel and kill 'em all," Jorgensen suggested. "Dead men can't take delivery of any sort of shipment, except maybe a coffin."

Rockham smiled. "Point well made, Pauli. Sometimes, I wonder if you have a death wish.

There's no way in hell we could walk into that Russian hotel, blow away two or three men, and walk out without being grabbed by either the police or the Security Service. Just because the Russians are former communists doesn't mean they're stupid. Our guys would be made the minute they stepped onto the street. Even though the Security Service is cooperating with us, there's no way they'd allow anything that overt."

"What about Sukov? Isn't he a native speaker of Russian?"

"Yes, he is. His folks spoke Russian at home all the time he lived there. They escaped from the old USSR in the mid-fifties, and they hate communists and communism. But John has a bit of a problem—he's picked up a Texas drawl from his friends and everyone else in that state. When he's under extreme pressure, it comes out."

Jorgensen shrugged. "That may be, but I've never heard him y'alling or yeehawing."

Rockham had to agree. "He's not that demonstrative. It's more an accent like Tex Ritter or that cute gal LeAnn Rimes." He paused, cleared his throat. "Now, back to what we have. CIA and the DDO say this information came from inside Rostov's organization, and they consider it legitimate. Which you all know directs us to the Pacific AO. I know you've all heard this a thousand times before, but the regulations demand it, so I've got to say it. All of this information is eyes-only, so don't write anything to the folks back home, don't advise them about it when you get your final phone call home, and don't discuss it with anyone outside this building at this time."

"Yeah, you're right, boss," Marks observed. "Only, who goes and who stays in reserve?"

"Not to worry, Ryan, that's already been decided. Gold was established as the primary on this op from the git-go. Green will remain in reserve, in the event the tip proves to be another bit of disinformation. Matter of fact, I'm going to send for Blue to come over as a final backup. That way if our two platoons are deployed, there'll still be a reserve."

"Cover all bases, right, boss?" Marks said through a huge white grin.

"Bet your ass. That's why there's a shortstop between second and third base. In case they've got a rundown going with first base or a short pop fly, second is still covered."

Fleming spoke up. "Hey, boss, did you ever coach baseball?"

Rockham blushed. "No, but I'm studying up for when Matty goes from T-Ball to Little League."

Strong support came from resident baseball fan O'Banyon. "That's the way, boss. Teach him up real good and I'll see he gets picked up by the Yankees."

Three or four SEALs echoed their sentiment over that. "Yeah, right!"

"Hey, guys, I'm serious. My cousin, Cammus O'Banyon, is a scout for the Yanks. I've steered him to at least three guys who became over .300 hitters. He'll listen, boss, I promise you," O'Banyon enthused.

Rockham chuckled. "Blarney, I'm not certain I'd want him to become a pro baseball player. Professional athletes have a damned short career, and not all of them make multimillion-dollar deals."

Grinning wickedly, Blarney O'Banyon asked, "What would you like him to be?"

"What would be wrong with him becoming a SEAL? It's been good enough for his dad."

"Talk about lousy career choices. Man, for every commander, lieutenant commander, or even lieutenant in the Teams, there are at least thirty or so enlisted men. And how long before a SEAL catches a bullet or a few chunks of metal from a grenade or an RPG? I'm not saying that they all die young, but a whole lot of us get all crippled up and ache like hell for life."

Rockham squinted at him. "Are you bucking for a transfer to a surface ship?"

O'Banyon looked hurt. "Fuck no! I'm a SEAL and damned proud of it, sir. You won't get me out without a crowbar. Which reminds me of a story. Seamas and Doolin were walking down the—"

"Shut up!" half of his squad yelled. They all suffered from an overload of his tall tales.

Laughing, Rockham slapped him lightly on one shoulder. "You're a good man, Blarney, carry on."

"Aye, aye, sir."

"So let's get back to it. Gold is going to head out tonight for Manila, Philippines, to rendezvous with the *USS Grayback* for transportation to their area of operation. The stand-by order for our departure will be 2240 hours tonight. By the time we arrive at Manila Bay, we will have worked out the details for a takedown, either in Vladivostok or aboard whatever ship they transport the weapons on. Until then, make everything ready and relax. Grab some z's if you can. As most of you know, sleeping aboard someone else's submarine is not easy."

Tarpaulin-covered, the MB-21 rocket launcher and its deadly cargo of missiles and warheads moved along by flatcar without notice by railroad employees or the guards at the occasional security check point. Grigoriy Rostov and his select team of six men rode in one of the three passenger cars. They would arrive in Vladivostok at 0445 the next morning, two days before they were to meet their customers. Their cargo would be off-loaded and spirited away before anyone noticed. The plan pleased Rostov. It certainly had been better organized than the pullout from Afghanistan. That had been an insult to his friends and comrades lost in the fighting there. Of that he was certain. It had been nothing but a sop to the Western governments to try to curry favor with them. And he considered that a shameful, disgusting, and totally unacceptable position for the Soviet Union to have been forced into. Consequently, he felt that some of the sacrifices he had made for his country had been in vain. The soft purr of his cell phone interrupted his gloomy thoughts.

"*Da?*" He listened, and then spoke swiftly. "I will come at once, of course. Unfortunately, my friend, I am stuck on a train. I must wait for a place to get off where I can purchase an airline ticket. Give me eight or ten hours." He hung up with an angry curse.

"What is it?" Tsinev asked urgently.

"As you know, Ivan Arkadyvich I have not been a man of great wealth. Now it seems those wanting to press money into my hands grow so rapidly I have no time to serve them all. That was Fyodor from Saint Petersburg. He demands I come at once to handle a difficult transaction. I thought I could trust him to do it for us without difficulty. Ah, well, my friend, I shall go and then join you in Vladivostok late tomorrow."

Until recently, Rostov had never been a particularly powerful or rich man. He had always seen the deliberate acquisition of money as beneath the dignity and honor of a true communist. Rocking steadily, sometimes violently, on the tired springs from the ancient, vintage 1930s cars, he reached up tentatively and smoothed down the fringe of hair that surrounded his large bald spot. His thoughts returned to the bitterness he felt over his military career.

In spite of his dedication to his duties in Spetznaz, and the additional responsibilities he accrued from his work for Fleet Intelligence Directorate's Third Division, he had always felt that his talent was wasted, that he had been *used*. Passed over for promotion three times since becoming a senior captain, he resented the less accomplished, soft-fingered, pudgy officers with more and better political connections. But he was out now, his military career and aspirations only part of a written record in some musty storage bin in Moscow and at Northern Fleet headquarters at Pachenga Naval Base.

Tsinev interrupted his thoughts. "Tell me what you are thinking, Grisha. You are scowling so much it must be about a lost love, is that not so?"

Rostov sighed. "No, my friend, it is not over a lost love. It is over a lost nation and a lost political system that functioned so flawlessly. Also, I mourn the death of my military career."

Tsinev made a wry expression. "That is a great deal for one man to worry over, Grigoriy Mikhailavich. Why not worry instead about the lack of a dining car and some good vodka on this wreck of a train?"

"We are here for important business. When we arrive, the initial payment will be handed over by electronic transfer to our account on Grand Cayman. The fool Americans will never dream that their favorite offshore secure bank is also used by us."

Tsinev beamed at this revelation. "That is why you chose the Barclay Trust Bank instead of our usual

Swiss connection? It's brilliant. If everything goes totally wrong and we're forced to go into hiding in South America, we will be close to our money."

Rostov nodded acceptance of the praise and reached into a deep pocket of his naval greatcoat to withdraw a newspaper-wrapped five hundred milliliter bottle of vodka. "Here, I have a little reward for us."

"That is most welcome, thank you." Tsinev reached for the liquor. "Tell me, if these Chinese give us the payment in cash, what do we do?"

"We have them accompany us to a bank and have one of them fill in the transfer slip, and then we put in the routing number and account number, making sure they cannot see us write them down. From there it is all done by satellite transmissions."

"Is it not miraculous, Grigoriy? Think of it!" His excitement was contagious. "Less than ten years ago, we could not do that. The state owned all the banks and had none of the technology to make it work." His words grew soft, thoughtful. "Sometimes I suspect that our glorious leaders and the whole Politburo wanted to keep us nothing but stupid peasants," he stated hotly.

Rostov, the true believer, gave him a cold, hard look. "That comes close to blasphemy. Take care what you say around these doctrinaire communists we're dealing with."

"And around you as well?" Tsinev prodded, never slow on the uptake.

Rostov ignored the jibe. He studied the train

schedule in his hand. "It says here that we have an hour layover at Tomsk, in order to leave off cars and change locomotives. The schedule claims there is an excellent restaurant in the terminal building where we can get a meal. It is about time. It is there also that I shall take the airplane for Moskva."

"Well then, we eat and maybe we can get some sausages and cheese, some fruit and boiled eggs, to take along. Also we buy more vodka. Must not forget the vodka."

"*Da.* It is mother's milk. We'll have a drink together before I leave."

All four squads of Gold Platoon boarded the converted Boeing 747 for the long journey to Manila. At a maximum speed of more than six hundred knots, it was faster than any military aircraft with similar capacity. For many of them, it would be their first trip to the Philippine Islands. The long-range airliner belonged to Air America but bore the markings of an Asian private corporation. The flight plan, Rockham had been told, included a refueling stop in Singapore, where a flight plan to Manila would be filed. From there they would taxi to a hangar in the General Aviation sector of the airport and off-load. Closed trucks would transport them to the harbor, where a pair of swift charter fishing boats would take the squads to a rendezvous with the *Grayback*. Rockham explained all of this to Gold Platoon and asked for questions.

Paul Lederer raised his hand. "Commander, how come we go through all this changing of transportation?"

"Simple, Tall Paul," Rockham replied. "Because of the difficulty of getting accurate information on our target, we have very little time. The *Grayback* could not make it to a harbor in Italy in time or anywhere farther from Vladivostok than we'll be in Manila."

"Are we going to use these hot new IBSs?" Steve Handel asked, putting aside his highly prized Macanudo cigar.

Rockham nodded. "You bet we are. They're stowed in the cargo bay. Once we're out of sight of land on the island of Luzon and headed west, we'll haul them out and put them on the foredeck of the charter boats and make ready to transfer to the sub."

Daugherty, who had been asked by Rockham to come along on the mission, spoke up. "Then I would strongly recommend that we take along the two Plamya automatic grenade launchers we bagged off the green beanies, and plenty of those really nasty AP rounds with the iron and plastic needles."

Rockham shook his head. "If you want to put up with the extra weight, okay. Keep in mind that with the tripod and a full drum magazine, they weigh seventy-seven pounds. And they're not all that fast, just fifty to a hundred rounds per minute."

"Yeah, but that can bring a lot of scalding pee down on somebody, especially if we have to take a whole ship by force," Daugherty offered.

Rockham pursed his lips. "You've got a point. Okay, so they go with us. Set 'em up aft on the IBSs. Now, are there any other questions?"

Hunter spoke up. "What do we do with the Ruskie arms dealers if we catch them?"

Rockham gave him a cold-eyed glance. "What is it our friends at CIA say? Oh, yeah, 'terminate with extreme prejudice.' For these guys that's fitting. A dead arms dealer can't sell weapons to anyone—WMDs or otherwise."

A wicked smile appeared on Hunter's lips. "I like that. And the Chinese, what do we do with them?"

"They get the same," Rockham said, coming on as cold as the lockers in the county morgue.

"So we go in and waste them all?" Tinsley asked.

"You've got it. The only thing that might stand in the way is if the Russians change their minds and don't give us permission to act in their territory."

Sukov followed right up. "And what if they don't?"

Daugherty chose to answer that one. "Well, hell, John, we go in anyway."

Sukov laughed gleefully. "That's right enough in my book. I'll be handling the commo duties, right?"

"That's it, John. You're our best Russian speaker and you sure sound like a native." Rockham paused meaningfully. "Unless you get excited. So take your time, eh?"

Sukov looked at him in silent acknowledgment of all he had said. "You bet, boss. I'll have 'em all singing dirty Russian songs with me before we're done."

"Like what?" Hunter asked.

"Well, try this: 'I once knew a whore named Camille. Her box was as big as a Zil.—'"

"We don't want to hear it!" a unanimous chorus of SEALs rang out.

For a moment Sukov looked hurt. "What's wrong, guys?"

"You can't carry a tune in a bucket," Ed Lutz confided.

"Well, if that's all it is, okay. I'll leave it to your imagination," Sukov replied.

"Good!" they all shouted back.

"Okay, Shaun, pick two crews to man the automatic grenade launchers and see that they know every part and function. God knows we've got enough hours for you to get them qualified. Okay, now the takedown itself." Rockham paused and sighed heavily. "First and Second squads will go in and engage the target. Fourth squad will be in reserve. Third squad will secure the ingress and extraction routes."

Wayne Alexander raised his hand. "What if they have already gotten everything aboard ship?"

"Our local source, a deep-cover CIA field case

officer, will advise us in time to revise our tactics to fit the situation. If we go on shipboard," Rockham continued, "minus those in the autoweapons crews, we'll go in with first and third squads handling the caving ladders, second will be in reserve, the fourth will follow once we engage. Our information from CIA is that since they are going out by ship, it will be one hell of a big one. It will require everyone to take down the whole ship. Those of you on the *Plamya* crews, watch out for a signal for covering fire. The ship will be considered to be hostile since, according to CIA, although the registration will no doubt be Liberian or Panamanian, the crew will be from the PRC."

Wilkes spoke up, a note of awe in his voice. "Hey, guys, we're gonna be fightin' some really bad dudes."

"Taking on thugs from Red China bothers you, Pete?" Daugherty asked.

Wilkes responded with a grin. "Naw, LT. I was just thinkin'—we'll be makin' the big time."

Daugherty nodded at the young automatic weapons man. "You just have the *Plamya* ready when we need it and there won't be a SEAL anywhere who won't envy us."

Rockham called them back to the important facts. "Okay, moving on. No matter where we operate, it will be mandatory that our small arms are suppressed weapons. Set them on selective fire unless told otherwise. The only explosives will be flash-bang grenades. We don't want to risk the possibility of setting off any of those anthrax warheads."

"Nuts, I forgot about those," Quinn of Green Platoon squeaked. "Can a stray bullet crack one of them open?"

"Not according to our best authorities on chemical and bioweapons. It would take at least an electric M-6, or nonelectric blasting cap and an RDX booster to blow one apart. Think about it, kid—they've got to be safe enough to handle and do so somewhat roughly, or the folks who made them could not use them."

Quinn sighed with relief. "Yeah, that's good news. Is there any bad news?"

"Yeah, just a bit," Rockham admitted. "As of now we don't know where the hell we'll be operating. According to Colonel Wharton, we'll know that when we get aboard the *Grayback*."

"Well then, Rock, no matter how much I hate them, I can't wait to get on board that sub."

Laughing, Rockham replied, "I double that in spades."

For the next twenty minutes the briefing on the mission continued, and then the SEALs broke for chow.

CHAPTER 20

★ ★ ★ ★

For all his caution, Grigoriy Rostov had suspected this. His open war with the Russian mafia had unquestionably been reported to the Security Service. Seated in his roomette in one of the Pullman cars—ancient even by Russian standards—he reviewed what had transpired since he'd left the westbound train to Vladivostok.

At Tomsk station, he entered the restaurant. He ordered a double vodka, then selected the daily special—beef pirogi—along with a bowl of borscht. Unbidden, his stomach growled in anticipation. Without being asked, the waitress brought him a bottle of beer, and minutes later arrived with large steaming bowls of the meat-stuffed dumplings and rich beet soup.

He dug into the two bowls, each with a floating dollop of sour cream, with fresh-grated nutmeg on the boiled dumplings and some grated boiled beets on the borscht. To his surprise, the food was excellent. He fervently hoped that the former Spetznaz senior lieutenant would handle the off-loading of the launcher, rockets, and warheads and see to their safe stowage in the rented warehouse at the Rostok terminal. They could ill-afford to have their transaction discovered at this late date. Tsinev would be compelled to do some killing then, and that would bring the police. And *that* would bring a wretched cell in a horrid prison.

When he finished his meal, he paid with cash and left an overgenerous tip. Then he walked outside and down the street to the electric railway—which, he recalled, for some reason, the Americans called trolley cars—and took the route to the airport. It was on that short journey that he noticed the two men whom he had first seen on the train to Vladivostok. He had not seen them get off at Tomsk and had no idea what they were up to now. They could be mafia, bent on revenge for his destroying the crime family of Fyodor Sarinov. Then again, his necessary paranoia told him, they could be State Security. His concern diminished when he reached the airport and lost sight of them entirely. He approached the ticket kiosk and purchased a one-way to Moscow. To his satisfaction, he had only a half hour wait—something unheard of in the old Soviet Union—and he felt certain he had lost them when he boarded and headed for Moscow.

Except he hadn't. Now he had the bastards on his tail for sure. He located them instantly in the refreshment car. They were drinking tea, and he drank vodka. He rejected the idea that they came from the mafia. There was something about the polished way in which they handled the surveillance: they were not amateur thugs, they were professionals. When he followed them out of the refreshment bar, he learned that one of them occupied the compartment next to his. He would have to take care of that before they reached the transfer point at Vilnius. Sighing, Rostov slid from his seat and pulled a Spetznaz officer's dagger from the leather sheath strapped to his right leg. He gave his actions careful thought before stepping into the narrow corridor. He rolled his sleeves up to the elbows while he walked.

His knock was answered with a cranky voice. "Excuse me, Mister—ah . . ."

"Go away, I do not wish to speak with anyone," the man on the other side growled.

"This is your car steward. There is a problem with your luggage, sir."

"I do not have any luggage."

"Are you not Mr. Stefan Koretski?" Rostov hastily improvised a name.

A second later the door flew open to reveal a

very angry man. "I am not Koretski and I do not have luggage, you idiot!" he shouted a moment before Rostov sprang, throwing himself at the slighter man. Together, they crashed into the compartment.

"You fool, do you know who you are assaulting?" the security agent barked.

Rostov grunted out his reply with a powerful thrust of his knife. "Yes, you are State Security. I too have worked for an intelligence agency, and the first thing they taught us was that carelessness could be harmful to your health."

By then the agent's eyes bulged and his face had begun to drain of color as Rostov drove the tip of his Spetznaz knife up through the dome of the man's diaphragm. It might have been a cheap copy, but its edge was keen and slid without resistance into the dying man's chest cavity. Rostov shoved harder, and the blade sliced into his victim's heart. Swiftly, his chest cavity flooded with blood and he went stiff in Rostov's grip, then his knees gave out and the former Spetznaz captain laid the dead man's limp body on the extended bunk.

Quickly, Rostov washed off his hands in the small corner sink. He rifled the dead man's trousers and produced a State Security ID card and the compartment door key. He opened the door a crack and checked to see if the corridor was empty. Satisfied, he closed the partition behind him and locked it. On the steel plates that covered the coupling, he opened the upper half of a door and hurled the key away into the darkness. His breathing returning to normal, Rostov headed for his own compartment. He would have to find the other agent soon.

A man in the uniform with the rank of Captain on his shoulder boards approached the SEALs waiting on the dock in Manila Bay. "Are you Commander Rockham?"

Rockham came to attention and saluted. "Yes, sir, that's me."

"I'm Commander Harriman Ellis, XO of the *Kittyhawk*. There's been a change in plan. The *Grayback* is not going to be able to enter Manila Harbor. A U.S. submarine could attract too much attention."

"How do we reach the sub, sir?" Rockham asked.

With a smile, Ellis tapped his chest. "That's where I come in. The *Kittyhawk* is in port for a liberty call, and we received a request to lend a hand. Whaleboats will be coming alongside the dock here in five minutes. They'll take you out to the *Kitty*." Rockham started to protest, but Ellis raised a hand to stop him. "Don't worry, no one will see you board. We're due to go to sea again tomorrow morning. Once we get out of sight of land, you can take a helicopter to the *Grayback*."

Rockham smiled. "Quite a neat trick. So when do we reach the sub?"

"From the course I've laid, we should be within flight distance for the choppers a half hour before sunset."

"That suits me. Thank you, Commander," Rockham said, and concluded with a salute.

True to the captain's words, within five minutes three whaleboats drew alongside and waited turns at the landing platform for the SEALs to descend and come aboard. When all were loaded, the vessels sped off across Manila Bay toward the suburb where for sixty years the U.S. Navy had a huge base, complete with a repair facility able to handle anything up to a battleship in dry dock cradles. Even earlier, before World War II and during the last year of the war, after the Philippines had been retaken from the Japanese, three naval aviation squadrons were assigned to the airfield there.

Within minutes the tall derricks and concrete-sided dry docks came into view. In his whaleboat, Rockham informed those around him, "From here on in, guys, we're headed for some really deep shit."

When in doubt, ask one of the porters, Grigoriy Rostov reasoned. They would know where everyone was seated or in what compartment. A generous bribe would loosen at least one tongue. It took him less than ten minutes to find his man.

"Yes, the man with the scar on his left cheek? He is in *Bazah* 6702. I took his attaché case and single valise to the compartment."

Rostov's face was hard when he asked, "Which compartment in car *Bazah* 6702?"

"Compartment C."

"Thank you, comrade." He gave the porter a thousand ruble tip.

Rostov's knock was not answered, so he resorted to a set of lock picks he always carried. When the lock clicked, he opened the compartment to an empty room. Where was his man? Checking his wristwatch, Rostov discovered they were thirty-five minutes from the train station in Vilnius. He had to act fast so he would be ready to change trains. He turned to his right and started back toward the dining car and refreshment lounge.

Glancing in the narrow vertical glass of the window inset in the dining car inner door, Rostov saw his man seated at a white-napped table with real silverware. He was eating a juicy-looking sliver of rare steak and chewed lustily. From the presence of a salad, a broiled fillet of North Sea salmon, and three vegetable side dishes, he would be there for a while, Rostov reasoned. He drew away and waited on the far side of the coupling cross-over in the other vestibule.

Rocking hypnotically, the swaying cars had a soporific effect on Rostov as he waited for the second security agent he knew he must kill. He had no choice. He had left a corpse in the compartment next to his. He could not take the return train to Moscow. So he would fly out from Saint

Petersburg to Vladivostok, to avoid leaving a trail and for speed. *The man is a glutton*, he thought in irritation while the minutes sped by and Vilnius came closer.

At last the partition to the other car opened and the Security Service man came out. When he stepped onto the moving plates of the coupling housing, he glanced to his left and nodded to Rostov. Only a flicker of recognition in his eyes betrayed him. After he moved past, the Spetznaz-trained warrior struck with lightning ferocity. He whipped the sharp blade of his knife across the throat of the hapless security man, cutting deeply to sever the anterior and posterior carotid arteries, opening a gaping space in the esophagus and doing terminal damage to the vocal cords. Before the blood could flow onto the plates beneath them, Rostov had the door open and hurled the dying man out of the train. The body bounced once, then rolled down the embankment and into thick brush along the track.

Breathing heavily, Rostov headed directly to the restroom at the near end of the dining car and locked the door behind him. He washed away the blood that had splashed over the sleeve of his coat, his hands and face, then headed back to his Pullman car.

Tweee-eeeee-eeeee! The ascending and descending shriek of the boatswain's pipe sounded even shriller to Greg Rockham over the speaker system as they were piped aboard the *USS Kittyhawk*. The heavy mooring cables had been freed from the dock bollards and hauled aboard, and now they were underway, the huge brass screws turning ten knots as they exited from the bay. Commander Ellis had escorted his passengers to the Aviation Squadron officers' wardroom and saw them settled in. His face flushed as he spoke a few parting words of caution.

"I hate to have to bring this up, but while you are aboard, please do not mix with the regular crew or discuss anything about who you are or what you're doing."

Jay Hunter could not resist a mild rebuke. "We ain't exactly a flock of nervous virgins, Commander."

Ellis accepted it with good grace and cleared his throat before replying. "I understand that, sailor, but regulations are regulations, and you *are* on a top secret mission, so the warning has to be given. I have duties now, so enjoy your stay aboard the *Kitty*. The mess stewards will arrange to feed you an hour after the aviation officers clear the wardroom."

With that, he departed. Now, the officers and lead NCOs huddled around the long, maple table and poured over maps of the city and civilian facilities in the harbor at Vladivostok. Shaun Daugherty put a thick index finger on a long row of warehouses located in a crescent-shaped portion of the harbor, isolated from the sprawl of the city.

"My bet is here's where they'll do the deal. One of these warehouses could easily mask any transfer of the materials they're selling."

Rockham nodded, his lips pursed in his usual manner when engaged in serious speculation. "I think you've got it right, Shaun. But let's not overlook the other side of the bay. There are docking facilities and a number of warehouses sitting right up against the city limits."

"What we need are some good satellite photos, from one of those where you can read a license plate."

Rockham smiled and clapped Daugherty on one shoulder. "They're already ordered, my friend—as soon as we discovered that the bad guys were taking a train east to a Pacific port."

"That's cool. Everytime I see those fantastic photos, I wonder how in hell they can pull it off. They can't use low earth-orbiting satellites."

Chief Monday spoke up. "They don't. They way I understand it, they use the ones way out in geosynchronous orbit."

Hunter's eyes went wide. "Wow! They've got telephoto lenses that long? It must be one big hummer to be so detailed when the pictures are transmitted back to earth."

"You've got it, Crazy Horse. Only from what I've heard, they fix up a digital camera to a big ol' telescope on the satellite and take their pictures that way. Radio signals aim the scope. As long as they're over a specific area, they can see anything in range."

"Terrific," Daugherty approved. "When do we get to see the pictures?"

"Sometime this evening or first thing in the morning," Rockham said, "about 0430 hours, something like that."

A chorus of groans answered him.

"All right, here's how we take down the warehouse. Half of Green will provide security, while Gold breaches the door and goes in to take out any of the bad guys guarding the shipment. The other half of Green will be in reserve."

Mike Ferber posed the question on everyone's mind. "What if the stuff is already on a ship, headed for who knows where?"

"Then we find out from satellite surveillance which ship loaded from that warehouse and where it went. We shouldn't have any problem learning the name from a stern shot. After that, it's a chase-down and standard boarding maneuver, followed by a routine takedown of the ship. We've all been through it at least five hundred times in rehearsals, and several times for the real thing."

Daugherty's frown impressed them all with the seriousness of his words. "Only I have a feeling this isn't going to be routine. There's going to be someone on watch around the clock. Odds are we're going to have one hell of a job ahead of us."

* * *

Ivan Tsinev and Vladimir Frolik took charge of the large shipment as it was off-loaded from the train directly through the huge double doors and into Warehouse 5796 Southwest on Pier 6, Rostok Terminal. Once again Tsinev thanked their good fortune that Rostov had the forethought to have everything secured in a locked and sealed cargo container. The huge metal box resembled nothing more than a giant semi-trailer without wheels.

Concealed inside the windowless container, in addition to the launcher, rockets, and case of anthrax warheads was a large high-speed boat. Broad of beam, at over 9.5 meters and 24.4 meters long, the swift-running vessel was powered by twin Mercedes diesel marine engines. Dimitri Golovan, a former coxswain in Spetznaz, knew it was capable of turning enough rpm to deliver forty-five kilometers per hour even with a large load aboard. While they awaited Rostov's arrival, Frolik—a mechanical genius—directed a crew of his fellow Spetznaz troops in modifying the forward, covered deck to mount the launcher. They reinforced and shielded it to support the weight of the launcher and keep the back-blast of the rocket's exhaust from damaging the boat.

Frolik and Tsinev had drawn up plans and made blueprints of the work required. It began with cutting and welding small steel I-beams athwart ship, crisscrossed with shorter girders to reinforce the whole platform. This, Frolik intended to build from eight millimeters of sheet steel. The same forethought by Rostov included bringing along all of the materials and tools necessary for the task. Fine-beam laser cutters produced glass-smooth cuts through beams, bar stock, and plate with equal ease. An additional plus to this state-of-the-art technique was the lack of noise and very little flickering light such as would be made by a cutting torch or diamond-tipped saw blades.

Five of Rostok's crew did the donkey work. Nemec and Zabotin, both former demolitions experts, were likewise capable welders. Ironically, they used an American-made arc welder unit to join the pieces required to make the platform. Tsinev and Frolik kept constant watch and gave explicit instructions while the girders of the framework grew in size and solidity.

"Well, Vladimir Konstantinich, does our progress please you?" Ivan Tsinev asked Frolik after two hours of constant, hard work. "Another hour and we'll be ready for the launcher unit."

CHAPTER 21

★ ★ ★ ★

Long shadows fell across the flight deck of the
Kittyhawk from the six-deck-high island. They
had been at sea for over three hours. The command was given to reduce speed and turn into the
wind. A moment later the SEALs of SMD One
hustled out of the open hatch at the base of the island, directly under the CAG's open operations
bridge. The men, burdened with heavy gear,
rushed toward the helicopters waiting for them,
the twin main rotors drooping and unmoving.
Combat Air Group CO, Commander Norton Ballard, stood in his usual position, a life vest
strapped on, as per regulations, his second best
tan and "flying saucer" garrison hat rammed

down tight against the increasing breeze as the *USS Kittyhawk* turned sharply to port to come into the wind. The first four to board were the men bearing the bulky Russian *Plamya* grenade launchers and their tripods. Eyes squinting, the CAG watched the loading order closely, privately anxious—like some others—to get the dangerous special operators off his ship.

Turbine engines spooled up with a musical whine and the rotors began to slowly turn. Commander Ballard looked to his LSO and saw him lift the flare gun to fire a takeoff signal. During take-offs, the landing signals officer usually had little to do, except control the catapult launches. The crew chiefs of each conventional aircraft gave the pilot the signal to go to full power and await the shock of the catapult. The CH-46D helicopters launched vertically, so the LSO gave the launch signals. He fired a green smoke flare and studied the drift, then gave a thumbs-up to each chopper pilot, followed by a raised single finger, then two, three, and four, as the birds lifted off gracelessly and wallowed awhile in the wind across the flight deck before stabilizing and speeding away.

Ballard knew the destination of his helicopters, and wondered why in hell they did it this way. The big carrier was barely making headway, only enough to maintain steerage. As the choppers grew smaller, he lifted binoculars and scanned the surface ahead and to both port and starboard. Then he saw it. Far off on the nearly flat sea, the black silhouette of a Fast Attack nuke submarine's sail cut low through the water, the brightness of the setting sun behind it.

Both CH-46Ds cut wide arcs and pulled in close to the undersea craft. Ballard saw white spume blow up from the ballast ports and the sub rise higher, until its main deck was barely awash. Fascinated, the CAG watched while first one then another helicopter hovered over the deck and the SEALs slid down quick ropes to the rail-encircled conning tower. A hatch stood open, and two crewmen in faded dungaree shirts, trousers, and white sea caps helped them maneuver below deck. To Ballard, it seemed like no time at all before the last man disappeared down the internal ladder and the hatch closed.

The transfer had been completed successfully. Now he could leave the bridge, go below to the Flight Officers' wardroom and have a good, strong cup of coffee. Silently, he wished the SEALs good luck on this obviously highly dangerous and secret operation.

Even shriller than aboard the aircraft carrier, the boatswain's pipe squealed through the tube of the sub. "Now hear this! Now hear this! All hands to maneuvering stations. Stand by to dive." The chief of the boat's voice crackled over the speaker net aboard the submarine *USS Grayback*. Once more the boatswain's pipe trilled. A klaxon sounded harshly. "Dive! Dive! Dive!"

At his station just below the periscope platform, the talker took over for the COB and spoke urgently into the microphone which rose from the flat black base against his chest. "Flood forward ballast . . . flood ballast amidships . . . flood aft ballast."

Streams of bubbles rushed violently out of the ballast tanks as water replaced the air. Swiftly, the sub slid below the waves like a dropped stone. The gurgling roar sounded ominous to the SEALs, despite their frequent trips on submarines. Hunter winced, his red-brown, high-cheekboned face screwed into a vision of misery.

"That scares the crap out of me every time they do it," he confided to Sid Mainhart.

Mainhart cocked an eyebrow. "Why's that, Crazy Horse?"

Hunter wet terribly dry lips. " 'Cause it reminds me we're goin' underwater—*way* underwater—and the pressure is enough to crush a steel can. Worse still, we don't have any control about when we come up. It's not like when we're all on a dive."

Mainhart sought to reassure him. "Relax, buddy. If the pressure hull breaches, we'll be dead before we know it."

Crazy Horse Hunter gave him a gimlet eye. "Thanks. That really made my day." The deck tilted sharply and Hunter gasped involuntarily, reaching out with lightning speed to grasp the chain that suspended his bunk above a pair of deadly torpedoes. "Jeez, do they have to go down so fast?"

"It's a practice emergency dive. Didn't you hear what that dude said on the speakers?"

Hunter shook his head. "Naw, I was too busy stowin' my gear."

An odd expression flickered on Mainhart's face. "That's dumb. You've gotta listen to everything they say, and do what's required on a sub, or you get your ass handed to you. Sometimes you get it in one of those aluminum boxes . . . if they recover your body."

Hunter raised his hands in surrender. "Okay, okay, I'll listen, all right? But it still scares the crap out of me whenever we dive."

A veteran submariner, Mainhart shrugged and turned away.

A moment later the XO of the *Grayback* came forward to the torpedo room. "Commander Rockham?" he asked, looking over the assembled SEALs.

Rockham rise from a backless canvas folding chair next to a torpedo tube. "Yeah, what can I do for you, Commander?"

The lieutenant commander extended one hand with a sheaf of papers in his grasp. "I'm Jim Versch, exec of the *Grayback*." Rockham noted that he was big for a submariner. Actually, Versch was a wooly bear of a man, with thick forearms that bespoke a golfer or tennis player or perhaps a sculptor. "These came in just before we made contact and surfaced to receive you aboard."

"Thank you, Commander. I think these are just what we were looking for."

Versch nodded. As executive officer of a nuke attack sub, Versch had a top secret clearance, so he had been the one who received the photo message from the radio operator. "They look like high-altitude photos of a harbor area. I gave them a quick going over, and I'd say they're piers, docks, warehouses, and that sort of thing."

"Bingo! Those are exactly what we wanted. Thank you again."

After a slight hesitation, Versch asked, "I don't suppose I should ask what harbor those were taken in."

Rockham looked him in the eye and did not crack the slightest smile. "No."

"I thought so." Versch cleared his throat. After all, at the top of each page had been the bright red declaration, TOP SECRET FOR LCDR G. ROCKHAM ONLY.

Rockham checked his diver's watch. "Oh, what the hell, Commander, you have the same level clearance as the rest of us and you're going to find out in about six hours anyway. From what the cover sheet says, this is none other than Vladivostok Harbor."

Versch gave out a low, awed whistle. "I'll be damned. I thought I recognized it. I've seen it enough times through a periscope. Not exactly the safest place to be playing around in."

"So noted," Rockham responded with a dismissive shrug. "But where the head of NavSpecWar says to go, we go."

Versch pursed his lips. "And here all the time I believed that submarine duty was the most dangerous."

Rockham laughed out loud. "If you'd ask most of my men, I'm sure they'd agree with you. Truth to tell, I don't know of a SEAL who doesn't get a little twinge in the belly whenever they're on a sub that's diving."

Versch gave Rockham a mock punch on one shoulder. "You're all right, Rockham. Here I've been convinced that SEALs were all so full of themselves they wouldn't admit they took a dump like all the rest of us."

"Hey, Versch—"

Versch interrupted. "Call me Jim."

"Okay, Jim. I'm Rock. But face it, we all put on our pants one leg at a time."

"I'll give you that, Rock," Versch responded dryly. "But I've been told firefighters have their trousers set up so they can jump into both legs at once."

Rockham responded thoughtfully. "Yeah, I've heard the same."

"I tried to get our torpedo men to do that but it didn't work. It turned out a disaster. But then, their trousers aren't rubberized and they don't hang them up by red suspenders."

Rockham joined the laughter, and then sobered. "Sorry to cut you short, Jim, but I have work to do."

"Uh, sure, go on, get to what you need to do."

After Versch departed, Rockham called his officers and lead NCOs together to study the photos. He spread them on the long, narrow table where necessary work was conducted on torpedoes before loading and firing them. "Take a close look, gentlemen. We've got one hell of a job ahead of us."

Chief Monday bent close, picked up one of the magnifying glasses Rockham had laid out for their use and studied three photos in sequence. He nodded as he proceeded from one frame to the other. Then he went back to the first image. After a moment he jumped ahead to the pair that followed. At last he spoke. "I'm not so sure it's going to be as difficult as we thought."

"Why's that, Chief?" Rockham asked, not yet having viewed the satellite images closely.

"If you'll look here, boss, this is most interesting. See the prow of that container ship? Watch the progress it's making. See? Here . . . here . . . and here. These were taken early this morning according to the legend on the top margin."

Rock bent close, took a magnifier from a metal-legged stand. He slid it across the indicated photos. "Yeah, I see what you mean, Chief. It has Liberian registry and it's headed toward this concrete dock."

"You've got it, boss. Now look at this one and the next."

Rockham looked closely. "You're right. They tied up at that dock. There, at that warehouse. Do we have any other shots of the warehouse?"

Lieutenant Jorgensen went through the layout with a large magnifier. "Hey, here we go. Look at this. There is a railroad spur leading off to the shoreward side of the warehouse. It could be how this Rostov got his products to where the customer could pick them up."

"How do you mean?" Mike Ferber of Gold Platoon asked.

Rockham explained in a few words. "A lot of ships covertly owned and operated by the People's Republic of China sail under the Panamanian or Liberian flags. It's a convenient way for some countries to conceal a lot of what they're up to."

Ferber shook his head. "Doesn't that just frost your nuts? They never told us about that at the schoolhouse."

"Damn right," Henry Limbaugh chimed in. "I know that Shell Oil uses a flag of convenience, so do some of those fancy cruise ship lines. But I never expected a nation to use such a dodge."

"Well, the Red Chinese do," Rockham assured him. "Let's see what more we can make of this."

Before long they had uncovered surveillance shots from the previous day that revealed a flat car with shipping containers loaded on it. Eager to verify their decision-making ability and the soundness of their thinking, Rockham pointed to what the shots revealed.

"What do all of you make of that?"

"Looks like there's a pair of cargo containers there," Monday said.

"Yeah, now look at this one." He pointed to the other photos in time and date order. An LEO satellite showed the details of one of the cargo containers that had been removed. The four-by-four inch wood supports remained atop the lower car.

Jorgensen spoke out in surprise. "Hey, look at that. The top container is gone. When did that happen?"

"Some time during the thirteen hours that elapsed between overpasses by the low earth orbit satellite. Let's check one of the synchronal shots," Rockham suggested. After sorting through the long-range views, he selected one and studied what it portrayed. "See there, the top container is partway off the flat car. From the looks of that crane, they are going to haul it inside that warehouse."

"And you think that container has the weapons Rostov is going to sell?" Pauli Jorgensen asked.

Rockham looked hard at him. "Consider this scenario: the train comes in from western Russia and a flat car containing two cargo containers is put onto this siding right up against this warehouse. Now, here comes this crane and lifts the top container off and it disappears. Later we see the arrival of a container ship. Two plus two still equals four, right?"

Jorgensen gave the indicated satellite photos a closer examination. "I'll be damned. You're right, sure enough. Do we have any resource to tell us who occupied that warehouse?"

Rockham shrugged. "We can try. I'll see the captain about using the underwater high frequency system and call Danzig at CIA."

It took nearly an hour for a reply to come from Peter Danzig. "According to our agent in place, the warehouse on Pier 6 at Rostok Terminal is rented and occupied by Ivan Tsinev and Sons trading company. Tsinev was XO to Grigoriy Rostov in Spetznaz. He is not known to have any family except for a nephew. The nephew died in hospital about two weeks ago. The cause was anthrax-related pneumonia. Tsinev knew nothing about it until a couple of days ago."

"And our boy Rostov is supposed to have stolen anthrax warheads. Where were they taken from?"

Danzig's reply came swiftly. "From an old military storage facility some twenty miles outside Odessa." Then a thought struck Danzig. *If a dropped vial was responsible for the death of his only living relative, then Tsinev might be their inside informant.* It made his mind reel. He did not share his revelation with Rockham.

As though reading Danzig's mind, Rockham asked, "Then I wonder if Tsinev is still on board with Rostov? If the man thinks that any carelessness on the part of his leader's men caused him to lose his only relative, he might be a bit pissed off."

"My thinking exactly. But enough of that for now," he said, changing subjects. "Did you find the satellite photos useful?"

Rockham chuckled softly. "You know I did. We have a better than good idea where the WMDs are now located. Given what you forwarded, it seems the most likely answer. No idea of how many are guarding them or when they'll depart, but a container ship came into port and tied up at this dock earlier today. If I were a betting man, I'd say the container we found missing will be loaded on that ship before too long."

A pause followed. Then Danzig replied, "If it is, and it sails, your job will be a whole lot harder."

"I don't think so. As you know, we've taken down ships at sea before. It should be a lot easier than trying it right under the noses of the Russian security force."

"Keep me in touch, and hang in there," Danzig concluded.

Tsinev and Frolik stood together watching the final processes to complete their work. The electric winch had lifted the BM-21 rocket launcher over the gunwale of the power boat and settled it onto the welded steel platform. It took four men to swing it into place and see that the unit settled on the long bolts fixed to the metal deck. When the load was taken off the thin steel cable, the jury-rigged platform groaned ominously. To their relief, the noise quickly subsided and Frolik gave the signal to tighten the huge nuts on their bolts and secure the launcher.

Tsinev found a bottle of vodka and a rack of thimble glasses. He poured and motioned to the laboring former Spetznaz NCOs. "When you finish, comrades, come on down and have a drink with us." He handed a glass to Frolik and raised his own. "*Nostrovia.*"

Frolik clicked his glass against the rim of Tsinev's. "Yes, and to your health also. Four days from now we are going to single-handedly foment a war between the People's Republic and Taiwan. Think of it, comrade. It leaves a lasting impression, doesn't it?"

Knowing he had to carry through to avoid suspicion, Tsinev grunted reluctant concurrence. He was still ill at ease about what he had done earlier, not long after leaving the train the previous night. If anyone found out, his life would not be worth a ruble. But not to worry now, he sternly rebuked himself. They still had a lot of work to do before they could inform the ship's captain that the container was ready to load.

First they had to empty out all of the tools, welding equipment, and anything else not directly related to the rockets or their launcher. The warheads had been carefully packed in Styrofoam cartons to keep them protected until they were loaded onto each of the forty rockets. An hour before the indicated sailing time, the container would be loaded aboard the ship and they would join in the crush of late crew members who rushed to regain their ship before being stranded in a foreign country. After that, all they had to do was prepare and load the rockets, arm them all, and knock out the roof and one wall of the container. Once the rockets were fired, the fast boat was rigged to jettison the launcher and then speed away to safety.

Frolik was thinking the same thing, and excited by the prospect of creating such havoc. To his surprise, he discovered he had developed an erection and his member throbbed as though he was on his way to visit one of the fancy women in the brothels on the seamier side of Moskva. It would be a glorious day, he visualized, with Chinaman killing Chinaman until both countries nearly annihilated one another. No longer would they threaten Mother Russia. No longer would they arrogantly brag of their five thousand years of civilization. He smiled as he quickly swallowed down his vodka and hoped that there would be another.

CHAPTER 22

★ ★ ★ ★

0400 ZULU
One Day Later
Warehouse 5679 SW
Rostok Terminal
Vladivostok, Russian Republic

Rostov arrived that morning. He had finished aiding his underling in completing the transaction in Saint Petersburg and had to admit that it was a most lucrative sale. He went immediately aboard the cargo ship after speaking with his men. His only regret—and that a slight one—was having killed the two security agents on the train. Before he left the aircraft that brought him to Vladivostok, he'd verified that the money transfer had taken place to their bank on Grand Cayman. Now all that remained was to settle terms with the captain of the container ship.

Arrangements had been made in advance for the

loading and transport of a sealed cargo container, which was to be loaded last at the bow of the foredeck cargo area. The port inspector's certificate of content was given to the captain along with his payment. "You will find everything in order, Captain," Rostov assured him. "My men are prepared to have the container loaded at your convenience."

"Good. We are to sail at 1600 hours. Everything must be secured well before that. I understand that we are to stow this particular container on the top tier of aft deck cargo. Is that correct?"

"Yes, Captain, we will be first unloaded. You are to deviate from your normal course to the harbor facilities in Pamekasan Bay on Madura Island."

"But that will cause at least a twelve hour delay in my scheduled arrival in Nagasaki."

Rostov smiled. "Count what I gave you, Captain. I think you will find it satisfactory compensation for any penalty your shipping company imposes upon you."

Though tempted to protest, the captain refrained from doing so in the presence of this arrogant Russian. "Very well, then. We shall notify your loaders half an hour before making port at Pamekasan."

"You are most kind, Captain. Now, if you will excuse me, I have some pressing matters to attend to."

Unseen and unknown by Rostov, a U.S. satellite with a powerful camera system hung in geosynchronous orbit above Vladivostok harbor. At regular intervals it sent the images recorded back to a huge antenna disk on the back lawn at CIA headquarters in Langley, Virginia. There, the digitalized UHF signals were translated and rendered as photographs. These were regularly studied by photo interpreters and passed on to intelligence analysts. Two of those, as anonymous as most CIA employees, found a great deal of interest in them.

"Will you look at this," remarked the young man who had been assigned for the duration to Project 4510—the code name assigned to the Rostov case. "It looks like that ship is getting ready to sail."

His graying, matronly partner peered at the satellite photo through a large magnifying glass on a three-legged stand. A moment later she agreed. "They're getting ready to load a cargo container. It's going onto that ship we saw in the earlier photos docking alongside the warehouse. Now if we can only get a zoom-in shot on the stern and find the name of that vessel, we're going to be well ahead of the game. We can send this in real time to that lieutenant commander."

"And maybe whatever analysis comes out of it," the youthful analyst suggested.

His partner agreed. "You're right, we'll send it out as we get it. We'd better notify them at once and then get the stern shot close-up."

For the past half hour the *Grayback* had been cruising at antenna depth, receiving routine dispatches and some special, encrypted messages addressed to Lieutenant Rockham. As soon as they came in, these were delivered to the SEAL officer who took an encryption device from his staff RTO and began to break the communications into clear text. Lieutenant Commander Versch returned to his duties, after casting a quick glance over one shoulder to see Rockham hard at work, typing in characters and saving them to the disk.

When he was finished, Rockham punched the number indicated in the coded message on his sat-link unit, which had been attached to the sub's exterior antenna. After the two-way delay of six seconds, faxlike photos began to print out, sliding from the slot in the small, compact unit connected to the sat-link communicator. What he saw clarified the message and raised his hackles.

With the help of a magnifying glass, he identified a loading gantry extended from the quayside of Warehouse 5796. A large sling arrangement hung down from it and bore a metal-sided container. The powered drive unit moved the container slowly into position at the foredeck of the ship, on the top layer of other containers. To Rockham, it appeared to be the same container as the one missing from the flatcar that had rested beside the warehouse earlier the previous evening.

"This locks it up," he said aloud. "There went our WMDs."

Jorgensen bent over his shoulder. "What do you have there?"

Rockham looked up, a pleased expression on his face. "These were taken by one of our Keyhole satellites. We're getting continuous feed from Langley on this. It looks like our Russkie crooks have moved the stolen WMDs on shipboard. I hope the satellites zoomed in close enough to see—ah, there it is—just what we needed," he concluded as he lifted another photo from the fax/printer.

"By God, that's fantastic," Jorgensen said with fervor. "There's the ship's name and number. I can just make them out."

"Read them off to me," Rockham urged.

"It's the *SS Manila Star*, number 37095. That's a Liberian registry number, isn't it? If so, you can bet that's our baby."

Rockham seemed puzzled. "I'm not positive, but I'll assume that's correct. But why a cargo container? I'd say a container ship like that would make a damned poor platform." A thought occurred to him. "Unless, when they get where they're going, they off-load the contents of that container onto dry land or another, smaller craft. They might even have a fast-moving power boat inside that thing. It's a damned large container if you ask me."

Jorgensen seemed to like that idea. "I think you've got something there. If you're right, what do we do?"

"I'll be sending a request back to Langley, to the operators of the Keyhole that surveys that area of the globe. We'll want them to locate and keep track of that container ship once it shoves off from the pier."

"Damn right. I've never been one for putting all my eggs in one basket, but when we've got only one chicken," Jorgensen shrugged, "what can we do?"

Rockham chuckled. "That's quite an analogy. To continue it, once we discover where the egg is deposited, we crack it and scramble it. Now, the rest of what I got isn't such good news."

"Meaning what, Rock?" Jorgensen asked.

Rockham sighed. "Put it together with all of what Rostov's been doing, and it *fits*. This is what we've learned so far: thanks to Company assets inside Russia, it has been verified that the warheads stolen were empty, but designed to carry submunitions loaded with weaponized powdered anthrax. That much we knew. Now we know that the total number of 122-millimeter warheads stolen comes to a hundred, along with a hundred vials of the prepared anthrax spores also taken. Two forty-round launchers have also been verified. This is the same bioweapon we encountered up near the Arctic Circle during Operation Endurance. Now the Company's people have verified that at least one of the launchers and forty rockets, with accompanying warheads, are designated as being on the way to our Taiwanese turncoats. Each of the rockets is 122-millimeter as previously stated. Now add Rostov to that mix and we have one hellish stew."

"That really sucks, boss. But those rockets don't sound very big," Jorgensen observed.

Rockham continued the briefing. "The warheads weigh about forty pounds each, so one man can load them. The rockets can be fired in salvo, or 'rippled' in sequence or individually at selected targets."

"So if they get them deployed, we just might lose the whole ball game?" Jorgensen asked.

"You've got that right. To make matters worse, the launcher unit can elevate from zero to plus fifty degrees. It has a traverse of plus-minus 120 degrees and can be reloaded in ten minutes, although that probably won't be a problem for us. The maximum range for the rockets is about 2,750 meters.

"A radio intercept between the Taiwanese and the Black House has been translated, and we know the ship's destination. They will be heading to Madura Island. There's a good harbor there— only one, thankfully—so we'll know where to pick them up close to the other end. Only thing is, I want the ship kept under constant surveillance until then." As an afterthought, he added, "We'll go take a look at the sub's charts to find the best place to plan an interception.

"According to Sharon Taylor at CIA," Rockham went on, "we know that the officers and crew of the ship are Red Chinese. So if a few resist a takedown, they get blown away. However, we aren't to kill them all—the Agency wants a few to interrogate—but if we have to, we will. Once we've taken down the ship, we put what's left of the crew in lifeboats and scuttle the *Manila Star* so that any other nasty things aboard are put out of reach of those who might use them."

Jorgensen spoke up. "Too bad Rostov will profit from it no matter what we do."

"He won't if he's on board that ship. We're supposed to spare the crew if possible, but remember, Rostov and all his men are fair game."

"Good, this guy is one dangerous asshole. By the way, Rock, how did the Company get the information about all this?"

Rockham's expression became serious and wary. "Well, this is supposed to be absolutely hush-hush, but I can trust you guys. Russian intelligence established a source inside Rostov's organization, and they turned him over to the CIA. The Agency has been operating him ever since. He's given up all this latest intel on Rostov's operation. We even know the names of the men who accompanied the weapons package to Vladivostok. And a list of who worked to rig a launch platform on a high-speed power cruiser named *Leninayah Gubehrdost*—'Lenin's Pride.' Keep in mind that it has a twin screw, internal V-6, inline water-cooled diesel engine. It can develop 280 horsepower."

"Damn, that's fast," Chief Monday observed.

"Right you are. A boat this size can go like a bat out of hell, to a top operating speed of sixty miles per hour. Given the added weight of the platform, launcher, rockets, and their warheads, that speed might be reduced to around forty. Even so, it's one formidable piece of machinery."

"It's not a case of grab your ankles, bend over and kiss your ass good-bye, is it, Rock?" Jorgensen asked.

Rockham shook his head. "No, nothing that drastic, but we'll be hard pressed to close with them using the IBSs if they get away. Worse case scenario is if they don't pickle all those rockets at one time. If they have one or more left over to fire at us, we could quickly become SOL."

Jorgensen shrugged. "So, what are the plans for taking down this ship where we aren't supposed to harm the crew? And, while you're at it—and I don't want this to sound like a challenge or a criticism—why are we being so protective of the friggin' Chinese communists?"

Rockham produced a pained expression. "I asked the same question. The answer Sharon Taylor gave me was that China is our trading partner. The current administration does not want anything to happen that would interfere with good trade relations."

Jorgensen could not restrain himself. "Now isn't that a pretty crock of crap!" he piped up. "First it's interns in the Oval Office, now it's 'let's make nice to Communist China.' And this guy is *our* commander in chief?"

Rockham shook a cautioning finger. "Let's not

get political, Pauli," he warned, although he secretly agreed. "If the man is in the chain of command—which he is—then he should have the right to question any decisions that affects the military."

Jorgensen flushed. "Sorry. I've served in this man's navy for so long, I take the kind of crap that joker's handing out as a personal affront. Let's get back to business."

Rockham paused, and then gave him and his chief a broad wink. "To that end, I consider the crew as the enemy who are engaged in illegal activities and can be considered targets of opportunity. Listen up, men. This is my decision and I'll live or die by it. We no longer have to contain them without harm and take them off before sinking that container ship." Rockham's voice became brusque, an indication of his worry, as he continued with the details.

"Normally the BM-21 launcher unit is mounted on a Zil-135 flat-bed truck Somehow I don't think Rostov will have taken one on shipboard. In the Soviet version, the launcher unit weighs 3,500 kilos. The payload of rockets weighs 1,836 kilos. Even without the truck as a base, that's one hell of a load. If they plan to fire from this platform then jettison the whole damned thing and split, they'll have included some explosive bolts or some small shaped charges of plastic explosive to break it all free quickly and dump it in the sea."

"So, if we have to go after this little explosives

package shaped like a boat, what can we count on for backup?" Jorgensen wondered aloud.

Rockham smiled. "I'm glad you asked. If our final target is this speedboat, big as it is, the whole program changes from the plan to take down the container ship. We can probably never catch up to them, but we can take them out with the right munitions. We'll need some RPG-7s to stop that boat dead in the water. Or at least slow it down so we can board. The bad news is, we don't have any rocket-propelled grenades. Our job is to recover the WMDs, or failing that, make certain they cannot be used again."

"So if they use this big speedboat for their launch, if we can't board it, we sink it?" Jorgensen asked.

"You got it. Regardless, whether we go after the container ship or the fast boat, we will have support from Seventh Fleet, which Admiral Cromarty has arranged to make available to us for whatever need we have. Their aircraft can provide cover and a strike element if necessary. Okay, so taking down the cargo ship will follow standard routine. We put out four caving ladders. The point men go up first, secure the area around them, and then the rest of us go. Deck assignments will be made just before departure for the target. If any of Rostov's people are on board, we take them prisoner or kill them on the spot.

"Now, if we go after the fast boat, we'll be able to use only two caving ladders, so everyone boarding will have to scramble like hell to get on board in time. First thing is, slow that mother enough to be able to close and board. Once on board, divide into two units to take the open decks and belowdecks. First and third squads will go, with their own point men out, shooter teams as usual. Second squad will take the bridge. Command net and intercom to be individually maintained, ship-to-ship, with RTOs to keep touch as needed. Odds are it will be only Rostov's men, so we don't work too hard at taking prisoners. We should make sure to keep two or three to question in order to find out where the rest of the stuff is stored. Demo men will rig charges to sink the fast boat. We'll keep only one rocket and its warhead for proof of what was to go down and what we destroyed. Any questions?"

Jorgensen and the lead NCOs looked around. "None for now, sir," Jorgensen answered for them all.

"Excellent. We'll wait for more information, then refine our plan. That's it for now. Dismissed. Oh, hold it. Don't forget the availability of air support from Seventh Fleet. Anyone in a command position can ask for it at any time it's needed. Only hang-up is, it will take a good forty minutes to get where we want them. And finally, if possible, we'll hold off on air support until the cargo ship is secured."

"That's a great comfort," Ferber added sarcastically, although he had no real objection.

* * *

He had always loved the sea. Now Grigoriy Rostov stood at the railing near the bow of the *Manila Star* and let the brisk sea air ruffle his thinning hair. Despite the growing swells, a huge smile was plastered on his face, and he saw clearly how much they would gain in reputation for actually conducting this operation for the Chinese. Most of the international arms dealers were cowards, he thought disdainfully. A loud noise would make them jump. That was too bad for them. His thoughts strayed to his brief war with the *Mafiya Russiya*. With this coup, he would positively be held in awe by his peers, and somewhat in fear as well. His thoughts returned to the present when Tsinev joined him.

"Are we really ready for this, Comrade Grigoriy?"

Rostov turned a mild expression to his friend. "I think so. I don't have to like it, but I see no difficulties arising for us." He glanced over his shoulder and up to where their container rested on four-by-four supports.

"How do we get the launch vehicle off this ship?"

"We've been over that, Ivan Arkadyvich. We break down the container and use the ship's gantry and winch to off-load the speed boat into the water at Madura in Pamekasan Harbor. We'll be off and away before they can even haul in the anchors."

Tsinev shrugged. Now that he was stuck on this ship, he had no way of advising anyone ashore. "I hope you are right, Grigoriy Mikhailavich. If some far-ranging patrol aircraft saw us we'd get a nasty surprise in the Formosa Strait."

Rostov agreed silently but loathed admitting it to Tsinev. For all the good this would do their reputations, the danger and risks nearly outweighed that aspect. No matter, they would learn soon. Russians, he mused, were all fatalists.

CHAPTER 23

★ ★ ★ ★

2243 ZULU
The Next Day
28° 15' North, 140° 30' East
Twenty Nautical Miles West of Bonin Island
USS Grayback

For over ten hours the *USS Grayback* had been cruising west in search of the container ship *Manila Star*, headed south from Vladivostok. Three hours ago the sub turned to a heading thirty-five degrees. This would take them past the Japanese island of Bonin and place them in position to intercept the PRC-owned, Liberian-registered container ship with the WMDs aboard. Only minutes ago the vessel had gone up to periscope depth.

Lieutenant Commander Greg Rockham had been summoned to the Combat Information Center aboard the *Grayback* five minutes earlier, and already found himself burdened with new problems. Captain Aldrich stepped away from the periscope and descended the three steel steps to the CIC area. "We've got her," he declared with confidence. "She's just over the horizon, and by the amount of smoke she's making, it's certain there's a mighty heavy cargo aboard. She'll be in clear view within a quarter hour." He gestured to the Kollmorgan periscope. "Want to take a look?"

Rockham eagerly went to the periscope and peered through the eyepieces. A huge, elongated swath of orange light bathed the surface of the ocean, and a thick smudge of black smoke hovered on the near horizon. It told Rockham little and he remained unconvinced. Never having served as a submariner, he had no idea of how accurate observations made by periscope at surface level might be.

He asked uncertainly, "Are you sure that it's the *Manila Star?*"

Captain Aldrich nodded. "We're far enough off the normal shipping lanes, and there's nothing in the sailing notices we picked up from the *Kittyhawk* about any cruise ships in this area. Also, sonar says the cavitation sounds from her screws match those of the right class vessel. So, yeah, I'd bet my three gold stripes on it."

"Okay, so acting on that assurance, what do we do?"

Aldrich gestured to the bow plane driver. "We go deep—well below a hundred feet—until she's close. Odds are the *Manila Star* has no sonar and will go right over us without making contact. Once she's past, we come up to fifty feet depth and follow by sonar. Once we're certain she's headed for Madura Island, we'll come up to periscope depth and keep close tabs on her until we know what's going to happen with the WMDs aboard."

"Good enough, Captain. Is there any chance they'll discover we're tailing them?" With the ping of the active sonar and the faint sound of churning screws growing louder, that had become Rockham's major concern.

"Not a one. We're a mighty quiet design, even more than the Los Angeles class attack subs. We make like sort of a hole in the water." He turned to go back to the scope. "If you'll excuse me, I'll go keep a steady watch."

"Go ahead. And thank you, Captain." Rockham turned to Lieutenant Commander Versch. "Okay, Jim, do we launch our fast IBS boats from the bow deck behind the hangars, as usual?"

Captain Aldrich, who had been peering into the binocular eye pieces, bent sideways and interrupted with bad news. "We might not get you off for some time. Based on their current course and speed, the *Manila Star* will run in under some mighty black clouds not long before reaching Madura Island. The ache in my bones tells me there's gonna be some hellish rain squalls. The good news is that the rain that's moving in will help mask your approach once we've launched your IBSs."

"That's cool," Rockham answered, undeterred. "I've always loved riding in the rain."

Aldrich cocked one eyebrow. "Are you serious?"

Rockham smiled. "Sure am. You ought to see us during a SEAL reunion at Little Creek. If it rains, we stay outside, standing around in our canvas swim trunks, eating barbecue and fried chicken and drinking beer from paper cups. Hell, the beer companies bring in eighteen-wheeler refrigerated dispensers to handle the crowd. One time it's Budweiser, another time Miller's. We've even had Rolling Rock from Maryland."

"Okay, okay," Aldrich said, raising his hands. "I thought submariners held the championship for tall tales and beer consumption."

"Buddy, you ain't heard nothin' yet." He turned to the XO. "Let's go over the setup and launch for the IBSs. They aren't going to be as easy to deal with as our STABs. These babies—heavy and unwieldy as they are—carry two squads each and all their gear, plus a big load of ammunition. They also go faster than the STABs, with their twin hundred-horsepower Mercury outboard engines that move 'em at thirty knots. The IBS boats are faster and quieter too than those noisy little suckers."

Versch could not conceal a broad grin. "For all the bad things you SEALs call the IBSs, you for one seem to like them well enough."

Rockham chuckled. "Yeah, well, don't tell the other guys about it. It's tradition that SEALs hate the IBS boats. But I'd rather have one wrapped around me than two of those little inflatable jobs. Hell, Lieutenants Blackjack Macione and Larry Bailey modified some old trimarans to create the first ones. Fiberglass hulls with Kevlar armor and steel plate made the STABs nice but I'll opt for speed and maneuverability."

"Okay, back to business," Versch said, and pointed to a large map of the area of water around Madura Island. "Here's your AO. We'll be in close enough to see whatever they do with that cargo container. It will be up to you to turn that situation to your advantage—but of course I don't have to tell *you* that. You've been there, done that, far too many times. For which I am thankful it is you and not me."

Rockham chuckled. "If you don't mind a little off-subject question?" At Versch's nod, he went on, "What is it you'd like to do when you leave the Navy?"

Versch flushed and looked at Rockham from the corner of his eyes. "You won't tell anyone?"

Rockham shook his head.

"Okay, what I really want to do with the rest of my life is become an art instructor. I want to teach art to a bunch of skulls full of mush in a middle or high school so far from the sea I can't even find sand."

"That's odd. I had you marked as a lifer," Rockham responded.

"That's right, I am. Or I was. But let's face it,

Rock, look at me. I'm too damned tall to be a submariner. And I'm getting too big around for it too. And truth to tell, I hate surface ships. I get sea sickness all too damned easily."

"There's a word for that, from the sixties, you know. It's 'bummer.' "

Versch gave him a close look. "You're too young to have been a hippie."

"Yep, I was still wearing short pants to grade school back then. But seriously, what will we be facing in that piece of ocean?" He nodded toward the map.

"With the Philippines, Taiwan, and the Marianas along to the east side, and Korea and Mainland China to the west, the seas run fast through the Formosa Strait here and through this portion of the South China Sea. You can expect fast sea lanes—much like tidal bores—to be ripping through here. Cold water too, might even call it frigid. They are what the professor types claim caused migration to the Japanese islands and the Philippines, to begin human occupation in those places. These currents all seem to swing eastward, making a good case for that argument."

"Okay, that's a good geology lesson, so how does it affect our op?"

"Well, it doesn't by itself, only that if you have to drift and look for your target, you'll be SOL. Another thing, Madura Island is out of range of Taiwan for the rockets these Chinese are using, according to what you told me. So they have to go farther west to accomplish whatever it is they have in mind."

"Which I'm afraid," Rockham responded dryly, "is some very nasty stuff. At first it was believed that these Taiwanese were superpatriots determined to foment war with the Mainland by a sneak attack with nuclear and bioweapons. Closer looks by the Russian Security Service and the CIA revealed that they are in fact working for the PRC and intending to kill off as many Taiwanese as they can, plus fomenting a war of retaliation against the Mainland which Taiwan cannot win."

"The goal of which is what?" Versch asked.

"Any retaliation becomes a believable excuse for the People's Army to launch massive attacks against whoever is left alive on Taiwan and return the renegade province to the motherland."

Versch pursed his lips. "Evil, vicious bastards, these PRC military and political leaders, aren't they? There's a lot of Christians among the Taiwanese. What happens to them?"

"You can be sure, Jim, if their locations can be pinpointed, they'll be among some of the first ones targeted by the bioweapons."

Versch's face flushed with fury. "Then that's just another big reason these MFers have got to be stopped before they can pull this off."

For all the seriousness of their discussion,

Rockham cracked a tiny smile. "That's generally the reason we're here. If we can't take them down before they off-load the rockets, then you have to torpedo and sink the vessel. Your captain has sealed orders to that effect in the event we radio back that we failed."

"What a hell of a mess to be in. All right, look at this. My best estimation, given the range of the rockets, is right here in the Formosa Strait, if their target is Taiwan or the Mainland."

Rockham nodded. "That's the same evaluation that the analysts at Langley gave it. It makes it look more like the rockets actually came from the PRC."

"So, I'll let you know when we have a tight visual on the container ship."

Rostov's mood had changed. He now fretted at the long trip with seemingly no end in sight. When would they reach Madura Island? Never in all of his military service had he been so impatient. Why, then, was he so weighed down with worry and anxiety? Why couldn't the blasted captain hurry? Full speed ahead, he raged on in silence. He could not admit what truly bothered him was the proximity of the deadly anthrax.

He had little experience with such things. Granted, they had received the full series of immunization shots, and had antibiotics and protective clothing as well, yet they still had to load the

warheads with the submunitions—the lethal balls
loaded with the evil powder. That would begin
when the sun got higher. He had discussed it with
Tsinev, and neither of them liked the possibilities.
Among the men, the fear of what they worked
with was palpable. He decided it was time to give
them a cheering up. To that end, he asked for use
of the ship's communication system.

"Commander Rockham to the Control Room.
Now hear this: Commander to the Control
Room."

In spite of the fact that he'd gotten only a half
hour nap, by the time the last syllable faded,
Rockham started aft toward the area under the
sail of the submarine. Captain Aldrich and XO
Versch awaited him there.

Versch had a beaming smile and spoke first.
"We've got that mother nailed," he declared.

Rockham looked hopeful. "You have positive
ID, Jim?"

"Yeah, the bow number is correct, the container
with the number you gave us is the farthest forward on the foredeck stacks, and the logo on the
aft stack is that of the right shipping company.
We're waiting for a stern shot to verify the name,
but that's only so we go by the book. That's our
baby, all right, and regardless of how heavily
laden she is, she's making damn good time."

By then, faintly in the background, Rockham

noted the turgid sound of thrashing screws. Then his eyes strayed to the depth gauge. While he snoozed, they had descended to 120 feet. Now, as he stared at it, the needle began to move, indicating a rising attitude. "We're going back up," he remarked.

Versch nodded. "Yeah, she's far enough away now. We'll level off at fifty feet and follow her."

Already the sonar system aboard the *Grayback* began to mark the target, the loud *ping!* . . . *pong!* . . . *ping!* . . . *pong!* from the reflected ultra-high-frequency electronic pulses indicating the exact location of the *Manila Star* when translated to a two-dimensional grid-covered screen. A large green dot revealed the presence and rate of speed of the Chinese ship in relation to the sub. Too bad something like that didn't work on land, Rockham reflected. So far, experimental, backpack-mounted short-range radar units had not proven accurate, or even close to it. Such failings made working ashore exciting, although no one liked unpleasant surprises.

"How long before we reach Madura Island?" he asked.

Versch eyed his watch. "At the present rate of speed, I'd put it at around four hours from now. Say 2030 hours local time."

"Good, that gives us plenty of time to rig for a takedown of the cargo ship."

Versch looked incredulous. "You're actually going to board the container ship?"

"Yes. We would not be acting in good faith unless we exercised every means of verifying the presence of WMDs aboard that ship before you guys blow it out of the water."

"Yeah, I know, but it's going to be dangerous taking down the entire ship." Versch's mouth turned down in concern for this newly found friend.

"There'll be a couple of changes, Jim. First off, we need to surface far enough away to launch our IBS units and make the run in to the *Manila Star*. The second change is that you need to send a signal to the Seventh Fleet elements nearest to us to hold off on the air support until the ship is secured. We'll go in an hour after dark, at least an hour's sailing time from Madura Island."

"I don't envy you what you're about to do, but good luck, bro."

"Thanks Jim. We'll bring you back a couple of prisoners, if you like."

"Naw, but do me a favor—just do in all of those assholes."

Grinning, Rockham nodded approval of the XO's attitude. "You've got it, Jim."

Grigoriy Rostov sat at the small table in the crew's mess. He far preferred it to the officer's wardroom. The *Manila Star* being a military ship in name only, the amenities were not as sufficient as aboard a Kirov class heavy cruiser. With him were both Tsinev and Frolik. The subject of their conversation was the off-loading of their powerful fast boat and departure for the Formosa Strait. Rostov began the briefing with a reminder.

"Both of you remember the explosive bolts in the launch platform. Once we've launched the rockets, we blow the whole thing and head off as far away from Taiwan as possible in the shortest time. Youang is to meet us on Madura with the balance of the payment for the weapons, and we will have to take it with us until it is safe to make an electronic transfer to our numbered account." He went on, listing details of the rigging of the power boat for their intended action. Then he spoke of other matters. Finally, he concluded with a sincere desire for them to have success. As they started to depart to complete the tasks assigned them, Rostov spoke again.

"Oh, by the way, we will have to be most careful out on deck. It is raining furiously, as though the world has gone mad out there." As if to confirm this, grumbles wafted back to him as the former Spetznaz troops filed through a hatch and headed for the ladder to the open cargo deck.

Through the periscope, Captain Aldrich observed the pivoting I-beam of the ship's gantry swing out over the long, open cargo deck. With the superior magnification and superb clarity of the image, he could distinctly see the busy activity aboard the *Manila Star*. To his deepening concern, it appeared that all the bustling about centered on one particular container. He pulled his face away from the neoprene cups of the objective lenses of the Kollmorgan and gestured to XO Versch.

"Jim, come take a look at this, see if you conclude the same thing I did."

Versch moved into position and adjusted the focus. He muttered, swaying his weight from one leg to the other, using the subjective lens to cover the entire length of the container ship and always returning to the overlarge container first in line on the top row at the bow. At last he gave his opinion on what transpired on the distant cargo vessel. "If it made any kind of sense, I'd say those gooks were preparing to put whatever is inside the container over the side, into the water."

"Exactly," Aldrich agreed. "See those bigger guys? They have to be Russians, and they're getting ready to tear that container apart. My bet is, they have a real big, powerful boat inside just waitin' to be lowered over the side and put in the water."

"That means we were wrong about the *Manila Star* going into port here and off-loading the launcher and everything there."

Aldrich nodded. "Which brings up another problem. If Rockham and his SEALs want to take down that container ship before the launcher is off-loaded, they'll have to hustle, get it done quick like a bunny, and get back here so we can sink the sucker. To get ready for that, we'll have to drop back over the horizon and maintain contact by running our radar detectors full out and trust to sonar. Add to that, we'll be on the surface to launch those SEAL Swift Boats. If our chink friends have any pals around close enough to close on us, that will put us in some very deep stuff."

"I'm ahead of you, Cap'n. I'll advise Commander Rockham now, and as soon as we're in position and surface, they can man their craft and launch them."

"Thanks, Jim, I appreciate your forethought." Aldrich looked tired, more strung out than Versch had ever seen him.

"Uh, there's one thing more, Cap'n. What do we do about this hellish weather?"

Aldrich shrugged. "Same as always, I guess. We cuss it and learn to live with it. If those people get off that ship with the launcher and the rockets, we have no choice. Carry on."

A moment after his dismissal, when Aldrich returned his eyes to the scope, he called out, "Hold on, Jim. Pass the word to Commander Rockham. There's a really fast boat making for the *Manila Star* from Madura Island."

When Rockham learned of that, he did not like it at all. He let Versch know, then set about making preparations to pull the IBSs out of the torpedo loading hatch. It would take half an hour each to get them ready.

Heavy seas ran prow-on as Rostov stormed onto the bridge of the *Manila Star*. The vessel sailed now in total darkness except for the foredeck work lights. Not the least mollified by the arrival of their remaining payment, Rostov remained furious at the continued delays. "Captain, may I ask why the members of your crew seem to have ten thumbs?" Although only of medium height himself, Rostov towered over the diminutive Chinese captain of the ship.

"Pardon me, Comrade Rostov. I do not understand your reference," the captain replied coolly.

Exasperated, Rostov worked for an explanation in his imperfect Mandarin dialect. "For every step they take forward, some difficulty always arises that sets them back two steps. We appear no farther forward than before we set to work on opening that container."

Palms pressed together, the captain bowed slightly and spoke in a humble tone. "I am so sorry you have experienced difficulties. Perhaps it is the heavy weather, or the language barrier that interferes? My Russian is not so good as your Chinese," he went on, expounding on that theme. "So it may be that your men are failing in their efforts to communicate their needs to my crew. The solution may lie in you giving all of the orders for what your men require." He glanced uneasily out the big windows on the bridge.

Rostov's anger seemed to drain way. "An excellent idea, Captain. I will tell my foreman to relay his needs here to the bridge and I'll relay them to your crew." Rostov left without ceremony to find Tsinev and Frolik.

* * *

Great showers of foaming sea spray burst upward from the blunt prow of the *Grayback* as the submarine plowed through the rough water. Standing in the sail, Rockham studied the heaving breast of the ocean to the northeast of Madura Island. The sea's state was not conducive to launching even light boats from the deck of a sub. Drenching rain squalls swept across the slick hull as the SEALs made ready their IBSs for sliding over the side from the slatted afterdeck area. Nuclear subs, although much larger than their WW II counterparts, did not have wooden slat decking fore and aft. And the rain and the pitching of the boat added greatly to the danger of getting the IBSs in the water. Rockham watched his men work without showing any acknowledgment of the risk. Damn, it was great to serve with such men as these. Unbidden, his chest swelled with pride.

Fully inflated and loaded with gear, the IBSs were being secured to flange-shaped davits along the lee side of the sub. At last, the first of the four inflatable boats was hoisted and moved over the side. While Rockham watched with satisfaction, the thin nylon mooring lines snapped tight as the IBS hit the water. A sudden involuntary scream came from Ferber, leader of Gold Platoon. He lay thrashing against the pressure hull of the sub in obvious pain.

Immediately, three SEALs, who worked with

the others on the launch, went to help the injured petty officer. At once, Rockham saw what had happened. Ferber had stepped in at the wrong moment, and one of the mooring lines had snapped tight across the middle of his thigh. At the same moment, the sub had lurched in the heavy seas and rammed Ferber against the steel pressure hull. Pinned as he was, the men nearby could hear the bone snap and a groan of agony rise from the injured SEAL. Rockham was already on his way down the external ladder to the aft deck, deep lines of worry creasing his brow.

"How is he?" he demanded when he joined the trio as they attempted to free Ferber's leg from the line.

Henry Limbaugh answered him. "It's a damn shame, sir. There's no way in hell he's gonna go on this op. That leg's broken. We'd better get him below, where Jack and I can work on him, stabilize that thigh and splint it for now."

"How long will that delay our launch?" a worried Rockham asked.

"I'd guess at least half an hour."

Rockham hated the decision he had to make. "Too long. Get him below and let the sub's corpsmen take care of him. They've even got an MD aboard, right?"

Limbaugh looked troubled. "Yes sir, but beggin' your pardon, sir, Mike's one of *ours*. An' SEALs don't leave other SEALs behind."

Rockham sighed heavily. "You've made your point. But the mission comes first. Let's get him below."

As soon as Ferber had been lowered though the open hatch and placed on a bunk in as much comfort as possible, Rockham sought out Master Chief Monday. "Chief, we've got a problem." Quickly, he explained the situation, and concluded, "You're going to have to take Mike's place and run Gold Platoon on this op. The mission has to be a go. We can't afford the half hour delay Henry Limbaugh says it will take to rig Mike's leg, so grab a corpsman from our reserve platoon—thank God we've got them along—and have him take Henry's place. He can stay here as our representative. Do it like yesterday, Chief, and let's get our show on the road."

CHAPTER 24

★ ★ ★ ★

Even with the improved communications, Grigoriy Rostov still fumed over the slow progress toward off-loading and launching their high speed cruiser. For all of their hustle around the container, these Chinese deckhands seemed to have lead feet and permanent cases of mortifying lethargy. *Would they never get that damned crane into position?* Rostov wondered with impatience.

But slow laborers wasn't Rostov's only problem. Another headache appeared as the engines slowed and a boarding gangway lowered. *What the hell?* Rostov wondered.

In a few more seconds his question was answered as Youang climbed to the main deck and headed for the internal ladder that led to the bridge.

As a chilling reminder to both platoons as they made ready to cast off mooring lines, the voice of the battle talker rose out of the open hatch.

"Now hear this! Now hear this! All hands, man your battle stations surface. Load torpedo tubes one and four. Do not open outside doors. I say again, do not open outside doors. Stand by for action."

They made their approach silently, given the driving rain and howling wind. Fifty yards apart, two of the IBS boats closed on the *Manila Star*. The other two, bearing the reserve squads of Green Platoon, held off some three hundred yards while the heavily laden boats closed with the target. Green Platoon stood by, rigged out with all their gear and weapons, prepared to move in if the situation got too hairy aboard the container ship. Riding low in the water, all four boats gave out minimal radar signatures.

Now, as the SEALs ghosted in on the starboard side of the *Manila Star,* part of their minds were occupied with what situation would result in the *Grayback* firing those torpedoes before they were able to leave the ship. Seated in the lead boat, Greg Rockham contemplated those same thoughts. He fully realized that the main objective was, and had always been, to capture intact or utterly destroy the WMDs aboard that ship. If it cost all their lives, the big brass at NavSpecWar would only send the usual condolences to the surviving families via a chaplain and a ranking officer, probably not even making an inquiry into the reason why they had died.

Yet, such idle speculation would not deter them from making ready for the assault and takedown of the Chinese vessel. Tension mounted even for the veterans in the platoon as Waterstone and Grant, coxswains from SDV Team Two, throttled back the engines of the IBSs as the boats approached their target. The special mufflers and sound deadening on the motors kept the noise of the two boats to a low level. The black rubber vessels could not be seen against the dark ocean waters, even if someone were looking directly at them from only a few yards away. The SEALs themselves were silent as they approached their target, each man keeping his own counsel as they all did what their training had taught them to do.

While the coxswains sat in relative comfort at the rear of the boats, the rest of the SEALs were riding the tubes, crouching down and straddling the inflated sides of the rubber boat. It was the best way to maintain as low a profile as possible while still keeping solid contact with the IBS. But it was anything but a dry way to ride across the sea. The SEALs were long used to being wet and cold on an operation or during training—it was something they just endured.

The two rubber boats moved up and down the

peaks and troughs of the waves as their coxswains kept them on course. Waterstone and Grant would have to pull up alongside the container ship and hold their boats as steady as possible while their Teammates set the climbing gear in place. It was a tough job that called for rock-solid concentration and a lot of skill and maneuvering of the small boats—something both SEAL coxswains excelled at.

Finally, the boats reached the rusty flank of the *Manila Star*. One thing had happened to make their mission at least a little easier. The container ship had reduced its speed to barely over five knots due to the turbulent seas and high winds. The darkness grew deeper still, and the boats moved into the shadow of the ship. Waves slammed one of the boats against the hull, making little noise, but the SEAL riding the tube had to move fast to keep from being ripped apart by the razor-sharp barnacles that encrusted the rusty hull.

As the boats moved into the lee of the big container ship, they came into a slightly calmer area of the water. Immediately taking advantage of the situation, the breachers moved the painters' poles into position and set their hooks. The caving ladders had been hoisted into place, and the path to the huge foredeck of the ship was now open. A thumbs-up signal sent the SEALs swarming up the ladders in pairs.

As point men, Marks and Quinn came clear of

the water first, followed by their partners, Fleming and Mercer. Quickly, like eels sliding up the side and over the rail, they boarded the *Manila Star* near the stern. All four men took deep breaths to quell some of the excitement they felt. The ship's takedown had officially begun. While other SEALs pushed upward, the four spread out to cover the open foredeck space. Far ahead of their position, the yellow-white light of the deck illumination turned the cargo of containers into black silhouettes.

Covered by the hollow pounding of hammers and the screech of metal saws, the deployment of the SEALs went entirely unnoticed by the hard-working deckhands. A deep baritone voice rose above them, speaking in heavily accented Chinese. "Who is that? Show yourself." An instant later the angry words were followed by the harsh sound of a gunshot and a pitiful cry.

In a whisper, Jay Hunter translated what he'd heard and conveyed what he was seeing into his intercom radio. "Jeez, that has to be our Captain Rostov," he added. Privately, he wondered how Rostov could get away with killing someone on this ship, as he just had.

"Hang in there, guys," Rockham advised. "Let's move into position now and take this mother down."

First squad spread out to take out any guards covering the ladder and companionway that led to the bridge. Third squad took the ladder system that led to the engine room. Second squad headed toward the cargo-deck-level hatchway that gave access to the crew's quarters. Fourth squad remained in reserve, covering any approaches from where Rostov's men worked on the container. Rockham was now convinced that the container held more than the launcher and rockets. Keeping the Spetznaz men isolated at the bow would make the takedown easier.

First squad formed their train and advanced to the top of the large main ladder that connected to the bridge deck. On the four-deck-tall structure that contained the bridge, radio room, radar room and captain's quarters, mess deck, recreation room, and crew's quarters near the stern, it appeared as though nothing was wrong. Not even a single sentry had been positioned at the main deck hatchways. Rockham and the first squad entered swiftly and began the climb to the bridge deck.

Outside the radio room, they formed their train again and made ready. Ryan Marks, as point man, was also breacher. He positioned himself and fitted a Hooligan tool into the lip of the doorlike hatch. One solid reef on the long steel shaft popped the hatch open and the first shooting team entered in a rush. Soft *chuffs* from their suppressed Heckler & Koch MP5K-Ns spelled goodbye to the three Chinese in the compartment. Already Marks had moved on to the radar room door and made ready to breach it.

Silent in their crepe-soled shoes, the second pair

of shooters slipped into position beside him. With a nod for confirmation, Marks ripped the hatch away. Controlled three-round bursts cut into the two radar operators and a ranking petty officer. They went down without a sound. The squad formed its train again and headed to the wheelhouse hatchway with the others behind them.

Tensed for the moment, Rockham spoke softly into boom mike of his radio set. "First squad ready. Execute . . . execute . . . execute!"

At once, Ryan Marks burst through the single access to the wheelhouse. The shooters rushed in, but not fast enough to prevent one of the helmsman's assistants from recognizing an attack and crying out, "Attack! Attack!" They were the last words he ever spoke before he was killed by an H&K.

Less than a second later a burst of fire from a PRC Type-56 ripped open the quiet night from the direction of the crew's quarters.

It only made the old truism a lot truer. The best designed and rehearsed plan fell apart at the first contact with the enemy. What had started quietly suddenly burst into a full-fledged raging firefight. Unknown to their inside informant, a platoon of PRC special security troops had been placed aboard. Their mission: to protect the rockets and their launcher and ensure proper employment of them. The loud explosion of an RGD-5 hand grenade was followed by a chorus of shrill screams as the burst radius of the high explosive grenade sent slashes of jagged steel fragments into the tender flesh of PRC soldiers and ship's crew alike.

Type-56 assault rifles on autofire ripped through the crew's quarters, discharged by soldiers of the PLA unconcerned with which bodies the slugs struck. Many rounds took out Chinese sailors. Misses screamed and zinged around the steel bulkheads of the large crew compartment and flashed out the two access hatchways, to ring down the passageways outside. The men of the SMD ducked low and hurled two more Russian grenades into the space occupied by the PRC soldiers. More men screamed and died.

On the bridge, the captain and wheelhouse crew suddenly recovered their courage and snatched up their official PRC navy handguns, Type 54 Tokarev pistols, copies of the Soviet Tokarev, whose .32 subcaliber bullets literally bounced off the body armor of the SEALs confronting them. The hailstorm patter of multiple shell casings hitting the rubber matting on the steel deck announced the death of the Chinese sailors. Only two—one of them the captain—remained alive, gasping out their lives.

Rockham knelt beside the captain. "Rostov? Where is he?"

"He—I—He was here before you broke in. He must have left to join his own troops on the foredeck." A low gurgle rose in the captain's throat, then his legs arms and head spasmed briefly and he died.

* * *

From their reserve position in the IBS, Green Platoon heard the gunfire and muffled explosions of the grenades and tensed. Paul Lederer turned to the coxswain with concern clear on his face. "Bring us in there closer. There's an effing firefight."

"You're the boss for now, Tall Paul. In we go."

Three minutes later the loud cracks of explosive bolts carried across the water. "Son of a bitch!" exclaimed Grayson. "What's that?"

The SEALs inside the stern bridge structure heard the detonation of the explosive bolts. On the bridge deck, Rockham rushed to the open side well of the bridge and stared forward. Small clouds of dust blew clear from the container that likely belonged to the Russian arms dealers. As he watched, Chief Monday's head appeared in the hatch that led down to the engine room. To their momentary astonishment, they saw the top of the container lifted by the crane on the gantry and hauled over the side. There, a remote control triggered the release command and the container's roof plunged into the sea. More explosive bolts popped loudly, and the side walls of the container fell outward.

Then the man they believed to be Rostov shouted a command to the crane operator to reverse the unit from which the hook was depended. As the SEALs watched, fascinated, the hook was lowered and the Russians attached a large sling unit that lifted the boat inside from the four corners of the cradle. Swiftly, Rostov's men scram-

bled aboard. Slowly, majestically, the overlarge inboard engine power boat began to rise from
within the destroyed container.

"Well I'll be damned," Chief Monday said in
awe over the intercom. "Would you look at that
shit? Is that a rocket launcher?"

"You've got that right, Chief," Rockham answered softly. "It's a BM-21, to be exact."

"An' they got it welded to the foredeck of that
boat? What are they going to do with it?"

Rockham chuckled. "That should be obvious,
Chief. They're going to drop it in the water and
haul ass. We're after the wrong target here. Is the
engine room secured?"

"Roger that, Rock."

"Good. Any men you can spare, bring them
topside and close on that Rube Goldberg boat rigging. We'll be right down to join you. And keep
an eye out for a whole lot of PRC soldiers that are
breaking bad in the crew's quarters."

"Aye aye, Rock." Then Monday added as an
afterthought, "PRC soldiers? What the hell are
they doing here?"

"Tell you later, Frank. Now get those guys
humpin'."

Grigoriy Rostov shouted again at the crane operator. "Up! Take her up, damnit! Lift this boat now!"

Already, the slack had been taken out of the
four thick-braided steel cables attached to the

huge hook of the crane. The flooring of the container groaned as the weight was lifted from it and the power boat rose slowly into the air. From behind, Rostov heard shouts in Russian, some of them atrociously accented.

"Stop! Hands Up!" Like hell, the Russians all decided.

Swiftly, Rostov and his crew of six scrambled aboard the strange boat and the Spetznaz captain gave the signal to run the gantry truck out and lower the boat. A few shots flew in their direction but none came seriously close. The mechanism above them groaned and moaned and the floor of the container began to rise higher, then the wheels squeaked and the burden slid slowly out toward the port side of the blunt, curving bow. As the vessel dropped below the forward railing, the sounds of increased fighting came from the ship.

Closing with the container ship, the SEALs of fourth squad, Gold Platoon, opened fire on the green-uniformed soldiers of the People's Revolutionary Army who swarmed onto the deck. Careful to keep their buddies out of the kill zone, the men chopped down the enemy troops with methodically gruesome precision. A few moments later the roar of the twin diesel engines of the heavily laden power boat could be heard by all of the SEALs.

"Shit, they're getting away," Rockham growled.

A dark figure suddenly appeared; only a black

silhouette against the brightness of the deck work lights. Arms raised, the man came forward. *"Nyet vabeyesveyehl."*

"Do not shoot," Sukov translated rapidly, and as the man continued to speak, he added, "I am your friend. I am the one who gave the information. And I know where they are going."

Rockham nodded and gestured the man forward. *"Kto dayeela?"* Who are you?

"I am former Senior Lieutenant Ivan Arkadyvich Tsinev of the USSR Naval Spetznaz service. May I ask who you might be?"

"I am Lieutenant Commander Gregory Rockham, United States Navy."

Tsinev smiled and snapped off a crisp salute. "My pleasure, Commander. I am your prisoner."

Rockham frowned. "Why is it that you gave information to our intelligence service?"

Tsinev produced a rueful smile. "You see, I am the last living member of my family. Until recently, I had a nephew. Little Josef was only a boy of twelve when he died. He died because Grigoriy Rostov wanted weaponized anthrax to sell to some Taiwanese traitors. I could not bear to live with Josef's death on my conscience. And—I wanted revenge."

Moved by this declaration, Rockham placed a hand on the shorter Russian's shoulder. "Nothing for you to be ashamed about in that. It is tragic that the boy died. I have a boy. He's only eight," Rockham added with unusual candor. "Now, tell us, where are Rostov and his men headed?"

Tsinev hesitated for a moment, reluctant to go against years of conditioning and training, then said, "They are going to the Formosa Strait, between the Mainland and Taiwan. We were engaged to conduct the launch of anthrax-loaded rockets into Taipei and the military bases around the city."

Rockham made a quick mental calculation. "Then we had better get on our way. You will go back to the sub, under guard, and remain there until the mission is completed. They will sink this ship and then follow us."

Surprise registered on Tsinev's face. "You have a submarine? So that is how you found us so quickly. Yes, being your prisoner will be far better than being guilty of murdering thousands of more children."

By then, Green Platoon had boarded directly up the caving ladders and made quick work of the PRC soldiers. Bodies in their green uniforms—splashed with red—littered the open spaces of the container ship's decks. Rockham turned Tsinev over to Green's CO. They would make a swift search of the vessel. They found no more deadly bioweapons, rockets, or the second launcher. Tsinev, he thought, could probably provide that information.

And then Gold Platoon was speeding in pursuit of the fleeing Rostov and his men.

CHAPTER 25

★ ★ ★ ★

"There she is!" John Grant shouted over the roar of the IBS engines. "Son of a gun, it's a big mother."

"Can you close with him, Cochise?" Waterstone asked him.

"Hell, yes, Big Ed. Just let me concentrate," Grant replied.

Senior Chief Monday provided sage advice. "Be cool, Cochise. That rocket launcher can be depressed enough to blow us out of the water."

Grant grinned broadly, a wide, white slash in his brown face. "I don't think so, Chief. Those dudes have been pitchin' rockets over the side to lighten the load all along. By my count there ain't any left."

Monday gave him a gimlet eye. "Are you willing to bet your life on that, Grant?"

Grant gave that a little thought. "Well, as a matter of fact, no."

Everyone on board had witnessed the huge flash and mounting black cloud when the submarine sank the Chinese container sip. As a result, all along the course to the Formosa Strait, rockets had been removed from the launcher by Rostov's order and thrown over the side. It was necessary, he declared, to lighten the ship as much as possible. They would keep two rockets in reserve in case of need. "We cannot use them as a bargaining chip," Rostov insisted. "They would only sink us without hesitation. So we shall destroy them first." His glance went to the DSh-12 machine gun mounted on the cabin roof.

An hour later they realized their only hope lay in escape. If they reached the launch site unmolested, it would be foolish to fire the two rockets into Taipei. It would much better to use them on the men pursuing them. After that they could blow the explosive bolts, throw the jury-rigged platform over the side, and speed away to safety.

Now it looked like those plans had to be changed too. The high-speed vessel approached them, a huge white bow sprit curling back along the side. Rostov ordered the launcher to swivel right and lower, to as near a flat trajectory as possible, given its height above the heaving foredeck.

"Fire on them!" he bellowed.

The Russian machin gun opened up, but before Sergei Nemec could squeeze the rocket's firing mechanism, their pursuer ran in under the minimum declination available to both weapons. Rostov had only time to scream out, "Brace yourselves!" Then the SEALs opened fire and the prow of their rigid inflatable boat rammed into the speed boat occupied by the Russians.

Rockham stiffened when he saw the launcher leveled at them. "We don't dare call in air support now. I'm fairly certain—and John here will back me up on it—that Rostov would not try to run a bluff. There is at least one rocket and WMD in that launcher."

"So? What happens now?" Andy Bean asked.

Rockham gave him a brief grin. "Why, Bean, we do it ourselves. Like the pirates of old, we form a boarding party, ram, and take the boat."

He had gambled on the belief that Rostov would not fire a deadly anthrax warhead this close to himself. Two minutes later, Rockham saw that his guess had been right. They had run under the maximum depression for the rocket tubes. Following the violent collision between the IBS and the speedboat, the SEALs ceased fire momentarily, then leaped over the splintered gunwale of the other boat and closed with the enemy.

Fierce fighting broke out all over the power

cruiser. Down in the half-enclosed cockpit, the skirmish degenerated to hand-to-hand. Men struggled and died. One of the Russians had been split from sternum to crotch, his intestines spilling out onto the slippery deck. Forward on the launch platform, Frolik strained under the weight of one of the remaining rockets in an effort to remove it from its firing tube. Suddenly, Rostov broke off fighting with Paul Lederer and dashed forward to aid his trusted sergeant. Frolik had the deadly projectile out and lying on the deck.

Rostov nearly reached him when Rockham raised his suppressed H&K MP5K-N and fired a measured three-round burst. The first round caught Rostov in the side, tore through his abdomen two inches above his hip bone and exited after piercing his colon. He spun back toward Frolik, and the other two rapidly fired slugs struck Rostov in the back and shattered his ribs. Only one exited his body after piercing a lung.

By then Frolik had armed the internal destruct charge on the warhead. Satisfied with this act of at least limited mass murder, he looked up grinning and recognized an old enemy. His nemesis had come back to haunt him. The man in front of him had last been seen standing on the sail of a nuclear submarine that had risen from the ice in the White Sea. The men on board that submarine had saved their comrades, after being chased by Frolik and his men for hours across the frozen landscape. Just as they were about to be taken, fire streaming out from the rising submarine had killed a number of Frolik's men. The only word he remembered being shouted by any of the men on that submarine was "Bus!" And here, fate had put that man within his reach.

Rising up to his feet, Frolik screamed in rage, "By God—*bus*!" As he shouted, he fired a round at Monday.

The bullet struck Monday in his flak jacket and the chief staggered backward. Immense pain blossomed in his chest. Frolik fired again and missed, tried once again and found his weapon was empty. Monday charged him, his sidearm out and fired point-blank into Frolik's face. A puzzled expression formed for a second before Frolik fell dead. A second later Pyotr Adamenko sprang from the cockpit and smashed the gun from Monday's hand with a marlin spike, then swung the hooked pole like a baseball bat.

Monday readily blocked his attempt and answered it with a low spin-kick, driving his left leg into the Russian a few inches below the hip joint. It bowled Adamenko over. Yet, though dazed, the former Spetznaz trooper bounded to his feet and struck out with a hammer fist aimed for Monday's head as the chief stood up.

A windmill maneuver deflected the punch and spun the Russian to one side. Adamenko was beefy, well built, with thick, solid muscles, but he also had the speed and grace of a ballet dancer. He spun on the ball of his right foot and delivered a set of forceful blows to Monday's chest and stomach in churning pistonlike thrusts with both fists. He extended his middle knuckles and braced in a classical *schuto* position. Monday felt a rib crack but ignored it as he raised his left leg in a vicious front-thrust kick that sent Adamenko flying down the foredeck. Unstable on the heaving deck because of his injuries, Monday shuffled forward and closed with his stunned enemy. Adamenko managed to lash out with a lateral sweep kick aimed at taking Monday off his feet. The injured SEAL managed to jump above the swinging leg and aimed a steel-toed shoe into his enemy's crotch.

A high-pitched scream—more a wail of agony—came from Adamenko's lips as the kick landed in his groin. Against his will, his shoulders flopped forward, exposing his head in a vulnerable position. Monday wasted no time in following up his advantage. In a furry of blurred movement, he kicked Adamenko in the head, first with the left, then with the right shoe. "*Yeb vas!*" he shouted in the Russian's face. Fuck you! His fingers dug into Adamenko's throat, crushing his larynx and cutting off his air supply as his eyes bulged and he struggled frantically to breathe. Adamenko's legs and arms thrashed violently as he grew weaker and weaker, while Frank Monday knelt in the middle of his chest. Finally, the Russian made a gurgling sound and went slack. Not taking any chances, Monday recovered his stain-

less steel Sig-Sauer P220 pistol and put a .45 caliber round between Adamenko's eyes.

"Son of a bitch, he was one tough dude," Monday remarked as he came to his feet, then saw a
blur of rapid movement to one side.

At least one of the SEALs had not been so distracted by individual shooting or knife fights to
overlook the armed rocket. Sid Mainhart moved
rapidly to the railing on the lee side of the damaged speedboat, the 101.9-pound rocket and its
forty-seven pound warhead wrapped in his arms.
With a last, desperate look back at his comrades,
Mainhart went over the side, taking the deadly
weapon with him.

"No!" Monday howled as he watched Mainhart disappear over the gunwale railing.

Unable to prevent it, three of the SEALs
watched as Mainhart sank below the surface and
his features blurred in the saltwater of the sea.
Only a moment went by before they all felt the
"thump" of the rocket exploding as it spewed out
its deadly contents.

"Oh, God. Oh my God," Corpsman Jack Tinsley of first squad gasped out as the warhead exploded and anthrax powder spread deep in the
water. Silently, he made the sign of the cross and
muttered a quiet prayer. "Eternal rest grant him,
O Lord. And let perpetual light shine upon him
and bring him peace, through the mercy of God,
amen."

Rockham shot the last former Spetznaz trooper

between the eyes and turned to put comforting hands on the shoulders of Tinsley and Monday. His eyes were on the water. "The temperature of the sea water and its salinity will keep the anthrax from spreading. Eventually it will destroy it. What counts is that we wiped out the bastards. What matters is that we lost a damn good man. Rest in peace, Sidney Mainhart."

EPILOGUE

Once back on the *Grayback*, Rockham, his officers, and Chief Monday met in the officers' wardroom. While Rockham passed around the traditional post-mission cigars, Captain Aldrich produced the well-known hidden bottle from its place of concealment in a file cabinet in his compartment. In this case it was not the usual bourbon or scotch, but rather, Irish whiskey. He poured liberal dollops in five gray Navy coffee mugs bearing the wreathed dolphins and fouled anchor logo of the U.S. Submarine Service and passed them around.

"Gentlemen, may I say cheers for a job well done. Both of those vessels are on the bottom of the sea. No one will ever know how close the world came to another global war." They drank off the libation and Aldrich poured another around.

"Unfortunately, we lost a man," Rockham said grimly. "And we missed the sons of bitches who caused all of this."

"Yes, that is a shame. But at lease we recovered the body?" Aldrich tried an encouraging expression.

Rockham nodded in agreement. "Indeed. And the decontamination protocol was a bitch." He turned to Daugherty. "Shaun, I want you to know that this will be my last active mission as commanding officer of SMD. I am recommending you to take over command, including a recommendation for promotion."

Senior Chief Monday took a deep draw on his postmission cigar and exhaled a long, blue-white plume of smoke. His carefully prepared, studied words shocked them all. "This'll be my last mission too. I'm gonna hang up my Trident and spend my days fishing for grouper and barracuda. Florida looks mighty good to me."

Rockham forced himself to sound unmoved by this revelation. "Uh, damn, I hate to hear that, Chief—but good luck in your retirement. Now, if you gentlemen will excuse me, I have a letter to write home to the family of a lost SEAL."

After Rockham departed, Master Chief Monday took another draw on his cigar. The glow of

the burning tip matched the glow in the glass eye
of a stuffed bear in a child's room back in Virginia Beach—the child of a SEAL who had died
defending the world from terror.

Sep. 3rd
364.97
202.62